THE EARTH AND ALL IT HOLDS

Books by V. J. Banis available from New English Library:

THIS SPLENDID EARTH
THE EARTH AND ALL IT HOLDS

THE EARTH AND ALL IT HOLDS

V. J. Banis

NEW ENGLISH LIBRARY

First published in Great Britain in 1980 by
New English Library Limited

First NEL Paperback Edition November 1981

NEL Books are published by
New English Library,
Barnard's Inn, Holborn,
London EC1N 2JR, a division of
Hodder and Stoughton Ltd.

Made and printed in Great Britain by
Hunt Barnard Printing Ltd., Aylesbury, Bucks.

0 450 05001 7

Glory, the grape, love, gold – in these
are sunk the hope of every nation.

LORD BYRON

PROLOGUE

1892

1

How could she have known, when they first met, that she would love him all her life? The rain, the darkness of the California night, the small boy with dark, anxious eyes – memories etched on the mirror of her soul; she would carry them to her grave and, God willing, even beyond.

'Damnation.'

The rented surrey gave a violent lurch and came to a stop, rousing Jolene Perreira from exhausted sleep.

'What is it?' she asked in a frightened voice. She looked quickly about them and saw nothing but darkness. They had been traveling through Los Angeles when she had fallen asleep, but they had since left the city behind and were somewhere in the country. Not a light was to be seen in any direction through the falling rain, not even the glimmer of stars above.

'Something's broken,' her mother said. 'Here, hold on to these reins, keep a firm grip on them now.'

Jolene, a pretty ten-year-old with pale yellow hair, took the proffered reins, gripping them so tightly that her childish fingers ached with the effort.

Mama climbed down from the rig, her elegant slippers making sloshing sounds in the fresh mud of the road. 'What is it?' Jolene asked again after a moment.

'An axle, I think,' Mama said. 'This whole side's dragging on the ground.'

'What are we going to do?' To Jolene the darkness surrounding them seemed suddenly peopled with threatening shadows.

Mary Perreira sighed. 'I don't know, walk I guess, but it's miles to the ranch.'

'Won't someone come looking for us?' Jolene asked.

Mary snorted disdainfully. 'From French Hills? Not likely. Your Uncle Adam would be far more likely to put up barricades to stop us coming – not that it would. I can be just as stubborn as they can.'

Jolene was only dimly aware of the quarrel that existed between her mother and her mother's family – indeed, until a few days ago she had scarcely known she had an Uncle Adam or Uncle Jean or Uncle David. She had long ago questioned the absence of a grandfather, having learned that other children her age had one or even two, and so had learned that she had one as well, but beyond the fact that he existed, and lived at a place called French Hills, she had learned very little about him. At first she had fashioned him in her mind after a drawing of Santa Claus in one of her picture books, but gradually that image had faded, leaving a faceless ghost.

But however little she knew about her relatives, she knew a great deal about her mother, and she was willing to agree that Mama could be as stubborn as anyone. Hadn't Pappa said the same thing in regard to this trip?

'It's your stubbornness, Mary, your damn fool stubbornness, that's all it is, but this time it isn't going to get you anywhere.'

'It'll get me where I'm going. It'll get me to French Hills.'

'What the hell good will that do you?'

'I want what's mine – ours. I want it for Jolene's sake as well as my own.'

Jolene, listening to the sometimes bitter quarrel from the safety of her own bedroom, had heard her father's derisive laughter, which had set off a fresh string of abuse from Mama. But in the end, Mama's stubbornness had prevailed – at least with Papa. They were here, weren't they, headed for some destination Jolene could not even picture in her mind, though Mama had said they were going for her sake.

And I don't even know what it is we're after, Jolene thought wearily.

She jumped and nearly dropped the reins as something gave a ghostly howl in the distance. 'What's that?' she cried, eyes wide with fright.

'A coyote. Don't be frightened,' Mary said. 'My parents came all the way cross country without a buggy, I guess we can make it from here to French Hills. Come on, you'd better climb down.'

The coyote's howl faded on a diminuendo, as if washed away in the running water. In its wake, though, came another sound, the distant rhythm of horses' hooves, coming rapidly closer.

'Jolene, get down, stand here beside me,' Mary said in a tense whisper. 'There's no telling who that might be.'

Jolene, abandoning the horse's reins, jumped quickly down

from the buggy to stand within the protective embrace of her mother's arm. She peered through the gloom, unconsciously squinting as she did so, watching for a glimpse of the approaching rig. The rain concealed it until the last minute. Huddled together, she and Mama waited apprehensively. In the distance the coyote cried aloud once more; Jolene felt her Mama tremble, whether from the cold or from fear it was impossible to know.

Another buggy sped into view; it was almost upon them before the driver spied them and reined in the horses, coming to a halt alongside them in the muddy road.

'What the devil – what are you ladies doing out here in the middle of nowhere?' A florid-faced man with a dripping wet beard leaned out from the rig to peer at them curiously.

'We were on our way to French Hills,' Mama said, 'when an axle broke. We'd be much obliged if you could help us get to a farmhouse.'

'I can do better than that,' the stranger replied, 'I'm on my way to French Hills myself. Climb in before you get soaked.'

Mama pushed Jolene up into the seat and climbed in after her. 'You must be the doctor,' she said.

'That I am, Doctor Willis, at your service,' the stranger said, tipping his hat briefly, before starting up the horses once again. In a twinkling they were speeding once more along the darkened highway. 'But who might you be and what brings you to French Hills at this inauspicious hour?'

'I'm Mary Perreira, Claude Brussac's daughter, and this is my daughter, Jolene.'

The doctor's hands jerked involuntarily, causing the horses to whinny nervously. 'Why, I'd forgotten Claude had a daughter, it's been so long – you're the one married his . . . ' He hesitated; he had been about to say 'field hand' but the words stuck in his throat.

'His steward, yes,' Mary finished for him. 'But tell me, please, how is my father?'

'Why, it's hard to say, he was better, last I saw him, but when I arrived home this evening I had a message to come quick, that he'd taken a turn for the worse. There's cholera going around, you may know, plenty of the hands got it, I've been afraid there might be complications . . . ' He saw Mary bow her head and added hastily, 'Of course, till I see him myself, there's no telling.'

The buggy bounced and slid over the rutted track. Jolene, seated between her mother and the doctor, swayed back and forth drowsily. Once or twice she actually dozed off.

'Almost there,' Mama said finally. They had ridden some distance in silence, both the adults lost in their own reflections.

The announcement roused Jolene from her stupor. She sat upright, peering to either side of the buggy. There was not much to be seen at first, but as her eyes strained at the darkness and the still falling rain, she saw trees, and off to the right something else that struck a responsive chord within her – vines, rows upon rows of vines stretching up a hillside. It brought her sharp, almost painful memories of home, of riding with Papa through their own vineyards, of the rush and strain of harvest, when everyone was too busy to pay much attention to a young girl, and of the sweet-rotten smell of fermenting grapes. At once French Hills was less frightening to her and she found herself looking forward with genuine interest to what lay ahead.

'Look, all those lights,' she cried, pointing into the mist ahead. 'What is that?'

'Home,' Mama said, in a voice unlike her own.

Jolene turned to correct her – home, after all, was behind them – but with a shock she realized that the wetness on her mother's cheeks was not from the rain alone.

Although it was well past midnight the windows of the great house were ablaze, the rain making them seem to flicker and writhe. The smoke rose from the chimneys and, overwhelmed by the wet air, settled low across the yards, adding a pungent tang to the night air.

A servant came to take the steaming horses and as the three travelers hurried toward the house a man came out with a lantern to meet them. To Jolene's surprise, her mother had taken the lead, so that it was she whom the man with the lantern met first. Jolene, bringing up the rear, saw his quick look of shock as Mama threw back the hood of her traveling cloak, revealing her face to the light.

Mama spoke first. 'Hello, Adam,' she said.

'Mary! Good God, it is you, but how on earth . . . ?'

'I found them along the road with a broken axle,' the doctor said. 'Lucky thing for them I came along when I did.'

'How is Papa?' Mary asked, but before Adam could answer there was a shout from the yard and a boy, perhaps a little older than Jolene, dashed through the rain toward them.

'Señor, please, wait.'

Adam scowled when he saw the boy. 'Felipe, we've no time,' he said.

Felipe stopped in front of them, trembling but determined. 'My Mamacita, she's sick, very sick,' he said, addressing the doctor directly.

The doctor and Adam Brussac exchanged glances. 'The cholera,' Adam said. 'Half the people have it.'

'I know, it's near an epidemic.' The doctor's white beard wagged in the lantern light. 'I'll have a look at your mother when I've finished here,' he told the boy.

'But . . . '

'Please, I want to see Papa,' Mary said.

'We'll see to your Ma later,' Adam said sternly to the boy. He put a hand on the doctor's shoulder, piloting him inside. The others followed.

Jolene, bringing up the rear, would like to have expressed her sympathy to the boy, who looked so frightened and worried, but she was shooed inside by her impatient mother, and the thick oak door closed softly but firmly after them.

The night seemed endless. Jolene, struggling to stay awake, had tried in vain to follow the squabbling that had followed their arrival. Mama, of course, wanted to see her father, that much was already clear to Jolene; it was equally clear that the others did not want her to. First the doctor had to see him alone and afterward, despite Mama's loud objections, it was Adam – Uncle Adam, Jolene had learned, though she found it difficult to think of him that way – who had gone, leaving Mama to quarrel with the others.

The others were a roomful of relatives Jolene had not realized she had. Besides Uncle Adam, now absent in his father's room, there was his wife, a grim, cold-eyed woman who sat with pursed lips and said little; Uncle Jean, friendlier, though Jolene thought his laughter sometimes rang false, and his wife, plump and talkative, smelling of sachet as she gave Jolene a not-very-welcome hug; and Uncle David, who dressed like a monk but said that he was not. Jolene liked this last one the best, though he had the least to say. He, at least, looked glad to see her and Mama, though no one else seemed to care for his opinion.

The conversation droned on and on. Jolene, seated near the fire blazing on the hearth, seemed to drift in and out of the torrent of words, her head nodding in the direction of first one speaker, then another. She had all but fallen asleep when something caught her eye.

Seated as she was with her back to the fire, she was the only one facing the open door to the hall, so that she alone saw the boy, Felipe, dart past the opening. She blinked, wondering for a moment if she had imagined the quick flurry of movement, until, flattened against the wall, he stuck his head around for a furtive glance into the room.

He saw her watching him, and disappeared again.

'It wasn't like that,' Mama was saying. 'Of course Papa disapproved of my marrying José. Oh, I know what you're thinking, you're remembering what Papa said, about having nothing to do with me again, but you don't understand. None of you ever understood what it was like with Papa and me.'

Several of them answered at once. No one was paying the slightest attention to Jolene. Nonchalantly she stood and dusted off her skirt, pretending an interest in some bottles that stood on a table near the doorway. She strolled in that direction, paused to run a finger over one dusty bottle, and glanced over her shoulder. They were too absorbed in their argument to notice her. In three bold steps she was in the corridor and facing the frightened-looking Felipe.

'What are you doing spying on me?' he demanded in an angry whisper.

'What are you doing creeping around the halls like a thief?' she asked in reply.

'Looking for the doctor. Who's in there?' She told him. 'The Brussacs,' he said with a sneer.

'Aren't you a Brussac?' she asked.

The question startled him. 'What makes you say that?' he asked.

'You're here. And you look like Uncle Adam.'

'I wouldn't let them hear that, if I was you. They wouldn't like to think a Mexican looked like a precious Brussac.'

The derisive tone stung; she was only just learning of her own Brussac heritage and was suffering conflicting reactions to it: she wanted to be proud of that heritage, yet so far she had seen little that struck her as admirable. The Brussacs she had met were unfriendly and quarrelsome. Felipe's tone of scorn came too close to her own feelings, and loyalty made her defensive.

'At least the Brussacs are clean,' she snapped. 'You smell like you need a bath.'

He gave her a withering look and started away down the corridor. At once she was sorry to have been so tart. He was the first person since her arrival who had really paid any attention to her, and he also seemed the most interesting. Anyway, she had much rather be with him than listen to the boring conversation in the parlor.

'Wait, where are you going?' she asked, running after him.

'I told you, I'm looking for the doctor. My Mamacita's sick.'

'I'll come with you.'

'If you're not afraid of getting dirty,' he said.

Taking that for an invitation, Jolene trailed along after him. The house was built in the shape of a quadrangle, around a central patio – quite unlike the three-story gingerbread house which Papa had just built for them near Sonoma, in the north, and which she was missing sorely. She could hear the splashing of the rain in the fountain outside, and from behind them the murmur of the still arguing voices in the parlor.

'I've forgotten your name,' she said.

'Felipe.' He didn't bother asking hers. Ahead of them, gradually, she heard the sound of still other voices.

'El Patron's bedroom,' Felipe said, motioning her to be still.

'Who?' she asked in a whisper.

'Their father,' he said, with a shrug that made her understand that he meant the Brussacs she'd left in the parlor.

It took a moment for her to comprehend. Their father – he meant her grandfather, then. She was swept by a wave of panic. So far the Brussacs had not even let Mama go to him; she didn't want to think what would happen if they found her here!

'I don't want . . . ' she started to say, but he suddenly grabbed her, shoving her through an open door into a darkened room.

'Sshh,' he warned when she started to protest.

'I'll get the others,' a voice, Uncle Adam's voice, said from nearby. Felipe shoved her further back into the darkness of the bedroom. She had a glimpse of Uncle Adam going by in the corridor.

'Come on,' Felipe said.

'I'm scared,' she said.

He gave her a stern look, but apparently what he saw convinced him she really was frightened, because his expression softened. 'It's all right,' he said, suddenly appearing to be much older, 'Here, give me your hand.'

He took her hand in his own, leading her back into the corridor, and once again toward her grandfather's bedroom.

She didn't really want to go, and not only because she feared her relatives' reactions; she understood that her grandfather was dying, and while she had had no actual experience of death, she understood enough to know that she didn't want to know more.

At the same time, however, the feel of Felipe's strong young hand gave her a sense of well being that she hadn't had since leaving Papa at Sonoma. Reluctant to break the contact, she went along.

A single lamp, turned so low that it was little more than a candle flame, burned on the night stand. The gloom was so heavy that Jolene at first thought the room was empty. For a moment the two children stood in the doorway; despite the firmness of his grip, Jolene sensed Felipe's uncertainty. There was no sign of the doctor.

'Who's there?'

Jolene gave a quick whimper of fear at the unexpected voice, seeming to come from an empty room. What had appeared to be nothing more than rumpled bedclothes stirred slightly on the bed.

'Who is that? What do you want?' the voice asked from the bed.

'I was looking for the doctor, sir,' Felipe replied.

'Come here.' Weak though it was, the voice carried the unmistakable ring of authority. Felipe crossed the room toward the bed. Jolene would happily have stayed behind, but the grip on her hand was so tight now that she was forced to go too, though she hung back as much as she was able.

A draft stirred the lamp's flame, making the shadows on the wall dance eerily. 'Is it Adam?' the man on the bed asked.

'It's Felipe, sir.'

'Felipe.' He broke into a fit of coughing, making the coverlet shake violently. It was a moment before he could regain his breath.

'Felipe,' he said again, making almost a sigh of it. 'Meant to talk to you before . . . shouldn't have left it up to your father . . .'

Again he was interrupted by the coughing, harsh, labored barking sounds. Felipe stared in silent confusion. He had no father, only his Mamacita, and she was dying – just as, he thought, for the first time in his young life seeing things from a point of view other than his own, the man before him was dying too.

'I told you . . . I told Adam . . . I've made arrangements for you. He'll tell you . . . but you've got a right to know about your sister.' Still another bout of coughing, this the worst yet. 'I made no provisions – just as well she stay Juanita's child. She was happy enough to get her, her own baby dying like that . . .'

He paused, seeming to struggle for breath. Felipe's mind was awhirl. None of it made sense to him. He had no sister either, and no father. El Patron was talking crazy talk.

'I told Adam,' El Patron struggled to say, speaking more as if to himself, 'told him, no good, scattering bastards all over the countryside . . .'

For the first time, his eyes, sunken into his face like great gaping wounds, rested on Jolene. She had been staring in mute terror and confusion, the childhood images of a Santa-like man colliding with the near skeleton on the bed. A shudder passed through her at his gaze, and she had a horrible urge to pee.

For a long moment, so long that Jolene thought the man had somehow gone to sleep with his eyes open, he stared at her, his eyes seeming to grow wider and more intense with each second.

'Who's with you?' he asked.

Jolene would have turned and fled if she could but, to her dismay, Felipe gripped her arm in his free hand and tugged her forward, till she was standing at the edge of the bed. Those dark, nightmare eyes held her own prisoner. She could neither speak nor turn away, but only stand trembling at the bedside.

'Mary?'

She tried to find a voice, to explain that Mary was her mother, but though she moved her lips, no sound came forth.

'Mary – you've come home. I've always known . . .' The rest was lost in more coughing. A hand, so withered that the veins stood out in gaunt relief, appeared from beneath the coverlet, reaching toward her. She stepped back, pressing herself against Felipe, terrified of the hand's touch.

There was yet another bout of coughing. This time the sunken eyes closed. The coughing ended. She stared in horrified fascination as a line of pinkish foam appeared at his lips; one bubble grew and grew, until it was the size of a marble. Then it burst, becoming a tiny red rivulet running down his chin. He made a loud rattling sound in his throat, and the hand that had reached toward her dropped with a dull thump on the bed.

Suddenly there was no sound at all in the room; the silence seemed to rush in upon them. All at once, she knew: he was dead.

Her mouth flew open, and she uttered a long, high-pitched shriek; she turned from the bed, and somehow found herself wrapped in the protective embrace of Felipe's arms.

She was still there when, a moment later, her mother and the Brussacs burst into the room.

In the excitement of El Patron's death, the adults forgot to scold the two children. That was little consolation for Felipe, however, in view of the news that the doctor had already gone.

'We forgot,' Adam said. 'He's swamped with calls.' Seeing the boy's anguished look, he added in a softer voice, 'Look, I'll come out and have a look at your Ma in a minute, okay?'

There was nothing for Felipe to do but return helplessly to the shack he and his mother shared among the workers' quarters.

She lay blissfully unaware of the tensions and excitements of the big house. She was dreaming, of her own youth, and of a man with laughing eyes who had found her by a stream one day. So handsome . . . it was fiesta, and from the village plaza came the strains of music. Then she had loved to dance, her feet aching sweetly in the cool dust . . .

'Mamacita?'

Something stirred in her memory – the boy, something she meant to do, something to explain – but the man was there, smiling, inviting her to dance in the moonlight.

'Felipe.'

'They are coming, Mamacita, Señor Adam says he'll come.'

Adam. Yes, she knew an Adam, sometimes he came in the dark of the night, taking, never asking – but this was not he, this handsome caballero whose lips brushed hers, coaxing her into the trees, to the dry, shadowed clearing where they might dance uninterrupted . . . how sweet the music sounded.

'Felipe – your sister . . .'

The boy leaned low over the bed, straining to catch the whispered words. Again, a sister; El Patron had spoken of a sister too, but he had no sister. He started to speak, to remind her of this, but her lips were moving again, laboriously forming words.

'Your sister – look after her, care for her, you must promise me – Juanita is old . . .'

'Mamacita – '

'Swear it!' Her voice was a sudden hiss. One hand clawed at his.

'I swear.'

The hand relaxed its grip. He fought the tears, managed to ask, 'But who is my sister?'

She did not answer. She had gone dancing with the laughing stranger.

2

It was a day of the dead. Jolene's recently discovered grandfather was buried in the vineyards, beside his wife. Felipe's mother and a grapepicker who had succumbed during the night were buried in the little cemetery plot on the hill behind the storage sheds.

It had been Uncle Adam's suggestion that they all attend the latter funeral. Uncle Jean's wife had been willing, but Uncle Adam's wife had balked and Jolene's mother had refused altogether.

'I'm not going to some whore's funeral,' she had put it baldly, 'And I'm not going to legitimize her bastard with my presence either.'

In the end, the three Brussac brothers had gone alone, David in the coarse brown robe of the order of 'brothers' to which he belonged, the others in their work clothes, for it was harvest time and the work in the vineyards must go on, death notwithstanding.

Afterward there was a rather stilted lunch at which Jolene met her cousins: Nadine, Uncle Adam's daughter, who was nine, and Caleb and Harvey, eleven and twelve, who were Uncle Jean's sons. She found them a coarse and vulgar trio, the boys guffawing at their own private jokes and Nadine simpering idiotically. She was sorry when, after lunch, the three of them invited her to join them outside.

'Yes, why don't you go along and play,' Mama agreed. 'We're going to be reading the will anyway – which ought to prove interesting.'

Reluctantly, Jolene trailed along with her cousins. Secretly she had hoped for another meeting with Felipe. She felt herself drawn to him, without knowing exactly why – perhaps she sensed a kinship in his swarthy skin, so like her father's; or maybe it was nothing more than the loneliness she sensed in him.

The rented surrey that had broken down on Jolene's trip here had been replaced by a hired carriage that awaited her and Mama in the yard outside, the driver chewing rhythmically on a plug of tobacco.

'Your Mama's gonna be mighty angry about that will,' Nadine said when they were outside.

'My Mama doesn't care about any old will,' Jolene said, without conviction.

'She's sure come far enough for something she doesn't care about,' Caleb said.

'My mother says, just to steal what she can from us,' Nadine added.

'That's not true,' Jolene said hotly. 'Mama only wants what's rightfully ours.'

'Which,' said Caleb, 'is nothing.'

'Never mind about that,' Harvey said, interrupting the angry reply Jolene had been about to make. He gave her a big grin and came directly up to her. 'I've heard tell, a really pretty girl can get along just fine without any money. If she knows how to treat a fella, anyway.'

'I don't know what you mean,' Jolene said coolly, though she had a pretty good idea.

Harvey reached out and ran one dirty hand through her hair; she grimaced and drew back from him. 'No need for you to act all snooty,' he said, taking a firm hold on her long tresses. 'It don't do for poor relations to act too grand, you know.'

'We're not poor relations,' Jolene cried, slapping at his hand, though he refused to let go. 'Papa owns Brussac-America, and Mama says we sell more wine than French Hills any day in the week – and let go my hair.'

'I will, coz – soon's you give me a big kiss.'

'I won't. Let go.'

Harvey only laughed and, bending down, tried to kiss her. Caleb and Nadine joined in the laughter; both had found their new cousin altogether too pretty, and too refined, for their tastes.

There was a flurry of movement as someone ran across the

yard, and suddenly Felipe was there, hanging on to Harvey's back and pounding him with his fists.

'You let her go,' Felipe demanded.

Harvey, older and considerably bigger, threw Felipe off with hardly an effort, sending him sprawling in the dust. Before Felipe could recover, both the other boys were upon him, Caleb managing to get a hold on him from behind, while Harvey began pummeling him from the front. Nadine, watching from a safe distance, clapped her hands with excitement. It was an unfair fight, and though Felipe was kicking and swinging his fists valiantly, he was being soundly beaten.

'Stop that,' Jolene cried. 'You stop that this instant.'

She began to pound on Harvey's back and shoulders. He was so startled by this unexpected attack that he stopped beating Felipe. Caleb, equally surprised, let go of Felipe too, allowing him to sprawl once more in the dirt.

'Stay out of this,' Harvey growled.

'I won't,' Jolene said, thrusting her chin forward angrily. 'You let him alone or I'm going to tell Uncle Adam.'

Unwittingly, she had hit upon the one threat that carried weight. Exactly why Uncle Adam concerned himself with their Nemesis they had no idea, but they knew from past experience that they were courting a trip to the woodshed by beating up on Felipe.

'He's all yours,' Harvey said nonchalantly, spitting in Felipe's direction. 'We're not done with you yet, though, greaser,' he warned before sauntering away. Caleb and Nadine followed, casting their own threatening glances Felipe's way.

When she was sure they were really leaving and not playing some trick, Jolene turned her attention to Felipe, who was getting up from the ground, brushing the dirt from his clothes. There was blood on his face and one eye was already beginning to swell.

'Are you all right?' she asked.

'I think so.' He managed a crooked smile for her. 'What are you doing out here?'

'They're reading the will. Here, hold still.' She tugged a lacy handkerchief from her pocket and began to dab at his face. 'It's lucky for me you were around.'

The remark made Felipe blush. He had been where he wasn't supposed to be – hanging around outside the kitchen. Since those puzzling remarks of El Patron's the night before, he had been thinking about the cook, Juanita, and her daughter, Elena. El

Patron had mentioned Juanita, and somehow the cook had been connected with the subject of his sister, though he hadn't known he had a sister; and later, his mother had spoken of the same thing, and asked him to take care of his sister.

But how could he, if he didn't know who she was? Was Elena, the cook's daughter, his sister? She was about his own age, perhaps a year or two younger. He had tried to think whether she looked like him, but the fact was, he had only a scant idea of what he looked like himself. He had studied a mirror's reflection, but it had remained unfamiliar to him; when he closed his eyes, he could not conjure up that glass-frozen face.

It was for this reason that he had been hanging about; but this was all too personal, and too little understood by himself, to try to explain it to someone else.

'Ouch,' he said.

'They don't like you very much, do they?' she asked.

'They call me a bastard.'

Jolene, busy dabbing at the blood on his face, had a sharp, swift recollection of her mother using the same word earlier. And last night, before that horrible moment when her grandfather had died, he too had said something about bastards, hadn't he? She tried to remember, but at the time she had been so mesmerized by the sight of the dying man that the words had made little impression.

'What's a bastard?' she asked aloud.

'It's someone who doesn't have a father.'

'But that's ridiculous, everybody has a father.'

Before he could answer her they were interrupted by the eruption of a quarrel on the porch. Jolene's mother burst from the house, followed by two of her brothers, Adam and Jean. They were all talking at once, but it was Mary's voice, raised to a shout, that carried easily across the yard.

'It's outrageous,' she cried, tossing her head angrily. 'Pure robbery, that's all it is, you're trying to steal my birthright from me.'

'Mary,' Adam raised his voice to match hers, 'It's Pa's will . . . '

'A pack of lies, Papa never wrote any such thing . . . Well, he never meant it if he did write it. You know that was all bluff, he never meant to disinherit me. He'd have changed that will if you hadn't interfered. You're against me, both of you, because I married José.'

Jolene and Felipe couldn't hear what was said in reply; both Jean and Adam seemed to be talking at once, but whatever it was apparently infuriated Mary to the point that she could not even answer. For a moment she looked from one to the other of her brothers, her eyes flashing. Then, shaking her fist in their direction, she turned and flounced down the steps, in the direction of the waiting carriage.

'Jolene,' she fairly screamed. 'Jolene, come here at once, we're leaving this den of thieves.'

The sight of this beautiful and strong-willed woman in high temper was an awesome spectacle to young Felipe, used to the prim and proper wives of the Brussac brothers.

'Jolene.'

'I have to go,' Jolene said, with obvious reluctance.

'Wait . . . '

'Mama is furious.'

'I love you.'

'Jolene.'

She fluttered a hand at him and was gone, running across the yard to where her mother now stood half in, half out of the carriage. Mary yanked her daughter inside and the door closed noisily, but a moment later the curtain was jerked downward and Mary's head thrust through the opening.

'You needn't think I'm done with this,' she shouted, shaking her fist at them again. The driver, whether on her instructions or perhaps simply fearful of violence, started up the horses and the coach began to move, but Mary continued to lean out the window of the vehicle, shaking her first and shouting.

'You won't get away with it, I'll have my rightful inheritance, be damned if I don't.'

In her own seat, Jolene squirmed to get a glimpse past her mother of the young man she had befriended. She saw him staring wistfully after them, until the coach turned and he was lost to view.

She leaned back against the horsehair seat, paying no attention to her mother's shouted curses, her mind occupied with more personal reflections of her experiences on this singular trip. She was only dimly aware that she had made a conquest, and still less aware of just how she had accomplished it.

What she did have, however, was a new and strangely intoxicating sense of her own power over other people.

Particularly, it seemed, male people.

3

Felipe woke to the distant crowing of a cock. For a moment he could not trace the source of that delicious comfort with which he had slept. He knotted a corner of bedsheet between his fingers, lazily drifting between sleep and wakefulness.

Bedsheet. He sat up abruptly, his eyes flying open, blinking as the unfamiliar room crowded in upon him. Not a straw-filled mattress but a bed, with posters and linen and a warm comforter; a massive armoire in which his one change of clothing had been hung; a chest, old and nicked and scarred, yet elegant in its wear and age; curtained windows that opened onto a balcony.

He was in France. He was at the Chateau Brussac, from which the Brussac family had come to California long years before. Señor Adam had informed him the day of his mother's funeral that he was to be sent here.

'It's for your own good,' he had explained, while avoiding Felipe's eyes. 'I know the other children – well, kids can be cruel, especially when it's something you aren't to blame for . . .'

He had not asked if Felipe wanted to go. Felipe had been informed and that, presumably, was that. And in truth, had he been asked, Felipe would have been hard pressed to say whether he was sorry to be leaving. Sorry, of course, to be leaving Mamacita, but after all she had left before him, in a way of speaking. Except for her, French Hills had offered him precious little in the way of happiness.

Still, it had been his home for all his brief life. It was difficult to go out into an alien world. However unpleasant it was at French Hills, everything was familiar. He had drunk of the water of those hills, smelt the soil damp in the spring rains, crushed in his hands the pulp of the grapes. He was a part of French Hills, perhaps no more than the weeds that grew among the vines, or the rocks that washed down the ravines in the winter floods, but a part nonetheless.

Now, it was thousands of miles behind him, and he was in France. He had traveled for days on end across the great plains, had climbed mountains and crossed rivers so wide that they had seemed to his childish eyes like oceans.

He had been awed by the great cities, each larger than the last, culminating in New York. Then had come the ocean, so vast that it had filled his desert-nurtured soul with dread.

The last few days had become a blur of fatigue and over-exposure; his senses had balked at absorbing more, and he had plodded doggedly along at the side of Margarita, the maid who had been sent to accompany him on his journey. More trains, carriages, and finally, when he had thought that he had passed into some nether world of never-ceasing journey, they had come to an immense, crumbling wreck of a house, and perhaps the most astonishing of all the sights he had confronted, the mistress of Chateau Brussac.

She was old, as old surely as El Patron himself had been; she was, if Felipe understood correctly, El Patron's sister. But though he had been old, he had maintained to the last an aristocratic aura; his sister was a hag.

Her sparse grey hair was partially concealed under a dirty head scarf. Few of her teeth remained, and these were stained and blackened, and on her upper lip was a line of dark fuzz that gave her a mustachioed look. Her dress was so ragged and filthy that Felipe's mother would have long since confined it to a ragbag, and on her feet she wore the strange wooden shoes that in time he would learn were the shoes of peasants.

She wanted only a pointed cap to look the part of the witches that had haunted his fairy tales. Nor did her manner on meeting him for the first time dispel his anxieties at being entrusted to this creature's care, for it was plain that she did not welcome the intrusion.

In fairness to her, it seemed that the letter Señor Adam had written, explaining things, had gone astray, so that the arrival of an unknown boy accompanied by a maid servant in the late evening was an unexpected inconvenience. At first she had told them in French, and then in a sharp-sounding but intelligible English, that they must go to the inn, but Margarita entreated the woman to read the brief note of introduction that she carried and to this the woman had consented, albeit begrudgingly. She had led them along a dark, shadow-ridden corridor to a room paneled in wood so old it had gone black, and motioned them into chairs while she rummaged in a desk for spectacles. With these balanced precariously atop her nose, she had laboriously deciphered the note's contents, once or twice glancing over her glasses at Felipe.

Halfway through, she gave a great sigh, and sank into another of the musty chairs, sending a cloud of dust into the stale air.

'Claude is dead, then,' she said. She slid her fingers under the spectacles and pressed them briefly against her eyes. Felipe, drunk on fear and exhaustion, listened to the harsh rasp of his own breath and wondered if they would have to start out at once on the long journey back to California.

At length, though, she shook herself, like a dog shedding water, and again peered over the glasses at him. 'And this is the boy, this is . . . ' She paused, squinting at the note. ' . . . Felipe.' She fixed her gaze on him, studying him as she might have studied a strange bug caught between her fingers. He squirmed uncomfortably, unable to reply.

Her eyes drifted from him, seemed to see, beyond, something hovering in the gloom above him. She sat without moving for what seemed an eternity, contemplating she alone knew what.

'Well,' she said, rising with another of those peculiar shedding motions of hers, it's too late for the inn, you'll be wanting to rest, I'm sure. Tomorrow will be time enough to sort things out. Come with me.'

She paused at the door to say, more to Margarita than to Felipe, 'We've no servants here, nothing so grand, only an idiot who sleeps in the sheds and helps with the vines. You'll have to make do for yourselves.'

She had led them to a room crowded with white-sheeted ghosts that had, sheets stripped away, revealed themselves as furnishings – chest, bed, chairs. One for Margarita and, next to it, a room for Felipe.

And here, much to his subsequent surprise, for he had expected to spend the night trembling in fear, he had fallen almost at once into a deep and unbroken sleep, only dimly aware of the voices of the crone and Margarita in the next room, engaged in some lengthy discussion.

Now, he was hungry. It was early, but the strange mistress of the chateau had said they must do for themselves. He clambered from the bed and, having dressed, went in search of the kitchen.

The corridor was still dark. As he stepped from his room he sensed rather than saw something move at the far end of the passageway. Frightened, he turned in that direction. Something white fluttered briefly in the draft of an open doorway, then disappeared. He stared after it but it did not reappear and at length he told himself that it had been nothing more than a window curtain, but he did not go to investigate.

He went the opposite direction, down the great stairs. Their walls were marked with lighter patches where once paintings must have hung; the patches were like gaping wounds on the surface of the walls, testifying to the rape of this once grand manor. He wondered about the people who had lived here in the distant past; had there been a boy his age, rising with the dawn to descend these well-worn stairs? Felipe tried in his imagination to restore the house, to see it as it had been but his mind could not supply the missing pieces.

So many rooms. The house at French Hills had many rooms too, but it was easy to find your way about there, as the house was merely a square built about a central patio.

Here, however, rooms opened onto more rooms, and everywhere he looked were doors, all of them closed, all equally baffling. He found the dining-room at last – a long, battered table but only three chairs, and one of them with a leg missing – and from there the kitchen. While he was standing inside the door looking about, the mistress of the house came in from outside, a basket of freshly picked vegetables over one arm.

'*Bonjour,*' she greeted him. 'You don't speak French, I suppose?' He shook his head. 'A pity. My English is a bit neglected, I'm afraid.'

'You speak it well,' he said.

'Do I now?' She grinned, setting the basket down with a thump at a worktable. 'I learned it years ago as a child. Later I was – confined. I practiced it a great deal then for something to do. It has stayed with me. But I don't suppose that's what you had on your mind. Hungry, are you?'

'*Si* – I mean, yes, Señora.'

She began sorting out the produce, brushing away a speck of loose dirt, discarding a bad-looking leaf. 'Oh, I'm not your señora, don't go making me a Spanish lady, I've trouble enough being what I am.'

'What shall I call you?'

She thought for a moment, eyeing him reflectively. 'Um, yes, that's a puzzle, isn't it? But wait . . . ' She thought a moment more, then laughed aloud, a raucous cackle of a laugh.

'And why not,' she said, as much to herself as to the boy. 'You shall call me Tante Marie – Aunt Marie. And I shall call you, umm, not Felipe, not for a nephew of mine, they'll think the damn gypsies left you. We'll call you Philippe. No, that won't do, not for an American. Well, Philip then. I shall be your Aunt Marie and you shall be my nephew Philip Brussac, from America.' She cackled again.

'But I'm not a Brussac.' He was thinking of how the Brussacs would react to that announcement. Not too kindly, he'd wager.

'Indeed? Well – ' To his surprise she winked at him. 'Who's to say not, if I say so. There are Brussacs and there are Brussacs. They,' she emphasized the word, giving it some significance unclear to him, 'they aren't going to argue about it, are they? They sent you to me, didn't they?'

'Señor Adam said it was for my own good.'

'Um, yes, a little of theirs too. Well, never mind that, tell me something, do you know anything about wine?'

'No. But my Mamacita used to say I had the natural gift for the vines.'

'She did, did she? Blood tells, do what you will to hide it. Who was your Mamacita anyway, just a servant?'

'Yes.'

'And pretty, I suppose.'

'Oh, yes, she was beautiful.' It gave him a pang still to speak of her.

'Beauty can be a curse,' she said. She seemed to be looking not at him but beyond him, at some distant vista. He found himself wondering what she could know of beauty, this ugly crone. But for all her ugliness, he found himself drawn to this peculiar woman into whose hands he had been thrust. Despite her brashness and her odd ways, there was an underlying sympathy about her manner, as if she understood the hurts and longings that beset him. Unlike all the others, except for his mother and the beautiful girl who had appeared so briefly in his life, this woman seemed to care.

'Used,' she murmured, still lost in some private reverie. 'Used, and tossed aside, and the fruit of the seed as well. And they send you to me.'

She shook herself – already he had come to recognize that gesture – and said, 'Come with me.'

Taking a candle from a drawer, she lit it and led him through another door and down a steep flight of stairs, into a cellar of some sort. It was thick with cobwebs and stank of mildew and rot. Something squealed in the shadows and darted past their feet, but she seemed not to notice.

It was, or at least had been, a wine cellar. There were bins, empty now, and others that had been turned over onto the floor. The cellar appeared to have been ransacked ages ago, and left as it was, the dust eventually blurring the evidence of looting.

Marie kicked aside some debris with her foot, and tugged at a wine bin. To Philip's surprise the shelves moved, swinging noisily outward.

'This place was raided, oh, I don't know how many times, but they never found this, your grandfather built it in years and years ago.'

'My grandfather?'

'Your grandfather Brussac, you must remember that you are a Brussac while you are here.'

She saw his confusion, and the hard angry look of her eyes softened somewhat. She paused to put a gnarled hand atop his head. 'It is a game we shall play – you've played pretend games before, haven't you?'

'Yes, Señ . . . yes, Aunt Marie.'

She chuckled softly. 'Um, that's good, that's better. Mind what I tell you, we shall play this Brussac game, you and I, and who can tell, perhaps we shall find a way to win. Here, hold this light.'

She gave the candle to him. Philip lifted it over his head, illuminating the narrow recess beyond the door. It was another wine cellar, smaller and unravaged by the raids that had wrecked the outer cellar. Here moldy bottles of wine still rested in their racks. She selected one, examining the label and the cork, and finally tucking it under her arm.

'This was his first wine, the first he made himself,' she said, taking the candle and leading the way back to the kitchen. 'Long before you were born, before I was born as a matter of fact.'

She opened the wine with the skill of long practice, wiping the lip on her apron before pouring into two glasses; though everything about the house was rotted and crumbling, those glasses, he saw, were clean and unblemished.

'Here,' she said, thrusting one of the glasses at him.

He took it obediently, though he would rather have had one of the hard rolls sitting atop the cupboard. His empty stomach was beginning to growl. Still, he didn't want to offend his new friend.

'A toast,' she said, lifting her glass in salute. 'To my nephew, Philip Brussac, from America.' She chuckled to herself and lifted her glass.

Philip did likewise. The amber-red liquid tasted sour in his mouth and burned as it went down. Although he'd worked since infancy in the vineyards of French Hills, he had never tasted wine before and even this one swallow made him feel oddly dizzy.

Marie smacked her lips and peered at him over her glass. 'Well, what do you think of it?' she asked.

'It's very nice,' he said politely.

She made a face. 'It's bile, you've got no taste at all. But it's also history. This is your family, this wine, the blood of the Brussacs. Where the Brussacs are, there will be wine. Never forget that. Let others dig for rocks, carve wood or weave fabrics. Brussacs make wine.'

It was eerie to stand in the morning sunlight in this musty kitchen, and listen to the words of this half-mad old woman. His head swam from the wine and from hunger and from the strange sense of excitement that sprang to life between them. Somehow he felt that she had indeed made him a Brussac, and that these words expressed with such subdued passion were like an oath taken between them. Almost without volition, he found himself murmuring, 'I swear it.'

She cackled at that, revealing the all-but-toothless gums. 'Yes, yes, let it be our vow,' she said, putting the glass aside. 'Come, you'll want to see the vineyards.'

He didn't, not just now, not when his stomach was rumbling in protest at his neglect, but swept up in the heat of her enthusiasm and made light-headed by the wine, which seemed to grow and spread euphorically through him, he marched spiritedly after her.

Crossing the yard, he paused to look back at the house which was now to be his home, and as he did he stopped dead. 'Aunt, wait,' he cried, 'There's someone there, at that window.'

He looked away and when he looked back at the attic window there was no one there. 'There was someone,' he said, 'in a white dress.'

'Don't be alarmed, it was only René,' she said.

'Who is René?' he asked, disappointed; in his imagination he had shared the place with no one but this singular old woman. He felt a pang of jealousy directed at this intruder.

'René is my brother. He lives in the attic.'

'Why? And why does he wear a dress?'

'It's a wedding gown. René lives in a fantasy world,' she said.

'Is he crazy?'

'Yes, yes, but you mustn't be afraid of him, he's quite harmless, like a child. Look at these vines, they go back centuries, no one knows just how far.'

Her matter of fact attitude eased some of his fears, but nonetheless as they walked Philip found himself glancing back once more at the house. The figure in white was there again, at the window, watching them, it seemed. Philip's uneasiness returned, and he only half heard what the woman was saying.

It was not until the following night that Philip actually met the mysterious René, though in the interim he had remained aware of his presence. Often when out of doors he had looked up toward the attic and discovered the figure in white at the window, apparently watching him, and he had heard rustling sounds outside his door.

In the meantime too he had learned a little of the history of the household. The woman he now called Aunt Marie had been sister to Claude Brussac, El Patron of French Hills. When the Brussacs, Claude and his mother and the woman who was to become his wife, had fled France for political reasons, Marie, her brother René, and their father had been unable to escape and had been imprisoned for a great many years. Though she had been quite vague on what exactly their fate had been in prison, it was evident that it had been horrible and that her young brother's mind had been affected.

In time, with a change in the political winds, they had been released and had returned here to their old home, now in ruins. The father had died soon after, leaving Marie to care for the house and her brother as best she could.

'Of course they invited me to California,' she said. 'But what would have been the point? For me, for René, there would be no new life there. It was as well to stay with the old.'

Philip, settling into his bed for his third night at Chateau Brussac, was grateful that she had made that long-ago decision. He found the place wonderfully fascinating, and as it was a subject on which Marie liked to chat, he had already learned a great deal of its history. The house itself was ancient, its core dating back to the Romans. It had been an abbey for some monks in the twelfth century, and they had made wine, but there had been grapes and a press even before that. Marie had told him that the wine was the history of the Brussacs, and in the last two days he had come to understand a little of what she meant.

What did it matter to him that Chateau Brussac was crumbling and in ruins, that one wing was still blackened from some distant fire, or that there were no servants and one must run endlessly up and down broad stairs and long corridors to go anywhere or get anything done? It was his own private castle, to explore at will. His child's imagination supplied an army of kings and knights, and fair damsels who looked like Jolene. Each corridor, each beckoning door, was a new adventure.

Most of all, there was his new-found aunt. Like the house, she was ancient, but there was something childlike about her too that had allowed the two of them to become the closest of friends. She was the only friend he had ever had and, except for his mother, the only person who had ever been openly affectionate toward him. Of course, no one could replace his mother, but she was gone, even the place of her grave was thousands of miles distant, and though he would not have dreamed it possible, already the grief of her going had begun to fade a little. Aunt Marie couldn't take her place, but she could occupy one very close to it, a special place.

A warm bed, simple but plentiful food; yes, he was glad that fate had brought him here.

Thinking these sanguine thoughts, he was all but asleep when he heard again those rustling sounds outside his door. This time, however, they did not linger briefly, then go away as before; this time, after a moment, he heard the door to his room slowly creak open, and he had a glimpse of a figure in white on the threshold, holding a lighted candle aloft.

Frightened, and not knowing what to do, Philip pretended to sleep. He lay trembling, straining to hear. The rustling drew nearer and he could sense rather than see the light falling upon his closed eyes.

The intruder was by his bed now. Philip could hear the ragged breathing, and was sure that if he but stretched out his hand he would touch his visitor's gown.

At last the waiting became unbearable. Philip opened his eyes slightly, peering through his lashes, and saw René for the first time.

The reality was indeed less frightening than the contemplation of it. True, if one hadn't known, one would probably have assumed this was a woman, with the long, uncombed hair that fell about the shoulders, and the moldy gown that had once been white but now hung upon his spare frame in yellow tatters. His nails were like talons, long and curved under.

It was the face, however, that dispelled the fear, for the face was that of an innocent, a child's face, seemingly unmarred by the passage of time. Indeed, had this been a woman, it would have been a very pretty one, but for the rags and the filth.

René was studying him by the candlelight. Philip had left the window open and a sudden gust of wind sweeping through the room extinguished the flame.

Philip thought that René would probably go now, but instead he set the candle aside and knelt by the bed. Philip shuddered involuntarily as the withered hand reached up to stroke his hair. Slowly, curiously, the fingers moved over his face, outlining his features. Philip closed his eyes again. It was eerie to lie like this in the dark, neither of them speaking, nothing but the rasp of their breath, while those bony fingers traced a pattern of his face.

Then, when Philip thought that he must surely abandon his pretense of sleep, a peculiar thing happened. René lay his head upon the boy's frail chest and began to weep, faintly but unmistakably. Philip felt the warmth of tears upon his naked flesh.

He was embarrassed and moved, quite at a loss as to what to do. But after a moment, as the sobs seemed to increase in intensity, his arm lifted up and came about the trembling shoulders, and he began to pat the sobbing wraith comfortingly, as his mother had used to pat his shoulders when he had cried in her arms.

PART 1

1899

4

A long line of carriages slowly inched its way up Nob Hill, turning one at a time into the gates of a castle-like mansion whose windows blazed with lights. Along the street a crowd had formed to watch the arrivals, their sometimes rowdy comments adding a carnival-like atmosphere to the otherwise elegant scene. A trio of sailors drifted up the hill, passing a rum bottle among them; they were a reminder of the boisterous and ribald Embarcadero at the base of the hills, at the waterfront, whose commerce had raised many of the mansions lining the hill, a fact of which the mansions' inhabitants did not care to be reminded.

Mary and Jolene, in a hired carriage, slowly approached the open gates. A uniformed servant waited there, checking the names of each arrival against a long list; Jolene saw one carriage pull out of line, its window curtains slammed shut by an occupant who had been refused entrance.

The driver halted the carriage at the gate. 'Mrs Perreira, and daughter,' Mary said to the servant with the list. He glanced at it, and into the carriage, as if suspecting them of smuggling gate crashers inside. Finally he nodded to the driver and they pulled forward, taking their place in the line approaching the *porte cochère.*

'Jolene, please try to remember Mister Ecks' name this time, it's Joshua,' Mary said, nervously rearranging the folds of her gown.

'I'll try,' Jolene said indifferently. 'And for Heaven's sake, Mama, you try to remember that it's only a party and not the coronation of the queen.'

'A ball at the Ecks is not just a party,' Mary snapped. 'It's the first important event of the season. And, I might add, the first of the real Nob Hill events that we've been invited to.'

'Is that really so important?' Jolene stared out of the open window. Elegantly coiffed and gowned ladies alighted one by one and, on the arms of their formally attired escorts, swept up the steps to the doors, where more servants waited to see them in. Notwithstanding her remark, Jolene was well aware that the Ecks were royalty of a sort, the reigning monarchs of Nob Hill society.

'Important?' Mary was incredulous. 'You'll never take a place in Nob Hill society without Clara Ecks' approval, I can guarantee you that.'

'You and Papa . . .'

'Jolene, please, call him father.'

'You and *father*, then, have gotten along perfectly well without a place in Nob Hill society. And if it's so important, why isn't father here now?'

'You know your father doesn't like formal affairs,' Mary said sharply; her daughter had struck a sore spot. The truth was, Mary had coaxed, argued, even pleaded with her husband to attend tonight's party, all to no avail. They had parted earlier in frosty silence, and all during the ride here Mary had been turning over in her mind how to explain his absence to her hosts. It was quite bad enough as it was, without the necessity of quarreling with her own daughter.

'Notwithstanding your father's absence,' she said in a low voice, as they had finally taken their place under the *porte cochère* and the footman was hurrying around to open the door for them, 'these people are important to him as well, because they are important to Brussac-America wines. If someone as socially prominent as Clara Ecks were to take to serving California wines instead of French ones, it would be a tremendous boon to the California wine industry – and especially to Brussac-America.'

Jolene wanted to say that Brussac-America, as her father called his winery, seemed to be doing all right for itself without the boon of Clara Ecks' approval, but her mother was already alighting from the carriage. Jolene followed her, uncomfortable with the sight of the crowd across the street watching the arrival of the rich and the powerful. She felt a sham as she climbed the stairs at her mother's side. She was not rich, certainly not in a class with the Ecks, and she certainly wasn't powerful. She would, in fact, have been more comfortable on that side of the street, as one of the watchers.

In a way, she wished she could share her mother's Nob Hill aspirations, if only because she truly hated disappointing Mama. But it all seemed so shallow to her, so inconsequential. What difference did it make if Clara Ecks welcomed them into her house or not? It was a stuffy, overheated museum of a place anyway, and Clara Ecks was a stuffy, overheated bore.

Papa had been right to stay at home, even though it meant another of those lingering quarrels between him and Mama. By now Jolene knew all the signs; her parents' quarrels were like well rehearsed plays, each knowing in advance what lines the other would use and which response would have the desired effect. It was incredible that the oft-repeated barbs and taunts still had the power to anger or wound; or perhaps the emotional response was only habit as well.

Jolene was not unaware of the attention they received when they came in. The pretty girl who had dazzled Felipe some years before had grown into a young woman of striking beauty. Her hair was the same pale silk. Her tawny complexion had mellowed into a deep tan, a striking contrast to the San Francisco debutantes, who fashionably eschewed the sun's glare.

The recent annexation of Hawaii and the cession of the Philippines had brought a new awareness of the lands across the Pacific, and in the eyes of the nation moved California from the periphery to the center of events. One of the more visible results had been a rash of things Polynesian, and it was to be expected that the Ecks, whose fortune was built on Hawaiian sugar cane, would be quick to join the bandwagon.

That, Jolene reflected, must explain the brilliant tropical print of Clara Ecks' gown, and the orchid pinned over one ear. Still, she thought with a smile, one might be grateful that the hostess had not opted for a grass skirt.

'My dear Mrs Perreira,' Mrs Ecks greeted them, adding an extra *r* to the end of the name, 'And your adorable daughter, how nice to see you again, my darlings, but where is Mister Perreira?'

Mary murmured something about ill health. Jolene, looking past Mrs Ecks, barely heard; her attention had been caught by a man watching from an archway, with a boldness that bordered on rudeness. She wondered who he was. He was older, perhaps Papa's age, but quite handsome, in a dissolute way. Attractive, though she found his manner a bit off-putting.

He saw that she had noticed him – good Heavens, how could she not notice him – and smiled, nodding his head. Pretending she hadn't seen, Jolene looked away, but not before she saw that he had started in their direction.

Their hostess had excused herself. Jolene followed her mother toward what the Ecks referred to as the grand salon. The furniture had been removed or placed against the walls, transforming the room into a ballroom. There were potted palms everywhere, more of the Hawaiian craze.

A small orchestra had been crowded into one of the alcoves and the musicians were playing as if their fortunes depended upon it, which might well be the case – the Ecks were a powerful influence in local music circles.

The dance floor was filled with whirling, swaying bodies. Gaslights made the room as bright as day – too bright, Jolene thought; she much preferred the softness of candlelight, but Clara Ecks was a determinedly fashionable woman. Still, it was a lively scene and if Jolene was not much inclined toward Nob Hill snobbishness, she enjoyed a party as well as any young woman. She caught a glance from Clara Ecks' son, David. She had met him at one or two parties, less grand affairs than this, and though he was regarded as one of the town's more eligible bachelors, she rather thought he had taken an interest in her. Not that it was mutual; he was a bit too pompous to suit her. Still, it was flattering to be sought after by one who was himself sought after, and when he glanced her way again, over the shoulder of his current partner, she flashed him a dazzling smile.

'Mary – it is Mary, is it not?'

Jolene started and turned, finding herself facing the handsome stranger who had studied her so boldly a few minutes before.

'Richard Trémorel – I had no idea,' Mary said, looking even more surprised than her daughter.

'That I would be here?' Richard Trémorel cocked an eyebrow, looking amused. 'But surely you must have heard of my marriage – it was in the papers forever, it seemed.'

'To Doreen Ecks, yes, of course, but I thought – that is, since her accident . . .'

'Ah, yes, the "accident". Poor Doreen – the truth is, for all her upbringing, the girl had no taste. Flinging herself from a rooftop that way, it reveals a rather common mentality, wouldn't you say? I mean, there are genteel ways . . .' He left the suggestion of 'genteel ways' dangling uncomfortably.

'Yes, of course,' Mary said, flustered by the unexpected meeting and the awkward course of the conversation. 'What I meant was, hadn't I read that you were living abroad?'

'Until a week ago. Just until the press found something else with which to amuse themselves. But please, this is a subject that bores me, let us talk about something more interesting – such as this lovely creature at your side. The resemblance is unmistakable, of course – but have I forgotten a younger sister?'

'This is my daughter, Jolene – the Count Richard de Trémorel.'

'Your daughter – I can't believe it.' He looked surprised, but Jolene saw that his eyes were amused. '*Ravissante,*' he murmured, taking her hand in his and bowing to kiss it. 'Truly ravishing.'

The name, and the remarks on his marriage, brought vague memories to Jolene's mind – the highly touted marriage of the Ecks' only daughter, and her leap, less than a year later, from the roof of their townhouse. There had been hints of scandal, ugly rumors of strange goings-on, of sailors and ruffians from the waterfront seen coming and going from the house at odd hours.

The girl's parents had remained silent on the subject, and their apparent loyalty to their son-in-law, though he had gone abroad to live soon afterwards, had served as an acquittal of any charges against him. Richard Trémorel was handsome, sophisticated, and wealthy in his own right. Moreover, his French title was entirely legitimate, an asset of considerable worth in the current, status-hungry Nob Hill circles. How much this had influenced Clara Ecks' behavior no one could say, but her influence was such that no one cared to take her to question publicly, and in due time her strategy had been effective: the stories had become whispers, and then had ceased to be heard at all.

It was easy enough, Jolene thought, to believe the old rumors. Despite Richard Trémorel's well-practiced charm, his eyes were cruel and mocking, and the air of dissolution about him was unmistakable. A woman could see at a glance that this was a dangerous man with whom to get involved.

Yet, perversely, that fact only added to his attraction. His very smile, turned upon her with dazzling effect, was an invitation to illicit adventures; the insinuating way in which he ran one finger lightly across the back of her hand before releasing it hinted at an intimacy that was at once indecent and thrilling.

And, Jolene thought, withdrawing her hand tactfully but firmly, not entirely pleasant. She thought of a jungle snake, mesmerizing its prey, fixing its gaze, waiting for the right instant for its fatal strike. She had no doubt that Richard Trémorel's sting would be poisonous.

He had turned back to her mother, though not without letting his eyes slide, for the merest fraction of a second, over the fullness of Jolene's bosom. She felt in that moment as though the bodice of her dress had been stripped away, leaving her bare to his hungry gaze.

'It has been too many years,' he was saying to Mary.

'Yes, we must get together. We're in Sonoma. Perhaps you'd like to come to dinner sometime soon.'

'I should like that very much,' he said, with another of those quick sidelong glances in Jolene's direction. His interest was all too evident; Jolene was sure her mother must have noticed it too, though she gave no sign.

Someone called to him from nearby. He left them with apologies and promises that they would meet again soon. But the parting left Jolene vaguely troubled; as she and her mother were turning away, she happened to glance in his direction again. He was walking away from them, but he too had looked back, not at her but at Mama. It was a brief glance, so quick that Jolene could not even be certain afterward of what she had seen.

But it had looked, for a second, no more, as if he were regarding Mama with a look of pure hatred. So brief was it that when, disbelieving her eyes, she had blinked, it was over, he was looking elsewhere, and she was wondering if she had imagined the incident altogether.

Still, it lingered like a bad taste in her mouth. 'Who is he?' she asked.

'Richard Trémorel? You must have heard of him, he married—'

'Yes, yes, I know – what I meant was, how do you happen to know him?'

Mary said, 'I almost married him myself once.'

'Good heavens, I can't imagine—'

'I don't see why not,' Mary said coolly. 'I was considered something of a beauty, hard though it may be for you to believe.'

'Oh, I didn't mean that, you still are, everyone says so. I meant, were you in love with him?'

'I thought so at the time.'

'Then why didn't you marry him?'

'My family prevented it,' Mary said, an unmistakable note

of bitterness creeping into her voice. 'Your father had a hand in it too, though I didn't know it at the time.'

Sensing that she had ventured into a troublesome area, Jolene said, 'Well, it's probably for the best. I don't think anyone could be happy married to that man. He looks as though he beats his women.'

'Perhaps,' Mary said. She added, more as if to herself than to Jolene, 'On the other hand, perhaps today I would be the reigning queen of Nob Hill, and Clara Ecks would be contriving for my invitations.'

'You can't mean that,' Jolene said, dismayed. 'It wouldn't be worth the price.'

Mary stopped and turned to face her directly, ignoring an irritated 'Excuse me' from a gentleman whose path she had blocked.

'They say he drove his wife to her death – some, even that he caused it directly. Yet you see him here a free man, untroubled by any authority, earthly or otherwise. Great position means great power. These things are worth making sacrifices for.'

She continued on her way and Jolene trailed silently in her wake. But the exchange had troubled her. She couldn't help wondering how much her mother would be willing to sacrifice for the sort of position she sought.

Would she – the question came unbidden – would she, for instance, sacrifice her own daughter?

5

Although she ignored the mountains of imported caviar and the champagne that literally poured from fountains, Jolene was not inclined to pass up an evening of dancing, and, being young and beautiful, she suffered no lack of partners.

Soon after she had begun, she found herself dancing a waltz with a business acquaintance of her father. The gentleman was large and sweaty and had a habit of stepping on her feet, so that she was not at all sorry when a stranger asked to cut in.

'I hope you don't mind,' the newcomer said, waltzing her

briskly away from her former partner.

Jolene glanced up into his face. He was handsome, his dark eyes twinkling mischievously. A lock of chestnut hair had spilled across his forehead, adding to the boyish effect. She found herself squinting; her eyes had been weak since childhood, but she refused to wear the spectacles recommended by the doctor. Not even Papa's efforts had persuaded her otherwise, though Mama at least agreed with her.

'I'm grateful,' she said aloud to her partner. 'And my feet thank you as well, Mister . . . ?'

'Morrow,' he said, 'Sloan Morrow. But don't say it too loudly. My name's not on the guest list, and frankly I don't think the Ecks would welcome me.'

'But what are you doing here?' she asked; she found it hard to imagine that anyone could have succeeded in crashing the Ecks' party.

'I came to relieve some gentlemen of their money – now don't look so alarmed, please, I mean at a poker game, not at gunpoint.'

She stopped short, causing another couple to collide with them. 'You're a card sharp, you mean,' she accused him. 'You're quite right, the Ecks wouldn't welcome it, and they're very powerful people.'

'Powerful and rich,' he said, smiling as he pulled her firmly toward him and resumed the dance. 'But you needn't worry yourself about it – unless of course you're one of those gambling women who wants to sit in on a few hands – though I should warn you, I lose an occasional hand, but never a game.'

'You mean you cheat,' she said, though she remembered to keep her voice low.

'If you want to look at it that way, I could say I was cheated by being born to a cleaning woman and a down-at-the-heels gambler instead of a sugar baron. I prefer to think that with my cards I'm only righting injustice.'

Despite herself, Jolene laughed; the thought of anyone's taking advantage of the Ecks and their stuffy friends was too delicious for her not to.

She quickly recovered her decorum, however, saying, 'You're only going to get yourself in trouble.'

'With those gentlemen? They look all too eager to accommodate me, wouldn't you say?' He indicated a group of gentlemen nearby, waiting with ill-concealed impatience. As Jolene looked, one of the men nodded in Sloan's direction.

'I'm afraid they're waiting for me,' he said, leading her to a chair near the wall. 'I allowed myself to be talked into a little game with those fellows. You will save a dance for me a bit later, won't you?'

'I will not,' she said haughtily, snatching her hand away when he was about to kiss it. 'I have a reputation to consider, thank you, and dancing with a card-sharp isn't likely to do it any good.'

'Ah, but you mustn't forget your debt, Miss Perreira, I did come to your rescue.'

'How did you know my name?'

He shrugged. 'As easy as asking, same as every other man in the place has been doing since you came in. Never fear, I shall collect the debt one day. A man who lives by his wits as I do often finds himself in a fix. And now, I'm afraid I really must go.'

He bowed elegantly from the waist, though he retained his roguish grin. 'Do, please, save another dance for me.'

'I wouldn't dance the last waltz on earth with you.'

'Fortunately,' he replied, 'we're a long way from that. This band must have another hundred or two in them from the way they're sawing. *Hasta luega.*'

She watched him threading his way through the still-dancing couples. What a strange man, so unlike anyone she'd met before.

Mary joined her, staring after the vanishing gambler. 'Who on earth is that man?' she asked.

'His name is Morrow,' Jolene said matter of factly. 'He's a card player.'

'How peculiar, for this place. Where on earth did you find him?'

'I didn't,' Jolene said. 'He found me.'

Mary watched as Sloan Morrow joined the waiting gentlemen and, after a quick round of handshakes, they disappeared together through an arched doorway. She had not failed to notice the little smile with which her daughter had watched the man go.

Well, she thought firmly, whatever Mister Morrow's plans were, he was mistaken to think she would permit a flirtation between himself and Jolene. She had her own plans, for herself and for Jolene; and they did not include cheap card players, however handsome.

Mary had one consuming ambition, toward which she had

directed all her energies. She had worked hard with her husband, a husband she had long since realized was a mistake in her life, to make a success of their winery. Brussac-America's success was due as much to her shrewdness as it was to José's skills as a vintner. It was she who, in the course of difficult correspondence with her crazy Grand Aunt Marie in France, had conceived the idea of reinvesting in Chateau Brussac, ultimately providing them with a trickle of French wine but, far more valuable, the added cachet of French credentials for Brussac-America's wines.

She was the first to admit that their wines were not as good as those produced at French Hills. French Hills' wines were for the connoisseur who was willing to pay premium prices to buy the best. Hers were cheaper, and they sold to a clientele for whom 'Founded in France, 1430' printed on the label was more of a selling edge than the wine itself. People, she reflected wryly, like the nouveau-riche Ecks and the rest of the Nob Hill crowd, who needed someone to tell them what was good or bad.

Yet, though she scorned them, she coveted them too; and not only for the considerable sales boost that an endorsement could mean. It was position that Mary wanted, position and power.

She had exhausted the legal channels through which she had sought to regain the inheritance that her brothers at French Hills had stolen from her. What was gone was gone.

What was not gone, however, was her anger and her resentment. They – French Hills, her brothers, their families – were her enemies. She wanted to crush them. She wanted to repay them for the frustration and the humiliation she had suffered.

To do that, she needed more than money, more than a successful winery – she needed the sort of strength that emanated from Nob Hill.

It was toward this end that she had courted the Ecks and the others of their crass crowd. Nor had she any reservations about using her daughter to further her schemes. Doors that would not open to her might well open to Jolene – if, for instance, she were to make the right marriage. Perhaps David Ecks – she had seen his looks in Jolene's direction. Or perhaps even Richard Trémorel; scoundrel that he was, he was accepted on Nob Hill, however reluctantly, because of Clara Ecks' endorsement.

There were a dozen or more possibilities, and Mary had tirelessly pursued introductions to each of them. She was determined her daughter would marry well, and on her terms.

Her terms did not include Mister Morrow.

Aloud, she said to her daughter, 'I don't want you to have anything further to do with that man. Promise me you won't.'

Jolene, who sensed her mother's ambitions for her without fully understanding them, bristled at the tone of command. She herself had no interest in Sloan Morrow, but neither did she care to have her mother choosing her friends for her – friends of the Nob Hill sort.

'I can't promise that,' Jolene said, more from spite than from conviction. Privately she had already made herself the same promise.

Mary glowered at her daughter but for the moment she did not challenge the remark. She could afford to wait, knowing how stubborn her daughter could be when pressed.

And in the meantime, there were countless ways of discouraging unwelcome suitors, should they become a problem.

6

After her brief encounter with Sloan Morrow, it seemed to Jolene that the party lost much of its sparkle. She was half inclined, when David Ecks approached her to dance, to turn him down, but his look was so earnest, even hangdog, that she relented and allowed him to lead her onto the dance floor.

'Your heart doesn't seem to be in this,' he said, after a moment. 'You certainly seemed to be enjoying the dancing more a while ago.'

'I'm sorry, I'm afraid I've gotten a bit of a headache,' Jolene replied. 'Perhaps I ought to sit this one out after all.'

'What you need is a change of air. Come on, I've got an idea, maybe you can bring me a bit of luck.' He guided her through the crowd, toward one of the arched doorways.

'Where are we going?'

'Some of the men have got a game going. I'm usually not very successful at that sort of thing, but I thought maybe with you rooting for me it would change my luck.'

Jolene held back. 'David, I really don't care much for

gambling,' she said, realizing that the door toward which he had been leading her was the same one through which Sloan and his companions had disappeared earlier.

'Really? Then we needn't take part at all,' he said, 'we'll just have a look at how the game's going. Jim Straker's in the game and he's the one who always empties my pockets. I've got an urge to see Jim get his comeuppance.'

Reluctantly she went with him through the doorway. He led her into a smoke-filled game room. A group at the far end was engaged in a game of billiards, and two elderly gentlemen just inside the door were playing chess. The center of attention, though, was a group seated around a large round table playing cards. Sloan Morrow was one of them, she saw at a glance; she saw too that most of the table's chips were stacked in front of him. A sizable crowd of gentlemen had gathered to observe the game in progress.

As Jolene and David watched from just inside the doorway, one of the players laid his hand on the table. 'A full house,' he declared, reaching for the chips in the center of the table.

'That's Jim,' David whispered. 'Looks like that other fellow's beating the pants off him.'

Jolene wondered if David would sound so pleased if he knew that the 'other fellow' was a professional card-sharp. She was hopeful that seeing his friend trounced would satisfy David's curiosity and they might leave before Sloan Morrow saw her or created any kind of trouble.

As if reading her thoughts, Sloan said, 'Not so fast there.' He slapped his own cards down loudly upon the table, one at a time. 'Four kings takes the pot,' he said, raking the chips over beside the loot he'd won already.

'Four of a kind, again?' the loser said. 'I never saw anyone get such hands.'

'It isn't difficult,' said one of the observers, who had been leaning against the mantel behind Sloan, 'Not when you're using a marked deck.'

There was a moment of complete silence, punctuated by the thunk of a ball from the billiard table. Even the chess players had turned to stare at the card table.

Jolene had a premonition of what was coming. 'Let's leave, please,' she whispered to her companion.

'No, just a minute,' David said, speaking up. 'What's going on here anyway?' He strode angrily forward. Jolene, expecting the worst, shrank back into the shadows.

'Why, that's crazy, Jake,' the man named Straker said. 'That's a fresh deck of cards. I opened it myself.'

'You opened a deck, all right,' the other said. 'But this here fellow switched decks on you. Did it so slick I wasn't even sure I'd seen what I'd seen – till I saw him raking in the pots.'

'Gentlemen,' Sloan said, rising from his chair, but before he could say more someone had shouted, 'Hold on to him.' A chair was knocked to the floor as four or five of the players jumped up, grabbing Sloan's arms to keep him from leaving.

David swept the cards up from the table. He took them over to the nearest gaslight, examining them closely.

'Damn,' he swore aloud, suddenly flinging the cards to the floor. 'Jake's right, these cards are marked.'

'And here's the other deck,' someone said, producing the pack from one of Sloan's pockets. An angry mutter swept through the group. Only Sloan himself, Jolene realized, looked unperturbed.

'Who the hell are you, anyway?' David demanded, facing Sloan.

'The name's Morrow. Sloan Morrow.'

'Anybody know this guy?' The others exchanged glances, each of them shaking his head in turn.

'If you're a gate-crasher I'll see you get tossed in the jail,' David said. 'Let me see your invitation – if you've got one, which I doubt.'

'Sorry, friend,' Sloan said.

'To hell with the jail,' Jim Straker cried. 'Let's string the bastard up, teach all these card-sharps a lesson.'

There was a chorus of angry voices, some supporting Straker's suggestion, some not. Although it was nearly the end of the century, vigilantism was still active in California, particularly in the San Francisco area. Watching from the fringes, Jolene saw that even Sloan Morrow's cool façade had begun to crumble a little. His eyes flicked nervously from one angry face to another.

Before she'd even had time to contemplate what she was doing, Jolene stepped forward. 'Please,' she said, forcing her way through the crowd to David's side. 'Mister Morrow came with me this evening. I'm sorry if there's been any trouble.'

To her annoyance, Sloan Morrow grinned broadly, making her face turn crimson; already she was beginning to regret the hasty impulse that had brought her forward. Still, she could hardly see the man hanged – and after all, she was not so terribly fond herself of David and his crowd of snobs.

'Is this true?' David asked, looking from her to Morrow.

Sloan grinned all the more broadly and nodded. 'It surely is,' he said, 'I didn't want to say anything before, didn't want to embarrass the lady, but since she's spoken up – well, we are old friends. Matter of fact, you must have seen us dancing together just a little while ago. We were just talking about how much we owe one another, weren't we, dear?'

All eyes had turned toward her. Jolene managed a forced smile for David, ignoring his wounded look. 'Yes, that's true,' she said.

'In view of the fact that he's a friend of yours,' David said unhappily, 'we'll just forget all about this little incident. If, Mister Morrow, you'll be so good as to leave?'

Those holding Sloan's arms let him go, though a bit grudgingly. David after all was their host, and too powerful for any of them to argue with once he'd made a judgment.

'Most reasonable of you, sir,' Sloan said, bowing slightly from the waist. 'I'll just get my things. Jolene, you'll come to the door with me, won't you?'

She was on the verge of declining, but when she turned toward David she saw that his back was to her; the others only glowered. Taking her confusion for assent, Sloan took her arm gently but firmly and started toward the door.

'You forgot your cards,' one of the men at the table called.

Jolene felt Sloan hesitate for a fraction of a second, as if he actually meant to return for them. 'Oh,' she said over her shoulder, 'he won't need those anymore. I think he's learned his lesson.'

'Quite right you are too,' he whispered as they went through the door. 'A very sloppy job of marking. If I'd taken time to do them right they'd never have caught on to me.'

'Oh, you . . . ' she snapped when they were in the corridor outside. She jerked her arm free of his. 'You are a scoundrel. I ought to have let them string you up.'

'Which they were close to doing,' he said. 'Come to think of it, why didn't you?'

'Why, I . . . I suppose because I felt indebted to you,' she said, unable to answer the question to her own satisfaction.

'Really?' He looked amused – and unconvinced.

'In any case,' she said, angry with herself as much as him, 'let us agree that the slate is clean, because I really would like to see the last of you.'

'Ah, there is one little thing, though,' he said, 'call it a matter of accrued interest, if you will . . .'

'I don't know what . . .' She was unable to finish. Fully to her surprise he seized her in a quick but strong embrace, and his mouth closed over hers. The heat of the kiss, the demanding softness of his lips, shocked her into a momentary acquiescence, and she lay against his chest while his tongue parted her lips, invaded her mouth.

'Oh,' she tried to cry out, the sound smothered into an inaudible murmur. She struggled against him, suddenly furious at his daring to do such a thing. Unable to free herself, she bit down hard on his tongue.

'Ouch,' he said, releasing her so abruptly that she nearly lost her balance and fell into a potted palm. 'Why the devil did you do that?'

'Why did I . . . Oh, you monster, how dare you, I ought to . . .' She could think of nothing suitably unpleasant.

'You ought to thank me. It's quite obvious you've never been properly kissed before. Doesn't that swell know how to treat a woman?'

'He treats a lady with proper respect, thank you.'

'Not at all the same thing,' he said. 'But I'm afraid I'll have to save the rest of your education for the next time. I have a feeling it wouldn't be a good idea for me to still be here when the gentlemen come out.'

'There won't be any next time,' she told him firmly.

'Don't be ridiculous, how can I marry you if we're not going to see one another?'

'Marry—? Why, you're a madman,' she cried, stepping back from him with eyes wide.

'No, a gambler. But of course, you must remember, I play only to win. *Hasta luega*, my dear, till later.'

'*Luega* will never come,' she said, but he gave no sign he had heard; he was already on his way across the dance floor, dodging waltzing couples. She watched him go. His height made it easy to follow him, and though she knew that he had no breeding at all, he had somewhere along the way acquired an aura of sophistication and self-assurance that sat on him as gracefully as his fashionable clothes. She saw one or two women steal interested glances at him; people moved deferentially out of his way.

She shook her head, less angry than before, but still completely baffled by him. She remembered the burning intensity with which he had stared at her; it was as if he had been promising her they would meet again.

What rubbish, she scolded herself. There was no promise between them, and they would not meet again, despite his ridiculous pronouncement.

She put her fingers to her lips, still tingling from his kiss. He had been completely right about one thing, though: no one had ever kissed her like that before.

7

'You can't leave now. I won't hear of it.'

'I can, Mama,' Jolene said. 'Pardon me, I mean Mother – and I will.'

'But Richard Trémorel, what of him?'

'Mister Trémorel can go to the devil, for all I care,' Jolene said. 'I didn't ask him to come here, not the first time, nor the second time, nor this time.' She paused, doubling over while she tugged on one hightopped leather boot, then the other. When she stood, the boots covered the expanse of leg that would otherwise have been revealed by the shortened skirt of her riding-habit. Her mother had objected to the short skirt. Jolene, who liked to ride and found the ordinary skirts too cumbersome, had compromised with the boots, specially made after a man's pattern. It would never have done, of course, for riding with the San Francisco set, but here at the ranch, she had argued, who was to see?

'And another thing I don't like,' she went on, 'is the way he sits and leers at me the whole time I'm in the room – I feel like I've got no clothes on.'

'Jolene!' Mary was rightly shocked. 'No well-brought-up young lady would even think such a thing.'

'No well-brought-up gentleman would look at a lady like that. And don't pretend you haven't noticed. If it weren't that the elegant Mister Trémorel fits in somehow with all of your social schemes, you'd have thrown him out for it long ago. And Papa just might yet.'

'Your father happens to be in the vineyards. All this rain . . .'

'He was in the vineyards,' Jolene said, glancing out the window. 'Right now it looks as if he's going to be joining Mister Trémorel.'

'Oh.' Mary came to the window and looked out; yes, there José was, striding across the muddy yard, soaked to the skin and looking altogether out of sorts. 'Oh dear,' she added. José had made it plain from the first that he didn't care for Richard Trémorel and certainly did not want him courting his daughter. She had counted on his being in the vineyards most of the day; it had been raining for the better part of a week, ruining much of the grape crop. Despairing of a break in the weather that might allow a decent harvest, José and the workers had been picking what they could salvage. The losses would be staggering. Coming fresh from his struggles with this disaster, José would be particularly annoyed to find their guest in the parlor.

'You'll have to help me, I . . .' Mary turned from the window to discover her daughter disappearing through the door. 'Jolene,' she cried, running to the door after her, but Jolene only slapped her riding crop against the worn buckskin of her skirt and went on; in a moment her boots could be heard clattering down the uncarpeted stairs. A door opened and slammed below.

Mary hurried down the stairs in her wake. José had come in from the rear of the house, leaving muddy tracks along the tiled corridor on his way to the parlor. She met him at the bottom of the stairs.

'José, how lucky that you've taken a break just now,' she said.

She gave him her warmest smile. For a moment, as he watched her descend the last few stairs, some of the fatigue seemed to lift from his face.

He had been a beautiful youth, was still handsome, in a worn and faded way. A perhaps too deep devotion to the grape had added weight, a gentle piling up of flesh around the middle, a fullness of face that made him look heavier than he was. Years of working out of doors had turned his bronzed and satiny skin to old leather, prematurely adding the lines of age around the eyes and the corners of his mouth. It was not this that aged him, though, but rather a dullness, a lack of luster. His eyes did not gleam as they had done; his smile rarely flashed. He wore about him an aura of disappointment.

The warmness of her greeting surprised and deceived him; he looked, as he so rarely did now, glad to see her. It gave her an unexpected pang of guilt. Had she lived so long without that welcome in his eyes that she missed it only when she saw it? She felt a rare sense of affection for him.

'Don't tell me you were pining for my company,' he said, giving her his hand.

'Don't be silly, you know I miss you frightfully whenever you're not with me. I only meant, it's especially lucky just now, because we have a visitor. Mister Trémorel has come to call.'

'Again.' The gladness vanished from his eyes. Its going deepened her sense of guilt and made her angry.

'Yes, isn't it wonderful?' she said in the brittle tone that was her more usual way of speaking to him. She swept by him into the parlor.

Richard Trémorel turned from the big bay window at which he had been standing. It was impossible to say whether he had heard the exchange between husband and wife; he looked as aloofly polite as ever. It seemed peculiar to Mary, that friendly but distant manner he displayed toward her. Once he had whispered passionately into her ear; together they had planned to run away and marry, and but for her family's interference she would be his wife now, and not the wife of a vintner.

How she hated the wine, the grapes, the entire business. She had always hated them, the more so because she had forever been their prisoner. She had devoted herself to them, her mind, her soul, her energies, but it was not with her, as it was with José, as it had been with her parents and her brothers, out of love. She had escaped from French Hills with José, but she had not escaped from the wine. With Richard Trémorel perhaps that might have been possible – and perhaps, because he had bungled it, she hated him a little too.

Perhaps, she thought, that was what made polite strangers of one-time lovers. She could forgive him for being a scoundrel, forgive all his failings but one – his failing with her.

'I'm afraid Jolene won't be joining us,' she said aloud.

'Yes, I saw her ride past just now,' he said.

José, coming into the room after his wife, saw their guest's quick look at his dirty wet clothes, at his muddy boots leaving stains across the carpet.

Mary had seen it too. 'You remember my husband, of course.'

'Of course.'

'Joseph – (when, José wondered, had he become 'Joseph'?) – has been in the vineyards supervising the harvest.'

'It must be grueling work,' Richard said with a condescending smile; he had never done an honest day's work in his life.

'It is,' José said. He had a terrible urge to cross the room and bust the other man's jaw. Despite his intense – and he admitted, unreasonable – dislike for Trémorel, however, José's innate manners came to the fore. 'Brandy?' he asked.

'Some cognac, if you have it.'

'I'm afraid not. For obvious reasons we serve our own wines here.' José ignored his wife's disapproving glance and filled two glasses with the Brussac-America brandy, taking a certain pleasure from the knowledge that it was one of their less successful bottlings.

He carried one of them to Trémorel, who took it with another of his condescending smiles. Ignoring it, José went to look out the window at the still-falling rain. He felt mixed emotions over Jolene's decision to go riding: relieved that she wasn't here with Trémorel who, he had observed on the many previous visits, spent his time ogling her, and worried that she should be riding in the inclement weather. Several days of rain had brought warnings of flash floods in the hills. Although she knew the hills well, Jolene was too impetuous for her own good.

'Mister Perreira,' Trémorel said behind him, 'I want to talk to you. About your daughter.'

'Leave my daughter alone,' José said without turning.

'Joseph,' his wife said, shocked.

'Yes, please, Joseph . . .'

He did not let Trémorel finish. 'The name is José,' he said coldly.

The rains had turned the hills from brown to green. Riding without a cloak, Jolene reveled in the cool wash of the rain on her face. She seemed at times to burn with an inner heat, something more than sexual passion, though there was that too. At times she felt consumed by it, as if flames must leap up from her flesh, fed from some blazing core within. It was then she liked to ride, at night, in the rain, in the chill of dawn, till the fever had passed, the flames banked to smoldering embers.

She burned with the urge to live, to be free. It was unfair that women never could be free, they were slaves, first to their parents, later to their husband. Not even the widow or the spinster was truly free, for she was bound by chains of convention and conformity.

If I were a man, she thought as she rode, I would have ridden away long ago. A man, even a very young man, could come and go as he wished. A man might ride out as she had ridden out, and ride on, and on . . . How often had she dreamed of such a ride, but always the dream died with the same questions: where could she go? What could she do? How long before she ceased to be a hero and became a victim?

She reined in her horse at the edge of a deep gully, his hooves sending a shower of stones scattering down the ravine. Swinging down from the saddle, she paused for a moment, breathing deep of the damp air, holding it in her lungs until her temples throbbed and the sky seemed to descend heavily toward her. She looked across the rippling hills and valleys; sparse chaparral, scrub oak and here and there the redwoods that to the west grew in such magnificent profusion. A hawk swooped above her, seeming to mock her with his freedom.

She left the horse grazing in the grass and scrambled down the steep hillside of the ravine, a dry wash actually. She sought a sense of privacy, but when she was at the bottom the steep banks were like the walls of a prison, closing her in.

She knelt to pick a wildflower, nameless to her, but lovely anyway, yellow and gleaming with moisture. She plucked it, and it seemed on the instant to lose something of its brightness, to fade and wilt even as she held it in her hand.

If only she understood the source of the strange restlessness that drove her. It was as if she were waiting for something – or someone – to come into her life. Sometimes her skin tingled with the feeling that her destiny waited her, over the next hill, around the next bend; yet there was nothing, except the sense of waiting.

Someone shouted in the distance. She looked up and saw a rider on the hill far above, riding in her direction at a furious gallop. As he rode, he took his hat off and waved it, to get her attention, and shouted again – why, he had shouted her name. But who on earth . . . she squinted, trying to identify him – something familiar, yet not quite . . .

He disappeared for a moment into a little valley, appeared again at the rise, and then she recognized him: Sloan Morrow.

'Of all the nerve,' she said aloud, angry that he had come upon her here. She started to turn away, to scramble upward to her own horse, but the manner in which he was approaching made her pause. There was something so urgent, so frantic, about the way he waved his hat and shouted to her. She tried to make out his words, but they were indistinct, blurred by another sound, closer and not immediately identifiable, though oddly familiar, like a crumbling and scraping of rocks and earth moving. She glanced up the ravine; a hundred feet or so above her it disappeared about a turn. Perhaps there was a slide up that way, that would explain the eerie rumbling sound that seemed to be growing stronger.

She glanced back at the rider. He was closer now, close enough that she thought she saw the fear on his face. The rumbling had suddenly grown louder, drowning out his shouts. Only one word was clear to her: ' . . . Water . . . '

And in a horrible second of realization, she knew and understood: the rains, accumulating in the hills above faster than they could soak into the ground, or perhaps overflowing from some lake or pond, making in an instant a riverbed of the dry wash – a flash flood. A wall of water, rushing through the ravine, gathering force as it rushed downward, sweeping everything before it. She had heard of such floods uprooting trees, flinging aside giant boulders, even crushing houses in their path.

For a moment she stood rooted to the spot, listening to the rapidly mounting crescendo of sound. Then it was upon her. One instant there was nothing in the gully but her and the roar of sound echoing from wall to wall about her, and the next the water had swept about the turn and was rushing at her, a wall of muddy brown water, eight, maybe ten feet high, whipped into a foam at its crest.

There was no time even to run. She saw a scrub oak ripped from the ground as if it were a blade of grass. She turned, trying to scramble up the loose, gravelly hillside, but almost at once she was struck as if by a giant hand, sent tumbling head over heels into the roaring foam.

8

It was unlike falling into water, for in this she seemed to fall upward, lifted on the crest of the wave, up, up, as if into the sky. Then she came down, sweeping and sliding, like falling from a mountain-top in a dream. Stunned by the initial impact of the water, she was helpless in its grip, tossed this way and that. She was thrown against a boulder and tried desperately to get a hold on it, but she was swept away.

Something brushed against her thrashing leg, like fingers reaching for her. The scrub oak, bobbing along in her wake. She grasped at it, felt it slip from her hand, reached again, and caught it. She clung to it, swirling about with it. It rolled in the water, slipping from her grip, and the water closed over her head, but in a moment she had caught the tree trunk again; once more it dipped beneath the water, rolling from her grasp, and again she sank, only to take a fresh hold as both she and the tree bobbed to the surface. She was weak and breathless, and knew she could not hold on much longer. Where she was she had no idea. She had been too busy trying to keep herself afloat to notice her progress down the ravine.

A few hundred feet below the point where she had been swept up in the flood, the ravine widened somewhat, its sides sloping less steeply. The tree, with her clinging to it, was swept about to the side and lodged for a moment against a massive wall of rock. Although the rock was too smooth and too slick for her to climb up it, even if she had had the strength left, which she had not, the pause gave her a moment to catch her breath.

'Hold on,' someone shouted, astonishingly close at hand. She looked up and saw Sloan Morrow above her on the rock. He had a rope in his hands which he was tying quickly about his waist. He threw a loop of it over the horn of his horse's saddle and in a moment more he had plunged into the churning, swirling floodwaters. He disappeared beneath the muddy surface, reappearing several yards downstream, and she thought he had been swept away from her.

The rope – and the horse – held. She saw the rope leap from the water as it grew taut. He held to it, pulling himself hand over hand against the rush of the current, at the same time shouting to his horse. The frightened beast tried to run from the roar of the water, and as he did so he dragged Sloan closer to her.

But she was losing her grip. The water had continued to batter her against the rock, as if determined to dislodge her. Her hands were numb with cold and with exhaustion. A surge of water loosened the tree from where it had lodged against the bank, spinning it toward the center of the stream instead. Sloan shouted; the tree, she saw, would carry her past him, beyond his reach. Swallowing air and water together, she let go of the oak.

She sank at once beneath the water. She collided with something, but not until his arms had closed around her did she realize it was her rescuer.

'It's all right,' he was saying as she struggled to the surface, wrapped tightly in the circle of his arm. 'I'll take care of you.'

They were lying in the wet grass atop the ravine. Astonishingly, though it had seemed she was in the water an eternity, she had been carried only a few hundred feet. Her horse, having bolted at first from the sound of the flood and then discovered himself in no apparent danger, was grazing unconcernedly nearby.

'How did you happen to be here?' she asked.

'Looking for you.'

She raised herself on one elbow. 'But how . . . ?'

'Brussac-America is fairly well known. It was easy finding your place. Someone told me you'd gone riding out this way, so I came too. I saw you from up on the hill there – saw that water coming at the same time.'

She was silent for a moment, studying the handsome face: the dark eyes, so deep a brown that they looked black; the classical modelling of the cheekbones and the brows; the too-full lips that gave an otherwise austere countenance a blatantly sensual appearance.

'Why were you coming to see me in the first place?' she asked.

'I thought if we're going to be married we ought to start getting acquainted,' he said with a grin.

'Oh, you . . . you must think I'm as crazy as you are. Whatever would make you think I'd marry a common card-sharp?'

She started to get up, but to her surprise he seized her wrist, yanking her back down to the ground. She fell against him. His arms came around her.

'Let go of me,' she demanded, struggling against him.

'Be damned if I will,' he said in a husky voice, crushing her against him; she felt his hand trace a path down her back, across the dampness of her skirt.

'I rode all the way up here from the city,' he said, brushing his lips across her throat, 'I damned near drowned myself hauling you out of that water. I've earned the right to what I want and by God I mean to have it.'

'Stop it – don't,' she cried, but with one arm and the weight of his body he held her pinned to the ground. The other hand struggled for a moment with her blouse, freed one pale breast. His lips burned a path over it, came back to her throat, sought her mouth.

For a moment more she fought against him. Then, abruptly, her body relaxed. Her lips opened to his insistent tongue and her arms came up about him, feeling the breadth and power of his shoulders, the granite hardness of his neck.

'I've wanted you since I first saw you,' he murmured into her ear, kissing it as well.

She felt his fingers at her skirt, experienced for the first time the touch of a man's hand upon the bare flesh of her leg.

'Don't, please,' she whispered, struggling once more against him.

'I've got to.' The words were muffled against her breast.

'Please – not like this, wallowing in the mud, not my first time . . .'

He paused then, lifting his face to look into hers. 'Damn,' he swore. 'Why'd you have to bring that up?'

She managed a wan smile. 'A girl likes her first time to be more – you understand – more romantic.'

He sighed and sat back from her. 'Well, I sure can't take you into the fleabag hotel I'm staying at, not if you want any reputation left at all. And I can't see us going back to your place and asking your Ma if she minds our using one of the bedrooms.'

She leaned toward him, running one finger lightly over the heaving expanse of his chest. 'My mother's leaving in five days,' she said, giving him a veiled look. 'She's sailing for France, to look into our business investments. Some old chateau that we buy a little bit of wine from.'

'You want me to come up to the house after she's gone?'

'Papa's in the vineyards all day long.'

He studied her for a moment, seeking an answer to some unasked question. Then he laughed and relaxed slightly. 'Well, I guess I've waited this long, another five days can't hurt anything. You're sure . . .'

She scrambled to her feet. 'Come to the ranch next Tuesday,' she said. She paused, then leaned down again to kiss him, this time giving as good as she got.

'Hey,' he said when the kiss was ended.

'I have to go.' She ran lightly through the wet grass to where her horse was waiting, swinging herself into the saddle with the ease of the accomplished rider.

When she looked back, he had risen and was brushing the dirt from his once elegant clothes. 'You want me to ride back with you?' he asked.

She shook her head, blowing him a kiss. Then she reined the horse about and started down the hill.

'See you on Tuesday,' he called after her.

She did not reply, but waved her hand in farewell. She was remembering the burning intensity of his kiss. In a way, she was rather sorry she wouldn't be there when he came on Tuesday.

Of course, by that time, she'd be on her way to France with her mother.

9

Still, he lingered in her mind afterward. Even when she had arrived in France with her mother and was on her way from Paris to the chateau in which Brussac-America had invested, Jolene found herself thinking of Sloan Morrow.

Not that she attached any importance to his insistence that he would marry her. He was a gambler and a wastrel, a rootless drifter who lived as best he could by robbing others. Never mind that quite a few of them – David Ecks, for one – probably deserved to be robbed, just as they had stolen their wealth from countless little people.

Still, one could not deny that Mister Morrow had charm, and courage. He was handsome and could be amusing, if one didn't take him too seriously. She couldn't help imagining what might have been had Sloan Morrow had the advantages of a good upbringing, of family and money. She was not a social climber, like her mother. On the other hand, she could be practical too, and honest with herself. She had grown up in a comfortable sort of existence, and she had naturally supposed that when she married it would not be to a pauper. Of course, the important thing, the most important thing, was that she be in love, truly in love, with her husband-to-be, but she found it impossible to imagine that she, or any girl, would fall in love with someone as unstable and catch-as-catch-can as Sloan Morrow.

No, devil that you may be, she thought, you won't marry me, Mister Morrow – thrilling though your kisses may be.

'This can't be the place,' Mary said aloud, shattering Jolene's reverie.

'Chateau Brussac, Madame,' the driver informed her.

Through the open window Jolene had a glimpse of what passed for a gatepost, though it was so crumbled and covered with ivy that only a glimpse or two of stone could be seen through the greenery. Of its companion post, or the gate that must once have hung there, there was no sign. In place of a drive leading through the trees, there was a wagon track slicing through the weeds and wildflowers.

'Why, surely no one's lived here in ages,' Mary argued.

In reply, the driver lifted his whip and pointed through the trees. A thin finger of smoke, like a smudge against the sunset sky, could be seen lifting upward from some distant chimney.

'Well, let us go see, then,' Mary said. 'It will be dark soon.'

'Madame, I regret,' the driver said. 'The track is too rough for the carriage, and as you say, it will be dark soon – impossible to see a rock, a fallen branch.'

'But what are we to do?' Mary asked.

'There's sure to be an inn in Épernay,' he said. 'We could stay the night . . . '

'And pay you to bring us back in the morning, you scoundrel, not to mention your bed and board for the night.'

The driver said, a trifle smugly, 'Madame could walk, of course . . . ' He shrugged, implying that it was entirely up to her if she preferred that silly idea.

'Mama, why don't we?' Jolene said. 'It can't be far, and a good walk would do us both good after all this riding about.'

'Very well,' Mary said, with only a moment's hesitation. José had been opposed to this trip altogether, and to placate him she had had to swear to keep expenses down. He was entirely right, the modest supply of wines they received from Chateau Brussac hardly justified the expense of a visit to the chateau. She had argued that it was a practical way of providing Jolene with a European tour; not quite the 'grand tour' that was *de rigueur* to Nob Hill debutantes, unfortunately – José would never have stood for that. Still, it couldn't hurt to have it seen in the papers that they had spent part of the season at their ancestral chateau in France. After all, who in San Francisco need know about missing gates and weed-grown drives?

As to her real reason for wanting to come, she would not

have dared reveal that to José, who was forever criticizing her for her schemes. She had learned long ago of the young man in residence here: 'My nephew, Philip Brussac, of French Hills,' Aunt Marie referred to him, but Mary was too shrewd to be taken in by that. There was no Philip Brussac of French Hills, not among the legitimate children of her brothers to the south.

She had made discreet inquiries. Her father's will had indeed named a Philip Brussac, and had guaranteed that he could not be disinherited. A share of French Hills was his; moreover, provisions had been made for his upbringing.

If not a legitimate member of the family, Mary had concluded, then undoubtedly an illegitimate one – the bastard son of one of her brothers, perhaps even her father; she well knew that he had been a man of passionate lusts.

It was to meet this Philip Brussac and to unravel the secret of his parentage, if she could, that she had come to France. She had an idea that this mysterious young man might somehow be useful to her in her dream of regaining what had been stolen from her. Just how, it was impossible to say until she met him and knew more about him. She was convinced, though, that she could find a way to fit him into her schemes.

In the meantime, she must make pennies count. It would not do to have an irate José ordering them back to California before she had worked out the proper plan.

The driver rather reluctantly helped them down with their bags. It had not occurred to him that these overdressed Americans – both of them beautiful, he didn't mind admitting, especially the younger one, his lips smacked unconsciously whenever he glanced at her – would not have gone along with his suggestion. He had anticipated not only an extra fare, and a soft bed and a good meal at the inn, but a tip from his friend, the innkeeper, as well. Who would have thought they would want to walk; no expensively dressed Parisian woman would.

Mary paid him. He had cheated them on the fare, and she repaid him in kind with the tip, though she was rather sorry to stand in the gathering darkness and watch the carriage disappear down the road.

'We'll leave the large bags here behind the gateposts,' she said, taking refuge from her nervousness in activity. 'Someone can come for them later.'

The two women set out along the darkening path. Mary had written ahead to say they would be arriving. Surely Aunt Marie would have rooms and a warm meal awaiting them, though she had gotten the impression from her letters that Aunt Marie was more than a little peculiar.

The track was rough and difficult to follow in the fading light, causing one or the other of them to stumble every few yards. They wound their way about a stand of poplars, straining their eyes for a glimpse of the house.

'Maybe we should have followed the driver's suggestion,' Mary said finally, short of breath from the unaccustomed exertion.

'It can't be much farther,' Jolene said, though privately she was beginning to wonder. Oughtn't they to have seen a light at least by now? The wind billowed her cloak and rustled the leaves of the poplars with a sound like whispering voices.

They almost did not see the house when they finally came upon it, hidden as it was by the massive old trees surrounding it. Although it was now night, the windows were unlighted, so that the vine-covered house all but vanished into the shadows.

'Why, it looks deserted,' Mary said in dismay.

They had come to an abrupt stop at the edge of the trees. So absorbed were they in contemplating that dark and ruined structure that neither of them heard the thud of horses' hooves on the damp grass.

Suddenly a buggy swept around the corner of the house, followed an instant later by an old farm cart. Jolene gave a squeal of fright as the horses rushed toward them, threatening to run them down.

The driver of the buggy saw them at the last minute and veered to the right, shouting loudly at his horse. The rig rocked and swayed violently, almost pitching on its side, before it finally came to a halt.

The cart came to a stop behind it. Jolene had a glimpse of someone in a long white gown jumping down from the passenger side and disappearing into the deep shadows among the trees. The driver, a woman, got down more gingerly and hurried toward the buggy.

'Are you all right?' she asked its driver.

He ignored her concern and jumped to the ground, striding towards Jolene and Mary. 'Where the devil did you come from?' he demanded.

'We might ask the same of you,' Mary said angrily. 'You frightened us half out of our wits, coming around the house all of a sudden like that. What on earth were you doing, anyway, you were going like a house afire.'

'Having a race with Aunt Marie,' the young man said. 'Worse luck, I was winning. I'd have won for sure if you hadn't scared my horses.'

'Well, of all the . . . ' Mary exclaimed. 'Scared your horses? And what about us?'

He was no longer listening to her, though. He had come to a halt a few feet from them, staring through the gloom.

'Jolene,' he said, his voice little more than a whisper. 'You've come, at last.'

She was at a loss. His face was indistinct, veiled with shadows. She took a step toward him, unconsciously squinting as she tried to distinguish his features.

He was startlingly handsome, his complexion olive-hued, his hair raven black in the darkness; his eyes, so intense, staring at her, into her, as if awaiting some word from her, some sign. He laughed, amused at her confusion, and then some blending of light and shadow, some gestured recognized on an unconscious level, gave her the answer. For a moment she was a child again, at French Hills, and a boy was telling her, as she ran to a carriage, that he loved her.

'Felipe,' she breathed his name, and in that instant it was as if a bargain had been sealed between them, as if her soul had come home to its own. How could she not have known, all these years, that it was this, this reunion, this man, for whom she had waited so restlessly?

For she knew it now, as surely as she knew her name, as surely as they stood here before one another, not moving, not touching, and yet together in a way that defied words, a joining as instantaneous, as irrevocable as it was inevitable.

'It's Philip now,' he said, dazzling her again with his smile; he held out his hand to her. 'Philip Brussac. Welcome to Chateau Brussac.'

10

For Jolene the years that had separated them seemed like a long dream from which she had awakened to the morning of his love. There had been no real unhappiness in her life before, but neither had there been real happiness, only a sense of waiting for something, she knew not what, that would make of her existence a life. Now, the waiting was over.

All of this might have been intolerable in the company of her mother – after all, Jolene knew better than anyone that her mother intended for her to make a good match, and this penniless young man, living on charity, of dubious family connections, would certainly never satisfy her mother's requirements. But as it turned out, it was Mary herself who made things easier for the young couple.

'I want you to be especially nice to Philip,' Mary said shortly after their arrival.

'What do you have in mind, mother?'

'I want you to help me persuade him to come to California with us,' Mary had said. Already she was busy devising schemes for making use of this striking young man. He was handsome, personable, intelligent, and it was clearly he who produced Chateau Brussac's wine. Moreover, his parentage was as plain as the nose on his face; despite the swarthy complexion, inherited from whatever unfortunate servant girl was his mother, Philip was the spitting image of Adam as a young man.

Exactly how she could use her knowledge against her brothers she was not yet sure, but there was no doubt in Mary's mind that Philip Brussac would be a useful ally. He too was obviously being cheated of what was rightfully his, and he was a man, which was always an advantage in such matters.

Together, they would right the wrongs that had been done to them, she was convinced of it.

Determined to persuade Philip to her way of thinking, Mary threw her daughter and Philip together at every opportunity, and was pleased to see how co-operative Jolene was being for a change.

For her own part, Jolene could not have been happier. She and Philip spent long hours together as day sped quickly after day. He showed her the vineyards and the wine-presses, proud of what had been accomplished since his arrival at Chateau Brussac. With nothing but some part-time help from the village, he had tripled the vineyard's yield, at the same time greatly improving the quality of the wines. Although the district had long since been written off by serious vintners as a wine-producing region, Chateau Brussac's wines were served without complaint in homes and restaurants throughout the area and even in many of Paris's growing number of bistros. Most profitable of all were the American sales through Brussac-America, though he readily admitted that that had been Aunt Marie's idea and not his own.

'Someday I'll make fine wines,' he promised. 'My own wines.'

'California wines are getting better each year,' Jolene said. 'They say that someday they shall rival the best of France's wines.'

There was an awkward moment of silence between them; thus far neither of them had broached directly the subject of his coming to California, though it was on both their minds.

'Someday,' he said, speaking slowly, as if weighing this prospect for the first time, 'I must return to California.'

Fearful of seeming too glad, she asked a tentative question: 'Will you be returning to French Hills?'

'In time,' he said, a trace of bitterness creeping into his voice. It was the closest they had come to the subject of his relationship to the Brussacs, and to French Hills.

From the perspective of his added years Philip now understood many things that had puzzled him before. Although there were other, unanswered questions that haunted him he was sure that he was Adam Brussac's bastard son. His resentment of the way his father had misused his mother had grown into a passionate thirst to avenge her mean life and pitiful death.

Nor could he feel any gratitude toward his father for having sent him here to grow up, happy though that decision had been for him. He remembered the conversation overheard long ago between Adam and Claude Brussac: it was Claude, El Patron, Adam's father and his own grandfather, who had arranged for his upbringing. He knew that much, though he did not know why he had been sent here. To get him out of the way? But surely that could have been accomplished in simpler ways – a mission school, for instance. Or had that shrewd old man intended for him to learn the art of winemaking, as he had, as he would not have been permitted to do at French Hills? Had he perhaps intended that Philip should return to French Hills one day, qualified to claim his rightful place among the Brussacs?

Much as these questions troubled him, they paled into insignificance beside the one, the burning question: was Elena, dimly remembered from his childhood, the sister to whom El Patron had referred, whom he had sworn to his dying mother to care for, whose existence Adam Brussac had so firmly denied?

He had had much time to consider these questions, and in

his own mind he was convinced of Elena's identity. The death-bed vow that he had sworn to his mother was like a curse upon him. It would never let him rest until he had returned to French Hills, until he had found her and claimed her and fulfilled his boyhood oath.

But these were questions that he could not discuss with any-one, not even Aunt Marie, though he was aware that she knew a great deal more than she had ever told.

'I don't think the Brussacs are in any rush to have me back,' he said, in a lighter tone.

Jolene smiled and said, 'The more fools they.'

His fingers tightened upon hers. It was late night; the others had gone up to bed hours before, leaving the two of them to sip wine and talk in low voices before the fire. Now, with reluctant steps, he was seeing her to her room.

They paused at her door, the candle he held flickering in a draft of wind – there were no modern gaslights at Chateau Brussac.

'See you in the morning,' he said, without moving.

Jolene hesitated, staring up into his handsome face. She would gladly have invited him in except that she was afraid of shocking him or causing him to think that she was loose. She waited, hoping that he might take the initiative, but he did not.

'Good night,' she said at last, concealing her disappointment.

The village girl whom Marie had hired to assist with her visitors had been in already. A fire had been lit against the evening's chill and an oil lamp glowed on the bedside table. The bed had been turned down, and Jolene saw her nightdress draped across one corner of the bed. Something was lying atop the nightdress, something small and dark, though from across the room, in the flickering light, she could not make out what it was.

She started across the room, but stopped before she had reached the bed. Surely that wasn't . . . she took a step closer, her eyes widening.

Someone had placed a dead rat upon her nightdress, its neck broken in some cellar trap, a trickle of drying blood running from the corner of its mouth onto the pale silk of the gown.

She gave a cry of dismay and turned away, fighting an urge to retch. In a moment she heard Philip's anxious voice at the door.

'Jolene, are you all right?'

Ashen-faced, she opened the door to him, wordlessly indicating the macabre sight on the bed. He strode to it, swearing at the sight.

'Who could have done it?' she asked, though she thought she knew already.

'I'm afraid it must have been René – no, don't look any more, I'll get rid of it.' He scooped up gown and all, carefully concealing the lifeless form in the folds of the silk. 'I'll see if Aunt Marie can clean this for you.'

'No, please, I couldn't wear it ever again.'

He let himself out onto the balcony, returning in a moment to fling the soiled nightdress into the fire. The flames flared brightly, green and blue and yellow, then died to a warm glow again.

'Why would he want to do that to me?' she asked. 'Surely I've done nothing to offend him. I've hardly seen him since I've been here.'

It was true, she had seen René only fleetingly, and then at a distance. She thought his story romantically tragic, and had been willing enough to meet him. Privately she had thought Marie a little mad herself, but she had accepted Philip's assurances that she had nothing to fear, enlarging that to include René – until now, at any rate.

'He's jealous, I suppose,' Philip said. 'In all these years I'm the only friend he's had, besides Aunt Marie, of course. But since you've been here, I've barely seen him myself. Partly I've been with you as much as possible, and partly he's been avoiding me. I'd better have a talk with him about this, I suppose – or try to, at least. It's difficult to know how much of what one says makes any impression on him.' He looked unhappy at the prospect.

Jolene sighed. Now that the shock of the ugly find had passed, she could even feel a trifle guilty at having monopolized Philip's time at the expense of his pathetic friend.

'No, let it go,' she said, coming to rest a hand lightly upon his arm. 'Aside from the nasty turn it gave me, there was no real harm done.'

'Your gown . . .'

'I have others.'

He smiled gratefully. She was suddenly and sharply aware of his closeness, of the lateness of the hour, the intimacy of the setting. He had unbuttoned his shirt on his way to bed and now his chest lay bare before her, sleek and hard, as if carved from bronze. She felt an overpowering urge to run her fingers over the chiseled flesh. As if of its own volition her hand lifted; her fingers felt cold as ice, his chest hot and damp.

'Jolene?' There was a tap at her door. 'Is anything wrong? I thought I heard you cry out.'

'It's Mama,' Jolene said in a whisper, snatching her hand back. 'It'll be the devil to pay.'

'Don't worry, I'll stay out of sight,' he said. He caught her in his arms and pulled her briefly against him, covering her mouth with his. The kiss was electric; she would have fallen onto the bed with him on the instant, and be damned to her mother, but in another second it was over and he was thrusting her away from him with a low sound, half a chuckle, half a groan, in his throat.

'Jolene?'

'Just a moment.'

He darted to the open door and stepped onto the balcony, pulling the door to after himself. The curtains and the night concealed him from view.

'Are you all right?' Mary asked when Jolene let her in. 'What's that smell – good heavens, are you burning your clothes?'

'I spilled something on that gown,' Jolene said. 'I got angry and threw it into the fire – and burned myself doing it. That's when you heard me cry out.'

Mary gave a suspicious look around the room. 'I thought I heard voices,' she said.

'Perhaps from another room,' Jolene suggested. 'The windows are open.'

For a moment she thought her mother was going to go to the open doors onto the balcony, but at length she seemed satisfied with the explanation. There were other things on her mind.

'Have you spoken to Philip yet about coming to California?'

'Only in general terms,' Jolene replied, glancing uneasily toward the balcony.

'I'm going to talk to him in the morning, but of course I'll need your help in convincing him.'

'I . . . ' Jolene hesitated, painfully aware of the listener beyond the billowing curtains. 'Mother, I'm very sleepy.'

'Perhaps if you'd gone to bed instead of burning your wardrobe,' Mary suggested dryly. She started toward the door, but paused. 'I suppose by this time he's sworn his undying love for you?'

'Not quite. I'm sure he's fond of me – as I am of him.'

'Yes, well, he's a very nice young man, entirely likable. Mind, though, that it doesn't go beyond that, this is only play-acting, you know, entirely for the purpose of getting him to California. Men are such fools, aren't they? A woman has only to flutter her eyes and pat a man's cheek and he'll believe anything.'

Jolene could barely wait until the door had closed after her. She rushed to the balcony, sweeping aside the curtains and stepping outside.

The balcony was empty. Philip had gone; how long ago, or how much of the conversation he had heard, she could not guess. The side of the building was luxuriant with vines, he could have climbed down them to the ground, or to another balcony of the many on the wall.

She slipped from her room, pausing in the corridor to listen. She heard her mother's door open and close. Removing her shoes so that she would make less noise, Jolene hurried up the stairs to the third-floor room that she already knew was Philip's.

There was no reply to her knock. Finding the door unlocked, she went in, but there was no one there.

She returned despondently to her own room, but once in bed she was unable to sleep. She lay for a long while watching the shadows cast on the ceiling by the fire.

Much later she heard muffled footsteps in the corridor. Hastily donning a robe, she ran once again up the stairs, to Philip's room.

This time the door was locked, but there was no answer to her furtive knocking. At length, when it became apparent he would not answer her, and fearful of rousing the entire household, she stole back to her bed.

The shadows on the ceiling paled and faded long before she fell asleep.

11

Mary came down the following morning with the intention of speaking to her great aunt. She found Marie poring over ledgers in the room that was used as an office, though that term was rather grand for the litter-strewn cubicle.

Pausing for a moment unnoticed in the doorway, Mary observed the other woman. Marie's dress was patched and dirty and her hair looked as if it had not been washed or combed in days. She remembered the night of their arrival here, when the chateau's residents had been engaged in a race around the grounds.

Yet for all Aunt Marie's unkempt appearance and her peculiar behavior, Mary had an unsettling impression that she was not quite as crazy as she led people to believe. Certainly, even with the lack of help, she managed things here well enough, if a bit haphazardly. True, Philip had the responsibility for the chateau's wines, but it must have been Marie herself who had trained him.

Marie looked up just then and saw her in the doorway. 'I wondered if I might have a word with you,' Mary said, stepping into the dusty room.

'But of course, Madame. I have been waiting for you,' Marie said, giving her one of those toothy grins and shaking herself for all the world like some old dog waking by the fire.

'Really? But I've only just come down,' Mary said, contemplating a chair before the desk and deciding that it was too filthy for seating.

'I have been waiting, Madame, for ten years – since I first hinted to you in a letter of Philip's presence here, and who he might be.'

Like most inveterate schemers, Mary was shocked by the discovery of another's scheming. 'I don't understand this,' she said in a haughty tone. 'If there was something you wanted from me, why didn't you merely write and say so?'

Marie chuckled to herself. 'Umm, yes – and if I had written and said that I had your brother's cast-off bastard child here and that I had grown quite fond of him, and wanted to see if I could stop them from robbing him of his birthright, would you have rushed to his aid, Madame?'

'Perhaps.'

'And perhaps not. I wanted to see whether you might have an interest of your own in the boy's future. People do more when that is the case. This is why I wrote you, why I have done business with you, rather than those others. Philip needed an ally against them. Are you that ally, Madame?'

'And what interest can I have in Philip's future?' Mary asked, angry to see that she had been made use of, when she had thought it the other way round. 'What do you think I can possibly get out of all this?'

'Whatever you came here plotting to get, Madame,' Marie said flatly. 'I am too far removed from your land, from the Brussacs of California, to know or be interested in your quarrels. But I know that it wasn't that pitiful wine we send you that brought you here, it was Philip – like a cutting from the old vine, he is, but grafted to new stock – like your daughter too, if I'm not mistaken. No, don't think me presumptuous; our stock grows old, the Brussac stock, and I have sometimes thought that it is tainted, but theirs will take root and be fruitful in ways undreamed of by you and me. That is why you came to France, is it not? To take Philip back with you to California; to make use of him to further some plan of your own?'

'Yes,' Mary said, abandoning her pretense. 'I was robbed of my birthright too, by the same Brussacs who have tried to rob Philip. French Hills is mine as well as his. I want it back.'

'Um, yes,' Marie nodded, again giving her toothy smile. 'Someday that may be between you and him.'

'I will take him to California. I will support his claim to his inheritance. I ask only that he later support my claim as well. Will you help me persuade him to come to California?'

Marie's smile faded to be replaced by a sad look. 'Philip has brought a great deal of pleasure into our world, my brother's and mine, but he is entitled to a world of his own, and he has been robbed of what should be his. I will speak to him.'

'Thank you.'

'Do not thank me,' Marie said coldly. 'I do it not for your sake, nor for mine, but for his.'

And you are still a fool, Mary thought; Philip's visit to California would indeed be fruitful. This was the dream that had brought her to France.

Philip would be restored to French Hills – and through him, so would she be as well. It would all work out exactly as she had envisioned it.

Having spent half the night tossing and turning, Jolene woke late, to discover that Philip was already gone from the house. She looked so despondent, though, that Marie, who had a better idea of the relationship between the two young people than Mary did, told her where she might find him.

'There's a place by the river,' she said, indicating a path through the trees, 'he likes to go there to bathe, or just to be alone. Judging from the look he had when he went out, that's where he'll be.'

Thanking her profusely, Jolene saddled an ancient nag and rode out in the direction Marie had indicated. Impatient with the horse's leisurely gait, she tried to hurry him along, with only slight success; difficult to imagine, she thought angrily, that the night of her arrival this same horse had been engaged in a spirited race.

Philip was not hard to find. He was seated at the river's edge, idly watching the multicolored water flow past. Here a pool had been formed among the grasses, a perfect spot for bathing, or for solitude.

He watched her wordlessly as she approached and dismounted. She crossed the little clearing, stopping a few feet from him. They studied one another in silence. His expression was cold, unwelcoming. Her heart ached with all that she wanted to say, to express to him.

'I suppose you've come at your mother's bidding,' he said dryly.

She was slow in answering. To his surprise, she lifted her hands and began to unfasten the bodice of her dress. In a moment she was in her chemise, and then she was naked before him, stepping from her discarded garments with the unashamed grace of a wood nymph.

'Do you think this is my mother's bidding?' she asked.

Still standing where she was, she opened her arms to him in a timeless gesture of invitation. His breath quickening in his throat, Philip strode to her, closing her in his arms. He felt her body tremble and in a rush he felt an overwhelming need to shelter and protect her, to care for and comfort her. He gasped for air as a drowning man breaks the surface of the water, filling his nostrils with the scent of her, the river, the damp earth.

Together they sank into the tall, cool grasses.

Later they bathed in the river's cold water, and Jolene pricked her foot on something buried in the silt at the bottom. He dived to search for the culprit, and came up with the broken hilt of an old sword, rusted and crumbling from long years in the water.

'I wonder how it got here,' she said.

'Someone must have fought on this very bank,' he said, turning the fragment over in his hand. He wondered if it had been a Brussac. In the years since he had come here, he had gained a sense of history, history not only of time and place, but of blood as well. Here, where Brussacs had breathed and loved and bred, he had become a Brussac too.

He had often wondered at the others who must have come to this lovely spot by the river; was it some unconscious tie with those past generations that had brought him here, again and again!

He looked up and saw Jolene observing him with a tender regard. He smiled and said aloud, 'I'm glad we made love here.' Flinging the rusted sword back into the water, he clambered onto the bank, helping her out as well.

'You'll be leaving soon?' he asked.

'In a few days, yes.'

Aunt Marie had spoken to him earlier, but that was not the first time that he had considered the question of California. He was torn by conflicting emotions. He wanted to go, of course; not only because Jolene would be there. There were other, even deeper ties. A sister to find, a promise to keep. And a name to justify, to make truly his own. He could not be a Brussac, could not be himself, until he had claimed his rightful place as Adam Brussac's son. It was not land or money that he wanted; it was his heritage.

But if staying here was impossible, going would be no less painful, for this had been his first real home, his first real family. He loved the crazy old woman who had taken him to her bosom, given him, above all other gifts, the pride and self-esteem that the others had denied him. How could he ever hope to repay the priceless years that she had bestowed upon him?

'Will you come with us,' Jolene asked, 'to California?'

'Yes, I must,' he said, but his voice was sad.

Their parting was brief and, to the casual observer, unemotional, for neither Philip nor Marie was willing or able to reveal to others the depth of their emotions. They embraced quickly, and she kissed his cheek, the withered fingers of one shaking hand lightly brushing a lock of hair from his brow before she averted her eyes and stepped away from him.

'You'll come to California when I've gotten settled?' he asked, his voice husky.

'Yes, yes, I promise,' she said, though both knew it was a promise that would never be kept. She was ancient, far too old to plan a distant journey.

He glanced upward at the attic windows. A curtain fluttered and was still. He had gone earlier to say farewell to René, but he had gotten no reply and it was impossible to say if René understood his explanations; he had sat by the window, staring out wordlessly. Only the tears that streamed unchecked down his cheeks had indicated that he even understood Philip was leaving.

'We'll have to be going,' Mary said from within the carriage, 'else we'll miss the train for London.'

For a moment more Philip hesitated. Marie looked stubbornly down at the ground; the sunlight glinted from the moisture on her own cheeks.

'Well, then, goodbye,' he said, not trusting his voice to say more. He spoke to the driver, climbed into the carriage, and almost at once it was moving.

Marie stood and watched until long after it had disappeared through the trees. She knew that she would never see him again. His presence here, since the day when he had come as a small boy, had stood out like a golden day in the long darkness of her life. Through his lean, young body as he grew to manhood, she had been young again. His thrills of discovery, his joy of living, had been her thrills, her joy, just as his aches and his longings had been hers too.

Now he was gone, and she was left a mad old woman, far, far older than before, alone in a rotting house with a mad brother and a few bottles of wine.

'The damned Brussac wine,' she said aloud, spitting violently into the dust at her feet. There would be no more wine, not from here. The vines, the land were dying.

She was dying.

I must talk to René, she thought, making her way with shuffling steps towards the house. She walked, as she had not for years, like an old woman, back bent, legs stiff.

There was no reply when she tapped at his door. She let herself in, blinking in the unaccustomed gloom. At first she did not see him. Not until she had stepped into the room and the slippered feet, the once-white shoes now yellow and moldy, almost brushed her face, did she realize the significance of the long shadow dangling on the far wall, swinging slowly about in the draft from the open door.

12

It was a far different trip from the one Philip had taken as a small boy journeying to France. For one thing, he had traveled second class on that first occasion, and now he traveled first, with his own cabin; the third night out he and Jolene and Mary even had dinner with the Captain.

For another thing, he had traveled to France as an exile, an outcast without even an identity of his own; now, he was literally going home. He was a Californian. He was a Brussac, though others might try to deny that fact. Mary had promised to support his claim when the time came. And the time would come, he would not rest until he had gotten what was his.

Most significant of all, however, was the fact that he was with Jolene. The unloved and unwanted youngster had found love, had found it with a small boy's instinct for where it was to be found.

They were scarcely out of one another's sight throughout the ocean voyage and the long train trip that followed it. Together they crossed the great plains to the accompaniment of clacking wheels and an incessant shower of cinders, he marveling at how the cities and towns had flourished since his childhood, she content to share in his rediscovery of the land.

If there was one who was less enthusiastic about the enforced intimacy of the long trip, it was Mary. Belatedly she had begun to suspect that Jolene's romantic behavior, which had not abated, though it was no longer necessary to her mother's schemes, was not entirely an act.

It would not do, in her opinion, for her daughter to become seriously involved with Philip. True enough, he was a Brussac and entitled to some share in French Hills; but he was still a bastard and even if all of French Hills were his, he would not be the sort of match she intended for Jolene.

With a rueful eye, Mary watched the young couple and pondered how best to deal with this unfortunate development.

They arrived at the Oakland Mole to the accompaniment of blustery winds. Philip, who remembered a different California of long, hot days and gentle nights, braved the cold to stand on the deck as the ferry carried them across to the San Francisco side; he turned his head this way and that as if searching for a scent on the wind.

'Not much farther,' Jolene said, coming to stand by him at the rail. 'We'll spend the night in town, at the Palace; it's where everybody stays. Tomorrow we'll ride out to the ranch.'

'Which way will we be traveling?' Philip asked.

'Sonoma's north of here – that way,' Jolene answered, pointing in the general direction.

During their brief pause in Paris, Philip had found a book on California which he had studied diligently during their journey, but he found the reality of San Francisco far different from what the antiquated volume had promised him. That had made it seem like little more than a dusty village, while before him, spread across the hills, was a modern city.

'That's Rincon Hill over there,' Jolene said, pointing, 'where the oldest families live, and that's Nob Hill. Nob Hill is Bonanza wealth.'

'Anyone who is anyone lives on Nob Hill these days,' Mary said, having come to join them at the rail. Philip saw the little grimace of disapproval Jolene made; apparently mother and daughter did not agree on the merits of the Nob Hill society.

'The highest hill, with the trees and green spaces, is Russian Hill,' Jolene went on. 'And that's Telegraph Hill, where the Italian population live.'

'It's a beautiful city,' Philip said.

Mary sniffed; her adulation of San Francisco society did not extend to their city. 'All that dust,' she said. 'It's practically built on sand dunes. Mark my words, someday it will come down about their heads.'

After a moment, Philip asked quietly, 'And Los Angeles, it's the opposite direction, yes?'

'Yes, to the south,' Jolene replied.

He stared in that direction, though there was nothing to see beyond the green hills that surrounded the city. Again there was the unconscious gesture of an animal scenting the wind.

Mary heard and saw. She smiled to herself and nodded her head. It was true, the boy might be in love with Jolene – who would not be? But there was another, an older love, his first love, as it were. He would not forget French Hills. The longing to return was as strong as the longing for revenge. Nothing would stand in the way of that.

To Mary's surprise, José and young Philip hit it off quite well. At first, José had been suspicious and cool toward this mysterious young 'relative' his wife had plucked from France.

'If he really knows winemaking,' José put it to Mary on the night of her return, 'he'd be a far sight more valuable to us there. This way, we've got nothing but that crazy old lady to rely on. And, if he doesn't know wine, what good is he to us here anyway?'

'The French wines don't amount to two or three percent of what we distribute,' Mary pointed out. 'Their only real value is in the name, and I think we've got about all we can get out of that. Give the boy a chance.'

José, because he was inherently fair, did just that and was rather gratefully surprised. The first day, he offered to take Philip on a tour of the cellars where the new wine was breathing in its casks while the last year's wine was being 'fined', or cleared of its sediment. He poured a sampling of the older wine for Philip and, as he usually did for visitors, offered him a piece of cheese with it. Philip laughed and respectfully declined the cheese.

'In France they've got an old saying,' Philip explained. 'Serve cheese when you're selling wine, eat apples when you're buying it.'

José laughed with him, and memorized the old saying to use himself in the future. Afterward, they took a rambling tour through the vineyards, now pruned down to bare brown stumps for winter. The truncated vines were attached to shiny new wires, making the entire vineyard gleam like a giant spider's web in the afternoon sun.

By the time the pair returned to the newly built Victorian mansion, they were chatting like old friends.

Winter here was not much different than in France, only slightly milder. Philip fitted himself into the life at the ranch, quickly making himself useful; in a matter of a few weeks he was behaving more like José's partner in winemaking than a house guest, consulting with him on every little detail, making valuable suggestions, even going so far as to disagree vehemently when he thought José was in error, and once or twice proving his point.

Philip was happy. Yet from time to time Mary, who watched him with the unblinking gaze of a falcon watching its prey, saw him turn his gaze to the south, as if awaiting some signal, some sign that it was time. Like him she too listened to the wind, and waited.

It was nearing Christmas, and soon after that the year, and an era, would end. 1 January 1900 would begin the new century. Throughout the land, people spoke optimistically of new beginnings, of new frontiers. A few, like Philip, looked both forward and back.

It seemed to Philip as if the parties never stopped that December. The Californians were determined to usher in the new century with a vengeance. They seemed to be ever journeying from the home of one vintner to another, and even into San Francisco. Between times, a parade of elegant carriages and not so elegant buggies and farm carts snaked their way up the drive to the Perreiras' mansion in Sonoma. Wines were tasted and compared, toasts drunk.

On the last night of the century, a short time before midnight, Philip asked Jolene to marry him.

Mary had planned her own ball for New Year's Eve. Guests had been arriving since midday, when a group who had ridden all the way from Monterey showed up. After that, they came in a steady stream until all of the northern winemakers were represented.

For Philip, it was exciting and yet stifling. He was unaccustomed to dealing with large crowds of people, and as the evening wore on he found himself on the move about the house, unconsciously looking for a place to be alone.

At length, he sought refuge in the one place most familiar to him – the vineyard. As he walked, the sounds of the party gradually faded until they were a distant hum. It was a clear, cloudless night; the vines lifted their stumpy fingers toward heaven, as if in a gesture of supplication. Philip strolled and thought of the century that was about to begin. He must make a new beginning for himself as well. There, to the distant south, a challenge awaited him. Sometime soon, he must face it, for until it was resolved, he was doomed to live in a sort of limbo.

'Philip?'

He turned and saw Jolene coming toward him through the rows of vines. His heart lifted as it always did at the sight of her. There, of course, was the rub, for he could not bring himself to leave Jolene. To be away from her even for an hour or two was an agony to him.

Since Christmas he had been trying to summon the courage to propose. He had no doubt that Jolene loved him, and certainly he knew that he loved her. Though she had given herself to him beside the river at Chateau Brussac, they had made love only rarely here in California. Partly it was lack of opportunity; the fall and early winter were a busy time for the winemakers. Too, it was a token of his respect for her. He wanted her as his wife, not as his mistress.

Only his sense of his own inadequacy had held him back from asking her to marry him. He was all too painfully aware that he was a nobody, with nothing to offer of his own. Though he had been happy here and thought that he had earned his keep, his destination was not Brussac-America. His quest for identity had scarcely even begun. What could he bring a wife but questions with no answers, dreams that might never see fruition?

If these things mattered to Jolene at all, however, she gave no sign of it. She came now into his arms with a shiver of delight.

'I saw you come out,' she murmured, pressing her cheek to his. 'I've been stalking you since, but I lost you for a few minutes among the vines.'

The excitement of the evening, the combination of moonlight and her warmth in his arms, and the scent of her hair in his nostrils, weakened the last of his resolve. He heard himself asking, as if it were another, 'Will you marry me?'

'Oh, yes, yes, God in Heaven yes, I thought you'd never ask me,' she cried, clinging to him ecstatically. They kissed; after a moment she drew back, saying, 'We must tell everyone the news.'

He felt a pang of misgiving, all too aware that the announcement would not meet with universal approval.

'Jolene, perhaps we ought to discuss this quietly with your father first,' Philip said. He had a great deal of respect for the quiet, courteous man who was her father, and he rather thought that José might approve of him sufficiently to accept him as a son-in-law. But Mary was something else again, and Philip knew her well enough by this time to know that, for all her pretended helplessness, Mary Perreira was a tyrant who brooked little interference with her own plans.

It was hardly likely that her plans included a marriage between Jolene and himself. Jolene must have known this too, yet still she insisted on making their announcement at once. There was something almost frightening in the urgency with which she hurried him over the ghostly fields, toward the lights and noise of the party in progress at the house.

In the yard outside the house stood the inevitable brass bell used to summon the workmen. Philip made a final, half-hearted attempt to dissuade her.

'Jolene, I really think this ought to wait,' he said.

She laughed, sounding for that brief space of time oddly different, yet familiar too. He frowned as it came to him, her laugh sounded strangely like Aunt Marie's – but of course, he thought with a sense of revelation, she was a descendant of that crazy old woman, as close a descendant in fact as he was. He wondered fleetingly if perhaps there was a trace of madness permeating the Brussac blood.

He had no time, though, for pursuing that train of thought. Jolene had begun to ring the bell, its clamorous summons bringing people rushing from the house almost at once. Asking excited questions of one another, they poured into the yard, forming a colorful throng while Jolene continued to ring the bell.

The crowd parted to make way as José and Mary appeared on the porch. Seeing them, Jolene stopped ringing the bell. She watched, breathing heavily as if she had just run a foot race, while her parents descended the steps and made their way through the now silent crowd of guests, all watching the scene with curiosity and evident relish.

'Jolene,' Mary said coolly, approaching her daughter, 'if you're ringing in the New Year, I'm afraid you're a few minutes premature. We've just been watching the clock in the parlor . . . '

'Oh, Mama,' Jolene cried, her eyes flashing brightly, 'we've something even grander than the New Year to celebrate. Philip and I are to be married. He's just asked me.'

There was a long, drawn-out stillness as everyone seemed to be weighing this announcement. Before Mary or José could reply another bell began to ring in the distance, announcing the arrival of midnight. A second later, another nearby, then another, and yet another, began to ring, from other farms, and from the distant town, until it seemed the hills themselves were pealing their joy. The crowd gathered in the yard began to shout and cheer, some of them in welcome to the infant century, others in response to Jolene's announcement.

It was impossible to make oneself heard over the din, the

likes of which had never been heard in the California hills. Philip's eyes met those of Jolene's father, and he was heartened by what he saw. But when he turned to Mary, his happiness paled. She glowered coldly at Jolene for a moment. Then, whirling about, she made her way through a crowd of revelers, now singing and dancing and drinking endless toasts. One tipsy gentleman seized her and tried to kiss her cheek but she gave him a shove that sent him toppling into the watering trough.

She reached the shelter of the house without a single New Year's greeting.

13

'It won't do, it simply won't do,' Mary said.

'Mary, you're getting yourself all worked up for nothing,' José said; they were alone in their bedroom. The last of the stragglers had left a short time before, and the house had finally fallen silent.

'For nothing? Our daughter is about to marry a half-greaser bastard . . . '

'Mary!'

She flushed angrily, her mouth setting in an ugly line. 'I won't have Jolene repeat my mistake,' she said.

'What are you talking about, your mistake?' he demanded. 'In marrying me, you mean? You haven't done so badly, it seems to me.'

'We're doing better these days, but only thanks to my unceasing efforts. I've knocked till my hands were raw to get some of those San Francisco doors to open to us. And with a good marriage for Jolene, I'll make the rest of them accept us. With someone like David Ecks for a son-in-law, we could be welcome anywhere. What doors do you think Philip could open?'

'French Hills, maybe.' She made no reply. 'Isn't that what you had in mind? Isn't that what's been stuck in your gullet all these years? Maybe your daughter could give it back to you.'

'I don't want French Hills back. I want . . . ' She paused.

'You want revenge, is that what you were going to say?'

She was looking past him, at a spot on the wall. Her lips curved into an unexpected smile.

'Mary, whatever you're planning, for God's sake, let it be,' José said, speaking more gently. 'You can't stop Jolene and Philip from doing what they plan.'

'Yes, I can,' she said.

'Mary . . .'

But she wasn't listening to him; she rarely did. As if unaware he was still in the room, Mary slipped a warm wrapper over her nightdress and left the room, smiling to herself.

She paused at the door to Philip's room, her hand on the little china doorknob. There was no sound from within. She knocked softly and opened the door.

Philip was still fully dressed, standing beside the window that overlooked the vineyards. Outside, the sky was already taking on the translucence of dawn.

'Am I disturbing you?' she asked, stepping into the room.

'No. I've been expecting you,' he said.

She smiled and closed the door after herself. 'Of course, you knew I wouldn't sleep until we'd straightened out this nonsense between us.'

Philip sighed and came to meet her in the center of the room. 'It isn't nonsense, Mrs Perreira. Jolene and I love one another. Can you understand that?'

'Oh, yes, I understand love well enough,' Mary gave a bitter laugh. 'I understand the false hope it can fill you with, and I understand too how bitter can be the awakening to reality.'

'Ours is no false hope. I mean to marry Jolene.'

'Really? And what name shall you put on the marriage certificate? Have you a name, other than the one my aunt lent you?'

'You know my name,' he said grimly, his face slowly turning a darker shade.

'Ah yes, Felipe, isn't it – is there another, or is Felipe all there is?'

'My name is Philip Brussac,' he said through clenched teeth.

'Yes, we think so, you and I. And what if the Brussacs – what if your own father denies it? What will I call you then? What of my daughter, what shall her married name be? And your children, my grandchildren, do you want me to tell you what they shall be called: the bastard's offspring.'

He took a menacing step toward her, his hands clenched into fists at his side. 'Shut up,' he said.

Mary threw back her head defiantly. 'Go ahead, strike me if you wish, it will change nothing, beating me will not give you a name.'

For a few seconds he glowered at her. Then some of the anger seemed to leave him. He turned from her, his fists relaxing into hands again, and strode to the window.

Mary seized upon his confusion. She followed him, taking his broad shoulders in her hands. 'Don't you see,' she whispered, leaning her cheek against the firmness of his back, 'if you love her, as you say, you must resolve these things before you take her for a wife. It would be unfair, not only to yourself, but to her, and to the children you will have, to do otherwise. You will be cheating them all.'

'And you too, I suppose,' Philip said, a note of bitterness in his voice.

'We had an agreement, you and I. I have honored it thus far. I will continue to do so.'

'Marrying Jolene does not prevent me from returning to French Hills.'

'Would you abandon your wife as soon as you have married her? Or do you think to take her with you? There is doubt whether they will accept even you. Arriving in the company of my daughter is not likely to increase your chances.'

He turned back to face her, his eyes glinting dangerously. This time it was he who seized her shoulders, in a grip so fierce that she almost cried out from pain.

'And if I go to French Hills,' he said, 'if I claim my inheritance and am accepted as Adam Brussac's son – will you then permit your daughter to marry me? Would you accept a wealthy bastard in place of a poor one?'

She was suddenly and strikingly aware of his nearness, his maleness. His broad chest rose and fell under the fabric of his shirt. She was completely unprepared for the wave of desire that rose up within her. She tried to speak, but no words came. He saw her confusion, and for an instant she saw in his eyes that he understood, that he too had become aware of the intimacy of the setting, of her scant clothing, of a man-woman current between them.

They were spared the knowledge of what might have happened, for at that moment Jolene came into the room.

'Philip, I couldn't sleep,' she began; seeing her mother, she stopped short. 'Mother, why are you here?'

Philip's hands dropped to his side. Mary, shaken, turned

from him, avoiding her daughter's gaze as she did so. 'I came to talk to Philip,' she said, even her voice betraying her tension.

For a moment Philip looked from one to the other. Then, with a purposeful gesture, he strode to the heavily carved armoire that stood against the far wall and, opening it, took out his valise. He carried it to the bed and began to fill it with clothes from a dresser drawer.

Jolene ran to him, putting a restraining hand on his arm. 'Philip, what are you doing?' she asked.

'Packing. I'm going to Los Angeles,' he said. He shook off the hand on his arm and continued his packing. Unnoticed, Mary stole from the room.

'But you mustn't,' Jolene cried. 'Philip, I beg you – our wedding . . . '

'I've got to,' he said. 'Don't you see, until I do, until it's finished, I'll never be whole.'

'It will never be finished, I felt it in my heart. Oh, Philip, I'm so frightened.'

'Damn,' Philip swore, seeing the tears that had begun to run down her cheeks. He threw aside a stack of shirts and came to enfold her in his arms.

'There's no need to be,' he whispered, stroking her hair. 'We'll be married, never fear. It's just that I have this other business I've got to settle first.'

'I'm afraid you won't come back to me.'

'Don't be foolish,' he said. 'I'll never really even leave you. No matter how far I journey, nor how long, I shall always be with you.'

The words, which should have comforted her, sounded hollow to her ears.

PART 2

1900

14

'Your first visit to LA?'

Philip turned his attention from the train window to the gentleman seated beside him. 'My home is here,' he said, 'but I've been away since I was a boy.'

'You'll find it greatly changed, I'm afraid,' the stranger said. 'Towns and oil wells springing up all over the place like mushrooms.'

'Those groves of trees there, what are they?' Philip asked, pointing out the train window.

'Oranges. Used to be a vineyard there, but they say oranges are more profitable these days.'

In the north, Philip had heard repeatedly of the shift of the California wine industry from Los Angeles, where it had begun, to the central and northern portions of the state, but he had been unprepared for the dramatic evidence of the change. Countless acres of grapevines had been replaced by groves of orange trees or, in many instances, by fledgling communities, clusters of new houses looking, he thought, like sores upon the ravaged surface of the land.

It was not difficult to see how Southern California had lost its supremacy in wine. The land boom that had come with the railroads and peaked in the eighties had multiplied Los Angeles' population ten times over. The growing metropolis had simply devoured much of the good grape-growing land. Increased interest in citrus and walnut crops, which needed no bottling or years of aging to make them profitable, had done its share of damage, it seemed.

As for oil, he was surprised to find it still a source of speculation. Since the sixties, each decade had seen a rise of interest in the oil that was unquestionably beneath the California land, and each time speculation had floundered on the seemingly insoluble problems associated with California oil. The digging and drilling techniques used with success in the East were simply inadequate for the faulted and fractured California soil; even when the oil could be recovered from the ground, its composition made it unacceptable for heating or lighting purposes.

Apparently, though, the fortunes that had already been lost had not diminished the lure of the so called 'black gold'. Perhaps it was the early gold rush that had made California a get-rich-quick land. In France, the centuries of history had taught patience. Life here was shorter and faster; everything was boom or bust.

Did the new century, he wondered, signify the end of Southern California's wine boom? And if so, what would that mean to French Hills and the Brussacs?

The train had reached the station at last. Philip joined the noisy, jostling crowd emerging onto the platform, his ears assaulted by the variety of tongues and accents. In France, and in the US cities of the East and the midcountry, he had become accustomed to a more uniform language, but here in the raw, young land that was California it seemed as if no two voices were alike. One heard English, both the American and the British varieties, with countless variations in accent and inflection; Spanish was omnipresent; there was a smattering of German; a passing voice rattling off French like a native, and another what he took to be Russian. He guessed from their appearance that a nearby group was using one of the Polynesian dialects for their heated argument. And that couple just ahead of him, the frail little man leading his frightened-looking wife, were they Chinese, or Japanese? Philip had to admit Orientals looked much the same to him. A deficiency on his own part, and one that he really ought to correct, considering the numbers of Orientals he had seen since his arrival in California.

This thought was on his mind as he emerged from the station so that the couple that might otherwise have flitted across his attention without leaving any impression continued to attract his notice.

With scarcely a pause the couple crossed to one of the hackney cabs waiting outside the station. Philip, looking around for his own cab, would undoubtedly have dismissed them from his mind then had it not been for one of those ugly incidents that seemed to be an integral part of the western scene: a tall, surly looking cowboy brushed rudely by the Orientals, knocking the woman, who had been about to climb into the cab, to the ground.

'Here, I'll take that cab,' the stranger demanded.

Philip, who had known his share of bullying, felt his hackles rise. He strode angrily forward, catching the stranger's arm as the man was about to enter the cab.

'Excuse me,' Philip said, 'but I think these people had already engaged this cab.'

The stranger swore, jerking his arm loose and turning on Philip with an angry scowl. 'What the devil are you talking about?' he asked in a loud voice.

'I said, unless I'm mistaken, this cab is taken.'

The driver of the cab, seeing a dangerous and time-consuming fight threatening, said quickly, 'It makes no difference to me who rides my cab, mister, long's they pay.'

'You heard the man,' the stranger said. 'Besides, these Chinks ain't goin' anywhere special, and me, I've got important business to take care of, and I don't like no greaser bastard telling me what to do.'

The last insult was like a slap to Philip, bringing back memories of his cousins, Harvey and Caleb, who had tormented him so as a child. For a moment he was overwhelmed by memories of the past. He seemed to see Harvey's face superimposed over the cowboy's.

'What the hell are you staring at?' the cowboy demanded.

Philip, glancing around, realized that their dispute had already caused a small crowd to gather. He caught the muttered phrase, 'Damn foreigners,' and realized with another shock that it was he, as well as the Chinese family, that it referred to; he had forgotten that his swarthy appearance and the accent acquired in France made him a part of the motley assortment of arriving immigrants.

He was not eager for a fight on the day of his return to Los Angeles, and he suspected that if one were to start here it would go badly not only for him but for the hapless couple at his elbow.

'At you,' he answered the question aloud. 'It's so rarely one gets to see an unmitigated boor firsthand.' He turned his back and addressed the silent Oriental. 'Do you speak English?'

'Yes, Master,' the man said, bowing from the waist.

'Good, you can share my cab, then,' Philip said, deftly steering them away from the site. 'And I'm not anyone's master, thank you.'

The man was quick to size up the situation and in a twinkling was shepherding his wife away from the spot, ignoring the menacing crowd.

'Hey, you,' the cowboy shouted after them.

'Keep walking,' Philip said in a low, calm voice. Most of the crowd was made up of surly-looking cowboys, guns belted to their hips. He already knew that there was a great deal of resentment against the foreign immigrants here, especially the Chinese, it seemed, though it appeared to him they had made a number of significant contributions to the building of the state. Still, all of that would be moot if one of them were to be shot now, because of his intervention.

Behind them, the cowhand had apparently decided that his 'important business' was more pressing than the unfinished dispute. With a final coarse insult, which brought a ripple of laughter from the onlookers, he clambered into the cab and a moment later was on his way. The crowd, looking disappointed, began to break up. Philip breathed a silent sigh of relief.

'Climb aboard,' he said when they reached the second hackney. 'I'll drop you on my way.'

To his surprise the old man stopped, his wife huddling close at his shoulder. 'No, Master,' he said, bowing again. 'You have been brave on our behalf, but you have done enough, it would serve neither our interests nor yours to share this ride. And I do not think we will be going to the same places. May I ask your name, Master?'

'My name? Philip . . . ' he paused the slightest fraction of a second, ' . . . Brussac.'

'Then, Philip Brussac, the family of Lu Chen will be forever in your debt. My children, and my children's children, will honor your name, and await an opportunity to repay you.'

Philip, embarrassed by the elaborately stated gratitude, was at a loss to reply. He shifted his valise from one hand to the other, giving himself a knock in the shins as he did so. This earned a smothered giggle from the woman. 'You're sure . . . ?' He indicated the cab, its driver flicking his reins impatiently.

'Please to go on,' Lu Chen said, grinning. 'There, see, is another cab. Have no fear, we will arrive where we have set out to go.'

'Yes,' Philip said, grinning in return. 'I feel sure you will.'

He swung himself up into the cab, turning to wave at the couple on the sidewalk. 'Good luck to you then,' he said.

'And to you, Philip Brussac,' Lu Chen replied.

Philip gave the driver instructions and as the cab began to move, he looked back. Lu Chen and his wife remained where they had been, watching him depart. Philip waved somewhat awkwardly, and they returned the gesture. The cab rounded a corner, and they were gone from sight.

Riding through the strikingly modern city, with its paved and lighted streets complete with sidewalks for pedestrians, he supposed he had seen the last of Lu Chen and his family, even his 'children's children', elaborate promises notwithstanding.

15

Although the city had changed, and spread wide across the land, French Hills seemed much the same. Once past the outlying communities that had sprung up as suburbs to Los Angeles, Philip found himself riding through the same green-brown hills he remembered from his childhood. He was assaulted by a wave of nostalgia. Something in the familiar womanly curve of the hills, the sight of the chaparral, the purple and gray mountains that lay like a crown on the horizon, brought back sharp and clear a hundred memories that had lain dormant in the dark reaches of his consciousness: his mother, dying, but before that, striding through the vineyards with a small boy at her heels; the vineyards themselves, and the strange scorched earth left by some catastrophic brush fire of the past; the Brussacs, Jean and David and, especially, for it was he on whose welcome Philip's future might well hinge, Adam Brussac, his father.

Since he had first known in France that he must return he had dredged his memory for images of his father. They were few. Adam, shouting at the pickers among the vines. A dim, sleep-blurred image of Adam slipping through the door of their shack, late at night. Adam, explaining that he was to be sent away.

Of the memories to which a child ought to be entitled – after all, this man was his father – there were none. No kisses or embraces, no fatherly advice, no lazy sharing of the hot, dusty afternoons of summer. In blood only were they father and son. Yet though blood satisfied the definition, was it enough? Was 'father' no more nor less than the source of a seed? Or would some trace of hitherto unexpressed love have endured the years of separation and the barriers standing in the way of their relationship?

He would soon know. His mouth felt dry as he neared the gates and the drive that led to French Hills. He was returning home; to what, he could not guess.

There was a man with a horse a short distance beyond the gate, apparently checking the fences. He saw Philip and, leading his horse, came to meet him at the gate. Not until they were nearly opposite one another did Philip recognize him as Harvey.

Harvey showed no recognition, staring at him suspiciously as he rode up and swung himself down from his horse. 'You looking for something?' he asked in an unfriendly manner.

'Yes,' Philip said, 'my home.' He went to the gate and opened it. Harvey reacted with astonishment, followed by anger.

'Here, leave that gate alone. What do you mean, anyway, about home? Who the hell are you?'

'Your cousin, Philip Brussac, recently returned from exile. I see you haven't changed in the least, Harvey, you're still the same rude, loud-mouthed lout that I remember from my childhood.'

Harvey moved to block the way, his eyes narrowing as he studied Philip's face. Suddenly he gave an oath, his eyes popping open.

'Felipe! Jesus God, it's the greaser kid. I thought we was rid of you once and for all.'

'Far from it, as you can see,' Philip replied. 'Is . . . ' he started to say 'my father' but decided against it; 'is Adam home?'

'Not to you he ain't.' Harvey deftly drew a gun from his belt, aiming it at Philip's midsection. 'You might as well get back on that horse and ride back to France, greaser, there ain't nothing around here for the likes of you.'

Philip glanced at the gun, one of the six-shooters that seemed to be the universal choice throughout the West. 'That remains to be seen,' he said, wiping the perspiration from his brow. 'Mind if I remove my hat?'

Without waiting for a reply, he lifted the wide-brimmed hat from his head. With a quick flip of his wrist, he sent it suddenly sailing over the fence. Harvey fell for the trick. Instinctively his eyes followed the hat's flight. When he looked back, it was his turn to find himself staring down the barrel of a gun.

'Drop the revolver, Harvey,' Philip said evenly. It was a standoff, both men with guns drawn, he was counting on his memory that Harvey was a coward.

The gamble paid off. Harvey hesitated for a moment; then,

with an angry oath, he flung his weapon to the ground.

'The belt too,' Philip said.

Belt followed gun. Philip knelt, scooping them up. He tucked the revolver into his waist and looped the gun-belt over the horn of his saddle.

'Now I'll trouble you for those suspenders,' he said.

'My suspenders?' Harvey looked astonished. 'What for?'

'Maybe I just like the color of them, cousin.'

'Well, how the hell am I supposed to keep my pants up,' Harvey wanted to know.

'You've got hands haven't you? It'll keep them from more mischievous pastimes.'

'Now you look here, you goddamn . . . '

Philip lifted his gun, sighting down the barrel to a point midway between Harvey's blazing eyes. 'The suspenders, please,' he said, cocking the hammer.

Swearing under his breath, Harvey unfastened his suspenders with one hand and clutched at his pants with the other. He flung the contested elastic into the dust of the drive.

Philip picked them up too. Then, keeping a careful eye on his cousin, he swung himself once again into the saddle. He rode to where Harvey's horse stood grazing patiently and, taking the reins, led the beast alongside his own, starting in the direction of the house.

'Hey, what about me?' Harvey shouted after him.

'Harvey, there's one thing they taught me in France,' Philip called back. 'A man should never get caught with his pants down.'

'You son of a . . . ' Harvey roared, shaking his fist in the air and starting to run after Philip. His trousers, momentarily forgotten, dropped downward about his knees, tripping him. His shout of rage was muffled as he fell face downward in the dust. By the time he had scrambled to his feet again, this time remembering to keep a tight hold on his pants, Philip – and the horses – were fast disappearing along the lane.

Philip's laughter was short-lived, however. As he neared the rambling old house that he remembered so clearly, he grew sober once again. Baiting Harvey wasn't going to make things any easier for him here; if he was going to stay for a time, he would have to find some way of striking a truce with his cousin, and with Caleb as well. They had been bullies as children, who had delighted in tormenting him; he supposed it was unlikely that either of them would take kindly to being his equal now.

He would have his work cut out for him, just ensuring that a knife didn't get planted in his back at some careless moment.

He had a half-sister as well, Adam's daughter Nadine. He remembered her as pretty, a spoiled brat who had actively encouraged Harvey and Caleb in tormenting him. There was probably little likelihood that she would welcome him, particularly as a relative.

As for the others, it was difficult to say what to expect. David had always been the kindest of the brothers, gentle and soft-spoken, but the order to which he belonged set him apart from the others; there was something unworldly about David that would probably make him ineffectual even if he should become an ally. And, anyway, he hadn't lived at French Hills in years. As for Jean, he had always seemed reasonable enough, so far as a small boy might have judged. He was competent and hard-working, well enough liked by the employees, and unquestionably second in command to Adam.

Again, Adam Brussac. It was he who dominated French Hills, he who had taken the helm from his father Claude. When all was said and done, it was upon him that everything depended.

A pretty young maid answered the front door. Philip wanted to ask about old Juanita, and especially about her daughter Elena, but he decided the questions were premature. His meeting with Adam Brussac came first. After that, he hoped, there would be time enough for answering questions.

He asked for Adam, again hesitating when the maid asked who was calling. 'Tell him it's – tell him Philip Brussac.'

She looked curious, but she nodded discreetly and vanished around a corner of the long hall to announce him. Philip stood with his hat in his hand in the tile-lined foyer, looking about at the heavy carved oak furniture, smaller and less elegant than he remembered it. It was quite different from the Perreiras' mansion, and certainly unlike Chateau Brussac in France. Yet for all its rough-hewn grandeur, French Hills had an earthiness, a sturdiness that was typically old California. The colors were the colors of the hills and the earth and the scrub oaks; the wood was unpolished, gleaming with its own warm patina. The Perreiras' Victorian house was impressive, and Chateau Brussac had been a child's wonderland of crumbling grandeur, but this was a house in which a man, even a very rich man, could feel at home.

There were footsteps in the corridor. Philip turned and saw a man approaching him. His heart leapt up, but as the man came closer, he saw that it was Jean, not Adam, who was coming toward him, studying him with a puzzled expression.

'Felipe,' he said finally, the puzzlement vanishing. 'I didn't know you were in California.'

'I've only recently arrived,' Philip said, taking the hand that had been offered to him.

'You caused us a bit of confusion, adopting the family name like that,' Jean said, not exactly accusing, but not quite approving either.

'It adopted me,' Philip said simply.

They regarded one another for a moment, Jean apparently weighing the visitor and his intent. 'I'm surprised Harvey didn't let us know you were on the way up,' he said. 'He was working down by the gate.'

'I would guess that Harvey's on his way now. Unfortunately it will take him a while, since he's got to walk and hold up his trousers as well. By the way, if he's looking for them, his gun and his suspenders are on the porch.'

There was a gleam of amusement in Jean's eyes. 'Harvey trying to keep his pants up? That might be kind of nice to see for a change, come to think of it. What can we do for you?'

'I've come to see your brother. Is he here?'

'Adam? He hasn't been well lately, I don't know if you've heard that. Is there anything I can do for you? Are you looking for a job, or . . . ?' He left the possibilities open.

'I'd like to speak to him in person, if I may. If he's not well enough, I can wait a day or two. Or longer, if need be.'

Again Jean regarded him steadily for a moment. 'No,' he said finally. 'No, that won't be necessary. Come with me.'

Philip followed at a respectful distance, though he could have guessed the way himself; as he had suspected, Adam had taken over the room that had once been Claude Brussac's.

Though he had steeled himself for any eventuality, Philip's first sight of his father was a shock. The tall man with the forceful personality that he remembered from childhood had become an old man in a wheelchair, his legs wrapped in a shawl. Only the eyes, dark and baleful, were familiar; they glowered at him angrily from beneath gray-flecked brows.

'It's our Felipe, back from France,' Jean said in the way of an introduction. 'You remember my other son Caleb, and Maude, Adam's wife.'

Philip nodded to each of them in turn. Caleb was a shorter, stockier version of his brother. He stood near the mantel, eyeing

Philip with undisguised dislike while he picked at his fingernails with the tip of a Bowie knife. Maude sat in a straight-backed chair placed next to her husband. She was as prim and as tight-lipped as Philip remembered.

'What is it you wanted to see me about, Felipe?' Adam demanded, emphasizing the name. Philip saw that the left side of his face was stiff and unresponsive; he talked out of the other corner of his mouth.

'It's of a personal nature, sir. Perhaps your wife would excuse us?'

The thin line of Maude's lips tightened even more. She glanced at her husband, looking disappointed when he nodded. With a rustle of taffeta skirts, she rose and started for the door.

'My husband is just recovering from a stroke,' she said, pausing in front of Philip. 'The doctors have warned against any undue excitement.'

'I shall try not to cause any,' Philip said.

She gave him an angry look and swept by him, out of the room. Behind him, Philip heard the door close softly.

'Now then, Felipe . . . ' Adam began.

'It's Philip, sir.'

' . . . What is it that you want?' He ignored the interruption.

'Only what I'm entitled to.'

'And what is that, do you think?'

'I want to live at French Hills, at least for the present . . . '

'Why should you wish to do that?'

'It is my home, is it not?'

Adam's unblinking left eye seemed to see through him to the wall behind. 'Your mother lived here,' he said, 'if that's what you mean.'

'We only waste time with verbal fencing,' Philip said.

Adam gave a disdainful snort. 'It's a pity my legs aren't better, perhaps you'd prefer another form of fencing, eh?'

'I didn't come here to fight with you, sir.'

'Didn't you? You arrive with the news that you've appropriated our family name, a name both honorable and honored, I might say . . . '

'A name to which I am entitled, and that I've come to claim. That's the real reason I'm here.'

Adam's face seemed to turn purple and when he attempted to speak he could do no more than stammer. 'En-t-titled . . . ?'

'It is my father's name, is it not?'

'Adam,' Jean said, 'Remember the doctor's warning.'

For a moment more Adam's mouth worked noiselessly. Then, gulping for breath, he sat back forcefully in his chair. He breathed deeply several times, making an obvious effort to calm himself; when he spoke again, his voice was more even.

'You've no proof of what you claim,' he said.

'The proof is evident to anyone who would look at us, sir. Your sister has no doubts on the subject. She is willing to support my claim fully, if need be. And I believe if your father's will were made public, it would shed some light on this matter.'

The dark eyes glinted dangerously again. 'Felipe,' Adam began.

'No, father,' Philip replied firmly, 'not Felipe anymore. It's Philip now, Philip Brussac. Nor do I intend leaving here until you have acknowledged that fact.'

Adam's hands gripped the arms of his chair and with a great effort he hoisted himself to his feet, the shawl falling to the floor in a multicolored heap.

'You . . . you . . . ' He sputtered, shaking a fist threateningly, 'The bastard son of a Mexican slut . . . '

Philip's eyes flashed with the same black anger as his father's. 'Must I remind you, father, the Mexican slut was not only your mistress, she was my mother.'

'You . . . you dare to . . . ' Adam's voice failed him, though his lips continued to move. He took a faltering step toward Philip, his fist upraised as if he meant to strike him. Then, with a strangled cry, he pitched forward, crashing to the floor before Jean or the startled Philip could reach him.

'Adam,' Jean cried, dropping to his knees over the fallen form.

'Christ Almighty,' Caleb swore, stepping away from the mantel with the knife in his hand. 'You've killed him!'

16

Jean put his ear to his brother's chest, listening for a heartbeat, and with his thumb opened one of Adam's eyes. Standing, he gave Philip an angry glance as he went to the door and shouted for the servants.

'Is he . . . ?' Philip asked, unable to bring himself to say, 'dead'.

'He's alive,' Jean said. 'Caleb, you go for the doctor, I'll have him put to bed.'

For several minutes a sort of orderly bedlam reigned. Maude ran into the room, her eyes wide with fear. The servants came, and the prostrate form was carried gingerly to the high-standing bed.

Philip attempted to approach the bedside, but his father's wife turned on him in cold anger. 'Get out of here,' she hissed. 'Haven't you done enough damage for one day?'

Philip hesitated briefly, feeling that his place was at his father's side and yet not wanting to upset Adam's distraught wife any further.

'Do as she says,' Jean said. 'I'll let you know if anything happens.'

Reluctantly, Philip nodded. He left the room, retracing his steps along the empty corridor. As he was passing the drawing-room, someone stepped from the open door.

He recognized her at once as Adam's daughter Nadine. She had grown even prettier with the passing years. Her dark hair fell in sleek waves about her pale face, her steel gray eyes regarding him with a mocking expression.

'Welcome home, brother,' she greeted him.

'You heard, I take it,' Philip replied, surprised.

Nadine laughed, tossing her head. 'Of course, I listened at the door. I must say, you gave the old devil a time of it.'

'The old devil, as you call him, is my father. Yours too, in case you'd forgotten.'

She looked unconcerned by his coolness. 'Oh, don't bother being stuffy with me, I'm not going to have a stroke to please you – though I must admit, pleasing you might be enjoyable.'

She paused, looking him up and down. She had a shawl draped over her shoulders, which she now removed and threw over a chair-back. The modern cut of her dress emphasized her tiny waist and the voluptuous fullness of her breasts.

'Are we really brother and sister?' she asked, tilting her head coquettishly.

'I'm afraid so.'

'Pity,' she said.

He strode past her, angry and disgusted, not only with her, but with himself, for he was aware that her frank flirtation had not been without effect on him. Behind him her mocking laughter echoed through the corridors of the house.

Outside he stood for some minutes on the porch, breathing deeply after the close atmosphere within. Finally he went down the steps and began to stroll. He was halfway there before he realized he was headed toward his mother's grave.

Once there, however, he found no relief for the turmoil raging within him. He had scarcely been back an hour, and already he had botched everything. He had lost his temper at the very time when he had needed to be calm and persuasive. What had happened was his own fault. He ought not to have begun by antagonizing his father with the use of his name. That had started the interview off on a bad note, and from there everything had gone to hell fast.

What was to be done now? If his father died, the likelihood of his being accepted as a Brussac was virtually non-existent. Even if any of the family might have been willing to support his claim before, they would hardly do so now; they would blame him for Adam's death, and not without justification.

At length he made his way back in the direction of the workers' shacks. The one in which as a boy he had lived with his mother looked uninhabited. He tried the door and, finding it unlocked, went in.

It was little changed from what he remembered – cook stove, washstand, paint-chipped dresser. There was only one bed now, its middle sagging ominously, straw showing where the mattress ticking had torn. It was obvious the shack hadn't been occupied for some time; one of the windows was broken out and a thick layer of dust lay over everything.

On an impulse he decided to make the cabin his quarters. He would need some place to stay until affairs were resolved one way or another and, even if he were allowed to stay, he would be more comfortable here than at the big house.

He found a piece of canvas in a pile of refuse left in one corner and took it to the window, tacking it in place over the broken glass. While he was there, Jean came down the steps from the porch at the big house. He looked around, catching sight of Philip at the window, and came in that direction. He carried a bottle of wine in one hand.

Philip met him at the door. 'My father,' he asked while Jean was still crossing the yard, 'how is he?'

'Adam's had another stroke,' Jean said. 'He's paralyzed. He can neither move nor speak.'

'For how long?'

Jean shrugged. 'Maybe for a short while, maybe for the rest of his life. The doctors warned us there was a strong possibility of this.'

Philip turned back into the shack, Jean following him. 'This is my fault,' Philip said.

'Not entirely. The danger has existed for some time, since the first stroke – though I wouldn't say you were blameless, either.'

'I thank you for that.' Philip gave him a ragged half-smile. 'I suppose you've come to ask me to leave.'

'On the contrary, I want you to stay.'

Philip was surprised, and suspicious. 'Go on,' he said. 'You've got to have a good reason for that remark. Let's have the rest of it.'

'Are you familiar with this?' Jean handed him the bottle of wine that he had brought with him from the house. Philip took it, glancing at the familiar label.

'Of course – it's Brussac-America's red table wine. I've been a guest of the Perreiras since before Christmas. Your sister was instrumental in persuading me to return to California.'

'That's typical of Mary,' Jean said dryly. 'What do you think of their wines?'

Philip shrugged. 'Good drinking wines – *vin ordinaire* we'd call them in France.'

'Compared to ours?'

'There's no comparison. French Hills wines are as good as most French wines, a damned sight better than lots of them. As I said, Brussac-America is *vin ordinaire* – everyday stuff.'

'It's outselling ours two to one. It's light, sweeter, ready to drink right now . . . '

'It'll age poorly,' Philip interjected.

'It wasn't intended for aging. The point is, José and Mary are beating us at our own game. They're clobbering us in the marketplace.'

'Why are you telling me these things?' Philip asked.

'You feel that you're entitled to a share of French Hills. You ought to know that it's in danger of becoming worthless.' He tugged the cork free from the bottle and took a long swig of wine, handing the bottle across to Philip. Philip drank in turn, and handed it back.

'That's a pretty strong statement,' he said.

'We were operating cash short before my father died,' Jean said. 'Things haven't improved since then. There's never been enough money to replant that burned out acreage; we lost a lot of our best vines in a fire years back. Our equipment is outdated, falling apart. And we're undermanned.'

He paused, taking another pull at the bottle. 'I bow to no man in my knowledge of growing grapes,' he went on. 'But I'm not a businessman. Adam always took care of that end, and he was a better winemaker than I am, that's not modesty, just the plain truth. The trouble is, Adam hasn't been able to work for several months, and now, God knows when – or if – he'll ever be able to.'

He paused, looking Philip straight in the eye. 'I need help. I need someone who knows winemaking and grapes, and isn't afraid of working.'

'You have two sons,' Philip said.

Jean gave a dry bark of a laugh. 'You've met both of them. Harvey and Caleb didn't grow up, they just got bigger. Their knowledge of wines is limited to which end of the bottle to drink out of and, truth be known, they much prefer beer, or tequila. You've been making wines for Aunt Marie in France, haven't you?'

'You seem to know quite a bit,' Philip said.

'She wrote Adam some years ago – testing the water to see whether he'd let you come back. Unfortunately, Adam never answered the letter. Maybe he intended to and just didn't get around to it.'

'Or maybe he just didn't want me to come back,' Philip said, a note of bitterness creeping into his voice.

'You're here now.'

'And you want me to stay.' Philip regarded him steadily. 'Are you prepared to acknowledge me as Adam's son?'

Jean shifted his weight uncomfortably from one foot to the other. 'That's my brother's decision to make, not mine. But if you were still here when he recovered, if you'd already proven your worth, to him and to French Hills, that would make a difference, wouldn't it?'

'And in the meantime, I'm supposed to be somebody else, is that it?' Philip asked dryly.

'You've got a name, haven't you – besides Brussac. You grew up in this same shack, didn't you?' He glanced around the dust-covered room.

'What if my father never recovers?'

Jean was thoughtful for a moment. 'I'll tell you what, I'll have our lawyers draw up an agreement. You'll keep quiet about who you are . . . ' he held up a hand to ward off Philip's objection, ' . . . for a year. At the end of that time, if Adam's recovered, I'll do everything I can to persuade him to acknowledge you as his son. If he doesn't recover, I'll acknowledge you myself – and give you a share of French Hills.'

Philip was thoughtful for a moment. His instincts rebelled at the idea of pretending to be anyone other than who he was; he hadn't traveled all the way from France, after all, to continue to hide his identity.

On the other hand, Jean was offering him everything he wanted – acknowledgment of his name, his birthright – even an inheritance. It was only a year. After so many, surely another couldn't matter greatly . . .

He sighed and said aloud, 'My mother's name was Garcia. I'll be Philip Garcia – for a year.'

'I'll have the lawyers write up an agreement.'

'That won't be necessary,' Philip said. He held out his hand. For the second time that day, Jean shook it without hesitation.

17

'What a lovely Carmen,' Mary said, elbowing her way through the crowd in the foyer of the opera house. 'I do so love Spanish music.'

Jolene, who suspected that her mother's interest in opera had more to do with the fashionable crowd in attendance than with the music itself, said, 'It's French, mother.'

'What is?'

'The music. Mister Bizet was a Frenchman.'

The explanation was wasted. Mary was no longer following the conversation; instead, having found a safe place where they could stand without being too badly jostled or having their feet stepped on, she was avidly eyeing the crowd for noteworthy faces.

'Look, there's the Grahams, and the Dodges. And there's David Ecks, he's trying to get your eye – Hello, David, isn't it lovely – for Heaven's sake, Jolene, don't ignore the man, at least smile and nod.'

'I smiled at him earlier – he was watching our box during the first act.'

'Oh, really,' Mary's smile grew brighter at this piece of intelligence, but when she turned again toward David, he was engaged in conversation with a group of friends.

'Well, you've succeeded in discouraging his interest, if that was your intent,' she said to her daughter. 'I don't understand you, aren't you enjoying the opera? As I recall, it was your idea to come.'

'I'm enjoying it very much.' It was true, her mixed French and Latin blood had responded hotly to the music's peculiar blend of French and Spanish influences. She felt roused and stirred by the insistent rhythms and smoldering passions, her nerves tingling with a peculiar excitement. She had a sense of something momentous that was drawing rapidly nearer to her, though whether for good or for evil she could not say.

'Jolene, you are behaving peculiarly, I must say. I suppose you're still angry with me.'

'You did send him away,' Jolene said coolly. 'You did it deliberately, too, to separate us.'

'Nonsense, you know very well he was obsessed with his beginnings. It was something he had to do.'

'Eventually. But he would have waited. He'd have married me first, gotten himself settled. It would have retained its proper perspective for him, if you hadn't goaded him about it.'

'You don't know what you're talking about. Some day you'll understand and then you'll forgive me.'

A bell rang to signify that the intermission was ending and the next act of the opera was due to begin. The crowd had begun slowly to drift toward the doors leading inside.

'I will forgive you,' Jolene said, 'when Philip has returned to me, when we are wed. And if he does not return, God alone will have to forgive you.'

The words were spoken with such chilling intensity that for a moment Mary was frightened. She had done what she had done in the belief that Jolene was only going through a young girl's crush and that, with the object of her passion safely removed, she would soon enough get over it and turn her eye on other, more suitable beaux.

'Mesdames, the opera will be resuming soon. Will you permit me to escort you to your seats?'

'Richard Trémorel, how nice to see you again,' Mary exclaimed, grateful for the interruption. Glancing past him, she saw David Ecks moving in their direction, scowling as he did so at Richard's back. Presumably he too had meant to escort them inside.

'The music will be starting soon,' Richard said.

'Thank you, but please, go on without us, we'll be in soon,' Mary said.

Jolene too had seen David approaching and knew what her mother intended. In a moment of spite, she turned to Richard, giving him the benefit of her warmest smile.

'You may take me in if you like,' she said, taking the arm that Richard offered. 'I don't want to miss a moment of the opera.'

She flashed a smile at her mother, ignoring the frosty look she got in return. As she went down the aisle with Richard, she found it ironic that a few months before she had been resisting her mother's efforts to bring her and Richard together, and now she was in his company purposely to spite her mother. How confusing it all was. She sighed aloud.

'How sad you sound,' Richard said.

'I was only thinking how much simpler everything would be if one were allowed to live one's life without interference.'

They had reached her seat. Richard held her hand for a moment. 'You must be prepared to do what suits you,' he said, 'regardless of what others might think.'

'That is not always an easy thing for a woman to do,' she replied, 'to go her own way alone.'

'Yet, if she need not be alone . . . ?' He cocked one eyebrow.

The lights dimmed; the opera was about to resume. Richard bent low over her hand, brushing it lightly with his lips.

'Thank you for your kindness,' she said.

'My dear Jolene,' he murmured. 'I hope that someday you may permit me to be of real service to you.'

He left, to the crashing of brass in the orchestra.

18

At Jean's suggestion, Philip left to him the task of persuading the others to accept his presence at French Hills. What arguments Jean advanced on his behalf Philip had no way of knowing, but to his surprise he dined that evening with the family.

Adam, of course, remained in bed. Jean's wife had died two years before in a spill from her carriage. The rest of the family was there, if not exactly welcoming him with open arms. Adam's wife Maude was openly hostile. As for Harvey and Caleb, Philip had no illusions regarding their feelings toward him.

Only Naline seemed perversely pleased with the turn of events. She kept smiling down the table at Philip, and once when he glanced up to find her staring searchingly at him, she winked conspiratorially. His face flushed, Philip concentrated his attention on the roast on his plate.

Yet though he suffered their rudeness, the truth was that with the exceptions of his father and Jean, the opinions of the Brussacs mattered little to Philip. There was really only one other person at French Hills whose approval he cared for, and she was not at this table, although his father's blood ran in her veins the same as it did in his.

He had come here ostensibly to claim his heritage, but there was another motive in his coming, private and in many ways stronger.

As a son, he had been no great comfort to his hapless mother. Too young to protect her against a rapacious world, and too late in grasping the truth of his parentage, he had been little more than a helpless witness to her decline and death.

There was a way, however, in which he could yet make amends for his failure in filial obligations. On her deathbed, for almost the only time ever, she had imposed a duty upon him, extracted a promise. Without knowing who his sister was, without even being certain that a sister existed, he had sworn to protect and care for her, as he had not protected and cared for his mother.

Now he knew, and was certain. If the Brussacs had rejected him altogether, if Jean had not offered him a compromise useful to both of them, Philip would still have remained long enough to find his sister and care for her. Whatever else he succeeded or failed in, on that point he was firm; he would not fail this stranger who shared his blood.

He set out that same evening to look for her. He asked Jean after dinner about the old cook.

'Juanita? She died some years ago. The food hasn't been so good around here since, but don't say I said that, or Inez is liable to poison me.'

'Juanita had a daughter,' Philip said, attempting to sound casual.

'Elena, yes – a pretty girl.' There was an underlying tension in his voice that puzzled Philip.

'Whatever happened to her?'

'She's around. What on earth makes you interested in her?' Jean asked.

'It's a long story. I promised to look her up, that's all. Where would I go about finding her?'

'We let her keep Juanita's old shack – the one out by the kitchen. You can try there, but my guess is you'll find her at the cantina, couple of miles along the road.'

'She works there?'

Again, there was the peculiar tense quality to Jean's voice. 'Yes, sometimes,' he said simply, leaving it at that.

It was nearly dusk by the time the chores had been finished. Philip splashed water on his face and arms from the horses' trough and put on a fresh shirt before going in search of his sister.

He stopped first at Juanita's old shack, finding it locked and empty, as Jean had indicated. Mounting, he rode the two miles to the cantina.

It was not difficult to find, an adobe hut set back from the road. Lamplight and the sound of masculine voices spilled from the open doorway into the rapidly descending twilight. To the rear, a tarpaper shack stood among a grove of trees.

Someone was strumming a guitar. Philip paused in the doorway, taking in the crude tables and chairs crowded into the small place, the bar formed of two boards resting on chair backs. From a back room beyond a curtain came the smell of greasy food frying; it mingled with the sharp tang of peppers, the stale cigars and the scent of hot, unwashed bodies, giving Philip's stomach an uneasy turn.

He swallowed and stepped inside. The strumming stopped, and a number of people glanced in his direction. He guessed that strangers were not common here.

An enormous Mexican waited behind the bar, drying his hands on a filthy rag. Philip ordered a beer: it was warm and flat and only partly cleansed his mouth of its bad taste.

There were two women seated at a table in the rear, one of them plump and sullen looking, the other gaunt and wide-eyed. They wore numerous cheap bracelets and enormous dangling ear-rings, and both had cheeks the color of roses, though they were plainly both past the season for such blossoms.

Neither of them, he was certain, was Elena. He asked the bartender for her.

'Elena?' The bartender looked around as if seeing the tawdry room for the first time.

'I was told she was here,' Philip said.

'Elena's out back,' the plump woman called, following her remark with a fit of giggling, joined in by her companion.

Philip started out. 'She may not want company,' the bartender said.

'It's okay,' Philip replied. 'I'm an old friend of hers.'

The windows of the shack were covered on the inside by thick curtains, but light showed around them. Philip made his way through the darkness to the door, stepping in filth and ordure along the way. He knocked, hesitantly at first and then more loudly. There was no reply, though he had heard a murmur of voices from within as he approached; now, everything was silent save for the strumming that had begun once again in the cantina, and a fresh spate of laughter from the two women there.

Philip knocked again, this time calling her name. After a moment's silence, a woman's voice from the other side of the door asked, 'Who's there?'

'It's Philip – Felipe, from French Hills.'

'Felipe . . . ?' Another pause, then the sound of a latch scraping on wood as it was lifted. The door opened a crack, giving him a glimpse of a dark-skinned woman clutching a wrapper about herself. She studied him through the narrow opening.

'So, it is you,' she said finally without enthusiasm. 'Welcome back.'

'Can I come in?' When she did not reply, he added, 'I'd like to talk to you.'

'I'm not feeling well,' she said.

'It needn't take long.'

'Elena, let him in,' a man's voice said from within the room. She flushed, but the door remained as it was.

'I'm sorry, I didn't know,' Philip said. He would have moved away from the door then, but before he could do so the door was yanked out of her grasp and swung open. To his surprise, Philip found himself once again facing his cousin Harvey.

'Well, don't stand out there gawking, come on in,' Harvey said, looking amused by the confrontation. He was in the act of donning his shirt, tucking the tails carelessly inside his trousers.

'If you're busy, I can come another time,' Philip said, still addressing Elena, though his hand instinctively went to his gun.

'I've already finished my business,' Harvey said. ' 'Course if I'd known she was all booked up tonight I'd've been glad to wait till tomorrow. Company first, and all that.'

Philip looked around the one-room shack with a feeling of dismay. It's chief furnishings were a rumpled bed and an unconcealed chamber pot. A rickety table pushed against one wall was filled to overflowing with dirty glasses and empty bottles, and the floor was strewn with litter.

Elena herself was scarcely more presentable. The wrapper, clearly all she wore, was filthy and tattered and the hand with which she held it closed over her breasts was grimy with dirt. Her long black hair was uncombed and lay in unsightly tangles about her face and shoulders.

It was almost a shock to discover that she was pretty, despite the filth and lack of grooming. Her eyes, wary and unwelcoming, were large and luminous, still the eyes of a child, looking out from a woman's body.

The squalor and seediness of the scene were like a physical blow to Philip. This was the girl whom he had vowed to protect and care for, this was what had become of her. In any other circumstances he would have turned his back on this creature in disgust. The urge to do so even now was strong within him.

'What do you want?' she asked, avoiding his gaze.

He swallowed his revulsion. Whatever she was, whatever the intervening years had done to her, she was still his sister – and his vow remained unchanged.

'I want to talk to you,' he said.

Harvey laughed coarsely. 'That's a switch,' he said. He had finished dressing and now took some coins from his pocket and made an elaborate show of tossing them onto the table.

'Caleb says he'll be by tomorrow,' he said. He started for the door, grinning in Philip's direction. 'Nothing like keeping it in the family, I always say . . .'

'Get out,' Philip said through clenched teeth.

Harvey made a show of laughing nonchalantly, but he did not linger. Not until the flimsy door had closed after him did Philip move his hand away from the gun at his waist.

Elena had looked embarrassed by the confrontation but now

she assumed a defiant air. 'Well, since you are here,' she said, swaying her hips exaggeratedly as she strolled to the table, 'would you like a drink? There's some tequila left.'

She did not wait for a reply but took two glasses from among the debris, dumping their contents onto the already filthy floor. She found a bottle with something left in it and poured two drinks, downing one of them immediately, and offering Philip the other.

'No, thank you,' he said. 'I prefer wine.'

She gave a harsh, ugly laugh, and emptied the other glass as well. 'The famous Brussac wine. Yes, I know that wine well, it is bitter, Señor, bitter.'

'It hasn't prevented you from keeping company with the slimiest of men . . . '

'What is it to you, Señor, who I keep company with?' she demanded angrily, her eyes flashing. 'What do you know about what goes on here, about the way it has been?'

'I know what I see, the way it is now.' He made a sweeping gesture that took in the room and its contents. 'You, him, this stinking toilet . . . '

She smiled bitterly and looked about at the filth and refuse. 'You do not like my little room?'

'You have a place, at French Hills,' he said.

Her smile vanished. 'Perhaps I like it better here.' she said. 'It is farther from the smell of grapes, and wine – farther from another stench, too.'

She poured yet another glass of tequila, spilling it over the sides of the glass.

'You don't need another drink,' Philip said.

'What I drink, Señor, is nobody's business but my own,' she snapped.

'You're wrong,' he said calmly, 'it's my business too.'

He crossed the room in two quick strides and snatched the bottle out of her hand, flinging it against the wall. It shattered, the yellowish liquor running downward in swift rivulets.

'And the name is Philip now,' he said, taking the glass from her hand and emptying its contents on the floor. He set the empty glass on the table with a bang, making the dirty glassware rattle.

For a long moment they stared wordlessly at one another, her face a confusion of emotions. Someone banged at the door and a man's voice asked, 'You all right in there?'

'Yes, yes, I'm all right,' Elena replied.

The door opened and the bartender from the cantina stepped into the room. His suspicious gaze took in the room and Philip, pausing at the broken tequila bottle and the stains on the wall, then returning to Philip.

'It slipped from my hand,' Elena said. 'The Señor will pay for the bottle.'

'He'd better,' the man said, scowling ferociously.

'Why have you come here?' Elena asked when they were alone again.

'I promised someone a long time ago that I would protect and care for you.'

She turned away from him, the defiance vanishing from her stance. 'Who did you promise?' she asked. 'My mother?'

He hesitated briefly. 'Yes,' he said at length.

Her shoulders had begun to tremble slightly. She put out a hand automatically toward the table where the tequila bottle had stood. Remembering, she snatched her hand back, hugging herself and swaying from side to side.

'My poor Mamacita,' she said, her voice cracking with emotion. 'She never knew.'

'Elena . . . ' He struggled for the right words, 'How did you . . . all this . . . ?'

She remained with her back to him, speaking in little more than a whisper. 'I could not help it. They came to me, they forced themselves on me . . . '

'Harvey and his brother?' There was a bitter taste in his mouth. Some day he would have to settle his scores with the two Brussac brothers; and the score was steadily mounting.

She nodded. 'At first I tried to fight them, but it was no use. They came together. They beat me unmercifully. After a while – I was so bruised and sore – I stopped fighting them. After that, it was not so painful, at least not for my body.'

'How did you come to be here?' he asked, hating himself for having to know.

'He brought me, Harvey. He wanted to show me off. They made me do things – all kinds of things. They gave me money. And tequila. I was grateful for the tequila.'

He was sorry now for having broken the bottle. He could not know how much pain it eased for her.

He looked around, saw a dress hanging on a nail on the wall. He went to it, taking it down, and tossed it to her. 'Put this on,' he said. He rummaged through a pile of dirty rags on the floor, searching for some shoes.

'What are you doing?' she asked.

'Taking you home – to French Hills.' He found one shoe and kicked it across the floor toward her.

'They will be there,' she said.

He paused, looking up and meeting her eyes, hopeful, frightened, grateful.

'So will I,' he said.

She rode back with him on his horse, her head lying against his chest. She was asleep before they had ridden a mile, looking, as she slept, incredibly young and fragile.

At the shack which was her home at French Hills, he dismounted first and, lifting her gently down, carried her inside. There was no light burning but the moonlight through the opened door showed him the way clearly enough. There was squalor here too, but nothing as bad as the room at the cantina. At least the bed was made up. It looked as if it had not been slept in for days.

He lay her on it, feeling a sudden tension in her body as he did so. 'Don't worry,' he said, giving her hair a reassuring pat, 'I didn't come here for that.' He found a blanket and pulled it up over her, tucking it under her chin. Her large eyes regarded him wonderingly.

'What do you want?' she asked.

He glanced around. 'I want you to get up tomorrow and clean up this place. Yourself too. I want to come back here tomorrow night and find that pretty girl that I remember from the past.'

She managed a wan smile. 'I will try,' she said.

He was going out the door when she thought of something and, calling his name, jumped out of bed. She found a bottle of liquor on the washtable and brought it to him at the door.

'You'd better take this with you,' she said.

He took it; it was half empty. 'You sure?' he asked.

She gave her head a determined toss. The moonlight had erased the ugly shadows beneath her eyes and the grime staining her face; when she smiled, she might indeed have been the innocent, happy girl he remembered. 'I'm sure,' she said.

He did not go directly to his own shack, but instead crossed the wide yard to the main house, letting himself in through the kitchen. The house was dark and still; the only light was the one showing from beneath the door of the room Harvey and

Caleb shared. Philip did not bother to knock. As he went in, he drew the gun from his belt.

Caleb was already in bed. Harvey was sitting on the edge of his in his long johns, examining a callus on his big toe. He jumped to his feet at Philip came in. Caleb, his eyes wide with fright, scrambled to a sitting position, tugging his quilt up to his chin like a frightened virgin.

'What the hell are you doing, busting in here?' Harvey demanded, sounding as much frightened as angry.

'Leave her alone,' Philip said, coldly and evenly. He leveled the gun first at one, then the other. His expression left no doubt that he would welcome an excuse to pull the trigger.

'Both of you,' he emphasized. 'Leave her alone.'

He did not wait for a reply. Not until he was in the darkened hallway and the door was closed after him did he put his gun away.

He waited for a moment outside the room. From within there was a murmur of whispered voices, followed by the sound of a heavy dresser being pushed against the door.

19

'Must you go?'

'I'm afraid I must.' Philip did not see Elena's anxious expression until he had finished strapping the bags atop the carriage. When he did, his preoccupied expression vanished to be replaced by one of tender concern. He came to where she was standing and took her hands in his.

'Jean thinks it's important,' he said, speaking gently, as he always did to her. 'For that matter, so do I. French Hills simply doesn't grow enough grapes of its own, we've got to buy from other growers, and with fewer grapes being grown in the Los Angeles area, our sources of supply have become undependable.'

'If you just knew how long you'd be gone,' she said.

'I'll be going from vineyard to vineyard, looking for the right grapes, and the right grower. If I'm lucky it'll take a few days. If not, maybe a month. It's just impossible to say.'

He did not add that, for him, the most important thing was

that Jean was willing to trust him with this responsibility.

Jean came out of the house then. 'All set?' he asked Philip. Jorge, who would be the driver, was making a final check of the gear.

'Ready to go,' Philip said. He gave Elena an encouraging smile, pretending that he did not see the anxiety behind the one she gave him in return. He understood the reasons for it well enough. This would be the first time since his arrival a month before that he had been away from her for more than a day.

His relationship with the Brussacs had not changed much in that time, except that Jean increasingly trusted him with responsibility for French Hills wines. Adam remained paralyzed from his stroke, unable to move from his bed or to communicate with his family. The others were resentful and cool toward him.

It was with Elena that he felt he had accomplished the most. In the past few weeks a remarkable change had been wrought; even Jean had been prompted to remark upon it.

'That's the first in a long time I've seen that girl sobered up,' he had said just a few days before.

Nor was it only a matter of sobering up. With sobriety, Elena had regained a sense of pride. She no longer went around filthy or in ragged clothes, and she had not been to the cantina since the night Philip had found her there. With her fresh-scrubbed face and her hair neatly tied back, often with a flower pinned in it, she had an innocent, even virginal look. Too much liquor and too little food had made her thin, but in the last month, with rest and a proper diet, she had begun to fill out. She was, as Philip had requested, the pretty girl he remembered from the past.

'Take care of yourself,' he said, giving her cheek a kiss. He was uncomfortably aware that as he had bent toward her her lips had parted, anticipating a real kiss. He knew that she was disappointed, just as he knew that she had grown quite fond of him in the passing weeks. Of course he was fond of her too, but it was impossible to explain their real relationship to her without breaking his vow to Jean. In the meantime, he was careful to express his affection for her, without allowing it to go beyond that. It was difficult for her, he realized, but the evidence of his good judgment was in her greatly changed behavior.

The driver was in his seat. With a final grin and a tip of his hat, Philip climbed in and the carriage began to move.

Elena stood watching until it had disappeared down the drive. Her smile had vanished with the carriage. Jean, having taken leave of Philip, strolled in the direction of the wine shed.

Left alone, Elena wandered listlessly among the olive trees that had been planted as a break for the Santa Ana winds that sometimes swept out of the mountains to the east.

Philip could never know what an ordeal the past few weeks had been for her. She had gone to great lengths to present him with a calm and confident façade, concealing from him the physical and mental anguish she suffered.

Liquor had taken its toll on her. There had been times when she had actually ached for a drink of tequila. She had lain for hours at night frozen with tension, unable to sleep, her mouth dry and thirsting.

If only she understood Philip better. She loved him, had loved him, she was sure, from that moment when she had opened the door of that shack and found him standing there. How fresh and clean he had looked, after the sordid experiences of her past. And how strong, how sure of himself.

She had taken her strength from him. Lacking confidence of her own, she had let herself be buoyed up by his confidence in her; that and the desire for his approval.

But it was more than his approval she wanted. Did he love her? Certainly at times she thought so, read in his eyes an unmistakable affection.

Yet when she would turn to that love, when she would gladly open her arms to it, he invariably turned away from her, drew back, as he had drawn back from kissing her properly just now. Then she saw something else in his eyes, something like a fleeting revulsion at the prospect of intimacy with her.

She had tried to convince herself that she only imagined it, but time and again it returned to trouble her. It taunted her dreams and longings, undermined her faltering self-respect. Did he find her repugnant because of the past she had lived, because of who and what she was? God knew, he had reason enough; she was sickened herself to recall some of what she had experienced.

Oh, Philip, she cried silently, you must love me, you must, I haven't the strength to survive this without your love!

The snapping of a twig behind her made her jump. She whirled about to find Harvey and Caleb standing just a few feet away, watching her.

'What do you want?' she demanded, angry at her own

frightened reaction; she was actually trembling. 'Why are you spying on me?'

'Why, we were doing no such thing,' Harvey said, grinning and stepping closer. 'were we, Caleb?'

'Not me, that's for sure,' Caleb agreed.

'Get away from me,' Elena said. She took a step backward and bumped into a tree.

'My, you sure are jumpy this morning,' Harvey said. 'Looks like your nerves are shot.'

'My nerves are none of your business,' she said. She pressed her palms against the rough bark of the tree. If only they would not look at her as they were doing. She remembered all the times . . . She shook her head, trying to clear it of the succession of ugly images that had swarmed into her consciousness.

'I'll bet I know what it is,' Harvey went on in that maddeningly insinuating voice that she hated so much; he had come to stand directly in front of her now. She avoided his eyes, looking down at his scuffed boots instead, praying that he would not attempt to touch her. Her nerves were taut with anxiety; she thought if he put a hand on her she would surely scream.

'I'll bet that greaser friend of yours don't know nothing about taking care of a woman,' Harvey said, dropping his voice to an oily whisper, 'so's her nerves don't bother her so much. Maybe he don't know too much about women. Maybe he don't even like women.'

'Shut up,' she snapped.

He grinned, showing the spaces between his teeth. 'That's what's bothering you, ain't it? Pretty boy's never laid a hand on you, has he? I saw him the way he kissed you when he was leaving, like a man kisses his sister, not the way he kisses a woman. Why, I'll bet he don't even know how to . . . '

Her hand flashed upward, slapping him resoundingly. She was nearly as surprised by the movement as he was. She fell back against the tree, frightened by the swift surge of anger in Harvey's face. Behind him, Caleb had finally lost his stupid grin.

'You little . . . ' Harvey seized her wrist in a vicious grip, twisting it until she cried aloud in pain and fright.

'Harvey!' It was Jean's voice, from the edge of the vineyards.

For a moment Harvey glowered down at her with unconcealed hatred. Then, with a muttered oath, he flung her hand aside and turned his back on her, striding quickly away through the trees.

Elena rubbed her wrist and watched him go. She was not deceived by the quickness with which he had let her go at his father's command. Harvey was not the sort to tolerate a woman's slap without revenge. He liked to think of himself as master of all he surveyed, and no woman would ever be permitted to resist him.

If only Philip hadn't had to go away now, so soon. She just wasn't ready yet to stand on her own two feet. He ought to have realized that; it was he, after all, who wanted her sober, chaste – that pretty, innocent girl he remembered from the past. But he had left her with men who wanted something different from her. She was willing, eager to be what Philip wanted, if only he would provide her with the strength; was that too much to ask?

The day stretched long before her. Philip had arranged for her to help with the kitchen work; having something constructive to do would help with restoring her self-respect. More to the point, so far as she was concerned, it helped to pass the time. Drunkenness had accounted for a great many of her hours in the past; sobriety could be long and slow.

She avoided Harvey and his brother throughout the day, though once or twice she saw Harvey glowering at her from a distance. His attention only added to her uneasiness, and when she returned to her own shack that night she made a point of being careful to latch the door. How she wished she could have a drink, just this once, to calm her nerves.

She filled the basin with tepid water from the pitcher and, stripping off her clothes, bathed quickly. Far from soothing her as she had hoped, the bath left her skin tingling. The room felt close and confining. She thought of the cantina along the road, its welcoming babble of voices, the musical cadences of her mother tongue; a cold bottle of beer, with perhaps a tequila to chase it down.

She lifted a nightdress over her head, shrugged it down over her body. Standing before the cracked mirror, she unpinned her hair, shaking it free. Her gaze flitted like a moth over her image, lingering nowhere for more than a second or so. Still the sleek blackness of her hair, the coppery sheen of her skin mocked her, as they had mocked her through all her years of envying the white-skinned Brussac woman and their friends.

She both hated and loved the Mexican-American heritage that had come down to her through her mother and her unknown father – loved the passionate feel for music that actually seemed to flow in the veins of her people, the sensual, elegant grace so natural it needed no rehearsing, the low, husky laughter that came so spontaneously, even in times of trial.

What she hated most was her non-whiteness – the 'greaser' and the 'spic' labels that came so easily to the lips of others, the sense of inferiority, of unworthiness that crowded in upon her when she had to be among pale-skinned people.

She was not especially intelligent, but she was bright enough to understand that it was herself that she hated. At least, she had hated herself until Philip had returned.

Now . . . but now was too confusing. If only Philip would love her, perhaps she could love herself.

With a sudden angry gesture she snatched up a shawl and, blowing out the lantern, she went to the door and stepped out into the cool night air. The yard lay awash in moonlight. Somewhere in the distance a coyote mouthed his ageless lament.

But Philip didn't love her, she saw it in his eyes whenever he came near to her. For the entire first week she had waited every night for him to come to her bed. He hadn't, and finally she had begun to see that something within him shrank from her whenever he came physically close.

Philip shouldn't have gone, not now. It was like a litany inside her head. Philip shouldn't have . . . shouldn't have gone . . . shouldn't have . . .

Someone stepped from the porch of the big house and started across the yard in her direction. When he stepped into the moonlight, she saw that it was Harvey.

She stood as if mesmerized, watching him approach, until he was close enough that she could see his toothy grin – or did she only fancy that he was grinning?

She stepped back inside, closing the door and lowering the latch into place. Outside she heard booted feet on the boards of the porch. There was a brief silence. He tried the door, finding it latched, and rapped lightly.

'Elena?' His voice had the thickness of liquor. Elena leaned weakly against the rough wood of the door, her eyes brimming with tears.

She had known, from the moment Philip told her he was going, that this scene was inevitable. She had been a fool to think for a second that her tormentors would let her off so easily.

The knocking was louder, more insistent.

Philip was worse than a fool to have left her like this. Wasn't he man enough to hold on to what was his?

Or wasn't she his? Hadn't she seen herself the revulsion in his eyes when they had shared even the briefest intimacy. He didn't want her, not as a man wants a woman. She was deluding herself. He thought she was not good enough for him, she was soiled from the men who had known her before.

The knocking had ceased. From that first tentative use of her name, Harvey had not spoken. She heard, or thought she heard, the harsh rasp of his breath on the opposite side of the door – only inches from her cheek, pressed against the wood.

The door suddenly shook and bowed from the impact of a booted foot. Frightened from her stupor, she backed into the room; she remembered finally the gun Philip had given her a week or more ago – 'Just in case,' he had said.

She tugged it from the drawer in which she had hidden it, more frightened at the time of the gun than she was of any threat from Harvey. It was incredibly heavy. She had to hold it in both hands to be able to raise it level.

The gun shaking to and fro, she faced the door, watching as the flimsy latch bent and finally surrendered to the determined kicking from without. The door crashed open, flooding the room with moonlight. Harvey swayed on the threshold, then strolled boldly in as if he were only making a neighborly call.

He paused when he saw the gun. 'What the hell are you doing with that thing?' he demanded, setting a bottle of tequila on the table. 'Put it away, before you hurt yourself.'

'G-get out,' she stammered. She tried to aim the gun at his midsection, found that she was aiming at his feet instead. Her wrists ached from the weight.

For an answer, he laughed and walked toward her. She tried to lift the gun and could not. Her frightened eyes met his, were held by them.

He snatched the gun from her hand, flinging it aside. His fist came up, smashing into her jaw, sending her reeling backward. She felt the warm taste of blood in her mouth.

Harvey followed her, grabbing the fabric of her gown in one hand, slapping her back and forth with the other. The gown tore in his grasp. He snatched it from her, ripping and tugging, jerking her this way and that like a helpless puppet, until she was naked and the blows he was raining on her fell on her body as well as her face. She staggered and half fell across the bed. A booted foot sent her sprawling across it, bleeding and gasping. In an instant, like a savage beast, he had fallen across her.

She lay pressed against the wall, whimpering like a child. How long he had been here she could not even guess, it seemed an eternity. Time and again he had mounted her, pummeling her with his body as he had earlier pummeled her with his fists, pausing briefly to rest or draw from the bottle of tequila he had brought with him.

Once, when she had refused the drink he offered her, he had prized her mouth open with his fingers and filled it with the fiery liquid. She had choked and gagged, but afterward she had been grateful for the relief it had given her.

He was done finally, belching loudly as he hitched up his pants. 'Here's a present for you,' he said, setting the half-empty tequila bottle down on the table with a bang. He started for the door.

'Oh, yeah, almost forgot,' he said. He drew a handful of coins from his pocket and tossed them onto the table as well. One of them fell to the floor, rolling across to where she lay and under the bed.

She waited until long after his steps had disappeared from the porch. Finally she could cry no more. She got up, staggering to the basin and splashing water on her face and breasts, turning the water a muddy red-brown.

He had left the door open. She stumbled across the room, closing it. As she turned back to the bed, she saw the bottle he had left behind.

She didn't wait to fill a glass, drinking instead straight from the bottle, tilting her head back and letting the tequila wash the bitterness from her mouth.

The litany continued: Philip shouldn't have gone . . .

20

Philip knew, almost from the first disappointment of seeing that she was not there to meet him when he drove up the lane.

He had intended seeing Jean first, to give him a brief report on his trip; instead, he went straight from the carriage to Elena's shack.

It was difficult to believe the filth that had accumulated in just over a week. The cottage looked even worse than when he had first arrived, with litter and dirty clothes scattered everywhere and a forgotten dish of stew molding on the table. Elena was not there.

There was a footstep on the porch and Philip turned to find Jean in the doorway, looking embarrassed and apologetic.

'Do you know where she is?' Philip asked.

'I haven't seen her myself. Caleb says she's been hanging around the cantina again,' Jean replied. 'Philip, I . . . '

'Save it,' Philip said, brushing past him. In minutes he had saddled a horse and was riding toward the cantina.

He found her there, as predicted. He did not bother with the cantina itself but went straight to the flimsy hut in the rear, letting himself in without knocking.

She was seated on the edge of the bed wearing a torn and dirty wrapper. A nearly empty bottle stood on the floor beside her, within easy reach of her hand.

She looked both surprised and frightened by his sudden appearance. She did not move at first, but sat staring wide-eyed at him from the bed.

Philip took in her disheveled appearance and the squalor of the room, his stomach giving a warning turn. He caught sight of a large purplish mark on her arm and, crossing the room in three long strides, he seized her wrist and lifted her arm for a closer look.

The bruise spread from the wrist halfway up her forearm. He dropped her wrist and, taking her chin between his fingers, turned her head this way and that, seeing the ugly bruises that still had not faded. A bad cut on her lower lip had bled again recently, leaving a black line over the tender flesh.

'Harvey?' he asked.

'Yes,' she said, her voice so little and frightened that it was almost inaudible.

'And Caleb?'

'Yes.'

He made a sound that might have been an animal growl. 'Get dressed,' he said, turning from her. 'Walk home. Wait for me there.'

He did not wait for her reply but went out again into the night. She did not move at first but sat staring after him until she heard the clatter of horse's hooves disappearing swiftly in the direction of the ranch. She got up then and began to dress, pausing from time to time for a drink from the bottle.

The vines, which had looked like gnarled, arthritic hands thrusting up from the ground, had begun to show a patchy fringe of green. With the coming of early spring the plants were about to enter upon a period of rapid growth. For the vintners it meant a period of hard work. Vines must be trimmed and tied as they grew, and if a late frost threatened, fires must be lit and tended throughout the vineyard in an often futile attempt to protect the infant plants from danger.

Philip found the two brothers in the farthest section of the vineyard, where some new vines had been planted during the winter.

They saw him approaching at a distance and were standing waiting for him when Philip rode up. He dismounted and came to stand a few feet in front of them.

'Well, how about that, Caleb,' Harvey said with a show of braggadocio, 'looks like the greaser's back.'

Caleb looked less confident than his brother, but he managed a watery smile. 'Looks that way, doesn't it,' he agreed.

'What can we do for you, greaser?' Harvey asked.

'I've come to take care of you boys,' Philip said. Neither of the Brussacs was armed. Philip slowly unbuckled his own gun belt and let it fall to the ground, noting Harvey's quick smile of relief as he did so.

Harvey was holding a shovel with which he had been digging up the soil around the vines. He tossed it aside and took a couple of steps toward Philip. Caleb advanced too, though lagging behind his brother.

'I told you to leave that girl alone,' Philip said, fisting his hands.

'I take what I want,' Harvey said, 'and I don't take orders from you.'

'You'll learn,' Philip replied.

He moved in, fists raised defensively. The brothers lifted their own fists, moving apart, so that Philip was forced to divide his attention between the two of them. Harvey began to circle him; following him, Philip turned his back on Caleb.

Caleb made a feint at him. Philip whirled, prepared to brush off the attack; then, seeing it was false, he swung back toward Harvey.

Harvey was faster, dashing in, bringing not his fists but a foot into play. He kicked Philip hard in the groin. Philip reeled off balance from the pain, falling to his knees on the ground. As he scrambled to get his footing, Harvey laced his fingers together to bring them chopping down upon his neck. Philip dived for his legs. Caught off guard by the unexpected attack, Harvey came down as well.

For a moment they grappled together until Caleb, seeing an opportunity for a relatively safe blow, joined the melee briefly, delivering Philip a box on the ears.

Jumping free of Harvey's flailing arms and legs, Philip made a dive toward Caleb. Yelping like a frightened dog, Caleb jumped back out of reach.

Philip let him go, judging that it was Harvey who was the greater threat, and Harvey was once again scrambling to his feet.

They closed together, exchanging blows. Harvey was clumsy but strong as an ox. He delivered another kick to Philip's groin, making him gasp with pain, but this time he remained on his feet. From the corner of his eye, Philip saw Caleb circling around them warily. In an instant Philip saw what Caleb was after – the discarded shovel lying a few feet away on the ground.

Harvey jumped to the side, again forcing Philip to turn his back on Caleb. Painfully aware of the danger behind him, Philip tried to manoeuver so that Caleb was in his line of view as well, but the brothers kept him circling about. Forced to trade blows with Harvey, Philip was defenseless against Caleb's expected assault.

Philip heard a rush of footsteps behind him. Unable to judge the direction of the blow, Philip dropped to his knees. The shovel whistled through the air above him, where his skull had been a second or so before; it struck Harvey instead, crashing into his face with a bone-snapping thud.

Harvey, his face splattered with blood, staggered backwards and toppled unconscious over one of the budding vines.

'Oh, Jesus,' Caleb sobbed, realizing his mistake too late.

In an instant Philip was on his feet again. Caleb, the blood draining from his face, made a futile effort to swing the shovel again, but Philip easily deflected the blow with his arm and, snatching the shovel from Caleb's trembling fingers, threw it aside.

'Don't hit me,' Caleb wailed, backing away from Philip with his hands raised imploringly.

'Stand up and fight,' Philip said, 'or I'll tear you limb from limb.'

He rushed in. Caleb made a half-hearted attempt to defend

himself but it was all too plain his heart was not in the fight. Philip delivered a crashing blow to his belly and another to his chin. Caleb groaned and dropped unconscious to the ground.

Breathing heavily, Philip wiped a streak of blood from his chin and, retrieving his belt and gun from the ground, remounted his horse and rode back to the house.

He found Jean in his office. 'I just whipped your sons,' Philip greeted him, swaying unsteadily in the doorway.

'Both of them?' Jean asked, without getting up from his desk.

'Both of them.'

'They look any better than you do?'

'A bit worse, I should think,' Philip said. He went to the bottle standing on a nearby table and helped himself to a drink of whisky.

Jean sighed and said, 'I don't doubt my sons had a good whipping coming to them, I've thought about it myself a time or two. But I'm not sure the girl's worth it, Philip . . . '

Philip banged his fist on the table angrily. 'The girl belongs to me,' he said. 'I want no one to forget that – not them and not you. Is that understood?'

The two men glowered at one another across the desk. 'Yes,' Jean said after a long silence, 'I understand.'

When he had gone out, Jean remembered that they hadn't yet discussed Philip's trip or the grapes he had been looking to buy. Jean sighed again and rose to stand by the window.

In some ways Philip was all too obviously a Brussac, he thought.

21

Elena was waiting at her cottage. She had made a hasty attempt to put the room and herself in order, with only partial success.

'You're hurt,' she cried when he came in. She ran to him, solicitously trying to examine the bruise on his jaw.

Philip brushed her away. 'It's nothing,' he said. 'I just need to clean up a bit, and rest.'

He had ridden most of the night in his haste to be home, some sixth sense warning him that things had gone badly in his absence. His body still ached from the fight with the Brussacs. There was nothing he wanted so much as to rest and sort out some of his troubled thoughts.

Despite his insistence that nothing was wrong with him, Elena insisted on stripping off his shirt and examining a large cut he had gotten in the scuffle. She brought fresh water and bathed the wound, clucking and scolding him for taking chances by fighting both the brothers at once.

Philip, dazed with exhaustion, sat lost in his own thoughts as she ministered to him. He was sorely regretting his vow to Jean to tell no one of his true identity. If he could talk freely with Elena on this subject, he would not have to worry about the obvious fact that Elena was falling in love with him; he was afraid that discouraging that love might destroy the tenuous relationship between them.

'Why do we stay here?' she asked, gingerly bathing his wound. 'The Brussacs are nothing to us. You can find work elsewhere. I can work too.'

'Elena, what if – ' he hesitated; 'what if I told you that I was a Brussac too?'

'But that is nonsense, if you were a Brussac, you would be a fool to live as you do, and not as they live.'

'But suppose it were true, suppose for some reason I'd kept it secret. Would you keep it secret too?'

'No,' she said emphatically. 'No, I would tell them, and I would spit in their faces – Caleb and Harvey and their father – yes and the old man too.'

He was silent for a moment. 'What if I said you were a Brussac too?' he asked.

'Why do you ask such silly questions?' she asked.

'Just wondering.'

She finished bathing his wound and came around to face him directly; she grinned, without any humor. 'Then I would kill them,' she said. 'One at a time, while they slept.'

She went out to empty the dirty water and bring fresh. Philip was seated on the edge of the bed. Intending to do no more than rest for a minute, Philip swung his long legs up onto the bed and lay his head gratefully on the pillow.

By the time she returned a few minutes later, he was already sound asleep.

For a few minutes Elena sat watching him with unbridled adoration, having already forgotten his silly questions regarding their relationships to the Brussacs.

Philip had fought for her. Despite all her doubts and misgivings, surely that proved that he loved her. And he had come back – later, when things were better between them, she would confess to him that she had even doubted that he would return, and they would have a laugh together. But here he was, in her bed even.

She struggled with his boots and trousers, got them off with no more than a muffled grunt from the sleeping man. She folded them neatly, laid them with his shirt on a chair. Then, quickly shedding her own clothes, she slipped into bed beside him. He had turned on his side. She pressed herself against him, fitting herself spoon fashion to the curves and bends of his body, her thighs pressed against the hardness of his buttocks, her breasts flattened against his back, legs entwined with his.

Clinging tightly to him, as if afraid of falling away from him, she too fell asleep.

Philip was dreaming of Jolene. How he had longed for her, the feel of her in his arms, the taste of her lips on his.

And now she was here, her flesh against his, seeming to sear him with its heat. In his sleep he turned to her, gathering her in his arms. She came gladly, eagerly, crushing herself to him, clinging hotly.

He rolled over upon her. Her thighs parted, welcoming him, her body arched upward to meet his urgent thrust.

It came to him suddenly, jolting him out of the half-sleeping state in which he had begun to make love to her: this was not Jolene, but Elena beneath him, her arms tightly encircling his neck, her body coupled with his.

'Oh, God,' he groaned aloud, desire leaving him in a rush.

He scrambled out of the bed. Night had fallen while he was asleep and at first he could not find his trousers. He felt about in the darkness, discovered his trousers on a chair, and got into them quickly. He struck a match and lit the lantern on the table.

'Philip, wait . . . ' Elena had gotten out of bed when he did. She came to him, putting a hand on his arm.

Philip shook the hand off. 'Elena, for God's sake, cover yourself,' he snapped, avoiding looking at her.

'Why? Am I so very repulsive to look at?' she demanded angrily.

'No, you're – you're quite beautiful. Please – ' He paused,

turning at last to face her directly. 'Please put on some clothing.'

She responded to the more gentle tone, hastily donning the dress she had worn earlier, brushing her hair back from her face. She rummaged among the debris on the table, found a not-quite-empty bottle of tequila, and poured a glass.

'Do you really need that?' Philip asked.

'I need – something.' She drained the glass in one swallow.

'Elena, I'm sorry. I want to help you.'

'You could help me, Philip.' She came to him again; he did not shake her off this time, but took her gently in his arms. Her cheek pressed against his bare chest.

'You could marry me,' she said. When he did not reply, she rushed on, speaking quickly and breathlessly, as if afraid he would not let her say it all.

'Oh, Philip, I can't do it myself, I'm not strong enough, you've seen that. I need you with me, to love and protect me.'

'Elena,' he said very gently, 'I can't marry you.'

He felt her stiffen in his arms, but he held her tightly to him, afraid of breaking the contact.

'Because you are ashamed? Ashamed of the men who have been with me, who have used me? I am dirtied? Soiled?'

'Don't be a fool, I never think of them.'

'You never think of them?' She threw her head back, staring up into his eyes.

He glanced away, embarrassed. 'They don't matter. What happened before isn't important, it's the future that counts.'

'And if they happen again, and again?'

'Don't talk like that.'

'There are men who are not ashamed, men to whom I can be a woman. I need you as a man, Philip.'

He let her go then, turning his back on her. 'Perhaps there is someone else,' she suggested. 'A girl in France, or up north?'

He had not mentioned Jolene to her before, afraid of undermining her fragile confidence, in him, in herself. He would have told her now, but before he could do so, she added, 'A woman with pale, white skin?'

He turned and saw the bitterness in her eyes, and the anger, but he saw too a silent plea, the faint glimmering of an almost desperate hope that he would deny what she had suggested.

'No, there is no one else,' he lied, afraid of the consequences of the truth. He felt as if he had betrayed her, himself, Jolene, yet there was comfort in the rush of relief on her face.

'But I still cannot marry you,' he added.

It was as if he had slapped her. Her face reddened, her eyes flashed.

'Then you should have left me with Harvey,' she said, snatching up a shawl and flinging it about her shoulders. 'At least he was not disgusted by me.'

'Elena – where are you going?'

'To find a man – someone who will love me. Someone who will make me forget how you turned away from me.'

She ran out the door. Philip followed her, catching up with her at the bottom of the steps. Sobbing, she fought him, trying to wrench free of his arms, but he held her tightly until at last she ceased struggling and again fell against his chest. A horse tied to the rail nearby whinnied nervously.

He could not tell her, not any of it. He had lived too long with his vow to care for her, to protect her. She was right after all, there was only one way he could protect her from herself. She must never know that she was his sister, it would destroy her by destroying the only comforting thing in her life, her love for him. If marrying her was the only way to save her, then he must do so. No one but him would ever know the truth of their relationship, and surely in time he could learn to forget it for minutes at a time, learn to pretend.

As for Jolene – but he could not let himself think of her, else he would never be able to do what he must do. Someday, somehow, he would find a way to make it up to Jolene, a way to make her understand. This, though, was something older and deeper. To fail Elena would be to fail himself.

'Elena . . . ' She stirred in his arms.

'Philip.'

'Elena, I will marry you.'

Inside the great house the old clock that stood in the foyer struck the hour, it's deep-timbred chime rolling across the yard like a knell.

22

'You're very pensive today,' Richard Trémorel said. 'Perhaps I've chosen a bad day to call.'

Jolene realized with a start that she had been daydreaming,

thinking of Philip instead of listening to her caller's conversation.

'Not at all,' she replied, stirring herself to be polite. 'I'm afraid I slept rather poorly last night. Why are you smiling at me like that?'

'You know in polite society a young lady isn't supposed to mention the subject of sleeping when she's in a gentleman's presence.' His mocking expression robbed the criticism of any sting.

'Someone,' she said, 'described respectability as a cloak under which fools might hide their stupidity.'

He laughed, enjoying the remark. 'Are you so disdainful of respectability, then?'

'I can be, if it interferes with what I want.'

'And what is it that you want?' he asked, growing sober. 'Am I right in guessing that there is a connection with your sleeping badly?'

She stood up from the stone bench on which they were seated; they were in the garden at Brussac-America. It had rained the night before, and the young leaves overhead, glistening like emeralds, shivered voluptuously in the breeze.

'As long as I can remember,' she said, 'I've dreamed the same dream time and time again. It's so silly to describe – you know how dreams are.'

'Yet often they reveal great truths, when we learn how to interpret them,' he said.

'I see a broad road winding over hills to a city. For some reason, I don't know why, I'm eager to reach the city. Men and women are hurrying along and I feel a need to be one of their number. The city stands atop a hill, surrounded by great walls with battlements, and the broad, white road leads up to its massive gates. The crowd presses on – men, women, children, not talking to one another, their faces shining with anticipation. Why they, and I, so passionately seek what is within, I do not know, only that I am impelled urgently to go there.'

'Is that all there is to it?' he asked when she seemed to have finished.

'Only that I am certain that when at last I have passed through the gates I will find happiness.' She gave an apologetic smile. 'It is foolish-sounding, isn't it? You can't say I didn't warn you.'

He rose too. 'I think your mysterious city represents nothing more than the freedom you so obviously long for,' he said, taking her hand.

'Really? I should have thought freedom would be without the walls rather than within.'

'There are many kinds of freedom. To fly into the prison of a man's arms can be freedom of a sort.'

'Please . . . ' She tried to remove her hand but he held it tightly.

'Let me take you away,' he said with impetuous fervor. 'I will show you freedom, the freedom you were born for. Jolene, you know I'm mad for you.'

It was not the first such conversation they had had. Indeed, she was surprised that he still persisted in his protestations when she had so often discouraged them in the past.

Not, of course, that she wasn't flattered, as any woman would be. Despite the difference in their ages, he was still an attractive man and when he put himself out to be charming, as he had for the past several weeks with her, he could be a most agreeable companion.

Yet even if she had not regarded herself as engaged to Philip, she would still have been wary of Richard Trémorel's often proclaimed passion for her. Although she had chided herself often for imagining things, she had never quite gotten over the feeling she had that, even when he was being most ardent in pleading his love for her, he was at the same time mocking her. There was something almost frightening in the determination with which he pursued her, as if she were a point to be proven in some mental argument.

She had observed, too, in countless little ways that Richard was cruel. She was not stupid, and had made a hobby of observing people; she knew well enough that most men could be cruel, often unwittingly, but this was not quite the same. He had a habit of catching flies in his hand – there was nothing remarkable in this, even her father sometimes made a grab as one buzzed annoyingly about his head. But she had observed that Richard did not merely kill them, or throw them to the ground as her father did; instead, he pulled off their wings and then released them once more, hopelessly crippled.

The evident relish with which he watched their futile efforts to fly sickened her and she was always glad when, tiring of the sport, he freed them from their misery by killing them.

'They're only flies,' he had pointed out when she had objected, 'nasty little pests – it's one less to get in your food, you know.'

Mary stepped from the house into the garden. The constraint between Jolene and her mother had worsened in the weeks since Philip's departure. Jolene found herself unable to forgive her mother's interference, and as the weeks passed and she missed Philip more and more, her resentment deepened. Sometimes the two barely spoke to one another in days, though they shared the same house.

Now, though, seeing that her mother looked distressed over something, Jolene excused herself and went to her.

'What is it?' she asked. 'What's wrong?'

'I've – ' Mary struggled for the right words. 'There's a letter for you.'

She handed Jolene an envelope. 'It's from Philip,' Jolene said, recognizing the handwriting at once.

'Yes,' Mary said. She glanced past Jolene, to where Richard was still waiting. 'Perhaps you'd better come inside to read it,' she said.

Jolene felt a quick stab of fear. Wordlessly she went past her mother and into the first unoccupied room, which happened to be the dining-room. She tore open the letter with trembling fingers and began to read.

At first she could not believe what she was reading. Philip, married? But it wasn't possible; Philip was going to marry her, when he returned from French Hills . . .

Suddenly she could read no more. The reality of the words came home to her. With a strangled cry she crushed the letter in her hand.

Mary came into the dining-room. 'You know?' Jolene asked.

'Yes, he wrote to me too. My poor darling . . . ' Mary came forward as if to embrace her.

'Don't touch me!' Jolene recoiled from her as if from a serpent. 'I don't ever want you to touch me again.'

'Jolene, you can't mean that, you don't know what you're saying.'

'I know that you are responsible for this,' Jolene cried, flinging the crumpled letter at her mother's feet. 'Your interference, you drove him away. He would have married me if it hadn't been for you. I shall never forgive you.'

She ran past a horrified Mary and up the stairs to her own room. Flinging herself across the bed, she gave herself up to uncontrollable sobs.

Some time later – it might have been minutes or hours, her grief had erased all consciousness of time – one of the maids came to remind her that Mister Trémorel was still waiting in the garden and wanted to know if he should come back at some more convenient time for her.

'Tell Mister Trémorel he can go to the devil,' Jolene snapped, but a second later she said, 'No, wait.'

She sat up, blowing her nose loudly, and sat for a moment glowering thoughfully toward the open window. The dark clouds building against the horizon looked like the ruins of a great city.

'Ask Mister Trémorel if he will wait just a little longer,' she said. 'I shall rejoin him in a few more minutes. Tell him I should like very much to talk with him.'

If only, Mary was thinking, anxiously pacing the parlor, if only José were here. Ordinarily she resented the closeness between her husband and her daughter, but today it was the distance between herself and Jolene that bothered her.

Jolene still refused to speak to her, though she had returned for a short while to the garden, where she had conversed in low voices with Richard.

Mary came to an abrupt halt in her pacing. Richard, of course, he was still in the garden; if she could not speak with her daughter, she could speak with him, perhaps she could enlist his aid. After all, he had once nearly become her husband, they had come within minutes of eloping together. Though he seemed a stranger to her now, he must surely retain some vestige of his past feeling for her.

She started from the room but, catching a glimpse of herself in the mirror, paused to smooth her hair and rub some color into her lips and cheeks. She did not care to remind him, after all, that more than twenty years had gone by since he had whispered ardently into her ear. Truth to tell, she did not care to be reminded of it herself.

He started up when she came into the garden, though he looked a trifle disappointed when he saw that it was she.

'You were expecting Jolene?' she asked.

'Yes,' he replied, 'she asked me to wait for her here.'

'She's had some rather unpleasant news.'

'So I understand.' He was polite, charming even, and as distant as ever.

Mary gave him the benefit of her most bewitching smile. 'It seems so peculiar,' she said, 'after what nearly was between you and me that you should be involved in my daughter's romantic misadventures.'

'They say that history repeats itself.'

She found that remark a trifle unsettling under the circumstances, making it difficult to maintain her coquettish air.

Her laugh came out strained. 'So long as you hadn't planned to run away with my daughter,' she said.

'No, Mama,' Jolene said from the doorway, 'he hadn't planned that.'

Mary's relief was short lived; she saw to her dismay that Jolene had changed into a traveling suit and was carrying a portmanteau.

'Running away,' Jolene added, handing the portmanteau to Richard as he joined her, 'was my suggestion.'

'Jolene, what does this mean? You can't just leave with a man, what will people say?'

'To hell and damned with what people say,' Jolene replied. 'I can't bear to live here with you, not after what you've brought about. The very thought of it, the very sight of you, fills me with rage.'

Mary was struck dumb by the intensity of her daughter's emotions. She remembered her own youth, when she had been on the verge of running away with this same man. Her grandmother had prevented it by locking her in her room, and sending José to take care of Richard. It was too late now, though, to lock Jolene in her room, and anyway, as strong willed as she was, she would probably climb down a drainpipe. Oh, where was José? There had been a time when he'd driven her mad by sticking at her side, and now when she wanted him there, he was somewhere in his damned vineyards. Not for the first time she thought that he ought to have married a grapevine.

'Jolene, I forbid you to go,' she said icily.

'I am going,' Jolene said. 'Richard has generously offered to find me someplace else to live. And if you try to block the door, I shall throw you bodily aside.'

Mary, who had been about to do just that, stopped cold, staring in horror at a daughter whom she suddenly realized she did not know at all. She turned on Richard instead, her eyes flashing angrily.

'You, sir, are no gentleman,' she cried.

He gave her a mocking smile and made a slight bow. 'I believe that it is the general opinion,' he said. 'Come, my dear,' he added, taking Jolene's arm, 'I detest scenes.'

Mary could hardly credit her senses. They were leaving, just like that, without a thought in the world for anyone else.

'You'll ruin your life,' she made one last stab at discouraging Jolene.

'You've already done that for me,' Jolene said.

Their footsteps sounded in the hall. Not until the front door had closed loudly did Mary run after them. God in Heaven, why had she been such a fool as to encourage Richard's courtship of her daughter? She had intended, of course, that he propose marriage; even with a bad husband, it would have been a profitable match. But she was a good deal older than when she had nearly run off with him herself, and she knew enough to know that Richard would never buy what was offered free.

'Jolene,' she cried, flinging open the front door, but it was too late, his carriage was already moving down the drive.

23

'Here you are, my dear,' Richard said, letting her into the apartment. It was their second arrival that evening. Earlier, after the drive in from the ranch, they had freshened themselves here before going on to dinner.

Richard's valet, who seemed to be the apartment's only servant, hurried forward to take their wraps. Jolene surrendered hers reluctantly. She had made a tentative suggestion that she go to a hotel, but Richard had dismissed the idea at once.

'My dear,' he had said, aghast, 'a single girl, unattached and unchaperoned, arriving at the Palace Court? It would be a scandal, if they'd even let you a room, which I seriously doubt. No, I'm afraid you shall have to rough it at my place for the night, and tomorrow we'll make some sort of suitable arrangements for you. I have a friend, a woman, who sometimes accommodates young ladies in need.'

The reply had relieved her mind somewhat, if not altogether. At least he was being considerate of her reputation. In her anger at her mother, and her eagerness to be away from home, she had not thought ahead to living arrangements but had trusted in Richard's promises to assist her. She had very little money, too small a sum to provide for her needs.

She had a vague plan of finding employment somewhere, perhaps in an office. Young women were less restricted than they had been in the past, and though traditionalists scorned those who 'wed themselves to writing machines rather than husbands', she did not lack the courage to fend for herself in exchange for the freedom she had chosen.

If Richard's lady friend would indeed accommodate her for a few days, until she was able to find some sort of position, she would soon be able to stand on her own two feet.

And just as well, too, she thought ruefully. After their ugly parting scene, she doubted that her mother would ever forgive her, and as for Papa, she could imagine all too well how crushed he must have been to learn of her sudden departure. Dear Papa; the fear of hurting and shaming him had been almost enough to prevent her going.

Almost, but not quite. She gave her head a toss. It would not do to dwell on such morbid thoughts. Grief was still too real a presence within her, to be held in check only by careful self-control and by occupying herself with a job and with building a new life for herself as quickly as possible.

And in the meantime, she reminded herself as she went into the apartment's drawing-room in front of Richard, there was tonight to be gotten through. Thus far Richard had made no mention of the evening's arrangements, other than to discourage her going to an hotel. Perhaps he meant to retire to one himself; after all, no one minded a gentleman's checking into an hotel alone for the night. And aside from the two of them – and his servant – no one would know that she had slept here.

'Shall I fix you something to drink?' Richard asked.

Jolene feigned a delicate yawn. 'I think not,' she said. 'It's rather late, and frankly I'm exhausted.'

Richard smiled warmly. 'As you like. Come along then.'

She followed him into the apartment's bedroom, a large, high-ceilinged room furnished, as were all the apartment's rooms, in the latest fashion, even to the electric ceiling light with its harsh glare.

The bathroom with its marble fixtures and brass hardware was beyond. Jolene saw that her things had been set out there, her peignoir gracefully draped over a chair, her toilet articles on the commode.

'Will you want Ah Fong to assist you?' he asked.

'I think not,' she replied.

When she emerged from the bathroom a little later, it was to find Richard already attired in pajamas and dressing-gown. He was by the fireplace, drink in hand. He turned to admire her as she came into the room.

Jolene felt naked under his gaze. With the exception of Philip, no man had seen her dressed like this before, nor was Richard discreet in his admiring glances, which were too bold for her liking. She paused uncertainly in the doorway.

'Is something wrong?' he asked.

'Only that I was a little surprised to find you here, dressed as you are.'

'It is my bedroom, after all, I hardly find it odd that I should be here, dressed for bed.'

'When you suggested that I come here, you said that I might make myself quite at home,' she said.

'As, indeed, I trust you shall,' he said. 'So,' he added, beginning to remove his dressing-gown, 'since we are both at home, and in agreement on the lateness of the hour, shall we not retire?'

She flushed angrily. 'My mother was right, you are a cad. When you offered to assist me, you did not make it clear that I was expected to go to bed with you in return.'

'My dear girl,' he said in an oily smooth tone, 'you are no prisoner here. Go if you like, go back to your mother's protection, if you can still call it that, after what she did to you. Go wherever you like, I shall not hinder you.'

She swept by him angrily, but before she was half across the room she stopped. Where was she to go? She could hardly crawl back to her parents, not after her bitter leavetaking. How was she to fend for herself on the streets of San Francisco, late at night? No decent hotel would take her in, unescorted, at this hour, and even if one did so, she would be unable to pay for any but the meanest room. She would be an easy prey to the scum that still prowled the streets of this altogether bawdy city. She might, if the stories women exchanged in whispers were true, find herself an even more odious companion.

'Shall I summon Ah Fong to repack your bags?' Richard asked from behind her, his voice all tenderly solicitous.

'I – I don't know,' she said.

He moved nearer, his breath like a tentative finger on her bare neck. 'You seem in no hurry to go,' he said.

She hung her head. How foolish she had been, not to see that his fervent offers of help were nothing but a prelude to seduction. She despised him – and for the moment, she was at his mercy.

'I have no place to go,' she whispered.

He touched her shoulders gently, caressingly. 'But you have a place, my sweet,' he murmured, kissing her hair, the lobe of one ear, her throat, 'here, with me.'

'Richard, I . . .'

'You'll want to know about Philip, won't you?' His hands had grown bolder, touching here, there, where no one but Philip had touched before. 'I have friends to the south. Don't you want to know who he married, this girl, what is she like, how did they meet . . . ?'

At the mention of Philip's name a wave of despair had swept over and through her, robbing her of her resistance.

'Yes,' she sighed, letting Richard guide her gently toward the waiting bed.

'I can do that for you. I can do so many things.'

She sank back wearily on the pillows, closing her eyes to the leering face above her. Richard's skilled hands began to remove her few pieces of clothing.

Perversely, though she loathed Richard and herself equally, it was neither of them whom she blamed for what was happening. It was Philip. It was as if she were hurting him, punishing him for his betrayal by submitting to this despicable man bending over her.

And if in the course of it she must be hurt too, what did that matter in comparison to the pain she had already suffered?

For Richard, it had been an unsatisfactory experience. Not that the young woman who had shared his apartment for three weeks now wasn't as beautiful – no, more beautiful than any other woman he'd had. Indeed, he had hardly been prepared for the sight of her unclothed loveliness; it was almost sacrilege to cover up such beauty.

Too, he had had the revenge that he had so long contemplated on the Brussacs. Long years before he had been thwarted and humiliated in his plans to elope with Jolene's mother. It had been vengeance of a particularly sweet kind to exchange the daughter for the mother.

Yet he found it oddly difficult to savor the sweetness. There was something about the girl, some final wall that he could not penetrate, humiliate and subdue her though he would. He had lain with her, invaded her very flesh time and time again, yet she remained as distant from him as when he had first lain eyes upon her. She was subdued, but unconquered. She submitted to him the empty shell of a body, yet when he looked into her eyes, he knew that he had not touched her at all.

It was frustrating, and put him increasingly out of sorts. Had he thought it would serve any purpose, he would not have hesitated to beat her – it was still, in fact, a possibility that he was considering; but in his heart he knew it would change nothing. He had hurt her repeatedly, deliberately, in the course of his lovemaking, but she had scarcely seemed to feel the pain, or if she had, she had refused him the satisfaction of reacting to it.

He finished his drink – she had a way of making him drink more than was his custom – and went into the bedroom. Jolene was at the dressing-table, applying the finishing touches to her makeup. He came to stand behind her, watching in the mirror. She did not so much as glance at him, though he saw in the slight stiffening of her shoulders that she was aware of his presence.

Aloof though she might be from him, she was not unchanged by the events of the past few days. She looked considerably older, nor was it only the dark shadows that had appeared around her eyes. There was a brittleness about her, like music played just off key. She had lost weight and her skin was stretched taut like parchment over the suddenly jagged planes of her face.

Yet in every superficial way, she was the perfect companion, the ideal mistress. She neither questioned nor quarreled, but went and did as he bade. Even the revulsion had died from her eyes.

She was dressed now, as he had dictated, for a morning drive. Watching her, studying her intently, it was hard to believe that she was little more than a girl. She looked very much a woman of the world, and despite his misgivings he felt yet another resurgence of his desire for her.

He quickly stifled the urge. He had awakened this morning hours before his usual time, to the clear knowledge that control of this situation was rapidly slipping from his hands. He would never conquer her, she might well conquer him. What if, after all his tricks and schemes, it turned out to be he, and not Jolene, who was destroyed by the affair?

The thought – and the certain realization that it was indeed a possibility – had frightened him into an unaccustomed sobriety and driven him to a quick decision, which he had not yet revealed to her.

'I've told Ah Fong to pack your things,' he informed her.

Not even that was enough to induce her to look at him, though he saw she was surprised. She added a touch more rouge, being maddeningly precise, before she deigned to reply.

'Am I being cast off?' she asked, a humorless smile curving her lips.

'Don't talk nonsense,' he snapped, losing his temper in spite of his determination not to. 'I've decided that it won't do to have you continue on here. There's your reputation to consider, among other things.'

'It's a trifle late to be thinking of my reputation, isn't it?' she asked, turning from the dressing-table and rising. 'And what are the other things?'

'Quite frankly I find this apartment a bit small for two, it was never intended as more than a *pied à terre.* And as for your reputation, though you may think me a cad, I have hardly announced your presence here. Aside from ourselves and Ah Fong, and perhaps one other of necessity, no one knows you are here.'

'I expect my parents could make a good guess, if they knew where "here" was.'

'They don't – and won't. This address is kept quite private.'

'And this other person, this necessary other person, who might that be?'

'Julia Benson, the lady friend I told you about. That's where I'm taking you now. It will be altogether a more fitting place for you to stay, and you need have no fears of Julia, she's entirely discreet, and very much accustomed to helping young ladies of your station find the freedom for themselves that convention denies them.'

'She sounds a paragon of kindness,' Jolene said. She went by him and out of the room. When he followed her, he found she had already donned hat and coat, and was stretching her gloves over her hands. It annoyed him further that she had not waited for him to assist her with her coat. He could not think which bothered him more, her complete subservience or the occasional flashes of independence.

They spoke little on their way. Jolene stared out the window at the clouds of dust blown by the wind and tried not to think of her current situation. The pain and grief that she had suffered on first learning of Philip's marriage had given way to a sort of numbness, though there was too an underlying anger – anger at a world that allowed women so few options, that made them pawns at the mercy of men who used them, traded them, discarded them when they so chose; anger too at her mother, whose machinations had wrought such disastrous results; and, especially, anger at Philip, who had betrayed her.

Richard had kept one promise, at least; he had found out for her who Philip had married. The reality, however, was worse than her wildest imaginings. She had pictured some elegant and stunning beauty. She would have liked to say, 'It's painful, but I could never have competed with her – I can see why he did what he did.'

It was especially bitter to know that she had been thrown over for a common whore, a drunken Mexican woman he had picked up in a cheap cantina, who had lain with more men than anyone could remember, herself included.

As for Richard, her loathing for him was almost inconsequential, paling to nothingness in contrast to her other, larger hurts and griefs. It was this that had allowed her to endure his misuse of her with such disdain. It would have galled him to know that she had been only dimly aware of him and his use of her over the past weeks. He had, as he instinctively suspected, touched no more than the surface flesh of her; the rest she had drawn deep within herself, to nurse her bruises and consider her course.

What sort of woman was this Julia Benson, she wondered? Did this move mean that Richard was leaving her truly on her own, to do with her life as she chose, as she had always dreamed of being able to do?

As a single ray of light can gild a dungeon with its glow, so this small hope began to revive her, to rouse her from the mental and emotional stupor into which she had fallen. Tentatively she began to flex her emotional muscles, to probe here and there among bruised and tender feelings.

Julia Benson's house was on Van Ness, once a bastion of old-order families who disdained the garish *nouveau riche* of Nob Hill, though by now the street was becoming a trifle seedy.

They drove through the carriage entrance and entered the house by a side door. A black maid whom Richard addressed as Denise came to take their wraps and giggle at something Richard whispered in an aside.

While she went to inform the mistress that they were here,

Jolene took the opportunity to look around. As they had come in a pair of well-dressed young ladies had been ascending the stairs, and now another girl of about Jolene's age came down, pausing at the landing to watch as Denise ushered them into the parlor.

The impression Jolene got was of a good private school for girls. These were obviously young women of breeding, and there was nothing in their appearance or behavior, nor in the appearance of the house, despite its rather loud decoration, that was not entirely circumspect.

As for Julia Benson herself, she was a striking figure of a woman, the sort more often referred to as handsome than pretty, though she might have been that too when younger. She was tall, nearly as tall as Richard himself, with regular aristocratic features – a long thin nose that at the right moment could give her an oddly predatory look and hooded eyes that gave an impression of far-seeing shrewdness.

'You naughty boy,' she scolded Richard, 'you should have brought your young charge to me at once. And you, my dear, you are Jolene, welcome to my home.'

After the unvarying tension of the past few days, Jolene was grateful for the woman's smile and her warm and breezy manner. 'I hope I won't be a nuisance,' she said.

Julia waved aside the possibility. 'Nonsense. As you probably saw for yourself, there are a number of girls here now. Sooner or later they always seem to find their way to my doorstep. Of course, we must thank Richard for thinking of bringing you here.'

Jolene found it difficult to imagine thanking Richard for anything, though in fact she was grateful to be moving here and out of his apartment. She would be only too happy if she need never see him again.

'I don't want to be a financial burden,' Jolene said. 'I do mean to look for a job at once.'

Julia's shrewd little eyes fastened on her. 'Have you some particular skill that might make it easier to get a position?' she asked.

'No, not really,' Jolene admitted a bit shamefacedly. 'But I can learn quickly. I thought perhaps something in an office. I've heard more and more women are working in offices.'

'Yes, of course,' Julia said. After a moment, she laughed and shrugged the matter off. 'Well, we won't worry about that just yet. In actual truth, I'm not a wealthy woman, and expenses do mount as the household increases. But it is an unwritten agreement here that each of the girls contributes as she is able – often not so much in cash as in other ways.'

'I'll be glad to do anything I can to help,' Jolene said quickly. 'Cook, clean – I'm not afraid of work.'

Julia laughed again, this time more easily. 'Now, now, we needn't turn ourselves into drudges. That would only defeat our purposes, wouldn't it? After all, we do want to be our most attractive, in case just the right gentleman should come along. But let us not worry about these things at the moment. Suppose I show you to your room now and you can make yourself comfortable. Richard, you will excuse us?'

Not until they had begun to climb the rather steep stairs did Jolene breathe a true sigh of relief. She had believed until then that Richard was up to some sort of trick, that he would at the very end refuse to let her stay, or find some other way to hurt or humiliate her. She could hardly believe her good fortune at being away from him.

'I don't know how I'll ever be able to repay your kindness,' she said.

'In due time – but here is your room, do you like it?'

'It's charming,' Jolene said.

It was a small room, smaller than her own at home, but attractively furnished in pale blues and grays, with here and there a splash of yellow. The single window looked out over the carriage entrance below. As she glanced out, Jolene saw an elegant carriage enter and a well-dressed gentleman enter the house.

'There's a bathroom at the end of the corridor, just for this floor,' Julia was saying. 'Ordinarily there are several girls on this floor, though at the moment there's only you and Amy, next door. Two of our girls moved on to other arrangements just last week. So you see, this isn't the end of the world for you, though I suppose you've thought that a time or two in recent days. My charges do go on from here to better things, once they've gotten on their feet.'

'I'm sure I shall soon be on my feet,' Jolene said. 'Though I think you're being modest when you speak of going on to better things.'

'You're very sweet,' Julia said. She glanced around, pausing to plump up a pillow on the tiny love seat by the door. 'I must go down now, I'll have guests arriving any minute.' She paused, as if weighing her words, though she continued to smile in her warm, friendly manner. 'We sometimes have gentlemen in to tea – all very proper and above board, of course. I know you won't want to bother with that right away, this is all too new for you, but in a few days . . . you might enjoy yourself.'

'I'm sure I shall,' Jolene said.

Julia was half out the door when she paused and turned back. 'Your mother was Mary Brussac, wasn't she?'

'Yes – do you know her?'

'I was her governess. A long time ago,' Her half smile deepened. 'I knew your grandfather very well.'

'My parents don't know where I am,' Jolene blurted out. 'I left rather abruptly.'

Julia laughed, tossing her head. 'My dear, I'm not likely to tell them,' she said. 'You're prettier than your mother, you know. And more sensible, hmm? Please, make yourself at home. There's dinner at eight-thirty for those who haven't made plans, and if you need anything, you've only to pull that cord there to fetch one of the girls.'

'Miss Benson . . . '

'Julia, please.'

'Julia . . . ' Jolene hesitated for a moment before rushing on. 'Has Richard – will I be expected to see him before he goes?'

'Why, that is entirely up to you, of course. I was under the impression that he was your benefactor, but if you'd rather not . . . ?'

'I would rather not.'

Julia's only reaction was a slight raising of the eyebrows 'I will give him your regrets,' she said, going out.

24

Jolene had been alone only a few minutes when there was a faint tap on the door and it was opened a few inches. A rather plain young woman with a pale, freckled face stuck her head into the room.

'Can I come in?' she asked.

'Of course, please do,' Jolene said. She had been sorting through the few clothes that she had brought with her, trying to decide what would be best suited to job-hunting. She meant to start out early the next day. Although she was deeply grateful to Julia Benson, especially for freeing her from Richard Trémorel's dominance, she had been sincere in her insistence that she did not want to be a burden.

'I'm Amy, my room's just next door,' the newcomer introduced herself, coming into the room and closing the door after herself. 'And you're the new girl.'

'Jolene. How do you do.'

'I've brought a little something to welcome you. Look,' Amy said, holding aloft a fruit jar half-filled with an amber liquid.

'What is it?' Jolene asked.

'Poteen.' Seeing Jolene's puzzled expression, she added, 'Irish whiskey. Don't worry, it's the real thing, don't let this old jar fool you. I have to hide it from Julia or there's hell to pay. Have you got any glasses?'

Jolene glanced around uncertainly, discovering a glass on the washstand by the pitcher and basin. 'Yes, here's one – but I don't know if I ought . . .'

'It's your first day here, isn't it? Anyway, if you won't, I will.'

She sounded so offended that Jolene, who was glad for an opportunity to make a new friend, relented. 'Well, perhaps just a little,' she said. 'But there's just the one glass.'

'That's all right, I'm used to drinking out of the jar. Here, try this.' She poured an alarming quantity of the whisky into the glass and handed it to Jolene. 'Here's looking up your address – one of my gentlemen friends taught me that,' she said, speaking the phrase 'gentlemen friends' with obvious distaste. She tilted her head back and took a long drink from the jar.

Jolene took a tentative sip from her glass. The raw whiskey burned a path down her throat. 'It's very . . . very strong, isn't it?' she said, trying not to grimace.

Amy laughed, animation making her plain face rather attractive, though there was something almost hysterical about the quality of her laughter. 'You're a real riot,' she said. 'A real lady, aren't you?'

'I suppose so,' Jolene said. 'Aren't you?'

The laughter vanished, to be replaced instantly by a withdrawn sullen look. 'I was brought up one,' Amy said. 'That was a long time ago, though. Things change.'

Jolene found the tone of the conversation discomforting. There was a sound of carriage wheels and horses' hooves outside as some new arrival entered through the carriage drive. She stepped to the window, glancing down, as two elegantly dressed gentlemen alighted from the carriage. She recognized them at once as gentlemen she had met at one or the other of the fashionable parties her mother had dragged her to over the last year or so.

'Why, that's Vernon Jordan,' she said, naming the scion of one of the city's more prominent families. 'And the other gentleman – his name escapes me . . .'

'Probably Mister Holiday,' Amy said, without coming to look. 'They always come together.'

'Do you know them?' Jolene asked.

'Well enough,' Amy said, with a dry bark of a laugh. 'Never to fear, if you're here long enough, you'll get to know their ways.'

Jolene was about to ask her what she meant, when they heard Julia calling from the bottom of the stairs, 'Amy, the Judge is here to see you,' and, when there was no reply, 'Amy, aren't you ready yet?'

'Damn,' Amy swore, putting her ear to the door, 'she's coming up. Get rid of that glass.' Without waiting for Jolene to do so, she snatched the glass from her hand and emptied the contents back into the jar, clapping the lid on it. She looked around the room frantically. 'You'll let me leave this here, won't you?'

Jolene was reluctant. 'I don't know,' she said. 'If Julia disapproves . . .'

'Oh, don't be a prig, she'll give me the awfullest time if she finds me with it, she threatened to have a belt taken to my back.'

Julia's voice, still calling Amy's name, had reached the corridor outside. They heard her knock rather loudly at Amy's door.

Jolene dismissed her visitor's last remark as pure exaggeration, and yet the girl – despite her rather haggard appearance, she looked to be even younger than Jolene herself – looked so genuinely frightened that Jolene relented, with misgivings.

'Very well,' she said. 'But just for now, please.'

Amy flashed a quick smile, the first genuine-looking one since she'd come into the room, and shoved the jar out of sight behind the dressing-table, not a minute too soon. Julia tapped at the door and opened it.

'Have you seen – oh, Amy, there you are, you naughty creature, I've been calling myself hoarse.'

'I was just welcoming Jolene,' Amy said, her sullen expression robbed her face of any charm.

'The Judge is here,' Julia said. 'You are ready, aren't you?'

'I'll just get my wrap,' Amy said. She slipped past Julia and out of the room, without a backward glance in Jolene's direction.

Julia glanced suspiciously about the room, seeming to relax as she saw that everything was in apparent order.

'I should perhaps have warned you,' she said, 'Amy is a bit – shall I say, unstable. She came to us after a number of unfortunate experiences. It's taken a long time for her to quite recover. You do understand?' The sharp, hooded eyes seemed to peer within her.

'Of course,' Jolene said, suddenly not so sure that Amy's remarks had been pure fantasy.

In the next moment Julia smiled, and the hard, cruel look vanished from her aristocratic face. 'I'm so glad you've made friends with her, it might be the very thing she needs – and you too, for that matter.'

Alone again, Jolene went once more to the window, watching as another, and yet another carriage arrived, disgorging elegantly dressed gentlemen, all of whom came in by the side entrance.

After a time, she saw Amy emerge on the arm of an elderly escort. As they were entering a waiting carriage, he looked up to speak to the driver, and she recognized Judge Carver, one of the city's more prominent politicians.

One thing was certain, Julia Benson was well acquainted with the city's better families – at least, with the gentlemen, though their wives and families had been conspicuously absent from the parade of carriages coming and going below.

Jolene turned from the window, renewing her determination to be up and out early the next day, to find suitable employment for herself.

For all her resolve, however, Jolene's job-hunting proved fruitless. Although she rose early and spent her days going from office to office, where she did indeed see a number of women working, there were simply no openings for one with her lack of experience or qualifications.

As the days passed, her anxiety over her position in the house deepened. She took most of her meals out, having only a cup of coffee at Julia's expense in the morning, and making do with bread and cheese, and perhaps some fresh fruit, for lunch and dinner.

Each day Julia questioned her about her search for employment, and each day she was warmly sympathetic, insisting that Jolene must stay as long as she liked and not worry so about a job. And each day, she pressed Jolene to meet some of the gentlemen who called. Under other circumstances, perhaps, Jolene might not have been so reluctant, but she had had experience recently with the sort of help she could expect from a 'gentleman', and she preferred to succeed on her own.

Julia accepted her excuses graciously, yet it seemed to Jolene that the hooded eyes grew narrower, her tone more insistent.

With renewed determination, Jolene would start out again the next day, but always the results were the same; and always, when she returned to the house on Van Ness, Julia was waiting to greet her.

Jolene confided her deepening worries to Amy, with whom she had formed a tentative friendship; their relative isolation on the second floor set them apart from the other girls and at the same time rather encouraged friendship between them. Although Jolene had met the others and found them friendly enough, she rarely saw them, being gone throughout the day and staying in her room in the evenings, exhausted from her job-hunting efforts.

'She doesn't want you to find a job, that's for certain,' Amy remarked. They were in Jolene's room, which for some reason Amy seemed to regard as a haven. Whenever they were both free she was there; often she shocked Jolene with her coarse ways and raw language, yet there was little doubt that, as she had informed Jolene, she had been raised a proper lady. As to her story, Jolene knew little, only that Amy's mother, widowed and fallen on hard times, had remarried a wealthy, older gentleman. Amy had run away from home soon afterward, but exactly what had happened to her, then or in the time until she arrived at Julia's, was unknown to Jolene.

'But that's silly,' Jolene argued. 'Julia surely can't wish me to remain unemployed. As it stands, I'm only a burden to her, contributing nothing.'

Amy gave her a studied look. 'She'd like you to contribute, all right. Hasn't she been trying to coax you to one of those teas of hers?'

'Every day,' Jolene admitted ruefully. 'Oh. I'm not a complete fool, I know that she arranges introductions between some of the girls here and the gentlemen callers, but though I'm not personally interested, it seems a harmless enough occupation.'

Amy laughed rudely. 'That's rich, I must say. "She arranges introductions",' she said in a parody of Jolene's remark. '"A harmless occupation." In a pig's eye! This place is a proper bordello, haven't you got that figured out for yourself?'

'I think that may be putting it a little strongly,' Jolene said, a bit annoyed at being thought so ignorant. 'You know we aren't allowed even to have gentlemen callers upstairs, let alone in our rooms.'

'The gentlemen who come here can afford rooms aplenty. And this way, Miss Julia Benson keeps her nose clean.'

'Amy – ' Jolene hesitated briefly. 'You've been introduced to the callers, you've gone out with some of them. Do you mean that . . . are you expected . . . ?'

Amy threw back her head and laughed, making Jolene flush angrily. Before she could comment on her companion's rudeness, however, there was a tap at the door and Julia came in, wearing one of the floral dressing-gowns that she favored.

'Have I missed a good joke?' she asked, smiling tentatively.

Amy's laughter had ended abruptly, to be replaced by the sullen expression she usually wore when Julia was about. 'Just something Jolene said,' she replied. 'You wouldn't find it amusing, I'm afraid.'

Julia looked crestfallen. In a more businesslike tone, she said, 'Well, I'm afraid you'll have to cut your amusing chatter short. The Judge is calling for you.'

'I don't want to see him,' Amy said. She had suddenly the frightened look of a hunted animal.

'Don't be foolish, he's an adorable man,' Julia said. 'And quite generous, I might add. Did you show Jolene the lovely stole he gave you?'

'A new stole, how nice for you,' Jolene said, trying to cheer her friend.

'I'll never wear it,' Amy said.

'I'm sure you may please yourself,' Julia said coolly. 'But now you will please remember your manners. Judge Carver is an important man, and important men do not like to be kept waiting.'

For a moment Amy glowered at her as if she would resist the other's direction; but Julia glared at her unflinchingly, and finally Amy got up from her chair and without a word left the room.

Julia gave a sigh. 'Really, she can be difficult, I wonder that you let her occupy your time so.'

'She's been very kind to me since I've been here,' Jolene said, adding quickly, 'as everyone has been, especially you, Julia.'

'Yes, well . . . ' Julia made as if to leave; then, apparently remembering something, she turned back, withdrawing a folded paper from her bodice. 'There, I almost forgot, I meant to give you this.'

Jolene took the paper and unfolded it, running her eyes over the column of figures. She went back to the top and read again, more carefully.

It was a bill, of sorts, for her room and board since she had arrived here. Virtually nothing had been overlooked, even her baths were noted and billed for, and each morning's cup of coffee. The total was nearly a hundred dollars, a staggering sum, in view of the fact that she had no more than a few pennies left to her name.

'I – I don't understand,' she stammered. 'No one told me I was expected to pay.'

'But of course,' Julia said, in wide-eyed innocence. 'A woman in my position, with no independent income – I could hardly afford to care for all the girls who come here. Mind you, I'm not meaning to suggest that I'm pressing you for the money, it's just that I thought you'd want to know how it was adding up.'

'I'm grateful. I'm afraid I haven't the money just yet – perhaps next week . . . ' Jolene's voice trailed off lamely.

'You have a prospect of a job, then?'

Jolene wished that she could lie, but she knew those hooded eyes would defeat her. 'I'm afraid not, not yet. But something's sure to come up soon.'

'No doubt,' Julia said, sounding quite unconvinced. 'You know,' she added, 'there are other ways . . . many gentlemen take real pleasure in being able to help out a young lady. The sum is a trifling one, for a man of means.'

Jolene had had a good lesson from Richard Trémorel on how men of means 'helped out' a young lady who was both attractive and in need.

'Thank you,' she said quickly, 'I'm sure I can manage something on my own.'

'As you wish,' Julia said, but her look and her manner were frosty.

It was late the same night when Jolene, who had lain awake for several hours worrying about the bill that Julia had presented to her, was awakened by a shuffling and scraping sound in the corridor. She and Amy still had this floor to themselves and so far as she knew Amy had not yet come home, meaning that she was alone on the floor.

The noise had stopped as she woke. She sat straining at the silence, waiting. It came again – a scraping at her door.

Jolene slipped from the bed and ran across the room, pressing her cheek against the dark oak paneling. 'Who is it?' she asked, her voice tremulous.

'Amy,' came a muffled reply.

Relieved, Jolene swung the door open – and gave a gasp as Amy half-fell into the room.

'Good Heavens,' Jolene cried. Amy's face was purple with bruises and stained with blood that had spilled onto her dress and her white gloves. She swayed and might have fallen had Jolene not grabbed her and guided her to a chair.

'Amy, what on earth happened to you?' she demanded.

'I don't want to talk about it,' Amy murmured, struggling to remove her gloves.

'But this is outrageous, you look as if you've been beaten. I'm going to call Julia – the police . . .'

'No!' Amy seized her arm with a grip so fierce that it made Jolene wince with pain. 'Please,' she said. 'Call no one. Just help me clean up, and – and if you would – in my room, in my hat-box . . .'

Her head swayed. Jolene forced her to lean back in the chair. Amy's eyes closed, her face looking a ghastly color beneath the bruises and the blood.

Jolene stole from the room and into Amy's next door. She found the hatbox with no difficulty, and inside, the jar of whiskey.

When she came back, Amy had revived somewhat. She was sitting up again, having removed her gloves and loosened the bodice of her dress.

The whiskey revived her still more and with Jolene's help she was able to get her torn dress off and bathe away most of the blood with her handkerchief dipped in water.

She would not, though, discuss what had happened with Jolene. 'Some things it's better not to know,' was all that she would say.

'But you must let me speak to Julia of this,' Jolene insisted, 'I'm sure she won't tolerate . . . '

Amy's laugh was all but hysterical. 'Oh, you are a caution,' she said. 'Julia doesn't care what they do to us, so long as she is paid. She's like a vulture, living off our flesh and bones . . . '

'Not a very pretty simile,' Julia said from the doorway. They had been so engaged in their conversation that neither of them had heard her come in.

'Julia, thank heaven you're here,' Jolene said. 'You must look at Amy, she's been hurt, beaten I should think . . . '

'And from what I've been told, not without some justification,' Julia said.

'Julia!' Jolene was shocked, but Julia ignored her, speaking directly to Amy instead.

'You've been quite disrespectful, I'm told,' she said, speaking coldly. 'You've offended one of our most influential friends. Not only offended him, I'm told, but caused him bodily pain. A kick, apparently, in a most sensitive region of his anatomy.'

'I wish I'd gelded him,' Amy said sullenly.

'Your temper is regrettable. Nonetheless, the Judge is a gentleman. He's even willing, in fact, to let bygones be bygones. I've arranged for you to have dinner with him tomorrow night. Of course, you'll have to apologize – and make amends . . . '

Amy had turned deathly pale. 'I won't go,' she cried. 'Not with him, never again.'

'Julia, please,' Jolene said, but it was a private battle being waged between the other two and both seemed to have momentarily forgotten her presence, or that they were in her room.

'You little fool,' Julia said, 'Have you no sense at all? The Judge is not only one of our most important visitors, but one of the most generous as well. Our expenses have been heavy this month, and some of the girls have been unable to carry their full share of the burden – ' She gave Jolene the briefest of sidelong glances. 'Fortunately for everyone concerned, the Judge has agreed to help us out with a small loan. But of course, we can hardly expect him to help those who offend and bodily wound him.'

'Damn you,' Amy cried, suddenly springing up from her chair. 'Are you blind? Can't you see what he's done to me?'

Julia looked unimpressed. 'Even the most patient gentleman can be forgiven for striking back when he has been hurt.'

'When he has been . . . ?' Amy looked incredulously at her. 'He wanted to tie me up, he wanted . . . to do the most unspeakable things. You can't ask me to . . . ' She suddenly burst into tears, burying her face in her hands.

Julia shook her head sadly. 'Oh, Amy, Amy, have you no idea how much trouble you could get into, telling such tales, and especially about someone in the Judge's position? No, my dear, your best course is to see the Judge and beg his forgiveness. I am assured that he is willing to forgive all, if you will only show the proper contrition.'

'I can't,' Amy sobbed through her fingers. 'You can't imagine how he'll punish me, what he'll make me do.'

'You're talking nonsense,' Julia snapped, losing her patience. 'You will do as I tell you, or else.'

Amy took her hands away and turned a tear-stained face to Julia. 'Or else, I suppose you'll put me out on the street, with nothing but the clothes on my back?'

'I will put you on the street,' Julia said icily. 'And the clothes on your back, may I remind you, belong to me.'

For a moment the two women regarded each other. Then, with a muffled cry, Amy ran from the room.

'Oh, Julia, you can't mean what you're saying,' Jolene said. 'There must be some way – if only I could help.'

'You can help,' Julia said, turning her cold gaze on her. 'There are other gentlemen of influence – some of them will be coming tomorrow for tea. Surely you could deign to meet them, I've asked nothing more.'

Seeing Jolene's indecision, she seized upon it, adopting a more coaxing tone. 'I assure you, all the proprieties are observed. Nothing goes on that couldn't take place in your own mother's parlor.'

'I – ' Jolene hesitated, but the thought of Amy's battered condition and her obvious terror undid her. If her meeting a few gentlemen for tea would soften Julia's cruel stance, how could she refuse? 'I will have tea with your visitors tomorrow. But I promise nothing more than that.'

'I've asked for nothing more,' Julia replied, smiling.

25

Jolene felt as nervous as a debutante when she came down the stairs the following afternoon. She had dressed as simply as possible in a dark skirt and shirtwaist and had pulled her honey-colored hair into a tight bun at the nape of her neck. She hoped to give an interested gentleman an impression of primness and aloofness.

She had stopped at Amy's room just before coming down. Though last night's bruises were not nearly so bad as they had looked at the time, they were ugly reminders of an unpleasant incident that Amy still refused to discuss. She had, in fact, been so morose and uncommunicative that Jolene had come away from her more despondent than ever. She must find a job for herself, lest she find herself, like Amy, a helpless pawn in Julia's machinations. She had made up her mind that if any of the gentlemen callers engaged her in conversation, she would press him for a legitimate job opportunity. Many of them, she knew, ran large offices or managed family businesses. On one occasion she had been coming in as a caller was leaving and had been introduced to a Captain Patterson of the local police; perhaps there was even the possibility of an opening with that agency. She could accept the help of a job offer with a clear conscience, because it was help that she could repay with hard work.

As it turned out, she did little more than make an appearance at Julia's tea. She had barely stepped inside the overdone parlor when a surprised voice spoke her name and she turned to find herself face to face with David Ecks.

'It is you,' he said, coming forward to clasp her hands in his own. 'But what on earth are you doing here, in this . . . ' He paused, embarrassed. 'Forgive me, I'm sorry,' he corrected himself quickly.

'It's quite all right,' she said, stunned herself by the unexpected meeting. It was as if for an instant a door had been opened upon the past, and she saw herself with her mother arriving at David's home for a party, remembered dancing in his arms and flirting with him harmlessly. How long ago, and how innocent, it all seemed to her now.

She knew that he was shocked and bewildered by her presence here, and she felt that she owed him some sort of explanation, though certainly not the entire story.

'I –I quarreled with my family,' she said, adding with a rueful smile, 'rather impetuously, I'm afraid, which seems to be my lot.'

'Have they disowned you altogether?' he asked.

She found herself smiling in spite of herself; how like David the question was. In a way, it was good to know that some things had not changed, though her own life was topsy-turvy. David was still the poor little rich boy, kind enough and still a bit pompous, though she was suddenly inordinately glad to see him.

'All those burning bridges,' she said, with a shrug. 'I'm afraid I made rather a mess of it. Anyway, someone brought me to Julia. I've been trying to find a job.'

He looked even more shocked. 'What? Like a common office girl?'

'I don't know that they're all that common,' she said, in a slightly cooler tone.

He was too busy looking about to notice. 'Look here,' he said, 'this won't do, this sort of thing is all right for these other girls, but not for you. Let's go for a ride, my carriage is just outside.'

'But I – I can't just leave, Julia . . .'

'Oh, damn Julia,' he said.

It was so close to her own sentiments that she could not help a little laugh. She found herself taking the arm he offered her and going gratefully with him out of the room and out of the house.

Julia, who had been only a few feet away, remained unnoticed by either of them. She had been close enough to overhear their conversation, including David's final oath. Far from looking offended, however, she smiled after the departing couple as if they had gone with her blessing; which, in a way, was the case. She was already calculating what she might expect from David in return for the introduction, which she was sure would prove to his benefit.

Jolene had not been fully aware of the strain under which she had been functioning until now. She sank back gratefully against the seat cushions, enjoying the cool breeze through the open windows.

David, perhaps sensing her feelings, did not try to distract her with conversation, though he held her hand. After a time the luxury of just riding without purpose waned, and she became gradually more aware of the man beside her.

'Thank you for letting me just relax,' she said, giving him a genuine smile. 'I'm afraid I'd forgotten what that was like.'

'Quite all right,' he said. 'I say, you don't have any kind of debt to Julia, do you?'

Jolene shook her head firmly. 'I owe her for my room and board, nothing more than that. As soon as I find a job – oh, David, you don't have any openings in the family business, do you? I've got no experience, but I'm willing to learn and I'll work hard.'

He patted her hand reassuringly. 'You leave that to me. We're going to have dinner together tonight. I'll get something worked out between now and then.'

She lay back again, glad to turn responsibility over to someone else, if only briefly. With another man perhaps she might have worried; indeed, she would have been reluctant even to go riding with just any gentleman, but she knew that with David she had nothing to fear.

He brought her back in an hour, feeling more at ease than she had since leaving her parents' home. 'You leave everything to me,' he insisted when he left her. 'I'll pick you up at eight.'

Jolene avoided the parlor where Julia was still entertaining several of her guests, and hurried up to her own room. The door to Amy's room was open and Jolene paused in the doorway. A dinner dress was laid out on the bed. Amy was in a wrapper, a towel over one arm; from the bathroom down the hall came the sound of a tub filling with water.

Amy gave her a sullen glance and continued collecting her toilet articles.

'I do hope this evening will go better for you,' Jolene said, feeling the inadequacy of her own words. Perhaps if she could get a job and get away from here, she could persuade Amy to come with her.

'I'm sure that it will,' Amy said. She took her jar of whisky from the hatbox and, uncapping it, took a long swallow, and a second one.

'Perhaps you shouldn't drink,' Jolene said.

Amy's eyes flashed angrily. 'I drink to kill the pain,' she snapped.

'From last night, you mean?'

'Of living,' Amy said, sweeping past her and going along the corridor to the bathroom.

In her own room, Jolene wondered if she dared speak to Julia about Amy; perhaps it really was a mistake to insist that she spend an evening so soon with the Judge. In a day or two both of them might see things differently.

On the other hand, her own standing with Julia was tenuous at best. Perhaps after all she could do more good for Amy by putting her own affairs in order first. Once she had a job and a place of her own, then she would be in a position to offer Amy something more than mere words.

She had only one dinner dress with her, of crushed garnet velvet imported from Paris. It had been made for her only a short time before, intended as a part of her trousseau.

The memory brought a stab of pain which was quickly thrust aside. There was nothing to be gained by clinging to past griefs. She had found that the world was a great deal harder and colder than it had appeared before, and that if she was going to survive in it at all, she would have to think of the future rather than the past.

For all of that, though, and despite her concern for Amy, she found herself in a surprisingly happy frame of mind. She was genuinely looking forward to dinner with David. At least it would be away from here and all the tensions linked to the place, and though he was dull and pompous, David was an easy companion.

She found herself singing as she got ready for the evening. She had intended to bathe but when she glanced out her door she saw that Amy still occupied the bathroom. It was already late and David would be returning soon to pick her up, but she kept a pitcher of water on the washstand for just such contingencies, and she settled for bathing from the basin.

It was evening by the time she was ready. She glanced from the window and saw that the fog had stolen over the city, blurring the lights into a pale shimmer. In the distance she could hear the clang of a trolley car and the deep basso voice of the foghorns from the bay.

There was a clatter of hooves below, and she looked down to see David's carriage arriving. She started down, but in the hall she saw that Amy was still in the bathroom. She felt suddenly guilty for her own tenuous happiness, knowing with what dread Amy looked forward to this evening.

It occurred to her that perhaps if she shared with Amy her own plans, for a job and a place of their own, it might cheer her a little. She started along the hallway, dark now with the fall of evening.

She was nearly to the end of the corridor when she became aware that her slippers felt damp on her feet. She looked down, lifting her skirts, to discover water standing on the floor. Her eyes slowly followed the water's course, to where it emerged from under the bathroom door. For the first time she realized that the bathwater that had been running when she arrived home was still running, a distant orchestration to the dread that was beginning to rise within her.

'Amy?' She tapped lightly on the door, then, fear fanning to life, more loudly. 'Amy, are you all right?'

There was no reply. She tried the door and, finding it unlocked, pushed it open. A wave of water washed over her feet, without her even noticing.

The sullen expression had gone from Amy's face, leaving in its place a dreamy, restful look. She lay with her eyes closed, and one arm draped gracefully over the side. On the floor, not far from the outstretched fingers, lay a gleaming razor, in a crimson pool only slightly redder than the water in which Amy reclined.

Jolene opened her mouth to scream but a hand was clapped rudely over it and she was shoved to the side, against the wall. She stared horror-stricken into Julia's eyes, no longer hooded but wide with her own fear.

'Shut up, you little fool, do you want to bring everything down about our ears?' When she was sure that Jolene was not going to cry out, she removed her hand, though her eyes continued to demand calm.

'Amy, she – she's dead,' Jolene gasped.

'I can see that for myself.'

'We've got to call the police.'

'Are you mad?' Julia hissed. 'Do you want a full-scale scandal, all our names splashed across the front pages? Have you any idea how many rich and important people come here? Leave this to me.'

'But . . .'

'Not a word, to anyone,' Julia insisted. 'Your escort is downstairs, you mustn't keep him waiting.'

Jolene started to leave but her eyes were drawn again to the grisly scene. 'Go on,' Julia ordered, shoving her toward the door. 'And remember, not a word to anyone, I'll take care of it.'

Numbly Jolene stumbled along the corridor, no longer even aware of the water that was ruining her pretty slippers and staining the hem of her dress.

She passed the still open door of Amy's room and then on an impulse went in and, grabbing Amy's whiskey jar from the hatbox where it was hidden, drank greedily from it.

The burning liquid helped restore her senses. She knew that she ought to put on some more makeup, give herself a few minutes to lose the ghastly pallor that the mirror revealed to her, but she was suddenly filled with a formless horror, she felt she must not spend another moment here, in this house. She fled down the stairs as if the dogs of hell were at her heels, and fairly flew into David's arms.

'I say, are you that glad to see me, or just awfully hungry?' David asked, surprised and pleased.

'Oh, David,' she cried, 'take me away, please, anywhere, just – out of here.'

He looked bewildered and seemed about to question her, but she tugged at his arm. 'Please,' she whispered.

He relented then, hurrying out the door with her. She had meant to obey Julia's commands not to speak of what had happened, but when she was in the safety of the carriage with David, so stuffy and safe beside her, her resolve failed her and she began to sob, quietly at first and then without reserve. David put an arm about her, holding her to him, and patted her shoulder with vague reassurance.

She found herself telling him in broken phrases of Amy, her dread of tonight's 'date', and finally of the grim conclusion.

'Good Lord,' David said when she told him of the discovery in the bathroom; he looked visibly shaken.

'Oh David, I can't go back there, I can't,' she sobbed.

The large, almost womanly-soft hand began to pat her shoulder again. 'Of course you can't,' he said. 'And you won't, you leave everything to me.'

'Are you going to call the police?'

'No,' he said sharply, adding, 'Julia's right about that, it would cause a major scandal.'

'But David, the girl is dead,' Jolene said.

'By her own hand. And anyway, making a lot of trouble for

everyone – me included, may I remind you – wouldn't bring her back. No, leave this to me, and don't worry your pretty little head over it.'

She sank back against the cushions of the carriage, trying to see the wisdom of David's reply. It was true, nothing would bring Amy back now; but shouldn't some justice be done? It was obvious that the Judge's behavior had driven Amy to do what she had done; nor was Julia blameless.

Nor, for that matter, am I, she thought despondently. If only she'd spoken to Amy sooner about her plans, or argued more vehemently with Julia.

The carriage had been traveling for some minutes when it came to a stop. The flow of her tears finally halted, Jolene peered through the window at an unfamiliar building.

'Where are we?' she asked.

'I wanted you to see something,' David replied, alighting from the carriage and coming around to help her down.

The house was an older one and had apparently been made into apartments. David let himself in at the front door and led the way up dimly lighted stairs. At the top, he unlocked a door and stepped aside for her to enter before him.

It was a small but elegantly furnished apartment, with a large window in front that afforded a view of the bay. Jolene gave the view a brief glance, and gazed around the room.

'Is there no one here?' she asked.

Looking a trifle embarrassed, David said, 'The apartment is empty.'

She strode past him into the bedroom, tiny but furnished, like the rest of the apartment, in flawless taste. The closet, standing open, was empty except for a discarded *peignoir*. David's face reddened slightly when she picked it up from the floor where it had fallen.

'The apartment is mine,' he explained, speaking rapidly. 'The young lady who was using it has departed. I – I thought you might like to stay here for a while.'

She eyed him speculatively. Her crying bout in the carriage had relieved a great deal of the strain she had been under, and she was thinking more clearly now.

She understood that he was inviting her to be his mistress, as no doubt the 'young lady' who had preceded her had been. Had he simply cast her out since this afternoon, she wondered, but she did not dwell long on that question; she had no need to be reminded that women on their own were so often at the mercy of their so called benefactors.

She thought of Amy and shuddered again at the memory. She had told David she could not go back there, and it was true, anything was preferable to that. Amy's frightened face and Julia's hard, cruel one loomed before her like ghosts, taunting her.

There was more to it than that, though. She had been the foolish innocent with Richard, and before that with Philip as well, blithely allowing them to manipulate her to their own ends. Now, however, she was being asked to make a real decision, to commit herself to an immoral relationship with this man whom she knew only on a casual basis, and with whom she was certainly not in love.

And yet, why not, she thought? Men had used her. Was it any more wrong to use them in return? She had tried, tried hard, to find some way of caring for herself, a means of support, but every door had been closed to her, not because of any lack of ability or aptitude, but because she was a woman. She had tried to breach the gates of this 'man's world', and had failed.

But there was, after all, another world as well, and ways in which men did want women, want them badly enough to pay dearly for the privilege. What she had given so lovingly to Philip, so helplessly to Richard, could mean power, power to live her own life as she chose. And if it meant that she must lie in the arms of this bland, pompous man whom she did not love – why, she had lain with worse, for less profit.

He had been waiting nervously, shifting his weight from one foot to another. She gave him a slow, langorous smile and, dropping the *peignoir* once again to the floor, came slowly across the room to him.

'It's a lovely apartment, David,' she said. 'and I'd love to stay here – if you're sure we can work it out between us.'

26

'Father?'

The shutters had been closed over the windows so that, after the bright sunlight of the vineyards, the room seemed as dark as night. Philip hesitated for a moment on the threshold before closing the door gently and crossing the room to the bedside. Not until he had actually leaned over the bed could he see that Adam's eyes were open and watching him, with what meaning he could not read. Only the eyes moved in his father's face, blinking, following his movements.

'I know you don't like me to call you that,' Philip went on hesitantly, intimidated as he always was by the rigidity of that frozen expression, bland, emotionless. 'But that's how I think of you anyway. When – when you've recovered, I hope that you will be glad to have me address you as father.'

The eyes blinked, offering no clue to the thoughts behind them.

Philip glanced around, uncertain of himself. His eyes had grown accustomed to the gloom, so that now he could make out the straight-backed chair by the bed and Maude's knitting on the table beside that; he had waited for days for an opportunity to speak to his father when she wasn't present.

'I wanted to talk to you,' he said aloud, pulling the chair closer and sitting down. Almost at once he rose again, unnerved by the unwavering stare of his father's eyes.

'They told you about the wedding?' he asked, as if an answer might be forthcoming. 'Yes, of course they did, they wouldn't know what it meant. But you and I know, father – don't we?'

He leaned over the bed again; the eyes were accusing. 'Yes, I know,' he said, sitting down again, 'I'm not a fool, whatever you may think of me. I know she's my sister.'

He paused, the words seeming to echo about him in the stillness of the room. Until now he had spoken them aloud to no one, and even now he found himself glancing uneasily over his shoulder, as if someone might be listening. Listening, to hear his shame and his guilt.

'Oh, God,' he swore softly, burying his face in his hands. He was half crazy with the knowledge of what he had done. His marriage was a crime in the eyes of God as well as the eyes of man. There was no forgiveness for his sin; and yet, wasn't that why he had come, why he had felt compelled to talk to the one man beside himself who knew, knew the full truth.

He stood up abruptly and began to pace the room, talking as much to himself as to the man unmoving on the bed.

'But she's not only my sister, she's your daughter, for God's sake, didn't you care about that? Why did you let things get the way they were? They were using her, didn't you know that? A word from you . . . They were ruining her life, her body, her mind. I had to . . . someone had to save her, from them, from herself – from your neglect, if you want the truth. I didn't mean it to happen the way it did. I didn't mean for her to fall in love, but when she did I was afraid to tell her the truth, I was afraid of letting her down. Only, now – now I think I've made things worse. I don't know what in the hell to do. I can't forget who and what she is. I can't tell her, and I can't forget it myself.'

He suddenly returned to the bed. 'Damn it,' he said in an angry voice, 'we were your children, didn't that matter at all? Oh, I know about meaningless lust, I understand how a man can sleep with a woman who means nothing to him. But we were yours, even if she wasn't. You had no right . . . '

He broke off, embarrassed by his anger directed at a helpless, frozen shell of a man who could not even reply.

'I'm sorry,' he said. 'I didn't come here to accuse you, I came to explain. I tried to right a wrong – your wrong, that's the truth of it, whether we like to admit it or not – and I've messed it up, father, I've created an even bigger wrong. And there's nothing I can do about it now but make the best of it.'

He paused, thinking he had heard an approaching footstep, but the house was silent except for a distant clatter from the kitchens.

'What I've done to her, maybe it's the cruelest thing of all the things that've been done to her, I'm not even sure anymore,' he went on. 'But I've taken a vow that she'll never know. I will spare her that, no matter what other crimes I've committed against her. I cannot be brother and husband both – very well, then, I will cease to be brother. Only you and I will ever know – and I pray to God that I may be allowed to forget.'

He was silent for a long moment. If only his father could speak, if only they, who shared between them his guilty secret, could share its burden.

'I – I guess I came because . . . ' Again he hesitated. He

leaned low over the bed. '... Because I need your forgiveness. Father, I know you can't speak, I don't even know if you can hear what I'm saying. But if you can hear, if you can forgive me, I beg you, give me a sign at least. Blink your eyes. At least I'll know you understand.'

The vacant eyes stared into his own. Philip felt as if he were sinking into their icy depths. Had his father even heard what he was saying, or comprehended it? If only he would blink ...

'What are you doing in here?'

Philip started and whirled about, to find Maude in the doorway, her eyes flashing angrily.

'I was visiting my father,' he said.

'He's not your father,' Maude said, coming to the bed. 'Get out of here, I won't have you disturbing him, you who did this to him. Get out, or I swear I'll have you thrashed and thrown out.'

'You will not have me thrashed, Madame, nor thrown out,' Philip said. 'But I will go, because I do not want to add to your unhappiness, or his.'

As he went out, she was bending over the bed, fluffing pillows and murmuring in the sort of low, soothing voice one used with a child. Philip thought of the angry words he had spoken, of the shame and guilt he had tried to unburden himself of. Had it meant anything at all to the man on the bed? Perhaps he would never know.

The possibility filled him with despair. He left the house and crossed the yard to the shack that had once been his mother's, and that he now shared with his wife. The family, though they were ignorant of Elena's relationship to him, had nevertheless objected to his marrying what Maude had termed a 'mere slut'.

'I won't be made to sit at a dinner table with her,' Maude had insisted.

Jean, though he had been more tolerant of the situation, had supported her in that, nor had Philip been particularly eager to move Elena into the big house, where she would be forced to share the company of those who disliked and had abused her.

The smell of beans cooking drifted to him on the breeze. Elena was cooking in the kitchen when he came in. He crossed to her and kissed her, fighting against the revulsion that inevitably rose up in him whenever he had to share any physical intimacy with her.

There was tequila on her breath, as there had been a number of times over the last few days. He glanced round the room, wondering where she had hidden it this time; he'd already found and discarded a half dozen bottles, but she always managed to find another.

At first he had been angry, he had sworn at her and torn the house apart looking for the concealed bottles, but gradually he had begun to understand that she drank to escape the inexplicable loathing she saw or perhaps sensed in him. How could he make her understand that the loathing was for himself, not for her?

'A letter came for you,' she said, turning her attention to the pot she had been stirring on the stove, but not before he had seen the quick look of hurt that marked her face.

His first hope, painful and exhilarating at the same time, was that the letter was from Jolene, but it was Mary's handwriting instead on the envelope. He opened it, carrying it to the window the better to read her cramped writing.

The message was like a physical blow. Without preamble, Mary told him of Jolene's running away with Richard Trémorel, a man she described as 'worse than a scoundrel'. Presumably abandoned by him, Jolene had gone to live in a San Francisco home that had a reputation as a place of assignations.

The letter ended with a plea to Philip to help dissuade Jolene from the ruinous path that she was presently following. He read it through a second time before crumpling it and throwing it to the floor.

Elena, frightened by the unfamiliar expression on his face, cried, 'What is it? Is something wrong?'

'I have to go to San Francisco,' he replied, going to the closet and taking down his valise.

'To San Francisco? But why – it is a busy time in the vineyards . . .'

'I have to go,' he repeated dully.

She ran to him, clutching at his sleeve. 'But you haven't told me what it is,' she said.

'Someone I know needs help.' He shook off her hand and began to throw clothes haphazardly into the valise.

She took a step back from him, her eyes narrowing suspiciously. 'Who?' she demanded. When he did not answer, she said, 'It's a woman, isn't it? You lied to me, there is another woman, up north. That is the truth, isn't it, you're going to her.'

'Yes.'

She threw herself in front of him and began to pound on his chest with her fists. 'Tell me her name,' she cried. 'Who is this slut, this whore who would steal my husband . . .'

He slapped her, twice, making her head jerk back and forth. She fell back from him, against the wall, her eyes wide with shock and fear, her hands flying to her bruised cheeks.

'Her name is Jolene,' he said in a voice like steel. 'You will never mention it, we will never speak of this again.'

He did not wait for a reply, but turned from her and resumed his packing. After a moment she began to cry softly into her hands, but even that sound did not penetrate the pain and despair in which he was enveloped.

27

'A nice party, wouldn't you say, Miss Jolene?'

'They're all nice parties, Walter,' Jolene said, sure that neither of the men in the carriage would notice the sarcasm of her reply. And she supposed, according to the standards of the crowd with which she now mingled, the party had been quite successful; to the best of her knowledge, only two or three of the guests had gotten so drunk as to pass out – one of them, it was true, in the fountain that ran with champagne instead of water – and although the usual number of fights had erupted only one person had been seriously hurt. Really, quite a nice party, in contrast to some she'd attended lately.

'I appreciate the lift,' Walter McCrea said, speaking more to David than to her.

'Don't mention it,' David replied. 'Montgomery Street, isn't it?'

'Right as rain. I've been shopping for a team, but you know what it is, damned near impossible to find decent animals at a reasonable price. You wouldn't believe what they're asking for a couple of broken down nags these days.'

Jolene smiled into the darkness, knowing as did everyone else acquainted with him that Walter McCrea was never going to buy a team at what he called 'a reasonable price'. He was a notorious cheapskate, living in rented rooms though he could well afford a mansion of his own on Nob Hill, and hitching rides to and from parties with his friends.

They had reached his corner. David rapped for the driver and the carriage rolled to a stop. Walter climbed down, thanking David profusely. He tipped his hat in Jolene's direction, letting his glance slide downward over the exposed flesh of her bosom. She pretended not to notice; ogling other men's women was one of Walter's pastimes, though he would never have expended the money himself to keep a mistress. She had heard that he visited the cheapest of the city's houses, in the vice-ridden Barbary Coast district along the waterfront; in another man, that might have been taken as a sign of courage, since disease was only one of several risks a man took on entering that notorious region; but in Walter's case, it only meant that he could buy his pleasures more cheaply there than elsewhere.

When the carriage was moving again, David chuckled softly and said, 'I wish I had a dollar for every time he's told me about that team he's been shopping for.'

She did not reply and pretended not to notice his hurt expression. They rode the rest of the way in silence, punctuated by the occasional clatter of a passing carriage.

Though she had adapted to the idea of being David's mistress, she had never been able to overcome a feeling of gloom that came over her whenever she ascended the stairs to the apartment they shared. She was always relieved when they had come in and the door was shut on the badly lighted stairs.

'Will you have a nightcap?' David asked.

Jolene draped her new stole over a chair and pushed a wayward curl back from her forehead. She replied, 'I'm a little tired.'

He poured two generous snifters of brandy and came to hand her one, kissing the back of her neck. 'You were very lovely tonight,' he said. 'I have a little present for you, by the way.'

'That's hardly necessary. You've been quite generous as it is, David.'

It was true, whatever fault she might find with him, he had certainly been generous since moving her into what he, to her annoyance, insisted on calling their 'love nest'. The closet was filled with new gowns from the best shops in the city; she had dozens of pairs of shoes, gloves, hats. And she had ample opportunities for wearing them; the last two weeks had been filled with whirlwind activity – operas, dinners at the finest restaurants, parties and balls, even a night dancing on a palatial yacht in San Francisco Bay.

Of course, there were places they did not – could not – go. A man, even one as influential as David Ecks, did not take his kept mistress into the best homes. They could hardly mingle with the élite social set to which David's family belonged.

Still, there was no shortage of places at which a wealthy man and a beautiful woman were welcome, their marital status notwithstanding. A few months ago she would have been insulted to be invited to the sort of 'fast' parties they had been attending; now she went and was glad, as it meant she needn't spend an evening alone with David.

Not that David was objectionable, not in the sense that Richard had been; he was gentle and quiet, and generally undemanding. If he was dull as well, weak willed and unassertive to the point of emasculation, the fault was not his, and at any rate it worked to her advantage. She had only to complain of fatigue or a headache and he was willing to forgo the physical pleasure he was paying for, though more often than not guilt would cause her to change her mind and acquiesce after all, earning his slavish gratitude.

There was another bonus to the fast life she was sharing with David; it left her little time to think of Philip. In a sense, she felt that she was spiting Philip by becoming a kept woman. He had thrown her over for a whore; she had become a whore. There was a neatness to it that gave her a perverse satisfaction, even while she hated herself for it.

David had taken a package from his pocket. She opened it and gave an involuntary gasp at the sight of a magnificent pink sapphire pendant from a chain of diamonds.

'David, it's – it's awesome,' she said, staring at the resplendent gems. 'But it must be worth a fortune.'

'You are worth a fortune,' he said, kissing her neck again. 'Put it on.'

'I'm almost afraid to.'

He smiled and, taking the pendant from her hand, put it about her neck. She was wearing a low-cut gown of burgundy silk; the deep hue of the dress and the creamy luster of her bare flesh set off the gem to perfection.

'You're very generous with me,' she said.

'No more generous than you are with me,' he replied, his chest swelling. 'I'm going to get out of these clothes. Will you come to bed?'

'In a few minutes – I think I'd like another drink.' She finished the brandy and handed him the glass. He frowned, as if about to say something, then thought better of it and went obediently to replenish her drink.

When he had disappeared into the bedroom, closing the door, she went to the gilt mirror by the entry way and studied her reflection. At first it was the sapphire pendant at which she stared, but after a moment her eyes drifted upward to examine her own face.

How much older she looked than she had even a few weeks before. Gone was the vulnerability, the innocence, the open, untroubled smile. The eyes gazing back at her were hard, unfeeling, the lips unsmiling, turned ever so slightly downward at their corners.

David's disapproving smile had not gone unnoticed. He was right, she was drinking rather too much. In the past a glass or two of champagne at a party was as much as she had taken. Now, although she was never drunk, after one awkward experience, had taught her that she did not like being out of control of her actions, she was also rarely without something to drink. She had discovered the pleasure of peaches in champagne for breakfast; late at night there was coffee flaming in cognac, and in between these times her social life seemed to rush forward on a river of wine.

She had heard that too much indulgence wrought physical havoc, and she leaned closer to the glass, searching for any telltale damage to her beauty. There, was that a tiny line beginning to appear at the edge of her eye? No, surely she was imagining things; she wasn't a sot after all, merely because she used spirits to soften the world's ugly edges.

There was a soft tap at the door, surprising because it was quite late, and because visitors never came here; the place was known only to David's most intimate associates, and she had formed no friendships since her abortive try with Amy.

She hesitated, wondering if she should call David; she could hear him whistling to himself in the next room as he prepared for bed, but the tap came again, impatient and furtive. She went to the door herself.

The corridor was unlighted and at first she did not recognize the girl outside. 'Miss Julia sent me,' the visitor said, stepping into the entry way.

Jolene recognized her then as Denise, Julia's maid; the visit was a surprise. She hadn't realized that Julia even knew of her whereabouts.

'There's been someone at the house, looking for you,' Denise went on, 'a gentleman. He says his name is Philip.'

Jolene's hand went to her throat. She felt as if she were suffocating. 'You mustn't tell him where I am,' she said, instinctively lowering her voice to a whisper so that David might not hear them. 'He mustn't come here.'

Denise gave her a knowing smile. 'Miss Julia is not one to give out information,' she said, lowering her own voice. 'But the gentleman is very insistent. He asked her to see that you learned he was here. He's staying at the Court.'

Jolene's head rang with the news – Philip, here, in San Francisco – searching for her. He must have heard . . .

'I have to go,' Denise said, jarring her back to reality. 'Miss Julia, she thought you'd want to know, right away like.'

'I'm very grateful,' Jolene said, recovering her wits. 'I – I haven't any money on me just now, but I'll send something in a few days.'

Denise smiled again. 'That won't be necessary. Mister David was very generous.'

Jolene winced at the reminder that David had after all bought her from Julia, plain and simple. Amy had called the place a bordello, and she had been right. It was more sophisticated than most, and more exclusive, but the business was the same.

The thought of Amy reminded her of that ugly episode. 'Denise,' she asked, 'what of Amy . . . ?'

It was as if a mask dropped suddenly over Denise's countenance. 'Miss Amy up and left us, the same night as you did,' she said. 'Didn't say a word to anyone. Mighty unfriendly of her, if you ask me.'

There was nothing in her voice or her expression to indicate whether she was aware of the lie. The wide, dark eyes met Jolene's evenly.

'I – I wondered what had happened to her,' Jolene said.

'She was a strange girl,' Denise said, as if that accounted for everything.

David called her name from the other room. 'Coming,' Jolene called back. She realized that Denise was staring at the sapphire pendant, smirking knowingly. It embarrassed and irritated Jolene.

'Thank you again,' she said, 'and thank Julia.' She closed the door on the girl and turned toward the bedroom, but on an impulse she went instead to the brandy bottle on the sideboard and filled her glass to the brim, half emptying it before she started for the bedroom.

David was in his dressing-gown. The bed was turned back, accusing her for her delay.

'Did I hear voices?' he asked.

'I believe there was someone in the corridor,' she said, unfastening the pendant and removing it thoughtfully from her neck.

He came to kiss her clumsily. 'Is something wrong?' he asked. 'You look like you've seen a ghost.'

'No, no, I'm all right,' she said too quickly. 'David, would you like to make love to me? Now, I mean?'

He beamed like a small boy. 'I was hoping we might,' he said, crushing her in a fervent embrace.

She had hoped that the heat of his passion might drive Philip from her mind, if only for a brief time, but when it was ended and David lay snoring beside her, she lay in the darkness and nursed the ache that Philip's memory had renewed in her.

28

For a second or two Philip thought he was facing a stranger at the door of his hotel room. He had all but given up hope that Jolene would receive his message or that, having received it, she would actually come to him; and now, just when he had thought he could not endure another moment of waiting, here she was.

Yet even a glance was enough to tell him that this was not the Jolene he had left behind a few short months before. She had changed, changed dramatically. The shadows under her eyes, the deep hollows of her cheeks where the flesh had stretched taut over the bones, the brittle air of sophistication that she wore as naturally as her elegant new clothes, added more than mere years to her appearance. She was cool and composed, though there was an underlying fragility to her self-control that made her achingly vulnerable.

'Jolene,' he said her name, feeling suddenly inadequate to the moment. Remembering his manners, he stepped aside, saying, 'Come in, please.'

She swept by him into the room, her chin tilted arrogantly. He ached with the desire to seize her, to clasp her to him and cover her mouth with kisses, to fall to his knees and beg her forgiveness.

Her green eyes glinted like gemstones as she turned them on him, freezing the words of love in his throat. There was no compassion in her expression, no trace of love or tenderness; she despised him. Even her brief smile was cold and unwelcoming.

'Hello, Philip,' she greeted him. 'How nice to see you again.'

'Would you . . .' He gestured helplessly, at a loss before this icy regality. 'Would you like to sit down? Can I get you anything?'

'I think not. I've only a few minutes to spare,' she answered, tugging at the fingers of one white glove. 'If only you'd let me know your plans, I could have been better prepared. I've been dreadfully busy lately, you do understand?' She cocked her head, lifting one eyebrow. It was the gesture of a coquette, and it gave him a stab of pain.

'You've changed,' he said.

The coquette's smile vanished, her lips tightened into a hard line. 'Changes have been forced upon me,' she said.

'I'm sorry. I deserved that,' he said. 'Jolene, can you ever forgive me?'

For a moment the eyes flashed with the fire that he remembered. 'Have you so easily forgiven yourself?' she asked softly.

'My God, no,' he cried in a voice of anguish. 'You can't know what I've suffered.'

'You have suffered it, at any rate, in matrimonial comfort.' She glanced round the room, though it was evident they were alone. 'Am I not to have the privilege of meeting your bride? Surely you did not leave her at home, so soon after your wedding. If you are not careful, Philip, people will begin accusing you of being insensitive to the feelings of women.'

'Stop it.' He crossed the room to her in two long strides and seized her shoulders, crushing her to him despite her struggles.

'Let me go,' she said, but before she could protest further his mouth had fastened upon hers.

For a few brief seconds she fought violently against him, but he was too strong. The taste of his lips was like a liquor that inflamed her senses at the same time that it made her limbs weak. Her legs seemed unable to support her and hardly knowing how it had happened, she found herself clinging hotly to him, her mouth opening to his assault, her entire being vibrating in a cosmic harmony with his. Philip, her heart sang, my beloved . . .

Reality returned like the swift, agonizing slash of a sword. He was not her beloved, he belonged to another . . .

She broke from his embrace with a tiny, whimpering cry. 'Please, don't, I beg you, if you have any mercy in you at all,' she pleaded in a whisper, turning her back on him. Tears had begun to spill from her eyes.

Overcome by his own emotion, Philip staggered to a chair and sank into it. What had he done to them? God in Heaven, how had he been so blind, so foolish?

'Why did you come?' she asked, in a voice filled with pain and confusion. 'Surely you couldn't have wanted to torture me further? Was I so sinful that you should condemn me to this hell, this hell from which there is no hope of redemption?'

'I would take all of your pain onto myself if I could. But all the pain in the world can't right what I've done – I know, I've suffered it already, a thousand times over, all the torture and the agony that man can know.'

He reached for her hand, clutching it in his, but she snatched it away and strode to the opposite side of the room.

'Oh, Philip, Philip, if only you'd loved me as I loved you.'

'Jolene, I beg you, don't say these things, you don't know what you're saying.'

She turned on him angrily. 'I know that you told me you loved me, that you would be mine forever, and here you are before me, married to another, to a – a common tramp!'

'Jolene!' He came to her, falling to his knees before her, grasping at the folds of her skirt. 'I beseech you. I do love you, I swear before Almighty God, I love you, you are my life. You cannot begrudge me a day with her, when every moment of my life since we met has been yours to command, when you own me body and soul.'

For a moment she weakened. He sounded so fervent, his protestations so sincere. She was assailed by memories – Philip as a child, at French Hills; Philip by the river in France; Philip in her arms at night . . .

'If you love me,' she said, speaking slowly and deliberately, 'then come away with me.'

'I – .' He hesitated. There must be a way, a way that he

could be with Jolene and yet spare Elena, whom he could not bring himself to destroy; and it would destroy her, if he simply left. 'I will work something out,' he said, determined. 'I will come to you, soon.'

She felt her compassion begin to wither within her. 'No, now,' she said. 'My reputation is already ruined, we needn't bother about that. And as for hers . . . ' She dismissed it with a wave of her hand.

'I – I can't.'

She snatched her skirt from his fingers. 'You can't because it's her you love, isn't it?' she demanded, furious anew. He made no reply. 'Answer me, you love her, don't you?'

He looked up and the anguish in his eyes seemed to her the answer to her charge. He did love her, this other woman, a love he hadn't even the words to deny.

'Jolene, if it is the only way, I will come with you now,' he said in an agonized voice.

'No. I hate you.'

'My God . . . ' It was like a wail of despair.

'I shall always hate you for what you've done. Don't get up, it will help to remember you groveling at my feet.'

'Jolene, in the name of Heaven, is there nothing I can say or do . . . ?'

She had reached the door. She paused to look back at him; he thought she had never looked more beautiful, nor more distant from him.

'Philip, if you ever cared for me at all,' she said, in a voice trembling on the brink of a sob, 'if there is any vestige of pity left within you, I beg you to spare me the cruelty of another meeting. What is done cannot be undone. You have chosen the path you wish to follow, and I, I must find my own way. Please, don't make my journey any more difficult than it is already.'

With that, she was gone, the silence and the emptiness of the room falling about him like a great, dark curtain. After a long moment Philip stumbled to his feet. He had had wine sent up earlier and now he went to it, pouring himself a glass, and half emptying it in one swallow.

He caught sight of himself in the mirror over the dresser. The eyes in the glass mocked him. Fool, they seemed to be saying, Fool, fool, fool.

He lifted the bottle and refilled his glass, realizing as he did so that he was drinking Brussac-America wine, bottled by

Jolene's own father, perhaps blended with the very wine he had shipped from France.

France. How distant it seemed, how long ago, when Jolene had come to him, and they had invested their blossoming love with all the ardor of their innocence.

He tilted his glass to drink again but the light caught it and turned the wine to blood. The blood of the Brussacs, Aunt Marie had called it.

Suddenly he could stand the mocking image in the mirror no more. He hurled his glass at it, watching the reflection vanish in a thousand shattered fragments. With a low groan of despair he flung himself across the bed, oblivious to the crimson rivulets that ran down the wall and spilled onto the floor.

29

Jolene was grateful that David was out when she returned to his apartment. She had sunk into a sort of waking stupor in which she walked and moved about mechanically while her mind and her senses were stunned beyond feeling.

She drank several brandies in quick succession, hoping that the shock of the raw alcohol would provide the shot in the arm she needed, but she might as well have been drinking water. In despair, she threw herself across the bed. She had hardly slept at all the night before and here at last the brandy did help; in a short while she had fallen asleep.

It was evening when she woke, the bedroom already cloaked in deepening shadows. She sat up, grimacing at the wrinkled condition of her gown, and saw from the clock over the mantel that it was nearly seven, though the silence of the apartment told her David had not yet come in.

She was glad that he had been delayed, as it gave her an opportunity to make herself presentable. Whatever she might be suffering inwardly, she had no intention of baring her personal griefs to David.

She bathed hurriedly and slipped into a fresh gown, combing out her lustrous hair so that it hung in loose curls about her face and shoulders.

She glanced at the clock again and frowned. It was after eight and still no David. She thought back over the previous evening's conversation; yes, he had definitely planned on being here this evening, they were to go to a supper a bit later. It was unlike him to forget an engagement, or even to be late.

Another evening she might have welcomed the time to herself, but tonight she did not feel like being alone. She found her thoughts returning all too easily to the scene with Philip.

She took down a book from the shelf and tried to read but the words kept blurring before her eyes and at last she gave up the attempt in exasperation, pacing nervously to and fro.

When at last, an hour later, she heard the key in the lock she was almost giddy with relief. She hurried into the little foyer, only to find herself facing not David, but his mother Clara.

'Yes, I can well imagine you're surprised to see me,' Clara greeted her curtly. 'David was under the delusion that I was unaware of his little love nest. No doubt you shared the delusion.'

'I really hadn't thought about it,' Jolene replied, recovering a semblance of poise. 'But do come in, please.'

'I'm already in,' Clara said, sweeping past her into the living-room.

'David isn't here,' Jolene said, following her. 'If you'd like to wait, I'm sure he'll be glad to see you.'

Clara gave her a wry smile. 'I'm sure you don't believe that any more than I do,' she said. 'Anyway, it would be rather a long wait.'

'I'm afraid I don't know what you mean,' Jolene said, though a new fear was beginning to form in her mind.

'I'm well aware David isn't here. Unlike you, however, I do know where he is.'

The fear grew stronger. 'Then perhaps you can tell me,' Jolene said, struggling to remain outwardly calm.

For an answer Clara went to the bay window, pulling aside the lace curtains to gaze into the fog-shrouded night. When at last she spoke, without turning, her words fell like blows.

'At this precise moment, David is on a ship, sailing out of San Francisco Bay.'

'I – I don't understand,' Jolene stammered, her self-control cracking as the import of Clara's words became increasingly clear.

Clara turned from the window with a smile of malicious triumph. 'He's on his way to Hawaii, to our facilities there.

He'll be working there for the next several months, perhaps longer, it all depends on how he behaves himself.'

For a long moment the two women regarded one another across the width of the room. Jolene swallowed hard, fighting for her self-possession. She saw now that she had been a fool to think that David could keep a mistress without his mother knowing about it; twice a fool, because she knew both David and his mother well enough to know how securely Clara kept her son tied to her silken apron strings. She could well imagine the scene between the two of them – had David argued for her at all, defended her, insisted that he was a grown man with a life of his own to lead? She doubted it; it was not David's way, to stand up to his strong-willed mother. Or, for that matter, to any other woman. For her, it had been a useful flaw in his makeup, but she ought to have been clever enough to see how easily it could work against her.

She drew her shoulders back and tilted her chin angrily upward. Very well, she might have been outmaneuvered by this shrewd, arrogant woman, but she would not give her the additional satisfaction of tears and distress.

'What you're saying,' she said with an icy composure that surprised even herself, 'is that you sent David away, to get him away from me?'

'Precisely.'

'That was rather drastic, wasn't it? You could have just forbidden him to see me, couldn't you?'

Clara smiled again. 'I could have, but then I already knew what a lovely creature you are, my dear – and how weak-willed my son can be. He might have stayed away for a time, but eventually he'd have gotten back to you.'

Jolene shrugged, going to the brandy and pouring herself a glass. She deliberately did not offer anything to the older woman.

'Would that have been so terrible a thing?' she asked. 'David is a normal young man, after all; it's hardly so shocking that he should be attracted to a woman.'

'To a woman like yourself, you mean. And David is hardly "normal", as you put it, he is an Ecks, with all the wealth and responsibility that entails. Even if your reputation is unimportant, his – and ours – is not. In time he must take his place as one of the pillars of society, but people can hardly be expected to respect and trust a man who keeps fancy women in shabby little hideaways.'

Jolene's eyes flashed angrily. 'My lineage is at least the equal of yours; my mother is the daughter of French aristocracy.'

'Your father was a grape picker. Your mother ran away from home with him because her father wouldn't have him as a son-in-law – you see, my dear, I know all about your aristocratic lineage.'

Although she was seething inwardly, Jolene managed a mocking laugh. 'Perhaps you know less about the pillars of our local society. I think few of them would be shocked by David's behavior. It's rather tame, I assure you, compared to most.'

'A subject on which I have no doubt you are expert,' Clara said sharply. 'But I did not come here to trade gutter talk with you, I came to tell you that your little idyll is over. You shall have to vacate this apartment.'

'That's for David to say, isn't it?' Jolene said with a show of false bravado, since she knew how little likelihood there was of David's disagreeing with his mother's decision.

'Not any more,' Clara said, undeceived by Jolene's air of confidence. 'It never really was, to be frank. David has no money of his own but the allowance I give him. It is my money that has paid the rent here, though to be honest it was described to me as an artist's studio. It was I who paid the bills for all those gowns and hats and other articles of clothing he showered on you so lavishly, just as it was I who paid for that brandy you are drinking now. So you see, I am entirely within my rights by ordering you from the place.'

Jolene's self-control wavered once again in the face of a rising sense of panic. 'Surely you can't mean to put me out on the street without a moment's notice. It's already late, I have no place to go . . .'

Clara smiled with genuine satisfaction at having finally pierced the girl's protective armor. 'I hadn't meant for you to leave quite this minute,' she said. Jolene breathed a quick sigh of relief, but it was dashed the next moment. 'You can leave tomorrow, provided you take nothing but what belongs to you.'

'I don't understand . . .'

'I'm referring to the clothes David bought for you – they shall be left behind. And of course, there is the necklace. I'm sure you wouldn't expect to keep that.'

'But these things are mine,' Jolene exclaimed. 'They were gifts to me from David. Surely a present becomes one's property.'

'Not, I'm afraid, in this instance,' Clara said. 'They were bought with my money ...'

'Money you had given David,' Jolene interrupted her. 'It isn't as if he stole it. Or as if I stole the things he gave me.'

'It is exactly as if they were stolen. I gave him no leave to spend a fortune on presents for you. He lied to me about the uses for the money. And as for you, no decent woman would have accepted such gifts from a man to whom she is not married.'

'And what of a woman who is at the mercy of men and their greedy lusts?' Jolene demanded hotly. 'A woman without money of her own is nothing but a pawn in the hands of men like your son. If there is any blame, let it be attached to the men who buy the symbols of a love they are unworthy to attain. Let it attach to a society which treats women like chattels. Regardless of what you may think of me, I am a person too, in my own right. David did not buy me, Mrs Ecks, only the use of my body.'

'This is outrageous. I demand that you return that necklace to me this instant, or suffer the consequences of your actions.'

'I'm afraid you're a little late with that threat,' Jolene said with a rueful smile. 'Now if you'll excuse me, I'm afraid I must pack if I'm to be gone in the morning.'

Clara Ecks was furious, her lips working for a few seconds in a wordless sputter. 'I warn you,' she managed to croak. 'I warn you.'

She left in a swirl of taffeta and a crashing of doors. When she had gone, Jolene stood for a few moments pondering the sudden change in her situation. At length she turned out the lights and made her way into the bedroom. She opened the door of the dresser and removed the velvet-lined box with the sapphire pendant.

It was at the moment her only tangible asset. She ought to be able to sell it for enough to live on for a considerable time.

But it was not merely economic necessity that had caused her to refuse to give the necklace to Clara Ecks. Despite everything that Clara had said, Jolene genuinely felt that she was rightfully entitled to the gems. She had earned them. After all, she had not gone to bed with David because she loved him nor because of any physical appeal on his part. Theirs had been a business arrangement, pure and simple. David had gotten what he wanted from the relationship; she had denied him nothing within reason. It was not fair now that she should be robbed of the gifts he had given her in return. Though the monetary value differed, his gifts were no more precious than hers had been.

Still, she was not so much a fool as to underestimate Clara's wrath. She made up her mind that she would rise early and be gone from the apartment before Clara returned to exert any more pressure on her. It would not take long to pack most of her belongings tonight. In the morning she would rent a hackney cab and set out to find herself lodgings, something simple and clean, and not too expensive. She would have to be frugal, but with the nest-egg the necklace would provide, she would be able to acquire training in some office skills. That would enable her to get a job so that in the future she would be able to provide for herself, without depending upon the dubious generosity of the Davids of the world.

At least, she thought wryly, there was one bonus to her present predicament: it hadn't allowed her any time to reflect on her meeting with Philip.

As it turned out, she had after all underestimated Clara's wrath. Though she packed her things the same night and rose with the dawn, she was not quite quick enough.

She was just putting on her hat before the mirror in the entry way when there was an imperious knock at the door and she opened it to find three men there, two in police uniforms and a third in a suit and bowler.

'Miss Perreira?' the man in the suit greeted her.

'Yes, but what . . .'

'Can we come in?' he asked, entering without waiting for a reply. The other two followed him. They went into the living-room, taking note of the packed bags sitting in the center of the room.

'What is this about?' Jolene demanded, following them.

'We've had a complaint about some stolen property,' the suited man, obviously in charge, informed her. 'Specifically, a necklace made of diamonds and sapphires – have you got such a necklace?'

'Why, yes – but it's mine,' she replied. 'It was a gift.'

He narrowed his eyes and his lips curled into a cruel smile. 'Can you prove that?'

'I . . .' She hesitated; how could she prove her statement? The only one besides herself who knew the truth was David, and by now he was at sea, on his way to Hawaii.

Taking her confusion for a negative answer, he gestured toward the bags. 'We can search those if we have to, but it'd be better for you if you tell us where the necklace is.'

Jolene felt as if she were drowning in the sea, sinking beneath great, smothering waves. Wordlessly she went to her valise and, opening it, removed the velvet case with the necklace.

The officer opened it, holding the gems up to the light. His little, animal eyes gleamed greedily at the sight, before he replaced them in the case and thrust the case into his pocket.

'I'm afraid you'll have to come with us,' he said.

'But I don't see why,' she said, her cheeks flushing angrily. 'You have the necklace, that's what you came for, isn't it?'

'Not entirely. We'll have to place you under arrest, don't you see?' He grinned again, plainly enjoying the sport he was having with her.

'Arrest? But you can't mean that. What are you arresting me for?'

'Theft. Possession of stolen property. A Mrs Clara Ecks claims these jewels were stolen from her. Also claims you're working as a whore – excuse me, a loose woman. Now, if you'll just come with us . . .'

'This is outrageous,' Jolene cried. 'I won't go, you can't make me . . .'

One of the uniformed officers took a step forward. The light from the window gleamed from a pair of handcuffs. Her face went pale as the blood drained from it.

'No, please,' she begged in a frightened voice; she had a horrible vision of herself being handcuffed and dragged through the streets in humiliation. 'Please, I'll go with you, only, don't use those things.'

The policeman hesitated until the suited man nodded. 'No trouble now, though,' he warned her, taking her arm.

'My things,' she gestured helplessly toward her bags.

'We'll take care of them,' he said, piloting her out of the room. 'Anyway, you won't be needing them for a while.'

His words struck an ominous chord in her already terrified heart. What was to become of her? Without the necklace, she was penniless. Worse, she was charged as a thief, and there was no one who could prove otherwise except David. Even if he could be returned from Hawaii, he would never stand up to his fiery mother, she was certain of that.

The police wagon was parked at the curb outside. To her

horror a crowd of onlookers had gathered to see what was transpiring. They gawked and shouted as she was escorted from the building on the arm of the officer. Jolene hung her head, trying to hide her face with her free hand. She tripped climbing into the back of the wagon and would have sprawled on the floor had it not been for the help of her companion, who climbed in after her. The two uniformed men took their places up front, and the wagon lurched off.

No sooner had they begun to move than the man with her scrambled across the wagon and fell upon her, pawing at her like a savage animal.

'Stop it, how dare you,' she cried, struggling against him.

'You're in a lot of trouble, sugar pie, don't give me that hoity-toity stuff,' he grunted, tearing at the bodice of her dress. 'It'll go a lot better for you if I put in a good word or two, believe me.'

'No, don't,' she said, helpless to escape his powerful embrace in the close quarters of the wagon. The fabric of her dress yielded to his efforts, tearing away to expose her breasts to his frantic efforts. He dropped his head, kissing and biting and making her yelp with pain, even as she felt a hand snatching and pawing beneath her skirt, his nails raking the delicate flesh of her thighs.

She bent and sank her teeth viciously into one large ear, feeling the flesh tear and tasting the blood in her mouth. He gave a bellow of rage and brought up a hand to slap her viciously. She was seized and thrown to the floor of the van like a rag doll, striking her head as she landed. Stunned, she lay helpless as he fell over her and she felt his brutal, tearing entry into her.

'You bitch,' he snarled, pounding her unmercifully. 'You think I ain't as good as those society fops you've been giving it to; well, I'm gonna show you what a real man's like.'

She lay sobbing and limp until she felt him stiffen and then collapse limply on top of her. After a moment he got up, rearranging his clothes.

'Get up, we're almost there,' he growled, wiping a streak of blood from the ear she'd bitten. 'And I hope to hell you rot in that prison they're going to send you to. Get up, I said.'

She managed somehow to crawl to the hard bench, in the farthest corner of the wagon from him. Her body ached with the savagery of the assault and she felt the prick of splinters from the wooden floor, but the physical pains were nothing compared to what she was suffering inwardly. She felt like a piece of cheap baggage, with no will of her own, and no purpose but to be used by animals such as the one still cursing her under his breath, despite having had his way with her.

Was this what it meant to be a woman, she wondered? She had always been taught to believe in a God of justice – was it possible that there were two Gods, one meting out justice to men and the other powerless, unjust, whose charges women were? Perhaps their God was a woman too, helpless in her domain as women were helpless here in this man's world.

She had been struggling to find herself, to find a place in that world in which she could live in freedom and dignity. But maybe, after all, her struggles were a foolish delusion. Wouldn't it be wiser to surrender, surrender to the men like this one, and David and Richard and yes, Philip too, who wanted to use her for their own purposes. They thought she had no rights of her own, that her body, any woman's body, was theirs to use, not hers to own. Perhaps they were right, perhaps women were lesser creatures than men.

Yet even as she thought this, an answering impulse rose up through the despair into which she had sunk. No, it shouted to her over the clamor of debasing voices, no – because to surrender would mean she valued herself no higher than the beast who had just so cruelly violated her; and it was a violation, it was a violation of everything that good and decent people believed to be true.

She could not prevent him, or others who were stronger or more powerful, from using her, but she need never resign herself to it. Resignation was a virtue only to the vanquished. Even if defeat were inevitable, accepting it only made it doubly so. Resignation was the slave's attempt to make a virtue of his slavery. Even though the man-forged chains that bound her might not be broken, she would remain a rebel to them. She would never acknowledge that the pain and fear and helplessness were good, or her God-given lot in life. Even if she had no longer the strength to fight, she would keep her freedom in her heart – the freedom to know and to say that what was done to her was wrong, no matter how in their might they justified it.

Men might overpower her, but no one but herself could defeat her. She fought down the sobs that had wracked her body, and gave her head a defiant toss, lifting her eyes to look directly at the man with her in the wagon.

He met the glance and misread it. 'Feeling better?' he asked with a leer. 'What do you think now about your society boyfriends? Don't measure up to a real man, do they?'

She managed a mocking smile, though her lips were cut and bleeding from his blow.

'You're unfit to call yourself a man,' she said in a low, even voice. 'You are a pollution, an obscenity.'

'Why, you little bitch . . . ' He moved toward her but to her relief the wagon came to an abrupt stop, and she realized that they had arrived at the station. Despite the nightmare ordeal that she knew awaited her, she could only be glad to have reached their destination.

And she had begun to form a plan – dangerous, perhaps, and certainly degrading – but preferable, overall, to the bottomless chasm that yawned before.

Better, she told herself grimly, than giving up.

30

Jolene was escorted into the station and to a desk where a florid-faced officer regarded her with obvious relish. Though her torn dress bared most of her bosom, Jolene no longer tried to preserve her modesty by holding the dress together; there were more important matters concerning her now.

'I want to see Captain Patterson,' she demanded before either her companion or the officer behind the desk could say anything.

The request produced immediate results. Both the men looked disconcerted. 'You're a friend of the Captain's?' the uniformed officer asked. The man who had brought her in looked positively frightened.

'We have mutual acquaintances,' Jolene replied. 'May I see him, please?'

After a moment's hesitation, the officer asked, 'Your name?' She told him and he scribbled it on a scrap of paper. 'Be right back,' he said, getting up from the desk and hurrying off along a corridor.

The man who had heretofore dragged Jolene about as if she were a piece of baggage had relinquished his hold on her arm and retreated several steps away, as if afraid contact with her might prove harmful. He eyed her warily as they waited, looking alternately disbelieving and cowed.

The officer was back in a few minutes, with instructions that she was to follow him. Ignoring the stares of the others about the stationhouse, who had begun to talk in low voices and glance in her direction, she tossed her head disdainfully and followed him to a closed door with the Captain's name printed on it in bold letters.

'In here,' he said, opening the door and stepping aside for her.

Jolene took a deep breath and swept into the room as grandly as if her dress were not in shreds and her hair in disarray.

The Captain, a tall, spare man with thinning hair and cold, intimidating eyes, rose from behind a desk as she entered the room.

'I'm told you asked to see me, Miss . . . ' He hesitated, consulting the scrap of paper that had been given him, 'Miss Perreira.' His scrutiny of her was rude and unfriendly. 'Have we met?'

'We have,' she said, refusing to be intimidated. 'Julia Benson introduced us at her house. I was just coming in as you were leaving.'

The mention of Julia's name caused the Captain's steady gaze to wave slightly. 'Ah, yes,' he said, managing a smile that did nothing to soften his manner, 'I believe I do recall – forgive me, I'm rather bad with names. Won't you have a seat, please?'

Jolene seated herself in one of the wooden chairs in front of his desk. The Captain seated himself behind it, taking a cigarette from a box atop his desk. He lit it with a kitchen match and exhaled a cloud of smoke in her direction. 'Would you like a cigarette?' he asked.

Jolene, who had always thought them odious, felt a need for something to give her courage. 'Yes, please,' she replied.

She took one, leaning toward the light that he offered her and puffing at it as she had seen him do. She nearly choked as the acrid smoke filled her mouth and nostrils, and she exhaled it quickly, making an effort to seem practiced at the business.

The Captain glanced again at the scrap of paper. 'These are serious crimes with which you're charged, Miss Perreira,' he said.

'No more serious than the crimes committed against me by one of your men,' she replied, taking another cautious puff on the cigarette. The smoke had made her curiously light-headed, which had had the effect of giving her the courage to pursue her course, though she knew it was a dangerous one; to anger the man seated across from her could have dire consequences. 'But I am sure that these matters can be dealt with in a civilized way.'

'You're suggesting that the charges be dropped?'

'I've no doubt they can be – for a friend of Julia's.'

'It might be necessary for you to go to trial,' he said.

Jolene stubbed out the cigarette in the dish on his desk. 'That would be unfortunate,' she said. 'Trials are such messy things, all sorts of sordid matters tend to be brought into the open. Surely with all Julia's influential gentlemen friends – yourself, judges, politicians . . . None of us really want a public display, do we?'

For the first time the smile that tugged at the corners of his mouth was one of genuine amusement, though it lasted no more than a few seconds. He got up, pushing his chair back noisily, and came around the desk to stand beside her. She resisted an impulse to shudder as she felt his hands, eerily cold, brush the back of her neck, stroking her hair. One hand slid downward, like a reptile gliding across her shoulder, to the exposed flesh of one breast, resting there ever so lightly for a brief space of time, before it was gone.

'You are a very beautiful woman,' he said in a husky voice.

She tilted her head, looking up to meet his eyes directly. 'Too beautiful to languish in a prison?' she asked, smiling boldly.

For a moment he returned her gaze. Then, abruptly, he turned from her. 'Please make yourself comfortable here,' he said, going to the door. 'I shall return shortly.'

She waited for what seemed hours, though it must have been no more than thirty or forty minutes. The cigarette she had smoked had left her stomach queasy, and after a brief stint of pacing the room, she sank into the wooden chair again and waited without stirring.

At last there was a footstep outside and Jolene rose from the chair, but it was not the Captain, it was Julia who came into the room.

'My dear child,' she said, coming across the room to peck at Jolene's cheek, 'how dreadful this all sounds. No, don't bother to explain, I've already learned that David has fled, and the rest I deduced for myself. I should have warned you that Mama would sooner or later intervene, she always does – but you seemed to know him so well.'

'Not well enough, apparently,' Jolene said dryly.

'A woman can never know a man well enough, not when she's at his mercy,' Julia said. 'That's why I make it my business to learn everything possible about them. But the dear Captain seemed to think it important that I come see you – tell me, what is it that you want from me?'

'I should think that's obvious,' Jolene replied. 'I want to get out of here.'

'And out of this difficulty?' Julia cocked an eyebrow.

'Yes, that too, of course.'

'Of course,' Julia paused to glance about the room, wrinkling her nose distastefully. 'Such things can be arranged. This is San Francisco, after all, anything can be arranged – with enough money.'

Jolene gave a mirthless bark of a laugh. 'Oh, come now, Julia, surely you haven't run out of wealthy gentlemen friends?'

Julia smiled in reply. 'No, indeed not. But as you've surely learned since last we met, the gentlemen who have the money almost always have – shall we say, expectations as well.'

'Have you someone in mind, someone who could help?'

Julia was thoughtful for a moment, her lips pursed. Then a slow smile spread over her features. 'Yes, I believe I do,' she said. 'However,' she added, the smile becoming questioning, 'he'll want a clear-cut understanding . . . ?'

Jolene returned the gaze frankly. 'Tell the gentleman he'll not regret his purchase,' she said.

'I hope not,' Julia said. She started for the door, then turned back as if suddenly remembering something. 'Oh, I nearly forgot, this came for you, by coincidence, just a short time before the Captain called me.'

She handed Jolene an envelope. Jolene did not need to open it to recognize Philip's energetic scrawl. Her hand trembling as she took it.

'I'll be back soon,' Julia said, giving a wave of her hand as she went out.

When she was alone, Jolene regarded the letter in her hand for a long moment. Finally, screwing up her courage, she tore the envelope open and removed the single sheet of paper from within.

It was a legal-looking document. She had to read it through twice before she grasped its full meaning. Philip had signed over to her all rights that he now owned or that might in the future revert to him in his family estate, French Hills.

Although it was hastily drawn, the document looked in order.

The stationery bore the imprint of a local law firm, and Philip's signature had been attested by two witnesses.

Her first reaction was one of astonishment. Here, in her hand, she held the very goal that her mother had pursued with such relentless conviction for so many years, the return of her inheritance, vindication of all the slights, real and imagined, that she had suffered.

Her astonishment gave way to angry resentment. She thought of her current predicament, and of what she had just promised in order to secure her freedom. Here was the money she'd needed, the wealth and power of the Brussacs. With this, she needn't sell herself to some stranger for the sake of salvation.

And yet, bitterest of all, it was worthless, this legal document, worthless to her because it came from Philip and, failing the one gift above all that she had wanted from him – his love – she could never accept another. To be beholden to the man who had used her and then so cruelly cast her aside to marry a common tramp? No, she would rather sell her body to Julia's client, whoever he might be; at least her soul would remain her own.

The Captain's cigarettes and matches were still on the desk. She struck a match and held it to the corner of the document. For a moment she was tempted – it would be so easy; use Philip, and his gift, as he had used her.

The paper began to burn. She held it until the flames were licking hungrily toward her fingers before she dropped it into the ashtray and watched it curl and shrivel into ashes, which finally she crumbled beneath her finger.

Philip was gone, and French Hills, and her mother's dreams. And gone too, she thought wryly, was the past that she had known, the girl that she had been. It was more than a legal paper she had burned, it was her life until now, gone in the fire and smoke.

Strangely, she felt almost relieved, as if born again. Her eyes fell on the cigarette box, and with a somewhat cynical smile she opened it and took out a cigarette.

As she lit it, she thought of how her mother would react to the sight; or, even more amusing, Clara Ecks and her Nob Hill cronies. It was still headline news for a lady of society to be observed smoking, though women of lesser station had been doing so for a few years. It was regarded as the mark of a loose woman, at the very least.

A loose woman – that was how the policeman who had

arrested her had phrased it. And all in all, it was an apt description, for a woman who lived and slept with men she did not love, who bargained to keep herself out of prison, who . . . she exhaled a cloud of smoke, finding this second experience easier than the first . . . a woman who smoked cigarettes.

That, after all, was the course which she was now traveling. It was a course she might not have chosen had she known the consequences of each of the steps she had taken, but it was a path to which she was now well committed, and she made up her mind that she would travel it without regrets, without looking back. Whatever came to her, she would deal with it unflinchingly, to the best of her abilities. Let others judge her or not, as they wished; her first obligation was to herself, to survive.

And that, she vowed to do somehow.

31

Jolene's relief at Julia's return was short lived. The sound of Julia's voice outside the office brought her from the chair in which she had been sitting impatiently, and after a moment the door opened, but it was Captain Patterson who came into the room. The smile that he gave her seemed particularly cynical.

'Everything's set,' he said, going to his desk and riffling through the papers there. He looked as if there were something more he wanted to say, but he restrained himself.

'You mean, I'm free to go?' Jolene asked, a bit incredulously; it had been altogther too easy, even allowing for Julia's connections. It seemed that in San Francisco even Justice was a loose woman.

He gave her a look that was difficult to read, though oddly enough she thought she saw a hint of sadness in it.

'Julia's waiting outside for you,' he said, 'with her friend, your benefactor.'

'But what about the charges against me?'

'They've been dismissed – lack of sufficient evidence, something like that.'

'Then – ' She still had difficulty believing with what ease she had freed herself from her predicament, ' – I'm free? I can go?'

'You can go,' he said. 'I don't know how free you'll find yourself.'

The words rang an ominous note. She edged toward the door, half expecting that at any minute he would stop her from going, revealing that he had only been taunting her.

The Captain remained unmoving at his desk, however, and with a last, puzzled glance over her shoulder, she went out into the corridor.

At first glance she did not recognize the man engaged in conversation with Julia. They heard the opening and closing of the door, and both turned in her direction, giving Jolene her first full look at the gentleman. She felt suddenly as if a yawning chasm had opened at her feet. She stood stock-still as the couple approached her.

'And this is the young lady we've come to rescue,' the gentleman said, smacking his lips audibly. 'I must say, Julia, you didn't exaggerate one iota, she is lovely indeed.'

'Judge Carver,' Jolene found the voice to say, 'this is an honor. I had no idea it was you Julia had in mind.'

'Have we met?' the Judge said, taking one of her hands in his and squeezing it so tightly that he threatened to break bones. 'Surely I'd remember . . .'

'No. but I know who you are,' Jolene replied.

'You know, Judge,' Julia said, looking altogether pleased with herself, 'your name is practically a household word in San Francisco these days.'

'Depending upon the house,' Jolene could not resist adding.

Far from being offended, the Judge found the remark hilarious, his booming laugh echoing along the gloomy corridor. Studying his round, porcine face, Jolene felt her initial dread growing with each passing second.

She had been duped by Julia, led to believe that her rescue was being arranged when in fact Julia, for her own cruel amusement or perhaps to punish Jolene for her earlier haughty behavior, had arranged an even more dreadful dilemma. She had seen and heard enough from Amy to know what sort of man the Judge was; it was he, after all, who had driven Amy to commit suicide rather than spend another evening in his company.

And now he had, to use her own choice of words, 'purchased' her. Short of Satan himself, she could not have chosen a worse man to whom to be obligated.

'The Judge has been most helpful in getting the charges against you dropped,' Julia said.

'Happy to oblige,' the Judge said; his florid face assumed a sober expression. 'That's not to make light of the gravity of the charges, my dear. I trust that you have learned a valuable lesson from this experience.'

'Indeed, I have,' Jolene assured him, unable to bear the sight of Julia's smirking face. 'And of course I am grateful.'

'That's all the reward I ask, your sincere gratitude,' the Judge declared, beaming. The greedy appraisal of his eyes gave a lie to his remark. 'Well, now, shall we be going, no need to hang around here, there's much nicer places.'

'I'm afraid I must be on my way,' Julia said, smiling sweetly. 'Jolene's call took me away from important business – though never too important to help out a friend, I always say.'

'So generous of you,' the Judge said. 'Now, just you go right ahead and run along; this young lady and I can manage for ourselves, can't we, little darling, we'll just use the time to get better acquainted.'

Jolene resisted an involuntary shudder as he took her arm and forcefully guided her along the corridor. She would sooner get better acquainted with a rattler. She moved numbly along at the Judge's side, trying not to think of what lay in store for her.

The Judge's elegant brougham waited at the curb. For a moment Jolene hesitated before entering, wondering if she dared try to run away; she knew it was futile, however, she could hardly expect to outrun a horsedrawn carriage, nor was the Judge likely to let her go without pursuing her. He no doubt had had to invest a considerable amount of money to secure her freedom. Considering that the charges against her had been brought by Clara Ecks, it was certain that the Judge had not purchased her cheaply.

She only wished that she could take some satisfaction from that knowledge, Jolene thought, entering the carriage. The Judge gave instructions to his driver and climbed in after her.

Jolene pressed herself into the far corner as the carriage began to move, but the Judge was unintimidated by her distance. He dropped a meaty hand upon her knee, squeezing until she winced from pain, his little dark eyes glittering brightly.

'Now, now, my pet, you mustn't be frightened, you and I will be the best of friends in no time. Yes sir, in no time at all, you'll see.'

'What – what exactly do you expect of me?' she asked in a dry voice.

He laughed aloud again, his massive belly trembling gelatinously. 'Why, I just want you to be nice to me, that's all there is to it. I'm a lonely man, don't you see, my wife died on me seven, no, eight years ago, a man gets powerful lonely in eight years. I like to have a pretty young thing like yourself around to take care of me. I have a lot of responsibilities, I need to relax and enjoy myself when I can. That's all it is, little honey, I just mean to have some fun.'

She wanted to ask his definition of 'some fun', but the words would not come. She could not erase from her mind the memory of Amy, trembling in terror at the prospect of another evening in this man's company; Amy, battered and bruised from his 'fun'.

The carriage ride was all too brief. Aside from the hand on her knee, the Judge had not touched her, nor had he spoken beyond his brief remarks on his intentions, but she had been unable to ignore the leering glances he had cast frequently in her direction. Now, he seemed all too eager to be out of the coach and inside the ornate Victorian structure that was his home. The closing of the elaborately carved front door after them sounded to Jolene like the sealing of a tomb.

'Are there no servants?' she asked, her voice seeming to echo through the still house.

'They're in their own quarters, in the basement, and they never bother me unless I call them,' he said. 'You needn't worry your pretty little head about them, you just come along with me.'

The stairs up which he escorted her were steep and dimly lighted. Her first idea was that he was taking her to a bedroom on the second floor, but he bypassed that floor and continued upward to the third, mounting an even steeper and narrower flight of stairs that ended at a closed door.

Instinctively, as they climbed toward the forbidding door, Jolene found herself drawing back, but the hand gripping her elbow tightly urged her on. With his free hand the Judge produced a weighty ring of keys and quickly unlocked the door. It swung inward and he led her into the attic room.

For a moment Jolene was confused by the unfamiliar furnishings, mostly things that she had read or heard about but had never actually seen before. Of course she was familiar with chains and ropes, and the buggy whip hanging on a peg by the door was no mystery; but she did not immediately grasp the significance of the manacles attached to the wall, nor the branding irons, nor the huge and rusted pincers atop a nearby table.

She stood turning slowly about, staring with ever-widening eyes, and slowly the horrible comprehension began to dawn on her.

'They're instruments of torture,' she said, hardly able to credit the words even as she spoke them, so unbelievably ghastly did they seem; and yet here was the evidence, before her, unmistakable in its purpose. 'This is a torture chamber.'

The Judge gave one of his coarse laughs and wagged a finger before her nose. 'A harsh term, I prefer to call this my playroom,' he said, 'and besides, you shall see, there's not a device here that isn't conducive to pleasure of one sort or another.'

'Surely not the victim's,' she replied.

'Oh, ho, pet, what a delicious wit you have, I can see we're going to enjoy our little time together immensely – indeed, I can hardly wait to begin.'

To her added horror he suddenly seized her in an embrace, crushing her violently to him and attempting to smother her lips with his own.

Jolene struggled against him, turning her face this way and that to avoid his kisses. His breath was fetid, and but for her terror of what might happen she would surely have fainted away on the spot.

'What – what do you mean to do?' she asked, gasping for breath in his smothering embrace.

He suddenly put his lips to her ear and began to whisper. She felt a tide of revulsion rising within her as the obscene phrases spilled from his mouth, like a stream of sewage inundating her. Though she had thought herself a loose woman and no longer a stranger to sexual matters, she could feel her face burning crimson – these were ways in which surely neither God nor nature had intended that flesh be used, a sexual vomit that seemed even to fill the air with a loathsome stench.

His breath was an excited rasp against her cheek. In his mounting heat he had somewhat loosened his hold on her and with a strangled cry she twisted free of his arms.

'God in Heaven,' she cried, 'you are loathsome!'

He shook his head, smiling sardonically. 'The ideas are just new to you. I assure you, when you've tried them . . . '

'Don't touch me.' She took a step backward.

'They all act the same at first, but you'll get used to it in no time. Why, before this night's over I'll wager your tune will be changed.'

Like a ghost, the image of Amy suddenly reappeared to her, not the lovely, love-starved waif who had come to her room to chat, but the limp and lifeless figure bathing in her own blood.

'You killed her,' she said aloud. 'You tortured and degraded her until she could no longer bear her own ravaged flesh, until she was so filled with shame and disgust that she could endure no more.'

His smile faded to be replaced by a menacing scowl. 'I don't know what you're talking about,' he said. 'Enough of this . . .'

'Amy. You drove her to kill herself.'

She saw him blanch at the mention of the name. 'I don't know anyone by that name,' he said angrily.

'But you did, I know that you did, and I know now what you did to her. Her death is on your hands.'

Her brutal accusations put him momentarily at a loss. 'They told me she'd run away,' he stammered. 'I don't know anything about anyone killing themselves.'

'You're lying,' she said, anger giving her courage. 'You know she died. I shall tell the city, the whole world, about it, about you, about this – this place . . .'

'You little fool, you'll tell nothing. Have you forgotten that I bought and paid for you, that I saved you from prison – yes, and using the same influence that let me keep her death a secret. Do you think I'd let you jeopardize my position in this community, when I've worked so long and hard to safeguard it?'

'You can't stop me,' she said. 'Unlike Amy I won't kill myself to protect your filthy secrets.'

He laughed again, but this time it was an ominous sound that sent a new tide of fear coursing through her. 'There are many ways to prevent talking,' he said. He saw the quick glance she threw toward the still opened door and, moving with an agility surprising in one of his age and build, he moved to block her path, at the same time again seizing her wrist, this time so roughly that she cried out in pain.

'Scream your head off if you like,' he said, chuckling. 'No one will hear you up here, and even if they should do so, they won't interfere – you're not, I might say, the only one who's ever screamed while she was here, though not all with displeasure.'

'Let me go,' she cried, struggling in his grip. His response was to clutch her wrist even more tightly, making her cry out again. He dragged her across the room, to the rusted manacles chained to the wall. With his free hand he seized the huge pincers she had noticed before.

'There's more than one way to stop a loose tongue,' he said, brandishing them menacingly. 'It won't wag if I pull it out with these, eh?'

She fought the faintness that threatened to engulf her, flattening herself against the wall. Her fingers brushed the length of chain and almost without thinking she clutched it in her hand and brought it lashing upward, into his leering face.

The unexpected blow stunned him, causing him to let go her wrist and stagger backward. In an instant she had darted past him and reached the door, but almost as quickly he had recovered and dashed after her, seizing her once again at the top of the stairs.

'You little bitch,' he swore, shaking her so violently that her head snapped to and fro, 'I'll teach you . . . '

Afterward, she was not entirely sure how it happened. The blow to his head must have left him still somewhat dazed, and with that and the violence of his anger he was careless of his step. He turned to shove her back into the room, but as he did so his foot went back and when he brought it down again, he missed the top step. He lost his balance.

For a moment he tilted precariously on one foot, a moment in which he could easily have righted himself – and in that moment Jolene brought her hands up to his chest, and pushed against him with all of her strength.

He seemed to hang suspended for a second or two, his eyes widening with a disbelief that became, at the very last, as he comprehended what was happening, horror; and then he was gone, toppling head over heels down the steep, narrow stairs, the banister breaking when he seized it in an attempt to stop his fall. He carried a piece of railing with him as he fell.

It took an eternity for him to reach the landing far below. There was a final dull thud, and all was still, the house lying in shocked silence about her. Still breathing heavily, Jolene remained motionless, staring downward, waiting for the crumpled form below to stir, to rise, to become Judge Carver once again – but it did not, and gradually she became aware of details that had escaped her before. She saw the way he was lying, the impossible angle at which his head was twisted to the side, and then she knew that he was dead and that she had killed him.

32

Horror at what she had done overwhelmed her, and for a minute or two Jolene could do nothing but stand shivering at the top of the stairs, staring downward, her mind a confusing whirl of thoughts, feelings, sensations.

The distant sound of a door opening and closing brought her back to the reality of the situation. She held her breath, pressing herself back against the doorjamb – was someone coming to investigate the disturbance? The Judge's fall had sounded deafening to her ears, but would it have been heard in the servants' quarters? Hadn't he told her that the servants had orders not to disturb him here?

She waited a full minute, two, and no one came, no one screamed, 'The master's been murdered!'

Murdered. The word stuck in her mind, came screaming back at her as if it echoed from the very rafters of the house. Murdered . . . murdered . . . murdered . . .

She could stand it no longer. She ran recklessly down the stairs, slowing her pace only as she neared the bottom. She paused for a second or two over the Judge's body, telling herself that she ought to examine him, to be certain that he was dead, but she could not bring herself to touch him. Although she did not regard herself as a particularly religious person, she nevertheless crossed herself hastily.

The house was empty. She ran breathlessly down the two remaining flights of stairs, half expecting at any second that someone would step from the shadows and block her path. And finally, there was the door to the street. She ran as if pursued by demons, flinging it open, dashing through – into the arms of the man standing outside.

'Damn it to hell, what do you . . . why, it's Jolene,' he said, trying to hold her still. In her terror she thought she had been seized and was struggling wildly against him. It took a moment for recognition to dawn on her and when it did she went nearly limp with relief.

'Walter McCrea,' she said; after all the times she and David had laughed at Walter and his penny-pinching ways, she could hardly believe how glad she was to see him. 'What are you doing here?'

'Coming to see the Judge on some business,' he said. 'From the looks of you, though, I think I ought to be asking you that question.'

He glanced past her, through the still open door, as if expecting to see someone in pursuit of her. 'The way you came through that door I thought the devil himself was after you.'

He made a move as though to step inside. She clutched frantically at the sleeve of his coat. 'Walter, don't go in there,' she cried.

He gave her a puzzled look, and glanced again through the door. 'What the hell's going on here?' he demanded. For the first time he took a good look at her. 'You look a sight, your clothes all torn and your hair hanging in your face. And those bruises . . . '

The tension caught up with her at last. Although she tried to hold them back, the tears began to scald her eyes, and she suddenly found herself sobbing into her hands, her body trembling uncontrollably. Even Walter McCrea's arms were comforting as they came about her in an unexpectedly tender gesture.

'Here, here,' he said on a more gentle note, 'why don't you just tell me what's been going on and maybe I can help you out.'

'Oh, nobody can help me now, it's hopeless, I've killed him . . . '

She felt Walter's body stiffen. 'You mean the Judge?' he asked, instinctively lowering his voice to a whisper.

She nodded her head violently. 'Jesus Almighty,' Walter croaked. 'Here, come back inside . . . '

'No!' She jerked back as if burned when he tried to usher her through the door. 'I – I can't go in there, please, I just can't . . . '

'All right, then, wait here, but for Pete's sake, stop that bawling, people are going by, the last thing you want now is a crowd of spectators, right?'

He let her go and, realizing the wisdom of what he was saying, Jolene made an effort to control the sobs that had been wracking her body. Walter started inside.

'On the stairs, the attic stairs,' she said. He nodded grimly and disappeared inside. She heard his footsteps, light on the stairs, and then the silence returned.

She saw a passing couple give her a peculiar look. The front of the house was shaded by a long porch. Jolene sat in one of the wicker chairs arranged at one end of the porch, trying to look inconspicuous. Her eyes kept darting to the open door through which Walter had disappeared.

It seemed hours before he returned, closing the door softly; a line of sweat beaded his upper lip, his eyes were wide with fright. She stood, and he took her arm, hurrying her down the steps to the street.

'I almost ran into one of the maids, on her way upstairs,' he muttered, glancing anxiously over his shoulder. 'If she goes on up there, all hell's going to break loose.'

'Did you – see him?' she asked.

'Christ, did I? He's dead all right, neck broke – did anyone see you in there?'

'No, only the Judge.'

He gave a dry bark of a laugh. 'Well, he won't be telling, that's for sure,' he said.

They found a hackney cab at the next corner. Walter fairly shoved her inside and, giving the driver directions, climbed in after her. She sank gratefully into the seat cushions, hardly able to believe.

'Where are you taking me?' she asked after a few minutes.

'Not to the police station,' he said, 'which is where you'd be headed if I hadn't come along when I did. Damn, this fool's taking the long way round.' He rapped for the driver, shouting for him to take the next street.

The realization that Walter McCrea had actually hired a cab for her suddenly struck her as amusing. In all the time since she'd known him, people had made jokes regarding his tight-fisted attitude toward money: 'What would it take to make Walter pay for a ride? was a sure way of getting a few laughs. And at last she'd found the definitive answer – one had only to kill a man. She began to laugh, softly at first, then louder.

'Here, stop that,' he snapped. 'Don't go getting hysterical on me, or I'll put you down at the corner.'

That suggestion sobered her quickly. Now that it appeared she actually had escaped the nightmare of the Judge's house, and the Judge's death, the future was even more of a blank than it had been before. Though he was the most unlikely rescuer she could think of, she was most certainly in Walter's hands.

The cab came to a stop. Walter got out and paid the driver, leaving her to get down unassisted. She glanced at the run-down building before them, once a proper mansion, now obviously a boarding house, and none too grand a one at that.

'You live here?' she asked when he came to join her. She did not miss the way that his eyes, less fearful now and far more confident than she had seen them before, moved quickly up and down her figure.

'The best I can do for you under the circumstances,' he said, taking her arm possessively. 'There's going to be all kinds of trouble over the Judge's murder. You're going to have to lay low somewhere till we see which way the wind blows.'

'I take it you don't mean to turn me over to the authorities,' she said.

For an answer, his hand slid around her waist, grazed lower over the curve of one hip. 'I figured we could work something out between us,' he said.

It soon began to seem as if she had traded one prison for another. Walter's 'laying low to see which way the wind blows' became a permanent hiding from view.

'All hell's broke loose over this thing,' he had informed her that very first day. 'Worst of all, they're looking for a mysterious woman known to be with the Judge when he was murdered.'

Although Walter assured her that her name had not been mentioned publicly, Jolene was all too painfully aware that there were those who knew the 'mysterious woman's' identity. Certainly Julia, and Captain Patterson of the police department, knew that she had left in the Judge's company only a short while before his death. That the police were actively searching for her she had no doubt, nor that the safest course for her was to do as Walter suggested and remain where she was, out of sight, at least until the furor subsided.

That did not make her confinement any more pleasant, however. She quickly came to hate the smell of frying fish – the daily meal, apparently – that drifted up from the landlady's kitchen, just below Walter's bedroom. A score or more of undisciplined children ran through the yard and up and down the building's corridors, their yelling and bawling punctuated from time to time by the landlady's shouted reprimands. Rats ran freely; once she had awakened with the dawn to find one regarding her steadily from atop the bed's headboard.

Then there was Walter. She could hardly complain that she was expected to cook and clean, nor even that he expected to be rewarded sexually for his efforts; after all, he had taken considerable risks in helping her and in continuing to shield her. No amount of cleaning, however, could make the filthy, shabby rooms they shared looked presentable, and it was impossible to prepare a decent meal from the limited foods of uniformly poor quality that he brought home, though he seemed to find them palatable enough. His appetite was not gargantuan; probably, she thought bitterly, because it cost less to eat lightly.

His sexual appetite, however, seemed boundless. At first he had approached her gingerly, with a slavish attitude, but with the passing of time he had become increasingly arrogant, increasingly demanding as he came to comprehend how completely she was at his mercy. The time of day or night mattered little to him, and no excuse would serve. If she attempted to be friendly toward him, it encouraged his desire; if she were cool, it was a challenge that must be met and overcome. She prayed for the times when he would go out, leaving her alone, but then the loneliness of her situation would weigh upon her until she almost prayed for his return, for human companionship and the sound of another's voice.

Nor did the furor that kept her a prisoner in this tawdry setting show any signs of relenting. 'The papers are still full of it,' Walter would report on his return. 'The police say they know just who they're looking for, and they mean to keep on it till they find her.'

'Couldn't you at least bring one of the papers home, so I could read the stories myself,' she complained, with no success.

'And spend my good money?' he replied, as shocked as if she had suggested some bawdy entertainment. 'Not a chance, not when I can read them free at the saloon.'

A week passed, two, a month; still she was his reluctant mistress. She chafed and fretted; with each day, the apartment seemed to grow smaller. She repaired the damage to her torn dress, made another from some cheap goods he brought when she insisted she must have at least a change of clothes. No matter how she tried to occupy her time, though, each day seemed longer than the one before.

'I want to go out,' she announced one evening as she was serving his dinner.

'Don't be crazy,' he said. 'Today's paper is just as full of this business as ever. Can't risk having you seen.'

'There's places that wouldn't be a problem.'

He began to eat noisily. 'I don't know what you're talking about,' he said.

'I'm talking about the Barbary Coast.'

He stopped his fork in mid-air. 'You *are* crazy.'

She went on, unintimidated. 'From what I used to hear, you know your way around down there. And it's certain we wouldn't have to worry about running into any of the society crowd, not in those places.'

'I can't take a lady to the Barbary Coast.'

She gave a yelp of laughter. 'It's rather late in the game to be worrying about my ladyhood, wouldn't you say?' she asked. Growing sober, she added, 'If you don't take me, I'll go anyway.'

'Go on, you haven't got a penny to your name.'

She grinned slyly. 'Yes, I have,' she said. 'I took your wallet out of your jacket when you were changing a little while ago.'

'Damnation!' He reached for the pocket, found it empty. 'Why, you little . . . ' His eyes narrowed.

'Call me whatever you like, I don't care. I want to get out of this apartment. I want to breathe some air that doesn't smell like stale fish and dirty children . . . '

'You think the Barbary Coast's going to be any better?' he argued. 'The place is filthy, rats running everywhere . . . '

'I've gotten used to them.'

He resumed eating his dinner, though with less enjoyment than before. 'You've gotten to be a real bitch,' he grumbled.

'It's a bitch's world,' she said; she noted that he stopped refusing. She attacked her own dinner enthusiastically, already thinking of how she could dress up her one clean gown. A short time before, she would have shuddered at the thought of visiting the infamous waterfront region with its cheap brothels, its gambling-halls and saloons; now the visit loomed like a tour of the Riviera.

33

A cacophony of sound poured from the open doors of the Golden Crest Saloon. Jolene tapped her foot impatiently, waiting for Walter to pay the cab driver. She ignored the cloud of cigar smoke and the stench of unbathed bodies too closely packed together. The babble of voices, the distant warble of an off-key soprano, the clink of glassware, were like a tonic after her enforced isolation, and when Walter finally joined her, she swept into the saloon before him looking scarcely less regal than the wealthy heiress who had once worn sables and silks to the opera.

The place was jammed, as indeed all of the saloons along the street had appeared to be, with crowds spilling over noisily onto the sidewalks outside. A drunk lurched against Jolene, mumbled an apology, and staggered on his way into a wall. At one time she might have been offended, but now she found the incident laughable. How good it was to see people, any people, enjoying themselves.

She maneuvered her way to an empty table, followed by a sulky Walter, and when a waiter with an appreciative eye for her bosom appeared, she ordered wine.

'Beer'll do,' Walter said.

'We'll have wine,' Jolene insisted.

The wine came with two dingy glasses, and when Walter grumbled that it wasn't worth the cost, she told him he had no taste, though in fact it needed no wine expert to know that it was a disappointing bottle.

Still, nothing could daunt her spirits at the moment; she was drunk on freedom, and she took in the scene hungrily. A makeshift stage had been erected along one wall, and the off-key soprano had given way to a juggler who was struggling to keep a half dozen or so apples moving through the air; from time to time one of the fruits fell into the audience, from whence it was returned violently, to the audience's roaring approval.

'I don't see what's so dangerous about this place,' Jolene said.

'This is one of the better-run places, believe me,' Walter replied. 'And they get their share of brawls and killings same as any other place down here.'

As if to prove his point, a fight suddenly erupted at a nearby table where some men had been playing cards. One of them accused another of cheating, and the accused leaped to his feet, brandishing a gun. With the swiftness of practice a bevy of waiters converged on the spot, one of them breaking a chair over the head of the armed man, with the result that a window was shot out but no one was wounded. The unconscious man was carried to the front door and unceremoniously tossed into the street outside.

'You see what I mean,' Walter said triumphantly. 'You'll end up getting us killed, traipsing around where we got no business being.'

'You've traipsed around here without getting killed,' she argued, though in fact she was a trifle shaken by the fight they'd witnessed.

'I went to a different kind of place, for one reason only,' he said.

'Well, I don't care, I'd rather be here than in that stinking apartment.'

'I'll take that as a compliment for the establishment,' a man's voice said from behind her chair. She looked over her shoulder at the tall stranger standing there, unconsciously squinting as she tried to identify him. He was very handsome, with the unruly chestnut hair and the dark eyes, twinkling now with a mischievous gleam; and he was familiar, but she simply could not place him.

'Have I met you,' she asked, suddenly frightened that he might be one of those society acquaintances she had meant to avoid.

'Why, Jolene, far more than met,' he said, grinning. 'We've even gone bathing together – no offense, my friend, the lady and I were fully dressed.'

The grinning face suddenly came into focus for her then. 'Sloan,' she cried, 'Sloan Morrow.'

He made a little bow from the waist. 'At your service, as always. But tell me, what brings you to my fair establishment? It's a little off your usual route, isn't it?'

'Your place,' she said, ignoring the question. 'You mean you own this saloon?'

'Don't say that too loudly, the customers here have some forthright ways of expressing their dissatisfaction. May I sit down?'

'Please do,' Jolene said, and Walter said, simultaneously, 'We were just talking about leaving.' He looked sullen until Sloan said, 'Can I buy a round?'

'Whiskey,' Walter said quickly.

Sloan signaled to waiter and asked for a bottle of whiskey – 'My private stock, ask Eddie to get it from the back,' he added.

It gave Jolene a moment to study him. She had scarcely thought of him in the time since they had last met, in the hills behind her home. What a child she had been then, and how long ago it seemed.

She was suddenly and painfully conscious of how she looked and the way she was dressed. And he, he looked dazzlingly elegant, the more so in contrast to the tawdry surroundings.

Sloan himself was using the conversation with the waiter to give himself time to recover from the shock of seeing her here, looking as she did.

He had seen her when she had first come in, but he had been unable to convince himself that it was really Jolene. She was the last person he'd expected to see in one of his establishments; the Nob Hill set did sometimes come slumming, but it was the fast crowd, of which she had never been a part.

From a distance he had watched and studied her, until he knew that it was no mistake, that it was really the girl of whom he had dreamed, the one he'd kissed by the bank of a flooding stream. His lips had kissed countless numbers of lips since then, yet he had still only to close his eyes to remember the touch of hers.

At last, unable to bear it any longer, he had approached the table, noting in dismay the shabby, patched dress – it could hardly be called a gown – that she wore, the pinched, drawn look of her face, the absence of jewelry and makeup.

Yet, strangely, she had never looked more beautiful; she was like a gemstone, lovely in its natural form, that had been cut, chipped, shattered, smoothed and polished, to achieve at last something nearing a perfect brilliance. The skin stretched taut over her face only served to accentuate the perfection of the structure beneath and the impact of her jade-green eyes, and though she had acquired something of a wanton air, she had at the same time retained a paradoxical aura of innocence which could not help but inflame a man's desire.

He could not imagine what she was doing with a scoundrel and a miser like Walter McCrea. A woman would have to be in love, or desperate, to accept a role as his mistress, and yet it was patently evident that Jolene had done so.

The whiskey came, and he saw that she drank it back with a gusto that equalled Walter's, smacking her lips with pleasure.

She saw his glance and had the grace to blush, but she gave her head a defiant toss and said, 'That's good poteen.'

'Funny, I always thought of you as the champagne sort,' he said.

'Well, you can't have missed noticing a few other changes,' she said, taking another swig of the whiskey. 'Seems to me you've changed a bit yourself. Been thrown out of any good parties lately?'

He laughed, cursing himself for letting his thoughts show. He hadn't intended to let her know how shocked or dismayed he was by her appearance, not at least until he knew the full situation. If there'd been some kind of trouble, maybe he could help; but he'd have to be careful of her pride, or he'd make an enemy of her – the last thing he wanted to do.

'Nowadays I'm the one who does the tossing out,' he said. 'Or rather, my bouncers take care of it. We try to run a clean place here – at least, by Barbary Coast standards. We do get a few of the uptown set – I suppose you heard of the place from your friends?' He was fishing, without much luck.

'We just wandered in,' she said. 'Walter, don't empty the bottle.'

Walter, left out of their conversation, had been greedily refilling his glass every moment or so. He shot her a hateful look. 'It's just going to waste sitting here while you two gab,' he said.

'It's all right,' Sloan said, dismissing it with a wave of his hand. 'Have all you like, there's plenty more where that came from.'

'Oh, look.' Jolene's attention had been caught by something at the next table. 'That man, he left his newspaper behind – reach it for me, won't you, it's been ages since I've read the news.'

'Damn it, I didn't come out and spend my good money so you could read the papers,' Walter said, getting up as if he meant to snatch the newspaper away, but Sloan had moved more quickly, easily reaching to the next table for the folded paper and handing it to Jolene.

She grabbed it out of his hand and opened it to the front page, her eyes scanning the headlines, then moving hurriedly downward. McKinley had won the presidential election, defeating Bryan and his free-silver platform – she had not even been aware an election was taking place; news of a fire in Chinatown; war in the Philippines.

'Are you looking for something in particular?' Sloan asked.

'It's not polite to read in company,' Walter said. 'If you don't put that away . . .'

'Judge Carver's murder,' Jolene said, turning to the second page and scanning that too. 'I wondered if there'd been any new developments.'

Sloan frowned, thinking back. 'Judge Carver – I didn't know he'd been murdered.'

'You must have read about it, a prominent man like that – about a month ago . . . ' There was nothing on the second page either.

'I heard he'd died,' Sloan said. 'An accident in his home, tripped and fell down some stairs, something like that. The newspapers didn't make too much of it – but you're right, that's been weeks ago, he's long since under the ground, and I sure didn't hear of any murder . . . '

It took a full moment for the import of his words to come clear to her. She lowered the paper slowly, looking venomously across it to a nervous Walter.

'You rotten skunk,' she hissed, growing more livid with each word.

'Now, Jolene,' Walter said, knocking over his chair in his haste to get up.

'You dirty, lying . . . ' She sputtered, unable to think of words odious enough. Walter turned to flee when she snatched up the whiskey bottle from the table. It caught him alongside the head, making him yelp and earning a roar of laughter from the crowd, who enjoyed a good fight immensely.

'Damn you,' she shouted after him, casting around for something else to throw, but by this time he had already disappeared through the street door.

She half started to pursue him; then, deciding after all that she would be happier if she never saw him again, she turned back to the table and dropped heavily into her chair.

'Of all the no-account bastards,' she swore, filling her glass with whiskey. The mere thought of how he had tricked and used her made her want to scream with rage. She glanced at Sloan and saw the eyebrow he had cocked at her language.

'Give me a cigarette,' she snapped, finding him the only convenient target for her anger.

'I can't abide women who smoke,' he said.

'And I can't abide people who don't mind their own business.' She reached across and snatched a cigar from his breast pocket. Walter had left his matches on the table and she struck one on the table's rough wooden surface, but before she could light up the cigar, Sloan calmly retrieved the cigar and thrust it back into his pocket.

Her frustration and her anger reached the boiling point and, without thinking, she slapped him. To her amazement, and still with his look of total calm, he slapped her back.

'What did you do that for?' she demanded, rubbing her bruised cheek gingerly.

'If you're going to go around slapping people, you ought at least to know what it feels like,' he answered.

'Well, I don't have to stay here and be manhandled by you,' she said, getting up again. 'I'm leaving.'

'No, you're not,' he said, grinning.

It was her turn to lift an eyebrow. 'And what makes you think I won't?'

'Because I'm telling you now that I'm not going to come after you the way you're expecting.'

'Why should I want you to?' she snapped, irked by the suggestion, since she had indeed expected that he would come after her in a conciliatory mood.

'Don't be a fool, Jolene. Without a man on your arm, you wouldn't get twenty feet outside that door. And if you think bedding Walter was a disappointment, wait until you've worked a week or two in a Chinese whorehouse.'

'A year ago you'd never have spoken like that to me,' she said. His slap had restored her senses sufficiently that she knew his warning was entirely correct.

'A year ago I'd never have run into you in a dump like this.'

Her eyes stung with tears. It was all too much for her. Abandoned first by Philip and then by Richard, betrayed by David and his mother, assaulted by the Judge, tricked into being a virtual prisoner of that odious Walter McCrea – she was literally at the end of her rope, penniless and helpless; and now Sloan Morrow, who had once sworn that he loved and wanted to marry her, was being as horrible to her as every other man had been.

Despite her efforts not to, she began to cry, quietly at first and then with increasingly noisy sobs that made her body shake convulsively.

The effect on Sloan was instantaneous. He leaped to his feet and cradled her protectively in his arms. 'There, there,' he crooned, speaking in a low voice as he would to a child. 'No one's going to hurt you. Come with me.'

'Where – where are you taking me?' she asked, though she offered no resistance as he shoved their way through the crowd.

'Just some place where you can cry without half the Barbary Coast thinking I've been beating you,' he said.

They went through a curtained doorway by the stage, into a narrow hall lined with dressing-rooms. He shoved the door of the first one open, almost hitting the soprano, who was in the process of changing costumes.

'Get out,' Sloan said with a jerk of his head.

'Listen, I've got to get this dress off . . . ' the soprano started to argue.

'You can take it off in Sancho's dressing-room, it won't be the first time,' Sloan said.

She opened her mouth to protest further, but then she got a look at his face, and thought better of it. She left, grumbling under her breath.

The room was little better than a closet, with a dressing-table and chair, and a narrow cot along the opposite wall. He sat her down on the cot and, going to the door, yelled for someone outside to bring him whiskey. When the bottle arrived a minute later, without glasses, he made her take a long drink from it, noting that she did so with the sort of expertise that came from familiarity.

The drink and the privacy had their effect, however; the sobs dwindled to an occasional sniffle. She took the bottle from him and helped herself to another drink. She squinted at the label and made a face.

'I guess I don't rate the good stuff any more, huh?' she said.

He brushed a wayward lock of hair gently back from her face. 'With me you rate anything your heart desires,' he said. 'This just happened to be what they handed me in a hurry.'

At the gentle touch and the tone of his voice she began to cry again, but more softly this time. He let her get it out of her system and when she was once again sniffling, he said, 'I gather it's been kind of tough for you lately?'

She managed a rueful laugh. 'Does a miner stink?' she answered. For the first time they smiled openly at one another.

'Want to tell me about it?'

'Just like that?'

'Just like that.'

And, to her own surprise, she did, just like that, pausing from time to time for another swig of whiskey. She started with Philip, not the childhood stuff, not even France, just with his leaving, and from there through the whole litany of mistakes and tragedies that had brought her to the Golden Crest Saloon on the arm of Walter McCrea. She made no effort to spare herself; indeed, it was a form of catharsis to bring everything into the open for once, like lancing a wound to let the poison drain.

Sloan was a good listener, attentive, offering an occasional word or phrase to encourage her to go on; but as he listened his lips tightened grimly and his eyes grew darker.

'. . . And this was where Walter brought me,' she said much later. 'The rest you know.' She glanced up at him, her red-rimmed eyes dry by this time. 'The usual story of a miss gone astray.'

'Not so usual,' he said. 'Do you want some more of that?' She had picked up the bottle again, to discover it empty.

'I suppose so,' she said. She lay back on the cot, yawning openly. 'I'm so tired.'

'Rest for a few minutes; I'll be right back,' he said.

She made no reply. He went out, and came back a short while later to discover that she was sound asleep. He stood for a moment staring down at her and he felt not only the burden of what she had suffered but a sense of panic entirely his own. He had been moved by her earlier tears as he had not been moved before. The women he had known in the past cried all too easily, pretending love for him that they did not, could not feel, to gain some favor from him, but he had known instinctively that Jolene's tears were not like that.

He knew too that the girl sleeping before him was, unlike the others, a threat to the freedom and independence he had always valued above all else. He had cherished his secret love for her, while at the same time its apparent hopelessness had prevented its being a threat. Now the situation had changed in a manner he could never have foreseen. He had risen from the station that had been his, while she had fallen. They were on common ground now, whatever their pasts had been.

It would be impossible for a man to see her, so lovely, so vulnerable, and not want her; but he was frightened by the knowledge that, in taking her, he would inevitably lose something of himself.

She stirred in her sleep and embraced herself as if she were cold. He looked around for some sort of blanket and, finding none, took off his jacket and laid it gently over her.

There was no room on the cot for more than one, nor had he the desire to disturb her sleep. He turned down the light and, tilting the chair back against the wall, made himself as comfortable in it as he was able.

Thus he spent his first night with Jolene, in a manner quite unlike what he had dreamed of for so long.

34

She woke wondering where she was – the tiny, cramped room, the hard cot; why weren't the children shouting from below? And the smell, where was the fish smell?

She swung her feet to the floor, bumping a shin on the wooden chair beside the bed. There was a dull throb in her head; but the empty whiskey bottle on the floor explained that. But how . . . ?

Sloan tapped at the door and came in, solving the mystery for her. She began to remember. 'Oh,' she groaned, burying her face in her hands.

'As bad as that?' Sloan asked, grinning.

She ignored the question and looked from him to the cot, and back to him again. 'Did I sleep here all night?' she asked.

'Most of it. Now don't be giving me that kind of look, you don't honestly think two of us could have squeezed into that bed, do you?'

'I guess not,' she admitted. 'Where did you sleep?'

'I managed,' he said. 'Look, I've ordered some breakfast. Are you hungry?'

'Hungry? I could eat a deck of cards,' she said.

He laughed. 'You wouldn't like it. I've had to do it a couple or so times. Come on.'

'Where are we going?' she asked, but she did not hesitate to go with him.

'My place.'

'You mean this isn't it?'

'Well, I've lived in worse. But no, I meant my apartment, it's upstairs. But the way you were blubbering last night, I didn't figure we'd make it that far.'

Since the assurance that she had slept alone and the mention of breakfast, she had been feeling rather kindly toward him, but that remark was not likely to cement a friendship, and when he had unlocked the door at the head of the stairs, she swept by him haughtily.

His apartment was a palatial suite of rooms positively teeming with gilt and red velvet. A rosewood square grand piano dominated one wall, a fireplace sheathed in marble another. The effect was garish and overblown but unquestionably expensive and, in its own way, effective.

'You can freshen up in there,' he said, indicating an open doorway. 'Food'll be along shortly.'

She found a complete bath with all the modern fixtures. The tub had been filled with steaming hot water, and an assortment of toilet articles had been laid out on the commode. There was even a dressing-gown draped over the back of a chair.

She bathed quickly and donned the dressing-gown. It was of black silk so sheer that it could almost be seen through, and trimmed in crimson-dyed feathers. It was tasteless and vulgar, but she could forget that in the thrill of feeling silk against her bare flesh once more.

'Doesn't it strike you as odd,' she said, coming back into the parlor where Sloan was waiting and smoking a cigar, 'that all the gentlemen I meet have ladies' clothing in their apartments?'

'That's because ladies and gentlemen have a way of becoming involved with one another,' he said. 'Or hadn't you noticed that?'

'I've noticed that it was no lady who wore this,' she said, ruffling the expanse of maribou feathers. She glanced around appreciatively. 'You've come a long way, Sloan.'

She saw the unspoken reply in his expression, and voiced it herself. 'I know, so have I.'

'You can put all that behind you.'

'It seems like I've got an awful lot behind me,' she said bitterly, 'and nothing in front of me.'

'You must be more near-sighted than ever. I'm standing not four feet in front of you.'

She gave him a measured look, but it was still impossible to be sure when Sloan was joking and when he was serious. 'How'd you come by all this?' she asked, changing the subject. 'The last time I saw you you didn't have a pot to . . . well, you know.'

'Now I've got a gold-plated one, and dozens of windows to throw it out of. I had a lucky streak, won a couple of big ones. My dad had always told me the time to quit was while you were out ahead; sad to say he never did follow his own advice.

Anyway, instead of losing it all back at the tables, I decided to run some tables of my own. I opened a little place, made some money, opened another place. I've got a dozen of them along the Barbary Coast now.'

'All gambling halls?' she asked.

His grin was almost sheepish. 'Not all of them.'

'You're running a bordello,' she said, making it a statement rather than a question.

'Two of them, though I prefer to call them fancy houses – they're a little dressier than most. And one peg house.'

'What's a peg house?' She had thought she'd learned all the terminology from Walter, but this was a term she'd not heard used before.

'Same thing, only the girls are boys. You'd be surprised; some weeks it's the biggest paying of the lot.'

She noticed the change in his tone. 'You sound disapproving,' she said.

'I try not to approve or disapprove of people's foibles, that's how I make my money, after all. Still, I can't help thinking it's a little demeaning for a man.'

'No more than it is for a woman. At least for a man there are plenty of other things he can do, but for a woman the choices are too often limited – by men, as it turns out.'

'You've picked up some funny notions,' he said, none too warmly.

She shrugged. 'The places I've been, you pick up a lot of things,' she said.

They were interrupted by a knock at the door. At Sloan's command, a man came in bearing an enormous tray and carried it to the carved mahogany table. Jolene's mouth watered at the aroma of fresh ham and just-baked bread. There were eggs baked in little cups, and an immense bowl of strawberries swimming in champagne.

So intent was she on the food that Jolene scarcely noticed the bent little man carrying the tray until Sloan introduced him.

'This is Weasel,' he said. 'Cook, major domo, pickpocket – in short, a man of many parts.'

Weasel grunted something that might have been, 'pleased to meet you', and deposited the tray on the table, deftly arranging the table for two with an expertise belied by his stubby beard and generally unsavory appearance.

'It looks delicious,' Jolene murmured, barely restraining herself from attacking the food without preliminaries.

'Weasel sailed as a cabin boy to a French Captain – he was rolling crepes when most boys are rolling marbles. Miss Perreira comes from French stock, Weasel.'

He shot her a respectful glance. 'Danged frogs are disagreeable but they know their food,' he growled. 'Soup's on.'

Sloan held her chair for her, a gesture that had vanished with her elegant past, but at the moment she had but one interest, the food before her. She was eating before Sloan had taken his seat, spearing a strawberry from the bowl, heaping jam on bread already dripping with butter. She bit off an enormous hunk of ham and stuffed it into her mouth, closing her eyes with ecstasy as she sank her teeth into it.

She opened her eyes to discover Sloan and Weasel both staring at her, the former with amusement, the latter with what might have been awe.

'It's wonderful,' she mumbled, still chewing. To her amazement Weasel gave her a wide grin, revealing blackened and rotting teeth.

'Danged frogs knows their food,' he said, going out.

She looked shamefacedly across at Sloan. 'I'm sorry,' she said, swallowing. 'I – I was just so hungry . . . '

'Don't apologize, eat,' he said. 'If it's any comfort, you've just made Weasel deliriously happy. I told him you were a true gourmet – I think he'd despaired of ever cooking for anyone who knew the difference between bad and good food.'

'This is . . . ' she tore off another piece of ham, ' . . . very good.'

Although he retained his relaxed smile as he watched her wolfing down her food, inwardly Sloan was seething. He was not ordinarily a man for vengeful, or even decisive, action, preferring as he had all his life the line of least resistance, but he had already sworn to avenge the wrongs that had been done this woman. Particularly, he wanted to settle the score with Richard Trémorel.

He was well acquainted with the man; Trémorel had long been an habitué of the Barbary Coast, and Sloan, who dealt in human weaknesses, knew him as a particularly despicable man. In actual truth, he was astonished that Jolene had gotten off so lightly in her experience with the man; he was inclined, once he had had his way with a woman, to prolong the experience solely that he might derive additional enjoyment out of making her suffer.

Sloan had known of Judge Carver and his sadistic habits as

well; many of his victims, after all, had come from among the Barbary Coast's unfortunates. But the Judge with his physical torture had been a piker compared to the ingenious cruelty of Trémorel's mind.

Inquiries during the night had brought Sloan the information that Trémorel had left town, apparently soon after delivering Jolene to Julia Benson's; but he would return. A rat might wander, but in time he scurried back to his warren; in this hell hole along the waterfront was all the filth and garbage that Trémorel's ugly nature fed upon. He would return.

Walter McCrea, that silly, trivial man, had already been attended to. As for the others, well, there was plenty of time.

He did not realize that in adopting this attitude, even in seeking to avenge Jolene, he had already accepted Jolene into his life, not as a fantasy but as a real and more or less permanent fixture. He was still awed by the miracle that had occurred. He had longed for her, and at the same time had known that she was not for him, that she was too far above him.

Now, suddenly, here she was, reduced to his level by the very men he sought to punish, and he was too stunned by the wonder of it, by her, her beauty so dazzling despite all that had happened to her that it caused a stab of pain in his chest each time she glanced up at him, to appreciate the irony of his actions.

Having finally assuaged her hunger, Jolene began to eat more decorously, but the unladylike habit of wolfing her food was one that would remain with her; for the rest of her life she would be haunted by the memory of too little and too poor food, and she approached each meal as if there might never be another.

Now, however, her appetite appeased, she became again aware of the man seated across from her. She managed a grateful smile that accelerated his heartbeat by several degrees.

'You can't know how wonderful it feels to have a decent meal,' she said apologetically.

'I've been hungry before,' he said, and the way he said it made her feel less embarrassed, as if he did, after all, understand just how it had been for her.

Weasel appeared as if by magic to clear away the dishes, and it was so evident that he was dying to ask her about the food that she couldn't resist saying, 'The eggs were outstanding.'

He fussed and looked embarrassed, but he asked, without looking directly at her, 'Didn't have too much cream on them, did they?'

'No, no, exactly right,' she insisted, and with complete honesty. 'But the seasoning, I couldn't quite decide – it was unique . . . '

'Cinnamon,' he said shortly, adding quickly. 'Don't tell anyone, I'm always getting pestered to tell, but I put a little cinnamon on them.'

He invested this declaration with the importance of a military secret, so that she knew his sharing it with her was a mark of respect. Oddly, she was more flattered by this wizened little man's gesture than by all the compliments to her beauty that had been heaped about her in the past.

'Thank you, I'll remember that,' she said, touching the back of his hand lightly with her fingertips. 'And I promise not to tell anyone.'

He went out beaming, but not before he had poured two huge cups of hot, black coffee. 'He's remarkable,' Jolene said, sipping hers. 'Where did you find him?'

'I saved his life in a gunfight – oh, nothing heroic, just happened he owed me twenty dollars and I figured I'd never get it back if I let him get killed. He's been with me ever since.'

'Do you make it a habit to rescue strays?' she asked.

He got up, his chair scraping on the hardwood floor, and lit a cigar from the humidor on the sideboard. 'Only the ones I have a use for,' he said, walking about behind her, so that he missed the angry flare of her nostrils.

'And by that you mean you plan to "use" me,' she said, resentment leaping up within her; she was all too familiar with the uses to which a man put a beautiful woman.

'I – assumed you'd be grateful, of course,' he said. He bent over her, running his fingers through her hair and lifting it aside to kiss the back of her neck.

She shuddered, but not, as he assumed, from rising desire. The phrases, the touch, the kiss – she had been through all this before. Gratitude; obligation; I'll do you a kindness, but the price is your submission.

He reached with one hand for her breast – and gave a yelp of pain when she sank the prongs of a fork into his palm.

'Damnation! What the hell . . . !' he swore, jerking back a bleeding hand.

'You're just like the rest of them,' she spat at him, kicking over her chair as she jumped to her feet. 'A few kind words, a free meal – only it isn't free, is it, I'm expected to pay, with the only coin of the realm you care about.'

'You can pay in glass beads for all I care, you've got no cause to stab me to death,' he said, wrapping a handkerchief about his hand to staunch the flow of blood.

'And you've got no cause to think you're entitled to paw at me, just because you gave me a meal. They're my breasts. I've got a right to say who may fondle them, and when. I'm not a keg of beer that you've bought for your saloon.'

He fetched a bottle of brandy from the cupboard and filled a glass, emptying it in one gulp. He was angry, not only with her but with himself for having handled things so crudely.

'You make me sound like the rest of them,' he said sullenly.

'Well, aren't you?'

'Hell no, I've never mistreated anyone, least of all a woman,' he said.

'Can you honestly say you've never taken advantage of a woman, gotten what you couldn't have gotten otherwise, just because she was hungry, or destitute, or needed your help?'

'Well . . . ' he hesitated, embarrassed by this line of reasoning. 'That's not the same thing.'

'It is to a woman,' she said. 'If a woman's got no other choices, she's forced to it, the same as if she were held down. Raped by acts of phony kindness is still raped. I know.'

This last, said with such quiet bitterness, took the wind out of his sails. 'I'm sorry,' he said, with obvious sincerity. 'But you kind of flew off the handle, too, without giving me a chance to tell you what I had in mind.'

She gave a disdainful snort. 'I knew what you had in mind,' she said.

He laughed, and some of the tension was dissipated, but not all of it. 'That too, sure,' he admitted. 'But that wasn't the whole thing. I wasn't planning on a quick toss and then throwing you out on the street.'

'I suppose you wanted me to be your mistress?'

'Of course.'

'Meaning,' she said dryly, 'that I'm to warm your bed so long as it suits you – a few months, a few weeks even. And whenever you get your fill, or get bored with me, then it's out on the street, and no better off than before?'

He paused for a moment reflectively. 'Actually I was thinking of something a bit more substantial than that. As I told you earlier I've got a number of businesses. They're not run badly, if I do say so myself, but they lack a woman's touch.'

'You want me to be the madam for your bordellos?' she asked dryly.

'Hardly that – both my houses have madams. I thought you could sort of oversee things, here as well as there. A lady sees things differently. If you're willing to try, and if it works out, I'd work out some sort of partnership arrangement.'

'Of course I'm still expected to be your mistress.'

'I'd be lying if I said that didn't matter,' he said frankly.

She studied him for a few minutes, weighing the offer. 'You're a fool,' she said after a while, 'to want as a mistress a woman who despises you.'

It was not entirely true; still, it did indeed rankle that she must now accept the charity of a man she'd once scorned as beneath her consideration. The lesson of Walter McCrea had not been wasted upon her.

'Does that mean you're accepting the offer?' he asked, apparently unconcerned by her professed loathing for him.

She shrugged and said, 'It's the only job in town.'

He came to where she was standing and gently opened the dressing gown, lifting it from her shoulders and letting it fall in a silken heap about her feet.

'You make it very difficult to love you,' he said.

'Then why bother?'

He smiled, encircling her with his arms and drawing her nearer. 'Because it's impossible not to,' he said.

Walter McCrea woke with a start as his door was kicked open. He sat up, to find two burly men standing just inside.

'What are you doing here?' he demanded in a trembling voice.

'We've come for you,' one of the men said, and the other added, 'You're going on a trip.'

'A trip? A trip where?' He was shaking from head to foot, clutching a sheet up about his chin.

'Shanghai,' was the answer.

He was filled with dread. A man venturing alone into the Barbary Coast ran a never-ending risk of being forcibly impressed into the crew of some ship, perhaps by being waylaid on the street, or even served a drugged drink in a bar. Since many of the ships sailing out of San Francisco were headed for Shanghai, the newly recruited crew members were said to be 'shanghaied'; it was a cruel fate. The lucky ones were gone for two, or even more years; the less fortunate ones died under the captain's lash for insubordination, or drowned trying to make an escape, or succumbed to any of the dangers of the sea.

'I won't go,' he cried, but one of the sailors slipped a wicked looking club from his waist band and slapped it menacingly against his thigh. Walter made no more protests.

The other sailor went to the clothes cupboard and, finding an empty valise there, began to cram clothing haphazardly into it.

'Why – why me?' Walter asked; they were a long way from the Barbary Coast.

'I'm supposed to tell you,' one of the men said, 'that you got to learn respect for a lady.'

Walter groaned and covered his face with his hands. Jolene, he thought, it was her, her and that fancy Sloan Morrow.

And to think, this was how he was repaid for everything he had done. It just went to prove what he'd always known – there was no justice for a man like himself.

35

Although it was a far cry from her high-society days, Jolene found that being Sloan Morrow's woman did give her a certain status. By Barbary Coast standards Sloan was a gentleman, and by any standards a wealthy one. She was treated with respect by the men and a usually restrained envy by the women with whom she came into contact.

Weasel had quickly become her ardent admirer. He was usually taciturn and invariably grubby to look at, though since her arrival he had taken up clean clothes and the habit of shaving, but she soon discovered that the elegant breakfast he had first served her was no fluke. Few of San Francisco's fabulous mansions boasted a chef as competent, and no one could boast a more devoted servant. He sought no reward other than her approval, having recognized her at once as a woman of the sort of breeding unknown to him before. She had learned that this wizened little man who had spent most of his life below decks had a penchant for Chopin, and nothing she did pleased him more than when she sat at the piano and played one of the waltzes or a nocturne while he cleaned and dusted about the apartment, rarely speaking, but smiling and humming to himself with pleasure.

For a long time, he was the only one she could truly have called a friend. The others treated her respectfully, but coolly. After all, it was evident that her background was different from theirs, and the fact that her experiences had left her withdrawn and suspicious of friendly overtures only reinforced the general impression that she was a snob.

One incident that occurred, however, did much to eliminate that impression. It was a Saturday, already busy though it was still early, and she and Sloan had enjoyed a particularly fine dinner in their apartment.

'I've got a little surprise for you,' he said, as they came downstairs, 'A new routine for the show. I think you'll enjoy this.'

The band, at his instruction, had waited for their appearance, and as soon as they came through the curtained doorway, the music began, and the girls of the chorus line pranced onto the stage.

It was, she realized with dismay, intended to be a cancan, which was now enjoying a vogue along the waterfront. She had seen the dance in Paris, and perhaps because of her own French blood she had recognized it instinctively for what it was, an expression of the exuberance of the French spirit, a young girl's kicking her heels in the air.

But this, this was such a heavy-handed and clumsy parody of what she had seen that, without even thinking, she cried for them to stop.

'What's wrong?' Sloan asked, bewildered.

'Everything,' she replied. 'You,' she said, waving a hand at the man who played the piano and also acted as conductor, 'it's not a funeral dirge, it's supposed to go like this.' She began to hum and snap her fingers, indicating how he was to pick up the beat. He listened for a moment, then began picking out a far more sprightly tune on the battered piano.

'And you girls,' she said, addressing the dancers, who had stopped with the music, 'you're stomping about like stevedores on the dock.'

'Nobody knew the steps,' one of the girls complained.

'It's not a ballet, the steps don't matter,' she said, mounting the wooden steps to the stage and taking a position in front of the footlights. 'It's the spirit of the thing that counts – like this.'

To the amazement of all, Sloan not the least of them, she hitched up her skirt and tripping lightly forward and back, kicked her heels in the air, twirling her elegant ankles with a gay abandon.

By this time, workers and customers alike knew who she was, but this was the first time they had seen her with her hair down, and after a moment of astonished silence a roar of approval went up around the room. The other girls, seeing how enthusiastically the crowd responded, began to fall into line with her, imitating her steps and improvising some of their own, but with the sort of infectious spirit that had been entirely lacking before.

It was like a catharsis for Jolene, and she gave herself up entirely to the music and to the wild dance, so that for the first time the San Franciscans saw a cancan as it was intended, and not a carefully choreographed routine.

But at the height of the frivolity, something totally unexpected occurred. Jolene, dancing to the very footlights and kicking one leg quite over her head, glanced into the audience and saw a foursome being seated at one of the tables. Even if she hadn't recognized anyone in the group, she would have known them for the Nob-Hill set, slumming; but she did know one of the girls casually, and when the stylishly dressed gentleman who was addressing the waiter turned toward the stage, she saw that it was David Ecks.

He saw her in the same instant, and his mouth fell open in dismay. For a moment she hesitated, losing the beat of the music altogether and earning puzzled glances from the pianist and the other girls on stage; but then she remembered how callously David had abandoned her, nearly causing her to be sent to prison, and with a deliberate wink in his direction and a toss of her head, she danced to the center of the stage, signaling for the others to give her room, and with a complete disregard for propriety turned a cartwheel.

By the time she had righted herself, David and his group were on their way to the door and the music was almost ended. She saw David pause before going out, giving her a pained look. For an answer, she finished as the girls had finished in Paris – she turned her back to the audience, bowing toward the rear curtain and, flipping her skirts upward, provided the cheering stomping audience with the briefest glimpse of a pantalooned derrière.

When she next glanced toward the doorway, it was empty. It was the last visit that David made to the Barbary Coast, and the last time she saw him.

She was known as 'the Queen of the Barbary Coast'. She would not set foot in Sloan's parlor houses, having seen her fill of such places while at Julia's; she was still often haunted by the memory of Amy. She did, however, oversee the operations and proved herself an apt manager. If a dispute arose between one of the girls and her madam, or between madam and customer, she was a fair and impartial arbitrator. If she learned that one or the other of the establishments was serving watered drinks, or that a customer and his wallet had parted company, the offending parties were summoned to the apartment over the Golden Crest and in no uncertain terms made to see the error of their ways, with the result that Sloan's houses, already known as safe and fair, enjoyed a reputation – and a patronage – like no other in the area.

Although she shunned these places, there was nowhere else along the Barbary Coast she was reluctant to go. She felt that she had seen already the worst of men, and when she had been a few days on the waterfront she offered it as her opinion that its vices were no worse than those on Nob Hill, only more openly practiced. She was known on sight in all of Sloan's gambling halls and saloons, and in a number of others as well. She went where no lone woman had gone before. It was true, she carried in her reticule a small pearl-handled pistol that Sloan had given her, and even the fiercest denizens of the Coast would be reluctant to risk the retaliation of Sam and Joe the two brutes that Sloan kept in his employ for protection; but her greatest protection was the awe and respect in which she was held by the waterfront's *habitués*.

Many of these rough men had never been so close to a true lady, let alone spoken directly with one. Her aristocratic lineage was no secret, especially since Weasel was wont to let it be known, but she herself never spoke of it. She could sit down with the roughest sailor and speak without coyness or mincing her words, while looking him straight in the eye. Though many a brutish heart burned with lust – and often more tender affections – she neither mocked nor encouraged their attentions; in public, her loyalty to Sloan was irreproachable.

If a man – or especially a woman – was temporarily down on his luck, he might receive a basket of food, always with a bottle of whiskey to relieve the pain, or perhaps a little silk purse with a few coins. There was never a name on these gifts, but it was common knowledge from whom they came, and when she went for a drive in her little carriage, men whom others had labeled the 'dregs of society' fought to tend her horses or hand her down.

And, lest all of this 'goodness' become cloying, she had two other qualities that especially endeared her to those among whom she now moved: she could swear like a sailor and drink with the best of them.

She was, in short, all that Sloan could have asked for in a business partner, which ought to have made him happy but in actuality only added to his frustration with their personal life. Jolene was as much a hellion with him as she was an angel with others.

She would not be cowed, try though he might to subdue her disdainful attitude toward him. She followed no dictates but her own, dismissing his threats of violence as easily as his protestations of affection.

'You're a fool to insist on loving me,' she told him offhandedly, and often added, 'I don't love you and don't ever intend to.'

She was deferential to him in public, a harridan in private, shouting and swearing and even flinging things at him if he dared to cross her will.

Inwardly, she was amazed by his patience, and though she loathed herself for her behavior, she felt a compulsion to test it continually with ever more outrageous conduct toward him. She had been cruelly abused in the name of love, and when Sloan spoke of his love for her it was as if two of her responded to test his love, one wanting the pleasure of proving his love real, the other the satisfaction of proving it as false as others had been. She was at war with herself, and it was Sloan who suffered.

On the other hand, let it be said that Sloan did not suffer in silence, or meekly. He tried spanking her, but when she woke him the next morning by breaking a water pitcher over his head – and leaving an ugly gash that took weeks to heal – he decided to forgo spankings.

He threatened to terminate their business relationship; she greeted the threat with scornful derision.

'Go ahead,' she said without a trace of concern. 'There's not a place along the Coast I couldn't get a job anytime I wanted one.'

He tried shouting her down, but the language she employed without flinching so shocked him that he was quickly forced into retreat.

There were times when he bitterly regretted his impulsive decision to make her his partner and mistress. His life, which had been before a fairly happy and uncomplicated one, was now in constant turmoil.

Yet when he saw her lying asleep, curled like a paper escaping the flame, he was touched by her look of childish innocence, and he saw her fiery bravado for what it was, a shield that she had raised against the vicissitudes of a world that had misused her. If only, he thought, he knew how to penetrate the shield.

He had thought at first to do so by making love to her, but their relations were as stormy in bed as out, and as infuriatingly unpredictable. One night she would welcome him into her arms with the fire of a tigress, engulfing them both in a scorching passion that left him weak and exhausted – and deliriously happy; the next night, his most tentative approach might send her into an angry rage against him. At other times she was so cool toward him that he warned her against the damage his 'delicate parts' might suffer from frostbite.

'It'd be no loss to me,' she informed him, unmoved.

'I can find other women to warm my bed, you know,' he warned her.

Jolene, already in bed before him, only shrugged and turned her back on him. 'Suit yourself,' she said. 'Oh, mind you turn out the light before you go out, I can't sleep with it on.'

He went out, slamming the bedroom door. For a moment Jolene thought guiltily of calling him back, but when she heard the outer door close as well, she knew that he was gone from the apartment. She tossed and turned, trying to console her nagging conscience with the reminder that she had never promised Sloan submission.

Finally she slept, only to be awakened late in the night by the sound of voices – Sloan's and an unfamiliar woman's – from the parlor.

Surely, she thought in surprise, he hadn't actually brought another woman here to the apartment? She sat up, just as the bedroom door opened and Sloan came into the room. Sure enough he was followed by a strange woman, simpering and playfully hiding behind him.

‘ ’Fraid we'll have to trouble you for the bed,’ he said, his voice thick with the effects of alcohol.

‘You must be mad,’ Jolene said, all but sputtering with anger. ‘To think I would vacate my bed, in the middle of the night, so that you . . . Oh, it's unthinkable.’

‘Suit yourself,’ Sloan said, removing his jacket and shirt. ‘Out of those clothes, sweet,’ he addressed the woman with him. She giggled and began to unfasten her dress.

‘What are you doing?’ Jolene demanded.

‘We're coming to bed,’ Sloan said, dropping his trousers and dancing around on one foot as he tried to get out of them. ‘With or without you in it.’

‘Well, I certainly am not going to lie here and watch the two of you rutting,’ Jolene snapped, flinging herself out of the bed. She flounced angrily from the room.

Once in the parlor, however, she saw that in her half-asleep condition she had done exactly as Sloan had intended. She turned back, changing her mind, but Sloan had anticipated this change of heart and, having followed her to the door, had quickly closed it after her. Before she could reach it again, she heard the key turn in the lock.

‘Sloan Morrow, how dare you do this to me?’ she shouted pounding on the locked door of the bedroom. ‘Open this door this instant.’

‘Sorry, love, not till we've finished,’ his muffled voice came back to her.

She pounded on the door for a few minutes more, with no results. The only sound from within was a spate of giggling that ended in a little squeal of pleasure.

Jolene abandoned the door and dropped heavily into one of the plush chairs. The autumn weather had turned cool and the fire had long since died out, leaving the room icy cold. She closed a window against the night fog but she could not shut out the chill. She was dressed only in the flimsiest of night-gowns and in her anger had not even thought to don a robe.

After a few minutes of shivering and rubbing her bare arms, she went back to the door and pounded on it again. ‘I'm freezing,’ she cried. ‘Let me in.’

There was no reply. She flounced around the apartment looking for something to wear, but her clothes were all in the bedroom.

Her eyes fell on the dining-table. It was covered with a fringed cloth that reached nearly to the floor. With an angry gesture she snatched the cloth from the table, scattering a crystal bowl and a luster which had stood there. She wrapped the cloth like a blanket about her and returned to the chair, huddling into its protective embrace and cursing herself for having gotten involved with a no-account like Sloan. She would happily have left, and she might even have braved the saloon downstairs, inadequately dressed as she was, but she had no intention of humiliating herself further by announcing to everyone that Sloan had cast her out of their bedroom for the sake of another woman.

Despite her discomfort, she did fall asleep finally, awakening to find the room gray with the light of dawn and Sloan standing over her. The bedroom door stood ajar.

She glanced suspiciously about the room. 'If you're looking for Miss Marcy,' he said, 'I sent her home about half an hour ago.'

Jolene dragged herself out of the chair, stiff from the cold and the unaccustomed sleeping position. 'I'm grateful for that, at least,' she said, too chilled and weary to feel like fighting at the moment. She plodded dispiritedly into the bedroom and threw herself across the bed, dragging the covers over herself.

'This bed smells of her,' she complained, wrinkling her nose. 'What are you laughing at?'

'She had the same complaint,' he said.

'Now what are you doing?' she asked when, a minute later, Sloan slipped into the bed beside her. 'Didn't you have your fill of the delectable Miss Marcy?'

'A mere trifle,' he murmured, attempting to gather her into his arms. 'Not the sort that lasts.'

'Let me alone,' she said, pushing a hand against his chest. 'I want to sleep.'

Sloan sat up with a sigh. 'What, still unaccommodating? Do you mean I'm going to have to go in search of yet another bed warmer?'

He started to get out of bed.

'You wouldn't?' Jolene asked. For an answer, Sloan swung one bare leg to the floor.

'No, wait,' she said, reaching for him.

To his delight, she surrendered herself to him meekly, her ardor belying any exhaustion. For the first time, Sloan thought that he had made some headway in establishing the proper relationship between them, and he went around the rest of that day whistling and grinning to himself.

His victory was short-lived, however. A few nights later he entered their bed, to find his advances met by another cold rebuff.

'Would you rather I go in search of a warmer companion?' he asked.

'As you please,' she replied, seeming unperturbed by the threat.

He hesitated, thinking that she would capitulate when she considered the earlier consequences of such behavior. When she did not, he got out of bed, but reluctantly.

'You're sure you don't want to change your mind about this?' he asked, one leg in his trousers, the other out.

She did not reply. Her back was to him, and she was making an elaborate pretense of sleeping.

He bent over the bed. 'I'm willing to forgive and forget, if you just say the word,' he whispered, kissing the back of her neck.

Her eyes flew open in mock innocence. 'Oh, you're still here?' she said. 'I'd thought you'd gone in search of a playmate.'

'Is that what you want me to do?' he asked petulantly.

'I want you to put out the light as you're leaving,' she said, smiling sweetly.

'*We'll* be back,' he announced as he stormed out a few minutes later.

His search proved less successful than anticipated, however. He began by approaching one of the dancers, Aleen, who had recently shown some ill-concealed interest in him. To his surprise, she was cool toward his suggestion.

'The Weasel, he said if any of us took a tumble with you, he'd put rat poison in our food,' she told him.

Grumbling at the betrayal in his own ranks, Sloan left the Golden Crest and, thinking to save time, went directly to one of his own parlor houses, only to find that all of the girls were tied up. At his other house he got a more truthful explanation, but it did nothing for his spirits.

'Miss Jolene, she let it be known that she would take it most unkindly if any of the girls were to trespass on her property,' the Madam explained.

'It so happens I'm not her property,' he argued.

'The girls understand about these things. Whores have their own principles, you know.'

'Damn it, these girls are working for me,' he snapped, but the Madam only shook her head stubbornly.

'I don't think you'll find a girl here to accommodate you,' she said. 'Not unless Miss Jolene says she don't mind.'

He left in a sorry temper. There were, of course, other houses up and down the coast, but he knew better than anyone the risks involved in visiting them; if a man didn't get the pox, he was likely to get drugged and robbed – or all three..

As it turned out, it was his night to sleep in the chair in the parlor – and Jolene who went around the next day smiling to herself.

36

Not even the Barbary Coast was immune to the special glow of Christmas. Indeed, the tawdry and often tragic circumstances in which its inhabitants lived seemed to lend a special poignancy to the season. Children begged a few pennies 'for the sake of the dear Lord', and women who seldom ventured out in the light of day could be seen bustling from shop to stall, their arms loaded with gaily wrapped packages and their faces aglow with childlike pleasure. From the churches further uptown the bells pealed their special songs, and hardy bands of carolers invaded the saloons themselves, often leaving with their hats filled with coins.

Jolene found herself looking back with awe on the events of the past twelve months. It had been a year ago New Year's Eve, at her parents' house, that she and Philip had announced their engagement. How long ago it seemed!

As a matter of choice, she did not think often of Philip. When she did so, she found that the unbearable agony had now been transmuted into a kind of dull grief. It was an ache that would endure as long as she herself did, but she had found that she could live with and despite it.

As for the life that she lived, however scandalous and improbable it would have seemed to her that previous year, she could not say that she was unhappy. For all the stormy nature of their relationship, and it had remained tempestuous, she and

Sloan had grown astonishingly close. It seemed each battle – and theirs were battles, not merely quarrels – only served as a prelude to an ever more torrid reconciliation.

She knew that the blame for most of their fights lay with her. It was as if the misfortunes that had befallen her had rubbed away some protective coating, leaving her emotions raw and painfully sensitive. She was quick to anger and, when angered, foolishly headstrong. Each quarrel, once begun on the slightest cause, seemed to have to run its own course, beyond any control she might hope to impose upon it, until cross words had become battle royal, ending at length with both exhausted and contrite in one another's arms. Still, each time they seemed to cling more tightly; she hated herself for the fights, yet in a perverse way it was through their fights that they came to know one another and to cement their unique relationship. The air cleared of charges and countercharges, the bitter venom of resentment drained as if from a lanced wound, they would bask together in a healing aura of forgiveness, each vowing, and pretending to believe, that the next time they would handle things diplomatically and not 'fly off the handle'.

Of late, however, things had been mellower between them; Jolene told Weasel, who was often witness to their differences, that it was the season, while Sloan, when alone with Weasel, said they were just running out of things to quarrel about. Weasel, close-mouthed as always, nodded and kept to himself his own explanation.

Jolene shopped extravagantly, taking pleasure in the freedom of money to spend. For Weasel, there was one of the new electric vacuum cleaners to make the presently onerous task of sweeping a mere trifle. Each of the employees was to be given a bonus as well as the day off, but the Madams and the managers of each of the saloons and gambling halls got individual gifts.

For Sloan, there were silk ties from France and a diamond-encrusted pocket-watch from Switzerland.

On an impulse, she ordered a box of fresh fruits, imported by refrigerated boxcars and outrageously expensive, to be delivered to her parents. She sent no card, afraid the gift would be rejected if they knew from whom it came.

Christmas Eve was crisp and clear, and for the first time in longer than she could remember Jolene found herself singing as she worked about the apartment, putting the finishing touches on packages, consulting with Weasel on the plans for the next day's festive dinner, tying a sprig of mistletoe over the doorway. Sloan was out, distributing their gifts among the employees.

'I'm off to get the tree,' Weasel announced, appeared bundled up as if about to brave a Yukon winter.

'Wait, I'll come with you,' she cried. Snatching up a coat and hat, she hurried along after him as he made his way to the lot where the trees were being sold.

She picked a Douglas Fir, so tall that Weasel grumbled it would scrape the ceiling, but when the salesman offered to have it delivered, Weasel insisted they would take it with them. Tying a piece of twine about the trunk, he dragged the tree behind them back to the apartment.

Sloan was there when they came in, standing at his desk with his back to the door. Jolene cried, 'Come see the tree we've . . . ' – stopping short when he turned and she saw his grim expression.

'Sloan, what is it?' she asked.

'It's nothing,' he said. 'A little business matter, that's all. But I have to go back out for a while.'

He closed the desk drawer and thrust his revolver into his waistband, under his coat, but not before she'd seen it.

'Why are you taking a gun?' she asked.

'You know what business is like on the Barbary Coast,' he said, making a poor attempt at nonchalance. 'Weasel, I've got to talk to you for a minute.'

The two men stepped into the hall and she heard the low murmur of their voices but she could not distinguish what was being said. She would have liked to join them and insist that Sloan confide in her as well, but that was so out of keeping with their relationship that she could not bring herself to do so. Instead, she stood waiting and wringing her hands helplessly.

They came back in a few minutes later, Weasel looking now as anxious as his employer had earlier and avoiding Jolene's eyes.

'Something's wrong,' Jolene said, coming to Sloan and clutching worriedly at his sleeve. 'Can't you tell me, please?'

'It's nothing to worry your pretty head about,' he said, bending to brush her cheek lightly with his lips. 'I'll be home in time for dinner.'

But he was not. It was Weasel who insisted on serving the dinner anyway, an hour and a half late. It was overcooked and cold, probably the first poor meal Weasel had served since she had been here, but had it been fit for royalty she would not have noticed. She could eat no more than a mouthful of anything, jumping up at the sound of each carriage in the street outside.

Weasel would tell her nothing. 'If he wants you to know,' he muttered in response to her importunings, 'reckon he'll tell you hisself.'

Weasel made a stand for the tree, its tip indeed scraping the ceiling as he had predicted. For trim, Jolene had strung strands of cranberries and popcorn and one of the women had baked decorated cookies in the shapes of stars and angels; for all Weasel's coaxing, however, she could not bring herself to approach the task she had looked forward to so eagerly for days.

'I want Sloan here to share it with me,' she insisted.

Sloan did not come. The fires burned low, were rebuilt, and burned low again. The streets outside had grown unusually quiet for the Coast, and still there were no steps on the stairs outside.

Each time that Weasel came in again, Jolene saw that his anxiety had deepened, and his fears served only to fan hers.

'Weasel, you must tell me what's happened,' she cried finally, unable to bear the waiting any longer.

'I promised him not to,' he said, but she could see that his nervousness had begun to wear away at his resolve.

'For God's sake, Sloan's in danger, he wouldn't have been carrying his gun otherwise. He may be bleeding and dying somewhere right this minute – can't you at least tell me where he's gone?'

'I don't know where he's at, exactly,' Weasel admitted reluctantly. 'He went to meet a man – an old friend of yours.'

'Of mine? I don't understand . . . '

'Trémorel.' Weasel spat out the name as if it were something disagreeable he'd found unexpectedly in his mouth.

'Richard?' Jolene put a hand to her breast. 'But – he's out of the city.'

'He's back, a few days ago.'

'But – but why should he go to see Richard, they've nothing to do with one another.'

Weasel forgot his place and spat a stream of tobacco juice that missed the spitoon and left a dark brown stain on the Turkish rug.

'Just shows how much you know,' he said. 'Sloan sent him a message, said he wanted to fight a duel with him.'

'A duel – but that's insane, this is the twentieth century, men don't fight duels anymore,' Jolene cried.

'Said it was the only way he could clear your honor.'

Jolene sank weakly into a chair, stunned by the explanation. 'And he didn't say where he was going?' she asked after a moment.

'Nope. Just said I was to keep you here and keep an eye on you.'

She remained seated when Weasel went out; she stared at the Christmas tree without seeing it. Sloan – fighting a duel to avenge her honor? But he'd never said . . . She began to cry suddenly, moved by the enormity of what he had done and her own stupidity in having so badly misjudged the depth of his feeling. She did not even know whether Sloan had any skill with a gun, though living as he had he surely knew how to use one; but she knew that no fight with Richard would be a fair one.

There was a noise, a footfall on the steps, not those that led to the now darkened saloon, but the back steps that led up from an alleyway below.

'Sloan,' she cried, leaping from the chair and rushing to the door, she threw it open – only to discover herself face to face with Richard.

'You!'

He brushed past her and came into the apartment. 'Not a very enthusiastic greeting for a former lover,' he said with a mocking smile.

She ignored his remark. 'Where's Sloan?' she demanded, peering into the darkness beyond the door as if she expected to find him hiding there.

'He's not dead, if that's what you're wondering. I just had him clubbed on the head.'

'You tricked him,' she said. 'You led him into a trap.'

Richard laughed. 'Of course. You know I value my life too highly to risk it in anything so melodramatic as a duel – really, my dear, he is a romantic, isn't he?'

'Where is he?' she demanded. 'I must go to him. What have you done with him?'

'You can't go to him where he is,' Richard said, reaching past her to push the door closed. 'I had him delivered to the Brady brothers.'

Jolene staggered backward from him as if he had struck her. She had been on the Barbary Coast long enough to know who the Bradys were. Everyone here knew – and feared – the name.

Any lone man who ventured into the area of the waterfront ran the risk of being shanghaied. If a Captain about to sail found his crew a man or two short, he or his mate, with a couple of loyal sailors, would set out in search of an unwary straggler.

Ordinarily they looked for young men, strong and healthy, who might be expected to last out the long and arduous voyages. They looked first for men who were already seasoned sailors, because they needed no training.

If the victim, being strong and healthy, was clever enough and lucky enough, he might find himself back in San Francisco in a year or two, a bit sadder and a bit wiser, but with life and limb intact and the experience of two years before the mast to tell his children and friends.

There were other ships, however, that sailed in and out of San Francisco harbor. There were ships whose crews had been decimated by disease or the cruelty of their Captains, requiring too many men for a Captain and his mate to pick up one at a time. There were skippers who regarded their crews as expendable; shanghaied men earned no pay, and if a crew could be gotten cheaply enough, what did it matter if another must be found at the next port?

It was ships such as these that the Bradys supplied. They dealt in quantity, not quality. For a price – cheap enough, all things considered – an uncaring Captain could buy a dozen, two dozen men on the spot, and if some of them were so old, so young, so frail that they could not be expected to last out a month on the high seas, what did it matter? They were worked mercilessly, fed little, and when there was no more to be gotten out of them, they were dumped unceremoniously overboard, to drown or be eaten by sharks.

Those shanghaied by the Bradys almost never returned to tell of their experiences.

'Better you had killed him,' she gasped.

'And to think,' Richard said, taking a step toward her, 'I came expecting to find you grateful to me for not killing him.'

'Stay away from me,' she warned.

He laughed and with a sudden movement darted forward and seized her wrist in a painful grip. 'You witch,' he said, forcing her to him, 'why do you think I came back to this city?'

'I – I don't know.'

'Because you've haunted me, day and night – like a song you can't get out of your head until you've heard it sung one more time. I came back for you, to have you, and be done with you, to break your spell . . . '

'No – let me go!' She struggled against him but he held her fast, bending to kiss her, his lips seeking for hers.

When Weasel came into the room, or where he had come from, she didn't know, but suddenly he was there, the blade of a kitchen knife flashing as he charged at Richard.

At the last moment Richard was warned by a sound, or perhaps by some instinct, and he whirled, throwing Jolene aside. The blade slashed at his shoulder, tearing his coat and opening a great gaping wound in his arm, but before Weasel could strike again Richard had recovered his balance and with a sweep of his good arm had sent the knife clattering across the room.

He fell on the frail old man, knocking him to the floor and dropping upon him to knock the wind from him. With his good hand Richard seized Weasel's throat, choking the life from him.

'Stop it,' Jolene screamed. 'You'll kill him.'

'I mean to,' Richard said without looking at her. Beneath him Weasel's struggles had grown feebler.

Jolene looked around frantically and saw her reticule lying on a table nearby. She dashed to it and snatched from it the little pearl-handled pistol that Sloan had given her for protection.

Without a moment's hesitation she lifted the gun and fired. The bullet struck Richard in the side, causing a little crimson stain to appear.

Sloan had warned her that the gun was too small to be lethal unless fired accurately and at close range, but the wound was enough to make Richard release his death grip on Weasel's throat.

Richard turned, smiling grimly at her. Weasel lay unconscious on the floor, whether dead or not she couldn't say.

'That was – most unkind of you,' Richard said, clutching at his side. He started to get up, found himself too weak, and grabbed at the end of a table for support.

'Stay where you are or I'll kill you,' she said.

'Don't be foolish,' he said, 'you know that you won't.'

She raised the gun until she was looking along its short barrel, directly into Richard's eyes, and the gun aimed between them.

He returned her gaze, still smiling, and used the table to pull himself slowly upright. Neither her eyes nor the gun wavered, rising with him.

Though he swayed slightly, he managed to stand without support. After a moment, he took a deep breath and began to advance slowly toward her, pausing with each step.

Her arm ached from the effort of holding the gun steady. She held her breath. He came closer, foot by foot, and still their eyes were fastened together, his confident, unafraid, hers frightened but defiant.

He was close enough to reach out now and wrest the gun from her. He raised his hand, reaching for the gun. A second or two before his fingers touched the cold metal, she squeezed the trigger and watched one eye seem to explode. For a moment the other gazed at her in bewilderment. Then he fell forward, into her arms. She stumbled backward, letting him crash to the floor, taking her now empty gun with him.

37

'It's your fault,' Weasel said, 'you ought to have been with him. You're his bodyguards, ain't ya?' He spoke hoarsely, his throat still purple stained from Richard's nearly lethal grip.

Sam and Joe hung their heads. 'He give us the night off,' Joe protested meekly. Since being summoned by Jolene, the two had neatly eliminated Richard's body by tossing it into the bay. It was not unusual for a body to wash ashore along the Barbary Coast, and no one would connect it with Jolene.

'Stop it,' Jolene snapped, 'we haven't time for blaming one another. The important thing is, we must get Sloan away from those men.'

The three men exchanged uneasy glances. 'That's a whole lot easier said than done,' Weasel said. 'The Bradys keep all their pigeons at a ranch down the Peninsula till it's time to load them on ship.'

'You know where this place is?' Jolene asked.

'Joe does,' Weasel said.

'I worked for them once, a few years ago,' Joe said. 'Worst

damn job I ever had. Quit it after three days. Never forgot that place.'

'Then all we've got to do is get some men and go there,' Jolene said.

'Place is a fortress,' Joe said.

'The Bradys keep fifteen, twenty men there,' Weasel explained. 'Tough sharpshooters. It would take an army of men to get in there.'

'Surely we can find enough men here on the Coast,' Jolene argued. 'Sloan is well known.'

'So are the Bradys,' Sam observed.

'No one'll want to fight them,' Joe said. 'They're part of the territory.'

His gloomy prediction proved correct. It was not only the heavy guard that the Bradys kept at their place, though no one was eager to go up against them either, the objections went deeper than that.

Hardly a man along the Coast had not in some way contributed to shanghaiing some unfortunate at one time or another; and though the victim might be someone well known, even respected by the Coast's denizens, this was still nothing more nor less than another shanghaiing. Most of them had long since inured themselves to the shame of the practice, and they had little enthusiasm for rising against the Bradys for something of which they were all, in varying degrees, guilty.

The Coast had its own, unwritten laws, and chief among these, expressed often and in succinct terms, was, 'Butt out.'

Christmas morning crept along and by noon the four had found no one to join them in attempting to rescue Sloan. Because of the holiday no ships were scheduled to set sail until the following day. Shanghaied victims were taken aboard ship shortly before setting sail, to minimize the risk of escape. This meant that Sloan was still in the Bradys' hands.

Ships would be sailing out of the harbor with the dawn, however, perhaps one with Sloan aboard, and once a ship had set sail, all hope of rescuing Sloan would vanish with the departing vessel.

'We must get him out of there tonight,' Jolene insisted.

'It'd take an army,' Weasel said yet again.

For a few minutes Jolene paced the floor, frowning thoughtfully. She stopped abruptly, staring at Weasel as if seeing him for the first time. Then she strode purposefully into the bedroom.

When she emerged a short time later, she was dressed to the teeth. She donned a hat and coat and snatched up her reticule, heading for the door.

'Come with me,' she said to Weasel.

'Where we going?' he asked, trailing obediently after her.

'We're going to get us an army,' she replied.

Captain Mike Patterson, a widower, had shed his uniform for the holiday. A stylish if flashy dresser, he was highly satisfied with his sartorial splendor as he left his boarding-house en route to his lone sister's house for Christmas dinner.

The cab he had arranged for was waiting at the curb, its driver already in his seat. Patterson was half into the vehicle before he realized that its interior was not empty. Instinctively, one hand went to the holster under his jacket.

'Oh, you won't need that, Captain,' Jolene assured him.

He hesitated for a moment; then, smiling, he entered the carriage and took the seat beside her. Almost at once the cab began to move.

'Miss Perreira, isn't it?' he greeted her. 'What a nice surprise, seeing you again – and looking so well.'

'I feel that I owe you my thanks,' Jolene said. 'I'm sure you must have had some influence in the way the Judge's death was handled.'

'An unfortunate accident,' Patterson said. 'My associates and I thought it best to play it down. The harsh glare of publicity can be unflattering.'

'Whatever the reasoning, it was to my benefit, and I'm grateful,' she said.

'Indeed. I wonder if the driver is going the right way?'

'He knows where to go.'

He had leaned forward in his seat. Now, with a sigh, he relaxed again. 'I have a feeling you didn't come to see me merely to express your gratitude,' he said. 'Tell me, Miss Perreira, to what do I owe the honor of your company?'

'The Brady Brothers,' she replied.

'I hope you're not planning on having me shanghaied,' he said.

'No. But a friend of mine has been.'

His eyes narrowed sharply. 'You don't mean Morrow, do you?'

She nodded, surprised. 'You're well informed, Captain,' she said.

'It's my business to know what's going on. I've known about Morrow since he's been in business on the Coast – and I knew when you moved in with him. You haven't exactly kept your light under a bushel down there, you know.' He shook his head thoughtfully. 'Well, well, so Morrow's gone, is he?'

'Not yet he isn't,' she said. 'There's still time.'

'Time for what?'

'Why, time to get him out of there. That's why I've come to see you.'

He laughed. 'I'll give you credit,' he said. 'You've got guts. And tell me, Miss Perreira – may I call you Jolene – what do I get out of this, outside of risking a bullet in the head?'

'You can have – ' she hesitated, lowering her eyes coquettishly – 'anything I have to give.'

He leaned back, letting his gaze move boldly up and down her body. 'We're alone in this carriage. What's to stop me from taking what I want anyway?'

'Nothing,' she said. 'Only, if I didn't kill you, the driver would.' She rapped on the roof with her parasol. Almost at once the communicating panel slid open and a six shooter was thrust through the opening. After a moment she rapped and the gun disappeared, the panel rasping closed.

'Impressive,' the Captain said, 'but hardly persuasive. I could kill him and you in a minute. You'll have to give me a better argument than that.'

'The public has been clamoring for over a year for the police to clean up the Barbary Coast. Breaking up their operation and arresting the Bradys would be a tremendous feather in your cap politically, Captain. It would surely mean a promotion.'

'Do you think the police haven't tried to break up the Bradys before? No one from down there wants to inform on them. We don't even know where their ranch is . . . '

'I know,' she said. 'I have someone who can take you there.'

He glanced at her with new appreciation. 'From what we've heard, they keep a dozen or more sharpshooters there.'

'Fifteen to twenty.'

'Fifteen or twenty men could hold off an army indefinitely,' he said.

'Our information is that they'll be taking the men out of there tonight, to a ship. We could set a trap for them, catch them outside.'

'We?'

'I plan to go too.'

The cab had rolled to a stop. Patterson leaned forward to glance out the window. He saw that they were in front of his station.

'You seem very sure of yourself, Miss Perreira,' he said, turning back to her.

She leaned toward him, the low cut bodice of her dress gaping to reveal an inviting expanse of alabaster flesh. One hand rested lightly upon his knee.

'You once indicated that you found me desirable, Captain,' she said in a throaty voice.

'You're asking me to risk my neck for a – a . . . '

The hand on his knee moved upward, stroking gently, the fingers teasing. 'Do you still want me?' she asked, wetting her lips with her tongue.

Their eyes met, hers bold, inviting, his reluctantly yielding. 'Hell, yes,' he said, seizing her hand and pressing it to his lips. 'Let's go to my place.'

'Later. After we've rescued Sloan.'

He squeezed her hand until she thought he would crush the fingers, his eyes all the while searching hers. 'And afterwards, you'll come with me? You swear it?'

'Hell, yes,' she said, echoing his words with a smile.

38

It was an unlikely group that gathered on a grassy knoll south of the city soon after dusk: Captain Mike Patterson, still wearing the suit he had intended for his sister's Christmas dinner; twenty uniformed policemen; Sam and Joe, looking decidedly ill at ease in the company of the lawmen; Weasel, who never carried a gun, bearing an antiquated rifle as long as he was; and Jolene. There had been objections to her accompanying them, but on this point she had been firm.

That she had been so quickly able to persuade Patterson to go against the Bradys was due as much to the climate of the times as it was to her persuasive charms. There had been, as she had noted, a recent clamor for police action against the city's criminal element.

Of course, the city's criminal element was not confined to the Barbary Coast; indeed, as Patterson well knew, there were more crimes, of greater magnitude, carried out in the city's board-rooms and mansions. Graft and corruption were rampant; the Southern Pacific dominated politics in the city, as it did through-out the state.

Against these giants, Patterson had neither the power nor the inclination to move; but the Bradys were a 'safe' target for action. They were notorious, they owned no votes, and paid no graft. Their arrest and the breakup of their ring would satisfy the general public that something was being done, and the city's bosses, public pressure removed, would join in the general praise for Patterson's actions.

At least, that was the outcome as he foresaw it, with but one major hitch – first, he had to arrest, or kill, the Bradys; and bitter experience had taught him that this was not an easy task to accomplish.

Jolene was left at the knoll. On this point, Patterson had been firm, and the others had sided unanimously with him.

'Ain't none of us going unless you stay here,' Weasel said, and Sam and Joe bobbed their heads in agreement.

The men, leaving their horses in her care, crept into positions surrounding the house that Joe had identified as the Bradys'. It was indeed built like a fortress, with a crude wooden stockade around it. Even with his present strength, Patterson had decided against trying to force their way inside; his men would have too little cover in the flat meadow outside the stockade, while those within would be virtually invulnerable.

Weasel, who knew almost everybody along the Barbary Coast, had learned that an Australian ship had limped into harbor a few days before, having suffered considerable damage and lost a large number of sailors in a typhoon. Its Captain had been seen in conversation with the Bradys, and the ship was rumored to be sailing with the dawn.

Patterson was gambling that the Captain would indeed be arriving during the night to pick up his new crew members. He had originally planned on rushing the stockade when the gate was opened for the Captain to enter, but Jolene had pointed out that Sloan and the others would probably still be inside and could all too easily be used as hostages. Instead, Patterson in-tended to wait until the ship's Captain and his 'purchases' were leaving. Five of his men would take places against the wall, and would rush the gate as soon as it opened. At the same time the others would dash from cover and follow them through the gate. The element of surprise would be on their side; even so, this would be no easy victory.

As if an omen, the moon rose bright and clear, an inland breeze sweeping away the fog that Patterson had hoped would help conceal them.

'Don't forget, it makes easier targets of them too,' he consoled his men, while inwardly cursing his luck.

An hour passed, and another. The men fidgeted. Jolene, safely out of sight, paced to and fro, pausing occasionally to caution the horses against any noise.

Midnight approached; Patterson had begun to suspect that Weasel's information had been false, when they heard the distant creak of wagon wheels on the road from the city and, a moment later, horses' hooves.

There were two men, one the Captain and the other who Patterson guessed to be his mate, armed with a shotgun. The Captain got down from the wagon and approached the gate; words were exchanged, too low for those hidden nearby to catch them, and the gate swung open.

When it had closed again, Patterson gave the signal and five shadowy figures crawled forward, taking positions on either side of the gate, pressed flat against the wall.

The transaction was handled quickly; it was not a business in which many social amenities were observed. Less than twenty minutes later they heard the warning creak of the wagon's wheels, approaching the gate from the inside.

The gate opened, the wagon started through. From his position, Patterson could see a dozen impressed seamen in the back of the cart, manacled and chained together. The ship's mate sat facing them, shotgun on his lap.

The horses were almost through the opening when someone called from within and the Captain reined them in. To Patterson's delight he saw all three of the Bradys – Michael, Vince, and the young one, Skip – approaching the wagon, which was now effectively blocking the gate, eliminating any possibility of its being closed when the attack began.

Careful to remain hidden in the shadows, Patterson raised his revolver, took careful aim, and shot a hole in the back of the mate's head.

All hell broke loose. The attackers were at the gate and

through it almost before those inside knew what was happening. The horses whinnied and stamped, bolting through the gate despite the Captain's efforts to back them into the stockade. Patterson saw Weasel dart toward the horses; the terrified beasts veered, overturning the wagon and spilling the Captain and the chained men on the ground. Before the Captain could recover, Weasel had the drop on him.

The shooting now was all in the yard within the stockade. Patterson moved to follow his men inside, but as he did so, the three Bradys dashed from inside. Seeing at a glance which way the wind blew, they had simply feinted to the side, allowing Patterson's men to rush inside. Now the brothers were making their escape.

Patterson aimed after the fleeing trio, but before he could shoot, they had disappeared into the shadows of a stand of trees.

Without the Bradys, the mission would be a waste. There was nothing for it but to go after them. He shouted for someone to follow him and, without waiting to see if they did, started running. He caught a glimpse of the three, silhouetted for a second against the sky as they ran over a hill, and a moment later crossing a moonlit glade.

Of a sudden he realized they were doubling back on a path that would lead them to where Jolene waited with the horses. He swore, crouching down as he crossed the glade. As he did so, a shot rang out and he felt a breath of air graze his cheek.

They knew he was after them; he'd have to be more cautious, even though that meant giving them the chance to escape. Getting himself killed wasn't part of his plan. They had enough of a lead on him, though, that unless someone stopped them, they were almost sure to reach the horses. Once on horseback, it would be hard to catch them.

And the only one who had any chance of stopping them was the girl.

'Damn,' he swore again, running right through a patch of brush that clawed at his clothes and tore his skin.

Jolene listened with pounding heart to the distant gunfire. The horses had begun to whinny nervously. She made no effort now to stop them, thinking the danger of discovery past and unaware that it was this very sound guiding the Bradys toward her.

She resisted an impulse to run toward the shooting. The men had been adamant about her staying away, but even more telling was her fear that something might go awry. If that Captain should manage to get away, with Sloan as his prisoner, she intended to see that he was stopped. From where she was she could look down on the road down which the wagon had traveled a short time before. Patterson had left a rifle with her, an eight-shot revolving Colt.

'Know how to fire one of these?' he had asked when he handed it to her.

'If I have to, I'll know how,' she had assured him.

Now, she kept the rifle trained on the road, watching and waiting. There was a rustle of brush behind her, but she guessed it to be the wind and kept her eyes glued to the road, wanting to take no chances of the wagon's escaping.

Patterson had seen and heard nothing for several minutes. He would have liked to shout a warning to the girl, but there was no telling where the Bradys were. They knew he was after them; one of them might be waiting, and a shout would tell them all too plainly where he was.

He crept forward, wanting to rush and knowing better than to do so. He stayed to the shadows, avoiding the moonlight that glared in the open. Unless his direction was off, she was over that hill there. As if to encourage him, one of the horses whinnied.

He mounted the hill, clinging to the shadow of a rock, and his heart skipped a beat. The meadow below was laid out like a stage, flooded with moonlight. Jolene was at the far side, her attention on the road beyond – and Michael Brady was no more than a yard or so away from her, creeping toward her with a knife raised to plunge into her back.

There was no time to wonder where the others were, or even weigh the pros and cons of what he did. Patterson stepped out from the rock, needing a clear shot because one was all he would get, and fired.

Michael Brady jerked and spun around, and fell dead; but Patterson had left himself open, and before he could seek the safety of the shadows, Skip Brady, who'd been watching for him, opened fire. Patterson fell forward, rolling a few feet down the hill before the trunk of a tree stopped him.

Jolene screamed with the first shot. She whirled about in time to see Michael Brady fall lifeless at her feet and, a split second later, Patterson felled by a shot out of the dark.

She threw herself to the ground, frantically crawling toward the patch of scrub bush nearby. 'Michael?' a voice called from the hill, and another, off to her right, said, 'He's dead, that cop killed him.'

'The girl?' the first voice asked. Jolene felt the hair rise on the back of her neck.

'She's still down there. She's got a gun.'

For a reply, Jolene lifted the rifle and fired in the direction of the first voice. The man yelped – wounded, but not dead. A moment later, a bullet smashed into a rock just inches from her head.

Two of them, somewhere in the dark surrounding her. She crawled backward, felt a rock with her foot, and crept behind it.

No use firing where the voices had been, by now they had surely moved. She thought, trying to fix each detail in her mind.

Only one of them had fired, and the one Patterson had killed had had a knife, but no gun – could the other be unarmed?

She smiled wryly to herself in the dark; small comfort even if it were true – one man with a gun was deadly enough.

Seconds crawled by. She wanted to run from where she was, but instinct told her that the first to move might be the first to die. She shifted the rifle, drying her hands on her blouse.

The minutes dragged by. The shooting had died down in the distance; the fight there was over, with what result she could not say. She wondered if she was going to die here on this scrubby knoll, alone in the darkness.

There was a scraping of boot on rock behind her. She turned and saw one of the Bradys, his wounded arm held close to his body, creeping toward her. He had his kerchief knotted between his hands, intending to choke her with it.

When she turned and saw him, he jumped toward her. With no time to aim and fire properly, she lifted the rifle to hip level and fired point blank. The man fell across her, dead.

By the time she struggled out from under him, though, and turned back to the clearing, the third man was standing there before her, his revolver trained on her.

'Come out of there,' he said. 'I'm taking you with me as a hostage.'

'You're taking nobody where you're going. They don't take hostages in hell,' Weasel said from behind him; he stepped into the clearing, his weapon aimed at Brady.

For a moment Brady glanced back and forth between the two of them. Jolene, scrambling to her feet, had her rifle trained on him now. He could kill one, or the other – but not both. With a shrug, as if it were of little consequence, Brady dropped his revolver.

Leaving Weasel to watch him, Jolene ran across the clearing and up the hill to where Patterson had fallen. He looked dead, but when she knelt and cradled his head in her hands, his eyes fluttered open.

'Don't talk,' she said. 'Someone will be here soon to look after you.'

'Too late for that,' he whispered hoarsely. 'The Bradys?'

'They're all accounted for.'

He was silent for a moment, as if contemplating her reply. 'Tell – tell me something,' he gasped after a moment. 'Would you – have come with me afterward?'

The lie came to her lips, but she could not utter it. This man had sacrificed his life to save hers. She owed him nothing if not, at least now, the truth.

'Hell, no,' she whispered.

'I figured,' he said. He tried for a laugh, coughed instead, staining his lips with blood, and died.

Patterson's men had succeeded in cleaning out the Bradys' stronghold. The Bradys' men were either dead or safely under arrest and their victims had been freed.

Sloan had been badly beaten and was still weak and dazed. Weasel commandeered a buggy that had belonged to the Bradys and drove it back to the city, with Jolene and Sloan riding in the back.

Jolene had to tell for the second time how the police had happened to make a raid on the Bradys at just this time. Sloan listened, unusually sober for him.

'I've still got a score to settle with Trémorel,' he said when she had finished.

'Trémorel's dead,' she said. She told him in a matter-of-fact voice how Richard had died, making light of her own part in the episode.

'And to think I once thought of you as a helpless little kitten,' Sloan said admiringly. 'Just goes to show you what a woman will do for a man she loves.'

'It shows no such thing,' she said sharply. 'I just didn't want the job of running all those businesses myself. You know I won't set foot in the houses.'

He made no reply, though out of the corner of her eye she caught a glimpse of him smiling foolishly.

'Besides,' she added after a lengthy silence, 'I think a baby ought to have a father.'

It was a full moment before the meaning of her words reached him. 'Jolene, you don't mean – you and I . . . ? Are you sure?'

'Pretty sure,' she said.

'Well, I'll be damned. I'll really be damned, if that doesn't beat everything.' He was silent for a moment. Then he said, 'Jolene, I want you to marry me. For the kid's sake. Will you do it?'

She shrugged. 'Might as well. There's no one else asking.' After a moment, she added, 'For the kid's sake.'

'Of course,' he agreed.

They were riding through the darkness of a grove of trees, and neither could see the other, smiling into the darkness.

39

Philip dismounted and walked his horse the last quarter mile up the lane. It was late, sometime well after midnight, and he saw no need to disturb all those who would be sleeping.

He had been to San José, to inspect their vineyards there, and had ridden since the previous dawn, hoping to get home to share at least a little of the holiday with his wife.

Not, he reflected bitterly, that his presence would make the holiday happy for either of them; there was no longer any happiness between Elena and him. Still, he felt that he owed it to her, especially in her condition.

A wave of self loathing swept over him when he thought of the baby she was carrying – his baby, his and his sister's. There had been times since he had learned of it that he had wished the baby would die unborn, though afterward he had been consumed with guilt for his wishes.

He reached the barnyard before he saw that, though the big house was dark as he had anticipated, there was a lamp glowing from the window of his own cottage.

He could have had electricity installed in the cottage, as it had been in the big house; for that matter, he could have moved into the big house if he had chosen. Adam had died in the first days of December and lay buried now alongside his mother and father. His widow Maude had quit the ranch, choosing to live in the city rather than, as she put it, 'with Mexican whores'.

True to his word, Jean had supported Philip's claim to his inheritance, though as it turned out his support hadn't been so essential as they had expected. Adam's will had made his relationship to Philip quite clear and had, in accordance with his father's wishes before him, left Philip a full portion of the estate.

Nonetheless, Philip had continued to live in the same shack in which he had lived as a child. He could not have explained why, though perhaps he simply did not want to dignify his marriage by transferring it to the big house.

He was Philip Brussac now, in name as well as in fact. He had accomplished what he had set out to accomplish, proved what he had needed to prove; but the difference between his shack and the big house served to remind him of how much he had lost: Marie and René were both dead – a letter had arrived from some provincial law office, informing him of the fact and asking what should be done with the chateau; the letter had gone unanswered.

Jolene was lost to him. He could not, even now, bear to think of her. Elena, the sister he had sworn to protect, loathed him, though not half so much as he loathed himself.

Jean, who had never cared to rule, now deferred to him in most matters pertaining to French Hills, making Philip its master, but their relationship was strictly a business one, fair but lacking any friendliness or warmth. His other uncle, David, had only rarely visited French Hills, and though he had been friendly, he too was gone now. The rest of the family – his family, though they hated acknowledging it – despised him openly.

Philip had intended to see to his horse, but the lighted window had begun to worry him. Elena's time was still nearly a month away; on the other hand, women did deliver early.

He tied his horse, still saddled, to a post and walked quickly toward the shack. She was not expecting him back for another day or two; perhaps, if her time actually had come, she would be grateful for his presence. It was the least he could do, to ease her unhappiness in whatever small ways he could.

It did not occur to him to knock, or signal his arrival in any way; this was his home after all. He stepped into the house and froze just inside the front door, taking in the scene in stages: Elena, naked on the bed, her belly bloated; Caleb, lying naked beside her, his hand lost to sight between her thighs; Harvey, standing by the table in his drawers, pouring a drink from a bottle.

It hit him like a blow in the stomach, and for a moment he was actually blind with rage and despair. He moved across the room, not even hearing Elena's squeal of fright, nor Caleb's oaths.

Harvey stepped into Philip's path. 'Phil, boy, listen here,' he said, slurring his words drunkenly.

Philip shoved him so violently that Harvey toppled right through the front window, glass and frame clattering noisily on the porch outside.

Caleb was dancing on one foot, frantically trying to get the other into his trousers. Philip seized him, flinging him hard against the wall. Before Caleb could get his breath, Philip was upon him, pounding his fists into his cousin's face and stomach.

'Let him be,' Elena screamed, trying to cling to Philip's arm. He flung her aside like a rag doll. She fell into the corner with a shriek. She started to get up, then groaned and clutched at her swollen midsection, sinking back into the corner helplessly.

Caleb had taken advantage of the distraction and had almost made it to the door, but Philip caught him, swinging him around and again pounding his fists into Caleb's already battered face.

Harvey, dazed and shaking his head, staggered through the door and attempted to help his brother, but Philip, stepping backward, snatched up a chair and brought it down over Harvey's head, knocking him cold.

Caleb ran naked into the yard, shouting, 'Help, help, he's gone loco.'

'I'll kill you, you son of a bitch,' Philip roared, but when he went to go after him, he tripped over Harvey's legs and fell to the floor. By the time he'd gotten to his feet and staggered to the door, Caleb had disappeared.

'Where are you, damn you?' Philip shouted, ignoring the lights that were rapidly coming on in the big house.

'What the hell's going on out there?' Jean shouted, but Philip ignored him too. He stumbled to the barn, flinging its doors open. He heard nothing but the uneasy shuffling of the animals in their stalls.

In the loft above him, Caleb fought against an overpowering urge to pee. He had always been frightened of the Frenchman, but never before had he seen him in such a murderous rage. If Philip found him now . . . despite his efforts, he felt a warm stream trickling down his leg.

He burrowed further back into the hay, and as he did so his fingers touched cold metal. He discovered the prongs of a pitchfork.

He felt a warm sense of relief. Philip was out to kill him. All right, then, it was kill or be killed; no one could blame him for defending himself against a madman.

He stood, careful to make no noise, and lifted the pitchfork from the hay, but by this time Philip had gone back out into the yard.

Caleb stepped to the hayloft window, overlooking the yard. There, in the moonlight directly below him, stood Philip, his back turned, looking toward the house.

The hayloft window was too small to allow him to throw the long pitchfork from within. He stepped to the opening, leaning precariously out and holding to the jamb with one hand, while with the other he raised the fork to hurl it down at Philip.

On the porch of the big house, Jean saw Philip, his back to the barn, and Caleb, poised to kill him. 'Caleb, no,' he shouted.

Caleb, turning his head in the direction of his father's voice, swayed drunkenly. The heavy pitchfork slipped from his fingers and fell toward the ground. A second later, Caleb lost his precarious footing and fell after it.

They landed almost at Philip's feet. He turned, in time to see Caleb impale himself on the prongs of the pitchfork. Caleb gasped and writhed for a moment; then his body stiffened and went limp.

'You killed him,' Harvey shouted, staggering up with a gun in his hand. 'I'll kill you for this.' He raised the gun but Jean, striding up, snatched it out of his hand.

'No,' Jean said, kneeling to examine Caleb briefly. 'We all saw what happened.'

'Is he . . . ?' Harvey asked.

'He's dead.'

'He killed him, Pa,' Harvey cried. 'You going to let him get away with that? Caleb was your son.'

'Caleb killed himself, like the fool he was,' Jean said. He took off the robe he'd grabbed when the ruckus broke out, and spread it over his dead son. 'Go to bed, Harvey, you stink of liquor.'

'No. I won't go to bed,' Harvey said. 'I won't stay here either to wait for him to kill me and steal everything from the real Brussacs.'

'You're drunk,' Jean said coldly.

'I may be, but drunk or sober, I know when I'm being robbed, and that's more than you can say.' He started for the house, shouting over his shoulder, 'I'm getting my things and riding out of here. But you, Frenchie, don't you worry, I'll be back one of these days, to settle things with you.'

He disappeared inside. Philip, drained of his anger, was aware of several of the work women running to and from his shack. He thought of Elena and the way he'd flung her violently aside, and moved to go to her but, when he glanced back, Jean had knelt again beside Caleb's body.

He went to Jean and laid a hand gently upon his shoulder. 'I'm sorry,' he said.

'You didn't do anything,' Jean said.

'Except come back.'

There was no reply and after a minute Philip returned to his shack, but the women barred his way, telling him that it was Elena's time, and they would summon him when it was finished.

Numbly, he went into the house, to the room that had been his father's study. He poured himself a brandy and seated himself behind Adam's old, work-scarred desk, remembering the day when his father, seated at the same desk, had informed him that he was going to France. It was the day of his mother's funeral; and the day, too, when he had first told Jolene he loved her.

'Señor?' It was one of the women. Philip rose and followed her through the night, to the shack, that looked crowded now with women. They parted as he came in, forming a path that led to the bed, where he could see Elena, her sweat-streaked face pale in the lamplight. She seemed to be asleep.

'Is she . . . ?'

'She is all right,' one of the women said. 'She lost much blood, but she will live.'

'Señor,' another said, 'your son.'

The first thing he saw was the twisted foot, looking almost like a devil's hoof. His fault? The stain of his sin?

'Would you like to hold him,' the woman asked, thrusting the tiny, wizened form toward him.

Philip recoiled as if she had thrust a serpent toward him. 'No,' he said, and again, 'No.' He turned from the shocked faces of the women and, stumbling to the porch outside, retched violently.

PART 3

1905

40

'Mommy, Mommy, come look.'

'I'll be right there,' Jolene called from the bedroom, where she had been trying on a new dress. She paused for a moment, critically examining her figure in the mirror. It was no use, cinch it though she might, her waist would simply never be as slim as it had been before. She sighed; the all-too-visible effects of marriage and childbirth.

Still, she consoled herself, tossing the dress aside for alteration, that was almost the only complaint she had. In the nearly five years since their marriage, Sloan had been a good husband; after what had gone before, she could all the more appreciate the happiness and ease of her present life. If only Philip . . . She frowned, resenting the intrusion of that name in her thoughts.

'Mommy.'

'Yes, darling, I'm coming.'

She came into the living-room to find her four-year-old daughter standing on the sofa to peer out the window. 'Zan, dear, be careful, you'll fall,' she said.

She crossed the room and lifted a squirming Alexandra from the sofa, kissing the top of her head affectionately. She supposed in reality that it was the coming of their daughter that had cemented the partnership between herself and Sloan. Certainly there was no question that he adored Alexandra as much as she did – and, she added ruefully, spoiled her frightfully.

'But Mommy, look,' Zan insisted, pointing at the window.

Jolene did, bending down to look outside. 'Good Heavens,' she exclaimed after one brief glance.

'It's a motor car,' Zan cried, wriggling out of her mother's grasp and dashing to the door.

'Zan . . . ' She was too late, Zan had already flung open the front door and raced down the steps, flinging herself into her father's arms.

Though how she could identify him as her father was a mystery to Jolene, following her more decorously down the steps. Sloan wore a long tan coat that looked like an overlong painter's smock – they called the coats 'automobiles' – and a rakish cap, with goggles that fitted closely about his eyes. His face was so blackened by dust from the streets that even when he removed the goggles, their outline could be plainly seen.

'Do you like it?' he asked her as she joined them, indicating the machine parked at the curb.

'It's – it's certainly awesome,' she said, regarding the contraption with a mixture of wonder and trepidation.

Awesome was perhaps an understatement; Jolene already could see neighbors peering from their windows, and one gentleman had already emerged from his house across the street to stare openly at the motor car.

It was white, with red trim and two elegant-looking armchairs upholstered in red leather. Massive fenders flared over the four rubber-rimmed wheels, and on either side of the passenger compartment were gigantic acetylene lamps that goggled at oncomers. Another wheel, wooden and considerably smaller, rose from a massive brass column directly in front of one of the armchairs – presumably the one to be occupied by the driver – and beside the same seat was an array of levers and pedals and a rubber-bulb horn that honked raucously when Alexandra squeezed it, to her delight. Stacked on a platform behind the red chairs were three replacement tires for the ones mounted on the running wheels.

'It's beautiful, Daddy – is it ours?' Alexandra asked, climbing up into the machine.

'It certainly is,' Sloan replied, beaming with pride. 'Come on, ladies, get your hats and coats, and we'll go for a ride.'

Alexandra squealed with delight and raced up the stairs to the house. Looking after her disapprovingly, Jolene asked, 'Do you think it's safe? For Alexandra, I mean.'

'As safe as a horse-drawn buggy,' Sloan reassured her. 'How about putting up a picnic lunch?'

'Judging from your appearance,' she said, going up the stairs with him, 'I'd do better to take a basin and a pitcher of water. You're sure Alexandra will be all right? What about her eyes . . . ?'

'I've got goggles for both of you, to keep the dirt out,' Sloan said, taking her arm in his.

Although the motor car was new, the tone of their conversation was not. Their battles with one another were still frequent and stormy, but on the subject of Alexandra's well being, they remained in unvarying agreement. Both parents idolized their daughter, only slightly more so than did Weasel, who was in complete thralldom to her. And both Jolene and Sloan were determined that their child would grow up better protected and cared for than they had been in their widely different backgrounds.

The fact that they were unlikely to have any more children only intensified their attitudes. Like all the women of her family, Jolene had had a difficult time giving birth, and the doctor had been firm in advising against any others.

For her part, Jolene had always felt that her own mother had been too wrapped up in her many schemes to regain French Hills to provide her with the kind of maternal protection she had needed. Was it not her own mother, after all, who had first thrust Richard Trémorel at her, hoping for an advantageous marriage? As a result, she had grown up vulnerable to men like Philip and Richard. She was willing to take the blame for the mistakes she had made, but she intended to see that Alexandra was shielded from making the same mistakes.

Sloan, on the other hand, had grown up with almost no restraints, and he had loved it. It was true that his father had been a ne'er-do-well, and that they had lived for most of his young years from hand to mouth; but he had survived and in many ways thought himself stronger for his upbringing.

It was not, however, the way he wanted his daughter raised, and he was quite as protective of her as Jolene was, with the result that Alexandra's existence was peculiarly cocoonlike. She was in many ways sophisticated beyond her years by virtue of her contact with Weasel and the Barbary Coast habitués who made up her acquaintance. At the same time, she knew no other children even close to her age and was as adamantly sheltered from those in the neighborhood as if in Oriental purdah.

Like a princess in a fairy tale, Alexandra grew in the sheltering love of her parents, without knowing the real world at all.

Within a short time, and over Weasel's dire warnings of tragedy, the three were soon ready to set out. Jolene and Alexandra had donned long raglan coats, with scarves holding their hats securely to their heads, and the goggles Sloan had brought them.

There were only the two seats, which meant holding Alexandra on her lap, but Jolene was just as glad for an excuse to keep a tight hold on her.

In order to start the car, it was necessary for Sloan to go to the front and turn a hefty-looking crank, which he did with every evidence that it was strenuous work indeed, his face contorting and sweat breaking out on his brow.

After a few loud coughs, the engine roared into life and Sloan bounded into the driver's seat, still breathing heavily from his exertions. A moment later, the carriage had begun to move along the street under its own power.

'Darling, don't squirm,' Jolene said, coughing as the dust rose up about them in a cloud. She held tightly to her daughter with one hand, while with the other she clung to the arm of her seat. A middle-aged couple, traveling the opposite direction in a buggy, glowered at them as they passed.

'What do you think?' Sloan called over the motor's roar, not unlike that of a steadily fired gun.

'It's certainly fast,' Jolene answered. There was no denying that the wind whipping in their faces combined with the sensation of speed to form an exhilarating effect.

'It'll do up to eighty-five miles in an hour.'

'Not while we're riding in it, I trust,' she said dryly.

'Think of it, Jolene – why, a man could travel from San Francisco to Los Angeles in a matter of hours, in the comfort of his own motor car.'

Though she was not so sure of the term 'comfort', Jolene had to admit that the speed and convenience of the motor car certainly opened the door to new attitudes toward travel. Aside from the requirement of roads – and there were roads of one sort or another virtually anywhere – there was almost no limitation on where a family might go; no longer need they be tied to railroad lines and schedules or to the slowness and rigors of horse-drawn travel.

She had a sudden and not altogether comforting vision of streams of motor cars racing to and fro in every direction across the land, belching smoke from their rears, their engines roaring at one another in passing. The horse, who had served man so nobly, almost since he had clambered from his caves, would vanish. Gone would be the elegant coaches and broughams; gone the riding free in the hills, horse and rider somehow mystically welded into one; gone that mysterious and romantic clatter of hooves just beyond the moonlit bend – who had not felt heart quicken at the sound?

They had left the city behind them and Sloan, spying a shady grove of trees only a short walk back from the road, said, 'This looks like a good spot.'

With Weasel's grudging help, Jolene had packed them a hamper of food before they set out, and now they lunched on cold chicken, grapes and cheese, washed down with lemonade for Alexandra and a bottle of wine for Sloan and Jolene.

Afterward, while Sloan stowed the hamper in the car, Jolene and Alexandra made their way to a nearby stream where Jolene used her handkerchief to wash some of the road-dust from their faces.

'There's one thing that can be said for motor car travel,' she remarked when they were once more on board and Sloan had, after considerable effort, cranked the engine into life again. 'It may be fast and convenient, but it is certainly dirty. I think that alone will prevent its ever really catching on with the upper crust. Aren't we going in the wrong direction?'

Sloan, instead of turning back the way they had come, had instead turned the other way, as if to continue on their journey.

'We've still got quite a distance to go,' he said.

For the first time since they'd started out, she gave conscious thought to the direction in which they had been traveling.

'Just where are we going anyway?' she asked, her eyes narrowing suspiciously.

'Brussac-America,' he answered simply.

'Sloan! Stop this car – you can't be serious.' She was aghast at the suggestion. Although she had sent an anonymous gift to her parents each year at Christmas, she had had no direct communication with them since she had left home in the company of Richard Trémorel.

She had thought of them longingly in the years of what she regarded as her exile. She missed the quiet depth of her father's affection, and she had even, with the passing of time, been able to forgive her mother for her machinations and their unhappy results; but whether they had ever forgiven her was another matter altogether. She knew all too well how stubborn her mother's pride was, and as for her father, her running away would certainly have wounded him to the quick. She had often contemplated writing to them, but the fear that her letter might be returned unopened had prevented her from doing so, and as time had gone on its way, the gulf between them had widened until it seemed to her quite unbridgeable.

'Never been more serious in my life,' Sloan replied.

'But – but what if they won't see us? They're very proud people, and very stubborn.'

'They'll want to see their granddaughter,' he said. 'Zan is our entry-ticket, and they'll have to take us in the bargain.'

Zan, stuffed with food and surfeited with riding, had fallen asleep on her mother's lap. Glancing down at her sleeping face, Jolene recognized the rightness of his reasoning.

'You've obviously thought ahead,' she admitted reluctantly. 'But why? I don't understand . . . '

'She's why,' Sloan said, indicating their sleeping daughter. 'Look at her, as lovely and as innnocent as a lamb – how long do you think she'd stay that way, growing up on the Barbary Coast. Do you know the latest word she's added to her vocabulary? Trollop. And God knows what others.'

Jolene was both shocked and amused. 'I hadn't heard that one,' she admitted, shaking her head. Clearly not by accident, Sloan had touched upon the one argument most likely to still her objections. Protecting Alexandra from unsavory influences had become almost a full-time occupation for her, and not, judging from Alexandra's increasing vocabulary of unsavory words and expressions, a successful one.

'You're speaking as if you mean to remove her permanently from the Coast,' she said aloud.

'Don't you think we should? It's been all right for us, I grew up in that sort of environment, and you had the necessary fortitude to make the adjustment, but it's no place to bring up a child – not our child, at any rate.'

'But your businesses – the Golden Crest . . . '

'Belongs now to a trio of bankers, though all the papers were drawn up in their lawyers' names. Wouldn't do to have their clientele know they were investing in gambling halls,' he said. 'They're all gone, Jolie, the bars, the houses, the lot of them, I sold them all off. We're not going back to the Coast, except to get our things.'

'But – but what are we going to do?' The news had been too big, and too sudden, for her to comprehend all at once. There had been no warning, no inkling – Sloan had been out a great deal, seeing his attorney often, but far from suspecting the truth, she had thought he was investing in yet another establishment.

'We're going to make peace with your family. And I'm going to offer to buy into Brussac-America, as a partner.'

'You know nothing about making wine,' she said, still bewildered by this unexpected turn of events.

'I knew nothing about running a whorehouse either, when I opened my first one. But I can learn.'

'And what if my father refuses your offer?'

The line of his mouth went grim. 'Then I'll offer again, and again and again.' He glanced sideways to look at her, though they could hardly see one another's eyes for the dust on the goggles they both wore.

'They're her family, her grandparents, the only ones she'll ever know. A child misses that, a family, roots, bloodlines – I know. She's got a right to them, whether they like it or not, and I intend to see that right acknowledged. They'll accept, all right, even if they don't like it. They'll accept it because it's the right thing to do.'

'You sound awfully sure of yourself, considering you don't even know my parents,' she said.

He grinned and said, 'They're Brussacs, aren't they? I've always heard the Brussacs are exceptional people.'

'It's true, my mother's a Brussac, but . . . ' She let the sentence go unfinished, her thoughts going back, as they had not for many years, over what she knew of Brussac history – the squabbles and the battles royal, her mother's never ceasing struggle to wrest from her brothers' hands the inheritance she thought they'd cheated her of, the passions bright, and dark, that were the landmarks of the family's past.

Exceptional, indeed, she agreed privately; and entirely unpredictable. She held her sleeping daughter on her lap and looked forward with both dread and pleasure to the meeting toward which they rushed with motorized speed.

41

The noise of its engine provided advance news of its arrival long before the motor car itself, with its occupants, came into view. By that time, most of Brussac-America's servants and field hands had collected on the porch and the lawn to watch.

At first, examining the crowd from some distance, Jolene did not recognize her parents. Not until the Mercedes was closer and her father had come down the steps from the porch, the others parting like waves before him, did she recognize that bent and limping figure as the man who had towered over her in the past.

It was easier then to identify her mother, though she had

remained on the porch. She too had aged, and there was no sign of greeting in the unsmiling manner in which she watched the arrival.

It seemed to take forever for the motor car to negotiate that last quarter mile of lane. Alexandra, awakened by the tension in the air, was standing on her mother's lap, squealing with excitement and waving enthusiastically at the gathering throng. The car had no more than stopped than she had jumped to the ground.

Jolene was almost as quick, running to her father and unabashedly flinging her arms about him.

'Papa, oh, Papa,' she cried, hugging him and pressing a tear-stained cheek against his. He patted her shoulder gently, still staring past her at the gleaming car, at the man who had brought it at last to a quiet stop, and the small girl who had come to tug at Jolene's skirt.

'So you've come back,' Mary said from the porch. It was said flatly, without emotion.

Jolene, recovering herself and remembering the estrangement of the last several years, took a step back from her father, and turned toward the house.

'Yes,' she said. She waited, but there was no word as to whether her return was welcome or not, and finally she said, 'This is my husband, Sloan Morrow, and this is my – your granddaughter, Alexandra.'

Sloan came forward without an invitation, pushing his goggles back on his head and shaking his father-in-law's hand enthusiastically. 'Pleased to meet you, sir, and you too, ma'am, mighty pleased to meet you both.'

It was an awkward meeting, not only because of past quarrels but because most of the people here had never seen a motor car before, and the appearance of those who had come in it, as well as the machine itself, dominated their attention, even though they might try to act otherwise. With their hats, gloves and long coats, and road dirt leaving an outline of goggles on their faces, the three could almost have come from another planet. One of the pickers shuffled forward cautiously to touch Alexandra's hair, as if afraid it might be of some alien substance.

Thinking that he meant to play, Alexandra gave a squeal of delight and darted behind her mother's protective skirts, peering around them with a wide grin.

A collective sigh of relief rippled through the onlookers, and the ice was broken. A number of people began to talk at once, some of them remembering and greeting Jolene, and others talking to one another excitedly.

'Perhaps we'd better go in,' Mary said. She still had not moved from the porch and now, without waiting to see if they followed, she turned and re-entered the house. Shooing Alexandra before her like a shield, Jolene went in after her, leaving Sloan and her father to come in together. She could hear Sloan asking him questions already about the near vineyards, and her father's monosyllabic answers.

José offered them sherry, and one of the maids brought lemonade for Alexandra. 'I was thrown from a horse,' José explained when Jolene inquired about his limp, but he did not embellish the story.

There were no questions about what their daughter had been doing since she had left their roof, and from that absence Jolene suspected that they knew something of her experiences.

Sloan had been right, however, for no matter how her parents might feel about her return, or the news of a new son-in-law, they were fascinated by Alexandra, who chatted with any and all in the room, blissfully unaware of any undercurrents of emotion.

Sloan exhibited an equally unconcerned manner, though Jolene knew that his, unlike his daughter's, was play-acting. Quite as if they were old acquaintances discussing a business arrangement, he explained to Jolene's father that he had recently liquidated his business interests and that he now had at hand a considerable sum of money, which he wished to invest. He paused at this juncture in his monologue, waiting for some reaction.

'Why should you tell me these things?' José asked.

'It's my hope to invest it in Brussac-America,' Sloan said.

'You mean you want to buy into our family?' José asked coldly.

'No, sir,' Sloan replied, unperturbed, 'I've already married into that. I want to buy into your business.'

'Why?'

Sloan shrugged and said, 'Because it's a good, solid business, and I've got to put my money into something. Because I want to restore my wife to her family. Because I want my daughter to know her grandparents, and to grow up somewhere where the air is clean and the nights free of curses and gunshots. Also,' he allowed himself a faint grin, 'I've always had a taste for wine.'

'Drinking it's a damn sight easier than making it,' José said. He got up, shoving his chair back angrily, and strode toward the french doors that would have carried him to the patio in the rear, but Alexandra was there, blocking his exit, and as he approached she pointed in the direction of the vineyards and asked, 'What are those?'

José, caught off guard by the question, stopped dead and followed her pointing finger. 'They're vines,' he answered, 'grape vines.'

'There sure are a lot of them,' Alexandra observed, adding in a confidential aside, 'We eat grapes at home.'

'Do you, now?' José replied. 'And would you like to see where they come from?'

'Oh yes,' Alexandra clapped her hands enthusiastically.

'So would I,' Sloan said, coming to join them.

For a brief moment José looked him up and down, as if weighing him. Then, without a reply, he turned and, taking Alexandra's hand, led her outside, Sloan following.

Jolene was left with her mother. They had never been close, and a bitter quarrel and five years' separation had not brought them closer. She was grateful when Mary offered her another glass of sherry.

'This – man of yours . . . ' Mary said, refilling both their glasses.

'My husband,' Jolene supplied.

'Yes, exactly. What sort of person is he?'

'He's a reprobate,' Jolene said. 'A gambler, a card-sharp, and a frequent trader in human vice.'

Mary permitted herself the ghost of a smile. 'Yes, of course, well, you would have him on a pedestal. But what I really wanted to know is, this idea of his, of investing in Brussac-America – is he serious, do you think?'

'Oh, entirely serious,' Jolene answered.

'And he actually wants to become a vintner? Would he be any good at it?'

Through the open windows she could see her father and Sloan, Alexandra skipping at their heels as they strolled the edge of the vineyard. Papa was explaining something, lifting one hand in a grandiloquent gesture; Sloan said something and they stopped, talking spiritedly to one another.

She realized that her mother was still waiting for an answer, and shrugged. 'Who can say? He told me years ago he intended to marry me and I thought he was crazy – but as you can see, when Sloan makes up his mind to something, he's likely to have it the way he wanted.'

'Yes, I would have thought that about him,' Mary said. She took her drink to stand by the window, watching the three at the vineyard. After a moment, she said, 'Tell your husband that Brussac-America would welcome his investment, as a partner.'

'Papa seemed unenthusiastic,' Jolene said.

'He looks quite enthusiastic now. At any rate, leave him to me.'

'I'm sure Sloan will be grateful . . .'

'I'm not doing it for Sloan, or for you – or even for myself,' Mary snapped without looking at her. 'I'm doing it for him. He's a fine winemaker but a poor businessman. I've had the responsibility of running this business, and now I long to hand the responsibility over to someone else. I've watched and waited and prayed for someone competent enough to take over, so that I could be done with it.'

She paused to look over her shoulder. 'Is your husband that man, do you think?'

'Sloan is a very competent businessman. I don't think you'll be disappointed.'

Mary's attention returned to the scene outside. 'He'll need something more than that, of course. What he needs is someone to share it all with him – not just the work of it, but the love of it as well. I hope your young man will do that too. I owe him that much for these years with me – all these years.'

'He's had you to share it all with him, and you've loved it with him,' Jolene said.

Mary turned, her eyes glinting. 'I've hated it,' she snapped. 'Always – every bottle, every vine, every last grape of it.'

Jolene was taken aback by the statement, delivered with such intensity that one could hardly doubt that it was true. 'I – I didn't know,' she stammered. 'Mama – I'm sorry . . . you always worked so hard at it . . .'

'It's because I hated *them* more,' she said, leaving no doubt to whom she referred. For a moment her face was contorted with bitterness, but it passed as quickly as it had come. She studied Jolene for a moment in silence, as if actually seeing her for the first time since her return. 'I was prettier than you, you know,' she said finally.

'I hope that it brought you better luck than it brought me,' Jolene said.

To her surprise, Mary laughed aloud. 'Yes, it can be a curse, can't it? There have been times when I've seen some lumpy-faced matron looking jealously at me and thought, if only she knew how much I envied her.'

Jolene, who was too well acquainted with her mother's vanity to take this remark seriously, said nothing.

'I tried to run away once with Richard Trémorel,' Mary said. 'They locked me in my room and when Richard came for our rendezvous, your father was waiting in my place, to trounce him soundly. Though I didn't know it was your father until some years later.'

'Richard is dead,' Jolene said; it was the first she'd told anyone except Sloan, and she hadn't really planned on telling her mother, but the news had seemed to slip out on its own.

'Did your husband kill him?' Mary asked, looking surprised.

'No. I did,' Jolene said.

'Did you, now?' Mary said, regarding her with renewed interest. 'Perhaps after all you're not such a fool as I took you to be. You must tell me about it later, when we can talk at length. I want to savor every detail to the fullest.'

The two, mother and daughter, smiled at one another across the room, and this time the smiles were genuine, and Jolene knew at last that she had come home.

42

The mariachi music guided him to the unfamiliar bar. Philip tied up his horse outside and went in, pushing aside the filthy curtain that hung in the doorway in lieu of a solid door.

The room was so poorly lighted and so thick with smoke that it was a minute or two before he could see clearly enough to identify anyone. Several tough-looking types studied him from a table just inside, but he ignored them, his eyes scanning the remaining tables and the bar.

She was at the far end of the bar, between two cowboys, one of whom had his arm about her shoulders. He had been through this so often by now that Philip no longer felt anger, only disgust and a pervasive sense of despair.

Nevertheless he elbowed his way through the bar to stand

behind her. 'It's time to go home, Elena,' he said, quietly but firmly.

She ignored him, though the cowboy with his arm around her shoulders gave him a dirty look.

'Better take your hands off her,' Philip said, speaking directly to the cowboy. 'I'm the lady's husband. I've come to take her home.'

'He ain't my husband,' Elena said without turning. 'Ain't no husband of mine.'

'The lady says you ain't her husband,' the cowboy said, without moving his arm.

'The lady's drunk, not to mention half crazy.'

'Who you calling crazy?' Elena demanded. 'You calling me crazy, and all the while it was you – it was you . . . ' She fumbled with the words, forgetting half way through the sentence what she had intended to say, and beginning to cry instead.

'You got the lady upset,' the cowboy said. 'I think you better move on out of here, fella, whatdyasay?'

Philip took a deep breath. He could feel the sweat beading on his brow. Their conversation had attracted the attention of others in the bar, who were watching with varying degrees of interest and even amusement. He saw a Chinese man standing in the door from the kitchen, and the bartender had been polishing the same glass since Philip had come in, all the while eyeing him suspiciously.

'I say, I'm taking the lady with me and I'm leaving this hole right now,' Philip said, reaching for Elena's arm.

'And I say,' the cowboy began, but Philip never heard what it was he meant to say. He had forgotten the cowboy's companion, seated on the other side of Elena, until he saw the sudden movement from that quarter, out of the corner of his eye. Philip ducked, but not fast enough; the beer bottle in the man's hand caught him alongside the head, making the entire room tilt sickeningly. Philip grabbed out, trying to catch his balance, but the cowboy brought a beefy fist crashing into his chin, and the bar room seemed to explode inside Philip's head.

And continued to explode, like a row of cannon being fired off one by one. He was momentarily aware of cold and damp, and the hard, rough surface of a street against the flesh of his cheek. He heard a whispering of voices, the words unintelligible – for Christ's sake, were they talking Chinese? Someone put their hands under him, as if they meant to lift him, but at the first movement the pain exploded again and he sank spinning into the blackness.

When he woke again, it was to discover that he was in bed. He forced one eye open, willing it to focus, and had a limited view of a bare wooden floor, a lattice-work screen, and beyond the screen, someone moving very quietly.

The room was unfamiliar to him. He lifted his head, which proved to be a painful operation, and took a better look around, but he was still unable to say where he was, or how he'd come to be there.

'Good, you are awake then,' a female voice said. He looked in that direction and saw someone looking through the screen at him. She stepped around it and he caught his breath.

She was as pretty and delicate looking as a china doll – or rather, he thought, his thoughts still turning slowly, a Chinese doll, for she was certainly Chinese. Her hair, black and sleek, hung straight to her shoulders, framing an oval face dominated by wide, dark eyes and lips that might have been formed of flower petals.

How long he had stared, or how much of what he was thinking showed on his face, he couldn't say, but her lips suddenly parted in a grin as if she had read his thoughts openly.

'Who are you?' he asked, 'and what am I doing here?'

'I am Anna,' she said, kneeling to examine a painful gash that ran across one side of his forehead. Despite the gentle touch of her fingers, he winced. 'You were in a fight . . . '

'I remember that much,' he said when she paused, studying his wound, 'though I wouldn't exactly call it a fight – more like I got the stuffing knocked out of me.'

She smiled again, to dazzling effect. 'They dragged you to the alley in back and left you there. When they had gone, my father and I brought you home, here. That was yesterday, and it is now night again. You have slept for a long time.'

She saw his eyes go to his shirt and trousers, hanging on the back of a chair at the foot of the bed. He was wondering who had undressed him, but she misread the glance.

'They took everything,' she said, 'except a gold watch, which they overlooked. Its chain was broken and it had fallen to the ground near where you lay, so perhaps they did not see it in the dark. I've put it atop the dresser there, for safe keeping.'

'I'm grateful,' he said. 'And to you and your father for bringing me here. I shall go now . . . ' He tried to sit up but the effort sent the room rocking and swaying, and he was forced to fall back upon the pillow.

'Whatever it is that you must go to,' she said, 'it has waited one day already, through no fault of your own. Surely it can wait another.'

He would have liked to reply and agree with her, but he was already drifting into unconsciousness, only this time he took with him an image of wide, dark eyes and lips the color of cherries.

She was still there when he opened his eyes some time later, the wide eyes watching him with concern. For a moment they gazed into his own and Philip had an uncanny sensation of something dark and heavy being lifted from within him.

' "Anna" isn't Chinese,' he said.

The remark jolted her, though it had been circling in his mind since she'd first spoken her name earlier. She laughed, an easy, musical sound.

'I am American,' she said. 'I chose American name, to the dismay of my honorable father.'

'To the displeasure of honorable ancestors,' a male voice said. Anna moved away – to Philip's immediate displeasure – and was replaced by an old man, who began to examine him.

'You – you were in the doorway in that bar,' Philip said.

The Chinaman nodded. 'I am humbly flattered that you should notice one such as I, Master Brussac,' he said. The nimble fingers prodded gently at Philip's ribs, making him wince.

'You know my name? The girl told me they'd taken my things.'

'This is true, but you and I have met before, Master, and Lu Chen does not forget those to whom he is indebted.'

'Met before? I . . . ' For a moment Philip could not remember actually meeting any Chinese and he was about to tell the man that he was mistaken, when memory came flooding back to him. 'Wait a minute – the train station, you and your wife . . . '

'No, not my wife, my daughter,' Lu Chen corrected him, inordinately pleased that Philip had remembered. 'My daughter, Anna.'

Looking back on the day he had arrived in Los Angeles, Philip could hardly credit that the frightened, shy little creature he'd mistaken for Lu Chen's wife was the same stunning beauty who'd been caring for him here. He had hardly gotten a glimpse of her face then, but he'd taken her for much older. Perhaps that was because the man with her had been older; or, he reflected, perhaps that had been a deliberate pretense on her part; an older woman, and a wife, might have been safer traveling than a beautiful young daughter.

'And you mean you recognized me right off in that bar?' he said aloud.

'This was not difficult. The woman had been there long time. She drank and talked much of her husband, whose name she mentioned several times.'

'None too kindly, I'll bet.' Lu Chen did not reply to this, concentrating pointedly on Philip's wounds. 'So, you waited till they'd finished me off . . . '

'I tell them to stop but they do not listen to a Chinaman,' Lu Chen explained. 'They threaten to take care of me also. I am not afraid for self, but if I am hurt as well, who will take care of Master? I run off, fetch daughter. When they leave, I bring you back here. So sorry that I must drag you part of way, there is much of you to carry. Anna is a good nurse, yes?'

'Anna is damned good medicine, yes,' Philip agreed. 'What did those gorillas do to me, anyway?'

'They worked you over good, but don't fear. Another two, three days, four maybe, you will be up again.'

'Another . . . ? Oh no, listen, Lu Chen, I've got to go, I've got things . . . ' He tried again to sit up, only to gasp as a sheet of pain seared his lungs. 'Broke my ribs, huh?' he asked when he could talk again.

'Some,' Lu Chen informed him. 'Not all, though. Another two, three days . . . '

'Yes, I know, or four maybe,' Philip interrupted him shortly.

'There is wisdom in changing what we cannot accept, and still more in accepting what we cannot change,' Lu Chen said.

As it turned out, Lu Chen's estimates were conservative, for Philip was there an entire week in the dingy little rooms above a laundry. And though he chafed when he thought of the work undone at the ranch, the truth was he was glad to spend the time with Lu Chen's daughter. She was a remarkable young woman, as he discovered over the incident of the bath on his third day there.

'It's unheard of,' Philip protested when she told him what she had in mind. 'You can't bathe an adult male who's practically a stranger to you.'

'It is for all our sakes,' she said, not quite succeeding in holding back a mischievous smile.

'Meaning that I stink, I suppose,' he said indignantly.

'Exactly right. And you have seen my father, even if he did not work day and night to scratch a meager living for us, he is too old and frail to turn you over.'

'I can turn myself over,' Philip said. She did not answer this, both of them knowing it was untrue. 'It's out of the question,' he finished.

'Then I shall ask my father's permission to go,' Anna said with a sad sigh and a shake of her head.

The threat had its intended effect; he was quite smitten by this lovely creature who had ministered to him with such tenderness.

'Go? Go where?'

She shrugged and said, 'Anywhere where the air is fresh. Perhaps I shall take my blanket and sleep in the doorway of the shop below.'

He was almost sure that it was a bluff, but no matter how he argued with her, or himself, he could not quite eliminate the last shred of doubt, the end result being that he submitted to her wishes.

She bathed him with a cloth, from a basin of warm water that had been scented with some unfamiliar lotion. It was both thorough and thoroughly embarrassing. She had no more than touched his bare chest when he experienced the predictable consequence, and though he still wore a shirt over the lower portion of his body, it was not sufficient to conceal his condition.

Worse, she did not even pretend not to notice, however unlikely that may have been, but giggled repeatedly, which had the result of reddening his face and increasing his turgidity. It did not, however, halt the bath, to his discomfort and frustration – frustration because, for all his embarrassment, he would have liked nothing better than to have shown her in no uncertain terms that it was not something to be laughed at, and to hell with broken ribs.

Afterward, though, he realized that there had been a subtle change in her manner toward him. Heretofore his condition of helplessness had seemed to offset any sense of man-woman feelings between the two of them; she had treated him, if anything, like a difficult but likable child. It was because of this that she had had no reluctance to engage in so intimate an activity as bathing him.

The result of the bath, however, had been to remind her that he was indeed a man, a very handsome one at that, and not as physically inconvenienced as she had thought.

She was still much the same with him, cleaning and dressing the wound at his temple, bringing his meals and helping him to eat them, though he was now able to sit up and could have fed himself.

Yet there was an undeniable change in their relationship, a tension that seemed to build like an electrical charge. Their hands would touch, accidentally, and both would start, as if actual sparks had leapt between them; or again, their eyes would suddenly meet, and both would pause, seeming to see one another for the first time in a new light.

The results of these brief interludes were evidence that he was recuperating. By the end of the week he was able to sit up by himself, and the next time he bathed Anna went out to tend to some shopping.

It was March, the end of the rainy season, and it had been drizzling for two days. Restless, Philip had managed to get out of bed for the first time since he'd awakened to find himself there. Using the furniture to support himself, he made his way slowly to the window, where he could watch the rain sweep down from the hills that encircled the city.

Tomorrow, he could start for home – could, and should. But even as he thought this, he glanced downward and saw Anna, dodging puddles as she ran along the street, and he knew that he was in no hurry to return to French Hills.

She came in, ushered by rain and wind, and for a startled moment paused, staring at the empty bed. She turned, even as he opened his arms for her and, almost without knowing how they had accomplished it, she was in his arms and his kisses were hot upon her lips, her cheek, her throat.

Her clothes and hair were wet against his naked skin and she shivered as he undressed her, discarding her clothes in a heap; but when he guided her to the bed, she struggled against him.

'No, wait . . . ' she murmured.

'I can't.'

' . . . Let me – it will pain you less.'

He sank back, closing his eyes. Her damp hair brushed his naked flesh as she knelt over him, and he reached up, clasping a handful of it and bringing it gratefully to his lips.

43

He was there for ten days, though he had sent a message to the ranch telling them he was all right and that he would be returning soon. Even so, it was only with great reluctance that he left.

'Is there anything I can do to repay you?' he asked Anna when he was ready to leave; he had said his farewells to Lu Chen earlier, and expressed his gratitude.

'Yes,' Anna said. He thought she meant to ask for money, and he was disappointed, but instead she said, 'You could give my father a job.'

'At the ranch?'

'He can do a great many things. And he works too hard here, for too little. It would be so much better for him there, with clean air and good food . . . ' She stopped, reading his expression.

'And you would come with him?' he asked.

'Of course. Who would cook and clean for him otherwise? And I could work for you too. I am a good cook, and I sew well.'

Philip shook his head, wishing that their parting could have been on an easier note. 'It wouldn't do, Anna,' he said.

'Why, because I love you?' she asked.

'Don't use that word,' he said, with such vehemence that it startled her. 'That word is a curse to me. It's only that – I have a wife . . . '

'Yes, I know.'

He caught the irony in her tone, and smiled ruefully. 'It's true, ours isn't a very happy marriage.'

'My father says she spoke as if she hated you.'

'Perhaps she does,' Philip said sadly. 'She has every reason to.'

'I do not know what you might have done, but surely a woman can find it in her heart to forgive her husband.'

'I don't see how,' he said, sighing. 'I can't forgive myself, God knows.' He swung himself into the saddle and, turning the horse around, gazed down at her. 'It wouldn't work. I couldn't have you there without wanting you, and I couldn't take you without being unfair to her. I've got too much on my conscience as it is.'

He waited for her to say something more, and when it became evident she didn't mean to speak, he said, 'Well, it's goodbye then. I'm grateful for everything.'

'Goodbye, Philip,' she said.

He wished that he'd kissed her again before he mounted. It was awkward parting with her like this, but it would be more so to dismount again. His horse pranced impatiently, and with a nod of his head, he rode off. He looked back at the end of the street and saw that she was still standing staring after him. He waved, but she did not wave back or even acknowledge the gesture, and he left with a conviction that he had handled things badly.

Jean came out to meet him as Philip rode up the lane. Philip saw the door to his own shack open, the boy standing in the doorway, and as he dismounted, he asked, 'Did Elena come home?'

'She's back,' Jean said. 'Not under her own power, though.'

'What do you mean by that?'

'She's dead, Phil.' Jean took the reins from him.

In some part of his mind he must have known that this was how it would end for her – the drinking, the endless chain of seedy bars and saloons, the nightmare of punishment that she inflicted upon herself; yet the announcement was like a blow to the stomach.

'How – what . . . ?'

'They found her in the river. Someone had beaten her and tossed her in. They brought her back two days ago. We've been waiting for you to get back before we buried her.'

'Do they know who did it?' Philip asked.

'Some cowboy she was staying with, they think, but no one wants to identify him,' Jean said. 'We put her out in your place.'

'Where's the boy been staying?'

'There,' Jean said. 'With her.'

Philip turned from him and crossed the yard, his legs feeling rubbery beneath him. Elena was dead, beaten to death by her cowboy-protector; perhaps on the same day, the same hour, even, that he had made love to Anna.

And would it have made any difference if I'd been here, he asked himself? He knew that it would not have. Elena had chosen her course, just as he had long ago chosen his, and she had been as doomed by that choice as he had been, swept forward by the relentless tide that was their selves – their lives, their passions, their follies.

Still, it did not stop him from aching with grief. He came into the shack and saw that one of the serving women was seated on a chair, and the boy was standing in front of the crudely made coffin.

His son, Roger, though he never thought of him in either way; was always 'the boy'. He stood now in a protective attitude that was touching in one so young, not yet even five. It was as if he meant to prevent Philip from approaching the body.

'He should be somewhere else,' Philip said to the woman.

'He would not go, Señor,' she said, rising from the chair. 'Always he screamed and fought and would not be still until he was allowed to return here.'

Philip did not know what to make of it. It was hard to imagine that the boy and his mother were close, but then he knew almost nothing about the child. He was reminded of his own childhood in this same shack, and of his mother's death. Had Elena and her child shared the same love that he and his mother had known? She too had been what many would term disreputable, yet her love for him had been like a cloak which, wrapped about, had sheltered him from all the winds of chance and from the neglect of his father.

That thought made him ashamed of the way he had shunned the child – his son, by whatever misfortunate pairing, and he approached the coffin with his hand outstretched toward the boy.

'No,' Roger shrieked, and flung himself in front of the coffin, arms outstretched to prevent any approach. 'Go away!'

Philip was shocked and hurt by the gesture; the ride out from the city had been a strain after his convalescence and he was gnawed at by guilt over Elena's death.

Roger began to cry, not quietly but in horrible rising screams and the sound struck upon Philip's raw emotions like the lick of a flame in the dry grass of summer.

'Stop that,' he snapped, his own voice rising to a shout. 'Stop it, I say.'

He reached to take hold of the boy. Roger responded by sinking his teeth into the back of Philip's hand. Blind with rage, Philip flung him aside.

It was the maid's horrified gasp that brought him back to his senses. He looked from her shocked face to where his son lay in a crumpled heap, sobbing softly now into the crook of his arm. His twisted foot lay at its own accusing angle.

Philip turned on his heels and strode from the shack. The servants were clustered on the lawn, drawn by the boy's agonized shrieks.

'Take her out of there at once,' Philip ordered, striding through their midst without a pause. 'We'll bury her now.'

It was a gray and dismal scene; not even the rain that had been promising came with its benediction. When it was done, Philip attempted to put his arm about Roger's shoulders, but the boy shook it off and clung instead to the maid who had been taking care of him. Philip did not press the matter, but left them wordlessly.

Jean, who had come to the burial, fell into step beside him. 'We've got a lot of business to discuss,' he said. 'Though I suppose it could wait till tomorrow.'

'No, today will do fine,' Philip said.

Boxes and trunks were being loaded into a carriage in front of the house. Nadine, having at last badgered Philip into buying out her share of her father's estate, was leaving, with no regrets on any side.

Adam was dead, as was Caleb. Harvey and Adam's widow were gone in their separate directions and in another hour, probably less, Nadine would leave.

Soon, aside from the servants, there would be only Jean and himself, and Roger – his family, and yet not his, just as French Hills was his and yet not; as Elena had been, and Jolene, and Aunt Marie – was there never to be anything, anyone, truly his?

'Those oil company people were here again,' Jean said when they were in the office.

'I hope you threw them off the place,' Philip said. At one time he would have been seated before the desk, and Jean, who had been running the place, would have been behind it. Now the positions were reversed, and it was Philip who riffled through the paperwork that had accumulated in his absence, making occasional notes.

'They're convinced the oil is here, Phil.' Philip, busy with his papers, made no reply. 'There's people making fortunes in California oil.'

'There's people lost fortunes, too,' Philip said. 'I've been all through this. It isn't like eastern oil, it's harder to get at, and even when you can get it out of the ground, it's harder to refine into anything usable.'

'Doheny and his bunch are doing all right. The men tell me they're getting almost a thousand barrels a day out of their land.'

'And turned it into a forest of wells. Tell me one thing: if we do that here, where do we grow grapes?'

Jean was thoughtful for a moment. 'There's the San José property.'

'The San José property has lost money for the last two years,' Philip said.

'It's the way it's run, not the soil. Adam made great wine when he was running things up there; it was only when Dad died and Adam had to come down to manage things here that things went sour up there. There just wasn't anybody to run it right.'

'El . . . ' Philip caught himself about to say, 'El Patron,' as he had used to call his grandfather. 'Your dad,' he said instead, 'believed that the future of California wine was here, not up north.'

'He was wrong,' Jean said, holding up a hand when Philip started to object. 'He was a good man and a great vintner, but he was dead wrong about that, Phil. He thought Los Angeles would remain a small cow town, and that San Francisco would become a huge city, crowding out those northern wineries – but it happened in reverse. Look at what's happened. There aren't a half dozen wineries in the Los Angeles area now, where there were once scores of them. They've all moved up north. The soil's better up there, the climate's better. If we concentrated our efforts there, we could produce as much wine out of that one property as we're getting out of both now, or damn near it, and better wine, too.'

'And grow oil down here,' Philip suggested.

'There's money in it. Enough money to make French Hills what it was before, the best damn winery in California. The way things are now, we're not making enough to pay the bills, let alone reinvest.'

Philip was thoughtful for a moment; finally he sighed. 'All right, I'll make you a deal,' he said. 'We'll go up to San José. It's time we found out for ourselves what those fools are doing anyway. And it may be you're right. Maybe we should be growing oil.'

'We don't have to give up wine, not altogether,' Jean said.

Philip seemed not to hear. He said, more as if he were speaking to himself, 'Aunt Marie said that wine was the blood of the Brussacs. She said wherever there were Brussacs, there would be wine.'

'And so there will. When your son . . .'

'Make the arrangements for the trip,' Philip interrupted him, returning to his paperwork. 'Plan it for, say, three weeks from today. We'll go by train, spend a week there. That ought to give us time to sort things out.'

Jean left, all in all pleased with himself that he had persuaded Philip at least to consider the possibility of oil. The conversation he had had three days before with the representatives of the oil company had left him convinced that their fortune was waiting beneath the ground, needing only to be pumped to the surface.

Jean was aware, as well as anyone, that French Hills had fared badly under his stewardship. He had never pretended to be a businessman, that had always been in his father's hands, and Adam's after him.

He knew, without rancor, that Philip was smarter than he was and had a better business head on his shoulders. But he was smart enough himself to know that things were too far gone for Philip to pull them back up by the bootstraps, not without financial help. If French Hills was to survive, it needed a healthy infusion of money, far more than they could hope for merely out of a vintage crop.

Oil could do it. If he could persuade Philip to his way of thinking on this matter, he could at least know in his heart that he had contributed something to French Hills other than its deterioration.

When he had gone, Philip sat for several minutes, staring into space. Then, taking a sheet of letter paper from the drawer and a pen, he began to write.

He had no idea where Jolene was now, but he would send the letter to her in care of her parents; surely they would know. And if not . . . but he refused to entertain that thought.

It had been an effort of will to force his thoughts from her long enough to concentrate on what Jean had been saying. Not even Elena's funeral had been enough to distract his thoughts from Jolene. He had felt guilty and ashamed, but he was unable to help himself. Since he had seen Elena's coffin lowered into the ground, one thought had seared his consciousness: he was free. Whatever the past had been, whatever foolish and tragic mistakes he had made, there was nothing now to stand in their way.

Nothing – unless Jolene had ceased to love him. She could hardly be blamed if she had. He had no right even to hope, and his hands shook as he wrote, so that his writing came out a quavering, spidery script like that of an old man.

'. . . I will be in San José on the seventeenth through the twenty-fourth of April,' he wrote. 'I beg you to spare me the time to see me, to talk with me. There is much that needs to be said . . .'

He finished the note and, signing his name, folded the sheet and inserted it into an envelope. He had just finished addressing it when one of the maids knocked and came into the room to tell him that he had visitors.

'Not those blasted oil men again,' he growled.

'I think not,' she said; he was too occupied with his own thoughts to notice the slyness of her expression. 'There are two – an old man and a girl. They say – *she says*, they have come to return something that belongs to you.'

She crossed to the desk and laid his pocket watch on it. He had forgotten it since he had last seen it, atop the dresser in Lu Chen's little apartment over the laundry.

He picked up the watch, turning it over in his hand. It almost seemed he could feel the gentle touch of her fingers upon it, as if they had left an indelible impression.

'Have them wait in the parlor,' he said, 'I'll be with them in a moment.'

'Begging pardon, sir, I did ask them in. They say they'll wait outside for you.'

'I'll be right out.'

When she had gone, he stared for a moment at the letter before him on the desk. Then, with a deliberate shake of his head, he finished the address and placed it in the box with the outgoing mail.

Harvey sat on a grassy knoll from which he had a clear view of the house far below. Beside him his horse grazed contentedly, saddlebags already packed with the few possessions he had taken with him when he left French Hills. Since then he had been living down the road, at the cantina, waiting, screwing up his courage. In a short while, a few minutes even, he would be leaving, leaving California for Texas. He was ready to go, except for one piece of unfinished business, and that he would be attending to shortly, with luck. He lightly fingered the rifle in his hand, and stared unblinkingly at the house which had been his home until two days ago.

He was only mildly curious about the couple that had just arrived, a woman and a Chinaman – looking for a handout, he supposed, or a job. It was the bastard he was waiting for; sooner or later, Philip would come out of the house. Harvey was prepared to wait until he did.

His wait was not a long one after all. He saw someone step into the shadows of the porch, and a moment later Philip came down the steps to greet the waiting couple.

Harvey raised the rifle, frowning as he sighted along its barrel. He wanted a clean shot; at this distance, it was a tricky business trying to pick one out of three. He waited, a bead of sweat slowly descending the bridge of his nose, growing as it went.

The trio moved in the direction of the porch; they were going inside. Harvey swore softly to himself. He'd have to chance it, no telling when he'd get another opportunity. His finger tightened on the trigger.

The shot rolled in lazy echoes over the valley floor. Below, the Chinaman jerked convulsively, staggered, fell – he'd shot the wrong man.

Harvey flung the rifle to the ground with an angry oath. No chance for a second shot now, and he didn't dare hang around here, they'd be looking for him in no time flat.

'But I'll be back, greaser, never you fear,' he vowed, swinging himself up into the saddle. He rode off furiously, already gone with the last dying echoes.

They found the rifle, and the trail that led off into the chaparral, but Harvey knew the hills too well, and in a few miles they had lost the trail altogether and had to turn back.

Despondent, Philip rode back to French Hills. Lu Chen was dead. He had little doubt who had fired the shot or that it had been intended for him, but that was cold comfort. If he had not loved Anna, if she hadn't followed him to French Hills, her father would be alive, and she would never know the tragedy of loving him.

Lu Chen had been carried into the parlor; Anna had been with him when Philip had ridden out. He came in now by the kitchen, seeing on the work table the water basin and the bloody towels with which they had tried unsuccessfully to stem the flow of his life's blood.

The maid came in with yet another basin of towels. 'Is she still with him?' Philip asked.

'Yes.'

He started from the room, pausing at the door. 'She'll need a place to stay,' he said. 'Prepare one of the shacks.'

'There are no empty shacks,' she said; her head was turned so he couldn't see her knowing smirk.

'My son and I shall be moving here, into this house. She can have that one,' he said. 'See that matters are arranged – to everyone's satisfaction.'

44

It was the dream girl again – the broad white road, leading up to the gates of a walled city, a great throng that hurried along the road, she hurrying with them. This time she thought she must surely reach the gates, must find what lay within that drew her so compulsively onward . . .

She woke with a start. The sky beyond the window was luminous with the approach of dawn, still some time distant. Sloan slept quietly, peacefully beside her, and the single dim lamp glowed through the open door from Alexandra's room.

Everything was safe, secure, the world at rest. Only she lay with labored breath and tried to still her thoughts, like the beating wings of a frightened bird.

Philip was in San José. He had arrived yesterday and would be there for several days more. So close, so very close.

She had not answered his letter; she had not dared to. Philip, free, begging her forgiveness, urging her to come to him. Come to him – come to him – come to him . . . it echoed through her mind, would not be silenced.

He had not said that he loved her; what need of that? She *was* his love, as he was hers, the word defined in the golden thread that bound them together, for always.

And yet, beside her, one arm resting protectively over her, lay her husband, whom she loved. She had not started out to love him, nor could she look back and pinpoint an exact time or place when she had begun to do so. She had simply awakened one morning to the knowledge, sure and complete, that something had happened between them, something warm and beautiful. Something not at all like what she had known with Philip, for it was at once less, and more.

There was her daughter too, her bed creaking faintly as she turned in her sleep. A loving, gentle girl who could not see a crippled bird without shedding tears.

There was home, for it had come to be that at last for her, the gingerbread house no longer so new and strange, her parents no longer idols nor devils, but simply a part of her, a part of what made her life complete.

It was too much, too much to throw away for the sake of an old fire that still burned unassuaged in her breast. For if she once went to Philip, how could she be sure of coming back? And even if, by some miracle, Sloan and Alexandra, and her parents were able to understand and forgive her, she knew that she would never forgive herself, because they deserved so much more from her.

Yet – and yet, the growing light of dawn was like the mounting heat of desire that grew within her, urging her to him, drawing them inexorably together.

She got quietly out of bed, thinking to get herself a glass of water; but she had taken no more than a step when there was an ominous rumbling like thunder and suddenly the house gave a violent shake as if it had been seized in the hand of an angry God.

Jolene grabbed at the corner of the dresser for support but the dresser itself toppled over and she fell with it. From throughout the house came startled cries orchestrated by other, terrifying sounds – the wild, jangling sound of smashing glass, an ear-splitting roar as some outbuilding collapsed upon itself.

Jolene struggled to get to her feet and as she did a portion of the wall directly before her simply vanished, leaving her staring at the dawn-gray sky beyond.

The first shock of the earthquake lasted only forty seconds, though it seemed an eternity. When it had stopped, Jolene managed finally to get up from the floor, but by the time she had reached the comfort of her husband's arms, the aftershock had struck, nearly as violent as the first.

By the time the sun rose above the horizon, Sloan had already made a survey of their damages, while José organized crews of workmen to clean up the rubble and to put out a fire that erupted in one of the smaller buildings.

Their losses were in property, fortunately, and not in lives. The main house itself had suffered the loss of that one portion of wall and several windows, as well as considerable breakage inside, and one of the storage sheds, the oldest and least substantial, had fallen into a heap of rubble on the ground, but José had expressed some concern about the building's stability months before, and was not entirely sorry to be saved the necessity of tearing it down.

The worst damage, at least in terms of financial loss, was in the cellars, where some whimsy of fate had chosen bottles at random to fling to the floor, while leaving neighbors to either side untouched. Even the unbroken bottles, however, had suffered from the shaking about, many so badly as to render them undrinkable for years, if not forever.

While the men tended to the more strenuous cleaning up chores, Jolene joined the other women in the cellars, cleaning up broken glass and spilled wine and examining unbroken bottles for other damage.

It was slow and tedious work and they were still at it when reports began to reach them through friends and neighbors of the damage to San Francisco, where the quake's main force had struck.

They heard of streets cracked and split open, of entire sections of the city reduced to rubble; stoves and fireplaces, overturned or ruptured, and how broken electrical lines had started scores of fires, while at the same time fractured water mains made fire-fighting difficult if not impossible.

They listened to these reports grimly, and it was agreed that as soon as order could be restored here, the men would journey into the city, to help there as best they could.

In the excitement of the quake and its aftermath, Jolene had had little enough time to think of Philip and his nearness; but in mid-afternoon another bit of news reached them that sent a spasm of fear through her.

While most of their news had had to do with the city of San

Francisco herself, there were reports as well of damage to surrounding cities, particularly those along the peninsula to the south. Even so, Jolene was totally unprepared for the information brought by the sheriff.

'San José's been hard hit,' he told them, Sloan had brought him to the cellars when the sheriff had specifically asked for Mary. 'Some winery was brought clear to the ground.'

Jolene, who had been only half listening, caught her breath. She wanted to ask a question but found that her throat was too dry, and was grateful when Mary asked it for her.

'What winery?' Mary asked.

'Don't know the name of it,' the Sheriff said, 'but there's been several men killed in it. They tell me there's relatives of yours among them. I figured maybe you'd know who they were.'

For Jolene the room seemed to rock and sway as violently as if the earthquake were being reenacted. 'Philip,' she said, hardly aware she had spoken the name aloud, or that others had turned to look at her. 'Philip – oh my God, Philip!'

All at once she remembered the letter, the dates Philip had mentioned. He was in San José, had been since yesterday morning. He had told her specifically that he would be living there, at the winery – ' . . . There are workers' barracks behind the offices,' his letter had explained, 'not very elegant, but I've slept in worse places . . . '

[illegible] had been kneeling on the rough floor, rummaging through a heap of bottles for any that might be salvageable; now she scrambled to her feet, oblivious to the fact that she had cut a nasty gash in one hand with a shard of glass.

'I must go to him,' she said in a daze, stumbling toward the stairs. 'I must go to him.'

'Jolene.' Sloan caught up with her and tried to take her in his arms, but she turned on him in a sudden fury, her eyes blazing.

'Let me go,' she shrieked. 'Let me go, I must go to Philip.'

'Jolene, you can't go there, it's the other side of the city, and the city's in ruins,' Sloan argued, but she only struggled with renewed violence to free herself from his grip.

'I will go, I must,' she cried. 'You don't understand, Philip is there, he's hurt, he may be dead. Oh my God, help me, please.'

She began to sob, tears streaming from her eyes. Staring at his wife, a moment before calm and capable, Sloan felt his own heart wrenched with pain. He could see that she was beyond reason, like a madwoman. He could restrain her only by force, and though one part of him urged that he do so, another voice warned that she would never forgive him; though she might, when she had recovered her senses, agree that he had been wise, he knew that if Philip were actually dead, or dying, she would forever carry in her heart a resentment against him for standing in her way now.

'Wait,' he said, but she threw her head to and fro with such fury that he half expected her neck to snap.

'I won't, let me go,' she cried, 'I must go to him, I must go . . .'

'Jolene, I'll take you,' he said grimly.

'You can't,' Mary said, and the sheriff seconded her opinion. 'You'll never get across the city.'

Jolene was still sobbing. 'Let me go, let me go,' over and over. Sloan gave them a despairing look.

'We'll take the car,' he said, 'and ferry across from Sausalito. There's bound to be some route through the city.'

Jolene, gradually absorbing the fact that Sloan meant to take her to San José, had grown calmer and was no longer sobbing, but she moved out as one in a daze, concerned with nothing but setting out.

Sloan left her in the car and hastily collected coats and blankets to take along; there was no telling where they would sleep that night.

'You'd better take a gun,' Mary said.

'It's an earthquake, not a war,' Sloan said.

'People do peculiar things when they're terrified,' Mary said. She brought José's revolver from his desk and insisted that Sloan carry it with him.

Less than twenty minutes after the sheriff had arrived, they were driving down the lane. Jolene sat huddled on the passenger's side, seemingly oblivious to his presence or to anything but the urgent need to reach San José and Philip.

A month before they had exchanged the Mercedes for a Peerless, one of the new limousine cars with doors on either side, rather than in the rear, as had been the custom. It was powerful and quiet as well as luxuriously comfortable, and under other circumstances the trip into the city had become a fast and easy one.

On this occasion, however, Sloan soon saw that he had made a mistake in bringing the motor car instead of a buggy, or even riding horses, who could more easily have avoided the rubble that frequently blocked their way or the awesome fissures that had been opened up in several places along the road.

It was evening and already growing dark by the time they finally reached the outskirts of Sausalito, though the distant sky glowed with lingering light.

It was not until they had mounted the last hill and were overlooking the bay itself that Sloan realized the significance of that peculiar glow.

Across the water, the entire city of San Francisco seemed to be in flames. They glowed here a pale yellow, and again blood red; there were shades of violet and green, perfect blues and rose yellows, and again and again, like the breath of some monstrous dragon, erupted the black, demoniac clouds of smoke as some new fire started.

'Good Lord,' Sloan breathed, staring disbelievingly at the holocaust, clearly visible even at this distance. He despaired of ever finding a way through that inferno. Only Jolene's uncomprehending presence beside him made him go on. She seemed oblivious of the scene before her, as indeed she was. Fear for Philip, for what she would find when she reached him, had crowded every other thought and consideration from her mind. She might have walked through a raging fire without comprehending it.

Realizing this, Sloan knew that he had no choice but to push on, frightened that if he did not Jolene would find some means of going on alone.

The little town of Sausalito was itself in a state of bedlam. Thousands of terrified citizens were fleeing across the bay from the stricken city, utilizing every available water craft. The area near the waterfront was like a scene from a nightmare, with panic-stricken people and horses vying for every inch of space. The crowds slowed the car to a crawl and finally to a stop.

'We'll have to leave the car here,' Sloan said. 'We'll find some way across and try to rent a carriage on the other side.'

Jolene offered no protests. He helped her from the car and held tight to her arm as he pushed and cursed and fought for a path through the mob, and she moved at his side like a sleepwalker. Several times she was almost torn from him by the crush of the crowd, and it seemed to Sloan for a while that they would after all have to abandon his plan of crossing here, and seek some other way of reaching San José. Perhaps, he thought, they should have circled completely about the city, and he might even have turned back and tried to do so had it not been for the certain knowledge that no matter which way they went they would find their way blocked by those fleeing the destruction of the city.

They reached the waterfront at last. Here the bedlam was even worse, incredible as that was for him to believe. Scores of boats of every description fought for room to disgorge their passengers, some of whom impatiently jumped into the water and scrambled ashore with their clothes and possessions dripping wet.

Sloan found one boat in the process of unloading its occupants and, jumping onto the deck, fought his way to the skipper.

'Will you be going back to the city?' he asked, shouting to be heard above the din.

'Are ye daft, man?' the skipper answered, waving a hand toward the distant glow of flames. 'The city's gone, look at it. Look at this stampede, everyone's trying to get out while the getting's good.'

'We have to get to the other side,' Sloan argued. 'I'll pay a hundred if you'll carry us over – and you'll make fifty times that coming back, if what you say is true.'

'It's true, all right.' The skipper hesitated, eyeing the wad of bills Sloan had dragged from his pocket. 'There's no telling if we can even get to the docks,' he warned.

'Put us down on the beach, then, anywhere as long as it's that side.'

'Done,' the skipper said, snatching the money from Sloan's hand. 'Let's be going, while we still can.'

Sloan leapt back to the dock and hurried to where he had left Jolene, but to his horror he saw that she was not there.

'Jolene!' He could scarcely hear his own voice above the roar of the crowd. He cupped his hands about his mouth and shouted her name again and again.

Finally he heard her answering call, and kicking and clawing his way through the mob, he found her, shoved back into the relative shelter of a doorway. She looked bruised and shaken, and her coat was torn in two places.

'They – they wouldn't listen to me,' she gasped when at last she was in his arms.

She seemed to have recovered somewhat from the daze she had been in earlier, enough so that Sloan felt compelled to ask, 'Are you sure you want to go through with this? It's bound to be worse over there.'

Her eyes met his and he could see the pain that her answer caused her. 'Forgive me,' she said, in a whisper that could barely be heard over the uproar around them. 'If you'd rather go back, I'll understand. I'll go on alone if need be, but I must go on.'

'Don't be a fool,' he said angrily. He seized her arm in a fierce grip and shoving her behind him, forced his way once again through the throng.

When they reached the boat he'd hired, he saw with dismay that two men had jumped aboard and were fighting with the skipper.

'You filthy pirates,' the skipper was shouting, laying about him with a broken section of two by four, 'You'll not be stealing my ship.'

'Get away, old man,' one of the cut-throats growled, circling the skipper with a knife in his hand, 'There's a fortune to be made this night, and we mean to make our share. Give us your boat, and we'll cut you in.'

'Otherwise,' his companion warned with a menacing laugh, 'we'll cut you up.'

Sloan jumped aboard, thrusting Jolene into the safety of the ship's cabin, and yanked from his belt the revolver that Mary had given him before they left.

It was too close on the deck to fire a shot and risk hitting the skipper, but he could use the gun as a club, bringing it down to good effect on one man's skull. The blow dazed the would-be assailant, and before he could recover Sloan had given him a mighty kick that sent him toppling into the water.

His companion, seeing the fight joined and himself now outnumbered, chose the better part of valor and jumped in after him.

Without a pause, the skipper shouted, 'Cast off that line before some more filthy buggers try to steal the boat. And it's hoping I am that you've both said your prayers, as this is a peaceful spring night compared to what you'll find over there.'

In a moment the boat was moving toward the open waters of the bay. Jolene came out from the cabin and went to the bow, staring straight ahead as if willing them to greater speed. Sloan came to stand protectively behind her, his eyes fastened on the city before them, approaching all too swiftly, it seemed to him. Eerily, though night had long since fallen, the light grew brighter as they went, the sky alive with dancing, writhing flames, and the surface of the water turned to a sheet of red-gold marble.

45

They were no more than a third of the distance across the bay when the engine of the little fishing-boat began to cough and sputter. For several minutes they floated idly while the Skipper tinkered with the engine.

'It's a fouled line,' he announced finally, starting it up again; to Sloan it sounded no better than before.

'Will it get us there?' he asked.

'I'm hoping that it will,' the Skipper said, without enthusiasm. 'Can't see what I'm doing out here.'

They crept forward at what seemed a snail's pace. Jolene fidgeted in the bow and at one point asked, 'Can't we go any faster?'

'Not unless you wanta swim and pull the boat,' the Skipper replied.

'He's doing the best he can,' Sloan consoled her, half afraid she might take the Skipper's suggestion seriously.

Although they had reached the outskirts of Sausalito soon after dusk, it had taken them a major portion of the night to secure passage to the city. With this new delay, it was close onto morning by the time they finally neared San Francisco's waterfront.

The holocaust that had looked so horrible from across the bay had grown infinitely worse as they had approached. They were all three drenched with sweat, for even here on the water, and in what should have been the cool before the dawn, the heat was stifling.

The Skipper had spoken truly when he had warned that the bedlam on this side of the bay was far worse than that they had left behind. As they had drawn closer they had found themselves going against a steady stream of boat traffic headed in the opposite direction, until finally the Skipper had had to veer from the usual course and had brought his boat in above the waterfront docks.

'Just as well,' he explained, cutting the engine altogether. 'Isn't safe going in there. The water's alive with people and all sorts of creatures trying to climb aboard any vessel doesn't stave 'em off. We'd be swamped afore we could get close.'

He had swung the boat in in the shadow of a freighter riding anchor, and taking up a long pole he ordered Sloan to use one of the oars attached to the side while he used the pole against the side of the larger ship to guide them toward the shore.

'Isn't there another oar?' Jolene asked, for the first time abandoning her place in the bow.

'There's no need,' Sloan said, but she went to the side and found the other oar.

'I can work,' she said, taking a place opposite him.

It was back-breaking work; the fishing-boat had not been planned for rowing except in an emergency. Neither Sloan nor Jolene had slept since the night before, nor eaten since a sparse and hasty lunch the previous midday. Fatigue and hunger combined with the roar and heat of the fire raging through the city, so that they were gasping for breath by the time the boat bumped into something and the Skipper said in a hoarse whisper, 'There, that's got it.'

He had guided them into a row of pilings with a rotted and abandoned boat dock that had proved of no interest to the mobs seeking to escape the city.

'You'll be all right here?' Sloan asked when he had managed to get Jolene onto the rickety planks of the dock.

'I will,' the Skipper said, 'providing someone doesn't find me afore I get this engine fixed, and commandeer my little vessel. But I wouldn't wager on how all right you'll be.'

Sloan followed his anxious gaze. From here it looked as if the entire city were one unbroken mass of flames; clouds of smoke billowed skyward, and a steady rain of ash and cinders fell on them from above.

One thing was painfully evident – the earthquake and its attendant fires had done what the city's fathers had not been able to do; wipe out the Barbary Coast.

'We'll manage,' Sloan said, with more confidence than he felt. He waved farewell and, taking Jolene's arm, hurried her forward, in the direction of the public docks.

So far they had traveled with little in the way of a plan, nor had he a concrete one now. He had a perhaps foolish hope that they might find someone at the waterfront with a carriage he could purchase, or even 'borrow' if need be. One thing was certain, they could not hope to travel far on foot in this raging inferno. Twice he had to stop and smother ashes that had threatened to set fire to Jolene's coat. Nor did he delude himself as to the strength that either of them might have remaining.

And they had only begun the journey to San José!

As if in answer to his unspoken prayer, Sloan heard the clatter of horses' hooves and a moment later a man came into view, leading a pair of horses pulling a buggy. The beasts were skittish, and their owner had apparently found it easier to walk with them than to drive them.

He saw Sloan and Jolene and shook his head wearily. 'It's no use,' he said, 'you'll never find a boat. The few that are left are practically swamped with people trying to get aboard.'

'We're more interested in your team and buggy,' Sloan said. 'Will you sell them to us?'

'Wouldn't do you much good if I did,' the man said. 'If the army or the Citizen's Patrol sees them, they'll confiscate them. They're taking every available vehicle for hauling dynamite and moving refugees.'

The night air was suddenly split by a thunderous explosion which made the horses rear and whinny in terror. Sloan leapt forward to help the stranger calm the animals.

'What the devil was that?' Sloan demanded.

'The dynamite. They're blowing up buildings to try to make a fire break at Market Street. Most of the water mains went in the quake. It's about the only way they've got left to fight the fire.'

There was another explosion, more distant and less violent. 'If I can get you on a boat to Sausalito, will you sell us the horses and rig?' Sloan asked.

The man gave him a suspicious look. ' 'Course I would,' he replied. 'They're no damn good to me, or you either, if we get burned alive. But where . . . '

'Come with us,' Sloan said, taking the leads from the man's hands and hurrying the horses onward.

This time they were in luck; the Skipper of the little boat that had brought them across was still at work on his engine and welcomed the promise of a paying customer on the return trip.

'Don't know how long it'll be, though,' he warned, indicating the troublesome engine.

'That's all right, I'd as soon be waiting on the water anyway,' the man said.

The deal was concluded with Sloan paying the stranger handsomely for the buggy and horses, and within a short time he and Jolene were on their way.

'Which way do you suggest to avoid the Army and the

Citizens' Patrols?' he'd asked before setting out.

'I don't know, they seemed to be everywhere,' was the reply. 'Where did you want to go?'

'South – toward San José.'

The man gave him a startled look. 'You'll not make it that way,' he said. 'That's where the worst of the fire is. They've long since evacuated everyone out of that area.'

'Then that's where we're least likely to meet anyone, isn't it?' Sloan said. He nodded at the stranger and the Skipper and, cracking the whip over the horses' heads, sent the buggy racing along the empty street.

Though it was not entirely empty now, for as the fires spread and the people abandoned the area, the animals – rats and mice, homeless or deserted cats and dogs, even a skunk – had taken to the streets, seeking some refuge. The charging horses sent them scattering.

The flames and the billowing clouds of smoke that seemed to hang over the entire city cast dancing shadows everywhere, though it was now the hour of dawn. Although they had been forewarned of the damage to the streets, Sloan had forgotten them in the ensuing confusion, and now he nearly overturned the buggy in a gaping fissure, righting it only with great skill and effort. He was more careful then, still urging the horses on with cracks of the whip, but keeping his eyes glued to the road ahead.

Beside him Jolene sat in a near stupor, all but unconscious from fatigue and fear. Dark, silent buildings glowered down on them from both sides as if they rode through a tunnel, but in the openings between buildings they could see the ominous red glow of the sky and the puffs of smoke chasing one another like phantoms.

The smell of smoke grew stronger, stinging their eyes and making them cough. From somewhere off to their left they heard a chorus of shouts. Remembering the warning about the patrols, Sloan whipped the buggy around a corner, heading away from the voices.

Another monstrous explosion made the ground beneath the wheels tremble as if with another quake, and the horses snorted their terror and danced sideways. Only Sloan's strong grip on the reins, and the whip, which he used incessantly, kept them under control, though he no longer tried to manage their speed.

Yet another explosion sent a tower of flame and smoke

spouting skyward. Sloan had thought to take them down Mason, and by mounting Nob Hill avoid the worst of the fire, but it was soon evident that to do so would put them among the worst of the refugees – and almost certainly result in the loss of the horses and buggy. There was no alternative but to stay with the fires, hoping that the flames would serve to protect them from the men now in control of the city. He sympathized with their plight, and under any other circumstances he would have gladly given the beasts over to them, and volunteered himself to fight fires – but his first obligation was to his wife, and having come this far with her, he was determined that he would see her safely through the rest. He knew all too well that should he leave her for any reason, she would do as she had promised and go on alone – and that prospect was too frightening to contemplate.

It was this thought that kept him going, though the horses now had begun to tire. As they drove on the fires grew worse, casting ghastly shadows like living demons that twisted and writhed toward them, and every few minutes the dawn was rent by another explosion.

They had been following a circuitous path through the city, and now at last they rounded yet another corner and came within sight of Market Street.

Sloan reined the frantic horses to a halt. Market Street was a solid wall of flames towering skyward; the tall buildings that had once lined the street were now either heaps of rubble or engulfed in fire.

Sloan stared at the scene in dismay. Jolene, her eyes burning from the smoke, turned to stare at his profile. How handsome he is, she thought, like some ancient god of fire, driving his chariot into the sun; and close on the heels of that thought came another: My God, what have I done? She had led them both to their doom.

Yet even as she thought this, she knew she could have done nothing else, for she was driven by something larger than herself, something wilder and fiercer even than the inferno that raged about them.

'What will we do?' she asked aloud.

Sloan, the sweat pouring in streams down his forehead, turned to look over his shoulder. Even as he did so, an immense cornice crumbled and fell from a building they had just passed, spraying them with dust and bits of stone. It would be impossible to return the way they had come.

'We'll have to go through it,' he said. 'Give me your petticoat.'

She did not pause to question his peculiar request, but hastily removed the garment, squirming about in the seat to do so. He took it from her and, leaping down from the buggy, handed her the reins, with instructions to keep the horses stopped.

Tearing the petticoat into strips, he approached the prancing, snorting beasts and tied the strips of cloth over their eyes, rendering them sightless.

'I'll have to lead them through,' he shouted. 'Hold tight to those reins and if anything happens – ' he paused only fractionally, ' . . . don't stop, keep going till you're out of the fire.'

He grabbed the leads and began to urge the horses forward. They pawed and danced and fought against him but, unable to see, let him lead them into the fire.

One minute the flames were like a solid wall before them and the next they had plunged into them. Jolene felt as if they had indeed ridden into the sun; the glare was blinding and her very skin felt as if it had erupted in flames. The roaring and crackling of the holocaust was deafening, washing over her in searing waves.

It could have been no more than a few seconds, yet it seemed they stumbled through the monstrous furnace for an eternity; then, suddenly, they were through it, the wall of flames was behind them, and she found that she could see again.

Sloan, his jacket flaming, staggered and fell to the ground. Jolene leapt down and ran to him, smothering the flames with the cloth of her skirt.

'I – I'll be all right,' he gasped. 'The horses . . . '

Still blinded, the horses were too terrified to do more than paw the ground. Sloan got wearily to his feet, and yanking the blinds from the horses' heads, helped Jolene into the buggy again, clambering in after her.

There were still fires and ruined buildings about them, but they had ridden into the section that had burned first, and here the worst of the holocaust was over already. They turned down a side street, and another and another, and the fire and heat fell gradually behind them.

Sloan saw ahead of them a small market that had been abandoned by its owners and had miraculously escaped the worst of the destruction. They would need food if they were going to make it to San José, and thinking he might find something here, he once again reined the horses to a stop.

'If anyone tries to take the horses or the buggy,' he said, handing Jolene the revolver that he'd carried tucked into his belt, 'don't waste time arguing with them, just shoot them.'

Although the area seemed empty, he knew enough about human nature to know that it would not be long before the looters and the scavengers returned to scour the streets.

The store had been burned, but one section of it appeared virtually untouched. He found some bread, dried out but edible, and a wheel of cheese. He tucked these and a bottle of wine into a bag and was looking about for something more, when he heard a shot from outside.

He rushed out, to find three men surrounding the buggy. One of them had hold of the reins while the other two were trying to climb into the buggy. One of the latter was struggling with Jolene, trying to get the revolver from her.

Sloan ran forward, seizing one of the men from behind and flinging him to the ground. He leaped into the buggy, prizing the other man's hands from Jolene's wrist and giving him a violent shove that sent him too toppling to the street.

The third man had started around the buggy to join the fray. Sloan seized the reins in one hand and the whip in the other, lashing out at the approaching assailant with the whip.

The man cried out as the whip opened a long wound across his cheek, and as he ducked back Sloan snapped the reins and sent the horses racing forward.

The two on the ground had gotten to their feet and were trying to climb back into the buggy, and from about the corner of a building came three more, looking for their own share of spoils.

Sloan struck out right and left with the whip, sending the horses straight into the midst of the new group. There were cries and oaths and a shot rang out, but the bullet missed them, and in a moment the buggy had outdistanced the pursuers and they were once again clattering through deserted streets.

46

The three-story brick winery had actually been built in 1870 at Mission San José, some twenty miles out of the town of San José. It had been designed and built by Mary's brother, Adam, who had butted it into a sidehill to provide the necessary cellars for the wine.

For a number of years it had been highly successful at the production of red wines, long French Hills' weak suit. Upon his father's death eight years later, however, Adam had been obliged to return to French Hills to manage that estate, with the result that the Mission San José operation had entered upon a long decline, both in the quantity and the quality of its production.

Jean's schemes to restore the property and move their wine-making efforts there might have proved successful; the soil was still good and the weather better suited to grape growing than it was further to the south. But it had been Adam's mistake to build his structure of brick, and it was exactly this type of building that suffered the most from the earthquake.

Even when Sloan and Jolene arrived exhausted late on the afternoon of the second day, workmen were still digging through the debris in search of bodies. Stepping down from the buggy, the couple could only stare in horrified silence; the entire building had been reduced to a pile of rubble.

For Sloan it was almost an anticlimax to stand and watch his wife make her way wearily up the slope that led to what had once been a functioning and prosperous winery. He had labored so long, endured so much to bring her here, it hardly seemed consequential now when a stocky, dark-haired man separated himself from the others in the crowd and started down toward her, at first slowly, and then at a clumsy, staggering run.

Not until Jolene herself had begun to run, and the two were actually in one another's arms, embracing, kissing, touching, did Sloan realize numbly that this was Philip – the Philip whose name his wife had murmured often in her sleep, whose danger had brought them racing across the bay and the length of the peninsula – Philip, whom his wife loved as she loved no other man.

'My darling – my dearest . . .'

'I heard . . . I thought you were dead . . .'

'It was Jean,' Philip said. 'I couldn't sleep – thinking of you – I'd gone outside. When it struck, they were all trapped inside. Twelve, thirteen of them, dead. One or two of them survived . . .'

'But you're unharmed. Oh, thank God, you're safe – I was so frightened –'

He kissed her brow, her cheeks, her hair. It was like a dream, to have her suddenly here, in his arms, crying gently. There was a stand of trees on a slope above them, long now with the shadows of approaching evening, and without even a thought for the man who'd brought her here, who was still standing below staring at them, Philip guided her gently uphill toward the trees.

Sloan watched them go with an odd lack of rancor. A moment before, Jolene had looked past her companion, had looked directly at him, and not seen him at all. She was out of herself, as if she had lifted the curtain of time and stepped through into another place in which he was not even known to her.

With a sad sense of acceptance, he knew that there was nothing faithless or disloyal to him in the embraces that she shared now with that other man, for these two were in another world in which he, and the shouting, laboring throngs of workmen, did not exist at all.

'My son?'

Sloan started, and turned to find a priest at his side; Sloan had not even heard him approach, and he thought, not without irony, that he himself had been as removed from his present surroundings as Jolene and Philip had been.

'There are still others lost inside,' the priest was saying. 'If you could help . . . ?'

The man looked as if he had been working since the quake; his habit was filthy with the red dust of the bricks, and his eyes stained with deep hollows.

'Yes, of course,' Sloan said. He went up the slope with the priest, not even pausing to glance toward the stand of trees into which the other two had disappeared.

It was night. Somewhere nearby a cricket played his monotonous tune, exactly as he must have played two nights before, and for him all the momentous events of the past two days might not have happened at all.

Jolene lay in the cool, damp grass where they had made love. Overhead she could see the stars through the lace-figured pattern of leaves. Although fires had been lit and some workmen still dug through the debris, the missing had by now been accounted for and the noise had died to a distant murmur.

They might almost have been alone in this glade, on this hill – in the entire world. Almost, except that she knew that Sloan was somewhere below, about one of those fires, waiting, enduring, because he loved her; she knew what that could be like, waiting, enduring, loving. She had had years in which to learn of such things.

And beside her was the man who had taught her. The wait had been so long, the struggle to reach him so great, that in a sense finding him again had been something of a letdown. It was true that he was still wonderful to her, just as it was true that her love for him burned unabated.

Yet – she could not forget – neither Sloan, nor that other, faceless woman. She could not forget that this was only a moment, snatched from the years rushing by, years of separation, longing, heartache.

Philip stirred and said, as it turned out, the wrong thing: 'That man, with you, he's your husband?'

'Yes,' she said. She sat up, the spell broken by the mention of Sloan.

'What will you do about him?' Philip asked.

'I shall do what I should have been doing long before now,' she said, standing and brushing the grass from her skirt.

'Which is?'

She turned to gaze down at the man still lying on the ground; the man she had loved so long, so destructively – and yet, in so many ways, a man unknown to her.

'I shall make him a good wife,' she said. 'I shall try to be as good a wife as he has been a husband.'

Philip scrambled to his feet, his eyes wide. 'Don't joke with me,' he said, seizing her wrists in a fierce grip. 'You know you must come away with me, it's the only way.'

'It is an impossible way,' she said simply, 'and one that we dare not follow, for the sake of our own decency.'

'For God's sake, Jolene, I love you, and I know that you love me . . .'

'Yes, that is true.'

He gave a nervous laugh. 'Well, then, there it is. You were joking all the time, or you're drunk with exhaustion. You will come away with me, won't you?'

She shook her head sadly, but firmly. 'No, Philip, I have never been more serious, nor more sober – nor have I ever seen myself more clearly. I have hurt many people – you and I not the least – because I was foolish and headstrong. But even a fool can learn. I'm going to try.'

'What are you going to do?'

'Find my husband. Return home, to our daughter.'

'And what about us?' he asked in a voice thick with anguish.

'There is no "us", Philip, perhaps there never was. There are only you and I, and our separate paths, which may never cross again.'

He suddenly crushed her to him, smothering her lips with his, a kiss that left her breathless and more shaken than she would have wished him to discover.

'You can't expect me to believe that you love them as you do me,' he said, almost angrily.

'No, I shall never love anyone as I loved you, Philip,' she admitted.

'Jolene . . .'

'Goodbye, Philip,' she said, disentangling herself from his arms. 'No, don't come with me, please. I've surely hurt him enough without adding that.'

'Jolene!' It was a cry of anguish, which echoed down the slope after her as she descended toward the fires below.

Sloan, standing by one of the fires drinking a cup of bitter coffee, saw her coming alone, and came out a little way to meet her. He saw, as she came nearer, that the firelight glinted off the tears that ran down her cheeks, and he waited in fear, trying to let none of what he felt show on his face. He had made up his mind to be strong; he would not stand in the way of whatever she wanted. If he could not be the man for her, at least he could love her enough to step aside.

She came straight to him, placing a hand gently on his arm. How weary he looked, she thought, and how frightened; surely only love, a deep, abiding love, could have painted those lines across his brow or lighted the fear that glowed in his eyes.

'Jolene!'

'I want . . .' she said, and paused as that cry came again, like a great dark hawk swooping down from the hill above them.

'I want you to take me home, please,' she said.

Sloan said nothing, but took her arm and led her to where the buggy sat waiting and the horses munched contentedly on the grass.

PART 4

1916

47

It was a time of turmoil throughout much of the world. Since the sinking of the *Lusitania* the year before, Americans had begun to take more notice of events in warring Europe; for some days now attention had been focused on a major battle taking place on the banks of the Meuse, at a place called Verdun.

Closer to home, the Mexican bandit Villa had invaded the state of New Mexico, catching a garrison of soldiers unaware and massacring soldiers and civilians alike. It had been a considerable blow to the image of American military might, and the lack of success with which the U.S. Army had since chased the bandit through the Mexican wilds had done little to improve the damage, or Mexican-American relations.

In Los Angeles the discontent of the working classes continued to cause unrest; though it had been six years since the ill-fated bombing of the Times Building by labor agitators, labor violence was far from ended.

Life at French Hills, however, seemed far removed from much of the world's turmoil. Philip, in fact, had largely turned his back upon the world beyond the gates of French Hills, finding plenty close at hand to occupy him.

He had yielded finally to the oil men, partly because he felt he owed it to Jean. Wells – only a few of them to begin with – had been drilled, and the promoters proved right; at least, to a degree.

The oil was there, as promised; but California oil was not like the oil being tapped in Pennsylvania and elsewhere. It was heavy and tarlike and difficult to refine. The wells had proved less productive, and their output less profitable, than had originally been supposed.

Having committed himself, and watched the black sludge spreading across vineyards that died under its flood, there was little Philip could do but agree to more wells, hoping to find in volume the profit that had eluded them.

The results were mixed; production was increased and some

of the oil was of a more marketable quality. The oilmen were saying that if he would only let them drill in the northern vineyard – the only one still planted in grapes – they were sure he would yet realize the fortune that had been promised to him at the outset.

And in the meantime, French Hills had all but ceased the production of wine. The loss of the San José facility with all its equipment and all its inventory had been a crippling blow. There had been no money to rebuild. For a few years grapes had been grown and harvested and shipped to French Hills, but the system had been too expensive to be profitable, and it had been several years now since the land had been put to any use. The vines, many of them brought from Europe by Philip's grandfather, the El Patron of his childhood, had withered and died.

Now, lying with Anna beside him in the bed that had once been El Patron's, Philip listened to the rattle and hum of the oil pumps and wished for the old days, when the same fields had rung with the laughter and curses of grape pickers; but he had promised himself when the roots of the vines had been buried under the shiny black tar, that his resistance to the wells would be buried with them. That was a part of the past, a past that had vanished with his old dreams; a past dominated by a woman who was lost to him. For the sake of his sanity, he had had to learn to close a door upon that past.

It was ten years since he had seen Jolene. His son was a young man now. Anna had long ago moved into the house as his mistress. Everything had changed.

'I wish . . . ' he said aloud, and paused.

Anna, lying with her dark hair fanned over his shoulder and the pillow as well, asked, 'What is it that you wish?'

Philip turned on the bed and ran his hand fondly over the gentle mound of her belly.

'I wish I were a young man,' he said.

'Why?'

'Because we'd be just getting started, instead of all finished,' he said with a grin.

She stretched lazily, her small, taut breasts straining upward. 'I've got plenty of time,' she said.

He had moved his hand downward, to the yielding warmth between her thighs, but his own sated flesh had refused to respond. Petulantly he swung his legs to the floor and got out of bed, refusing to look in the direction of the mirror on the opposite wall.

'Yes, you have,' he said, struggling into his pants. 'A damned sight more than I've got.'

'You're thirty-one,' Anna said, 'not even eight years older than I.'

'The difference is more than the years – you'll be young for a long time yet, but with every day that passes, I'm growing old.'

'Philip, it doesn't matter – '

'I know it doesn't, not to you, not now – but every day I must live with the possibility that some time, some morning or night, you will tell me of someone you've met – and he will be younger than I.'

'Everyone gets older.'

'But he will always be younger than I am.'

'Does that matter?'

'It does to me.' He paused, as if weighing his words. 'Anna, will you marry me?' he asked.

Her eyes went wide. 'Why?' she asked.

'Christ, do you have to question everything I say or do?' he snapped. 'Isn't it enough to know I want to marry you? Isn't that what you've always wanted?'

She got up from the bed and came to him, laying one hand gently upon his chest. 'It is, truly,' she said. 'But I have always known too that there was someone else in your heart . . . '

He made a gesture of rejection. 'She's married to another man. She'll never be mine.'

'There is always hope.'

He gave a short, sharp bark of a laugh. 'I've always thought the gods must have laughed among themselves when they included hope along with the evils in Pandora's box – the cruelest evil of all, hope, it persuades man to endure his misery to the bitter end.'

He turned away from her and went to the armoire, selecting a shirt from among those inside. 'Worst of all, it's nothing but an illusion, a play we put on for ourselves, pretending, always pretending – if this happens – if that goes another way . . . '

He paused in the act of buttoning his shirt and turned back to her, his expression somber. 'I want to ring down the curtain. I want to put hope back in the box, where she belongs with the rest of the evils, and close the lid on her.'

To his surprise she smiled. 'This is a very unromantic proposal,' she said.

He came back to her then, gathering her in his arms, and his lips, as they brushed her brow and lightly touched the tip of her nose, were gentle. 'Forgive me,' he whispered. 'At least I have never pretended with you.'

'And yet I too have known hope,' she replied. 'And I have found her kind and comforting.'

He held her at arm's length, studying her upturned face. She was even lovelier than the day he had met her. He could hardly believe his good fortune in having had her with him all this time, through the worst of his troubles. It was partly that that had caused him to propose marriage to her; more and more he found the things he had believed in, the things he had fought for or clung to, slipping away from him, like so many puffs of smoke vanishing on the wind. Her at least he could bind to him, make his own.

'What have you hoped for?' he asked.

'That you would love me.'

'I do.'

'And that you would someday ask me to marry you.'

'I have.'

'So you see,' she said, grinning, 'my hope has been good, and rewarding.'

'Then,' he said, lowering his lips to hers, 'I shall turn my back on the old hopes that deluded me for so long. In the future, I shall believe in yours.'

She returned the kiss, content to know that she would marry the man she loved, though she did not believe that the light of hope, once borne in love, could ever fully be extinguished. She knew that the lover and the beloved were travelers from different lands. It did not trouble her that he loved her less than she loved him, for she regarded loving him as a privilege in itself, of which she was barely worthy. Indeed, if he loved her instead it would be a condition fraught with fear, for always there would be the danger that someday he might go from her, to that other woman, taking his love with him; but as it was, though he might leave, her love for him would remain constant, unchanging.

The tender moment was shattered by the sound of breaking glass from the front parlor. They found Roger there, kneeling on the floor amid fragments of glass and milky green jade; his dog, a great shaggy mongrel, sat nearby, wagging his tail sheepishly.

'Oh, father's Buddha,' Anna exclaimed, clapping her hands to her face. The little jade figure had squatted inside its glass case for as long as she could remember, her father's most revered treasure from Old China. Philip's son, a gangly young man in his teens, looked so miserable that she could not help feeling sorry for him. After all these years, she still did not understand the peculiar estrangement between father and son, but she had gradually come to realize that it was mostly Philip who maintained the distance between them. She had long since taken for granted Roger's rejection of her friendship, but she could not help wishing that the boy received something more in the way of love and companionship from his father than he did. That Philip had love and affection to give, she was fully aware, but for some reason of his own, he did not choose to give it to his son.

'What happened?' Philip asked, coldly eyeing the damage.

'I was rough housing with Sport,' Roger said in a tremulous voice. 'I guess we just bumped the case . . . '

'You guess? Dammit, you've been told a hundred times, you're not supposed to be rough housing in here. You ought to have your hide tanned . . . '

'It's all right,' Anna said quickly, putting a restraining hand on Philip's arm. 'It was an accident.'

'It wasn't an accident, it was carelessness.' Philip's anger, fuelled by frustration, was ever close to the boiling point, and it seemed to take very little from his son to make it erupt. 'It's about time you started doing some growing up, young man. I'm going to make you pay for what you've broken – not just with part of your allowance, but with all your allowance, till you've paid enough to replace that piece – and I'd guess it'll take a couple of years, at least. What's more, you're going to apologize to Anna.'

Roger shot her a quick glance, his expression turning surly. 'I won't,' he said, looking down at the floor.

'Don't tell me what you will and won't do,' Philip said, striding across the room to jerk the youth to his feet by the collar of his shirt. 'I won't have you being churlish to my . . . ' He caught himself about to say, 'my fiancée,' but realized this was hardly the right time to break that news.

'Your Chinese whore?' Roger suggested in a small, dry voice.

Philip struck him without thinking, sending his son sprawling on the floor. Anna gave a gasp of horror.

Almost at once Philip was overcome by a wave of guilt. He moved toward Roger, extending a hand to help him up.

For an answer, Roger snatched up a shard of broken glass, holding it before him like a knife. 'Touch me and I'll kill you,' he said in a low, savage snarl.

Philip was not so much afraid as he was stunned, though there was little doubt that Roger was serious. Philip stood stock still as Roger, still brandishing the glass dagger, edged his way around toward the door.

48

Roger left the same day, hitching a ride with a Bible salesman into Los Angeles. For a week he lived hand to mouth in the alleys and side streets of the city, concerned only with his immediate needs – shelter from the spring rains, something to assuage the pangs gnawing at his stomach.

He was tall for his age, with a robust appearance. The club foot with which he had been born gave him a slight limp, not particularly conspicuous unless he was embarrassed, or conscious of it, at which times it seemed to become more pronounced.

He had left French Hills with better than ten dollars in his pocket, and a day washing dishes for a café had added two more to that; but a pair of seemingly friendly cowboys, correctly judging his familiarity with the ways of the city, had struck up a conversation, helped along with a number of beers, and he had awakened in an alley with a throbbing head and empty pockets.

Since then his luck had been mostly bad. He had made another dollar carrying coal for a widow's furnace, and she had fed him a dinner of cold biscuits and gravy, but a dollar, as he had quickly learned, did not last long in Los Angeles.

For two nights he slept where he could in the open, the weather being balmy. When the rains began, he was forced to sleep crouching in doorways.

He was, in short, miserable, and when, after two days with

little sleep and no food, he happened to pass by an open-air produce stand, it was almost inevitable that he should attempt to pilfer something to eat.

There they were, rows upon rows of the ripe, luscious oranges that had already supplanted grapes in the Southern California agriculture; figs, plump to the point of bursting; mountains of nuts, cartons of dates – he stood and stared, his stomach growling a leitmotif of hunger. The owner was occupied packaging the purchases of a thick, squat woman. No one was watching. It was evening, the sidewalks crowded with working people, hurrying home, crowds such as he had never seen until a few days before; surely, in all the confusion, no one would notice if he took a few things – an orange, tucked inside his jacket – a handful of nuts, thrust quickly into his pocket – some figs . . .

He became mezmerized by the food, by the sight and the smell of it. The cacophony of a bustling metropolitan scene faded into a muted background.

The richness, the splendor of the food betrayed him. The wit that might have told him to snatch and run was lost in the clamor of the hunger in his gut. He stayed, and stole – and stayed too long.

A hand clamped suddenly about his wrist. Startled, Roger dropped a fig and snapped his head around to find himself confronting the owner of the shop, a burly Italian with a wicked looking club in his other hand.

'Thief,' the man said, 'you'll go to jail for this.'

Panic stricken, Roger tried to break free of the man's grip. He was weak, though, from lack of sleep and lack of food; the man was strong, and filled with self-righteous anger. He began to beat the struggling youth about the head and shoulders with the club, all the while swearing at him under his breath.

Roger slipped on the wet pavement and fell. Stunned, he rolled to and fro on the ground, trying to avoid the blows being delivered with merciless regularity. He was only half conscious of someone – a girl – shouting.

'Labor violence! Labor violence! Management cruelty!' She was almost chanting the phrases – ' . . . Exploitation! Cruelty to workers! . . .'

One part of his dazed mind thought, that makes no sense, I don't work for this man – I don't work at all; but the litany went on: 'Labor! Labor! Labor!'

He realized two things all at once – it wasn't one voice now, but several voices, chanting the single word together; and, the blows had stopped.

He looked, and saw that a crowd had formed a semicircle. There were a few women on their way home from shopping, their arms laden with packages, and here and there a prosperous-looking gentleman in tall hat and neatly pressed trousers, but these were only onlookers. The bulk of the crowd – many of them chanting now and others shaking their fists and jeering – were working-class people. There were burly men in patched shirts and women with bandanas tied about their heads; men with shovels and hods, and two-day growths of beard. They were the poor, the used, the cheated – and at the moment they were angry, goaded on to increasing anger by a girl with frizzy red hair and thick glasses who was waving her arms and shouting loudest of all.

It was the most peculiar thing he'd ever seen, and Roger was divided between gratitude that the burly Italian had stopped beating him and had moved several steps back toward his store, and curiosity as to what was happening.

The Italian was trying to make himself heard, trying to justify his actions, but the unreasoning anger of the crowd was directed fully at him, and as Roger, still lying on the ground, watched wide eyed, a young man with no shirt under his suspenders dashed forward and, seizing a handful of the shopkeeper's own figs, pelted him with them.

A lusty cheer went up; another from the crowd followed suit, and another, dashing forward and seizing fruits to throw.

'Get up, quick.'

It was the girl, poking him with the toe of a badly scuffed shoe. 'Come on,' she urged him, 'while they're distracted.'

It took him only a moment to see the wisdom of her advice, and a moment later the two of them were pushing their way through the crowd, the girl leading. Once he almost lost her, but she looked back and, seeing him fall behind, urged him on.

'Here, this way,' she said, snatching his sleeve and guiding him into an alley. They ran until it had turned a corner; then, finally, they slowed their pace, both breathing heavily.

He started to say something, to thank her, but she gave her head a shake. 'Wait, we're almost there,' she said, though he had no idea where 'there' was.

They came to what appeared to be an abandoned warehouse of some sort, its windows boarded over. The door was set back from the alley in a shadowy alcove; to his surprise, she stepped into the alcove. The door proved to be unlocked, and he followed her into the gloomy interior of the building.

She led the way through a maze of boxes and crates. At the far end of the building, a large clearing had been formed, and, astonishingly, a pot-bellied stove gave off a faint glow.

'This is it,' she said, indicating the open expanse with her hands. 'Home sweet hopeless. Pull up a box and sit down.'

She opened the door of the stove and threw in some boards obviously broken off packing crates. Roger looked around; there were a half dozen or so piles of bedding arranged haphazardly around the edges of the clearing, indicating that she was not the only resident of this peculiar domicile.

'You mean you live here?' he asked.

'It's where we sleep – among other things. How are you feeling? He was really laying into you with that club.'

'Sure was.' He rubbed the back of his head gingerly, and brought his hand back with blood on it.

'Better let me look at that,' she said. 'Sit down.'

He sat on one of the boxes pulled up around the stove, and she stood behind him, cautiously parting his hair to examine the wound.

'Thanks,' he said, wincing as she probed gently. 'For coming to my rescue back there, I mean. But I'm afraid you made a mistake, I wasn't working for that fellow.'

'Doesn't matter,' she said. 'I know that bastard, he treats his employees like animals.'

He had never in his memory heard a woman swear before and it both shocked and titillated him. The increasing heat of the stove emphasized the damp odor of their clothes. He was conscious of her smell, musty and not quite clean. She left him and came back in a minute with a bottle of some liquid, which she poured on his wound. It had a sting that was not entirely unpleasant.

'Who's we?' he asked.

'What?'

'You said, "it's where we sleep"; I wondered who we was.'

She came around to stand before him and made a mock bow. 'Welcome to the headquarters of local chapter twelve of the Industrial Workers of the World. This is where we meet, talk, eat, sleep – and occasional other pastimes, depending on who's in the mood. My name's Stella, what's yours?'

'Roger,' he said automatically, and, a minute later, in a shocked voice, 'Wobblies!'

'Don't call us that,' she snapped, her eyes flashing angrily behind their thick lenses.

'It's what everybody calls you,' he answered, awed and a bit unnerved by the announcement; the Wobblies, as they were generally known, were the most radical of all the labor reformers, at the heart of much of the unrest and violence that had beset the Western states for the last several years.

'It's what General Otis and his *Los Angeles Times* calls us,' she said bitterly, pronouncing the names with chilling emphasis. 'To the workers of America, we're the hope for the future, their only chance of being liberated from the veneered cannibalism of industrial capitalism.'

He got up from the box shaking his head. 'I don't know about that,' he said. 'But I do know that wherever you people go, heads get busted.'

'Like yours?' she asked scornfully.

'That's different,' he said, though he wasn't quite sure how. 'Anyway, I'm not a worker. I'm a part of . . . ' He hesitated; he had been about to say, 'the capitalist class.' After all, he was a Brussac, scion of the French Hills wine and oil industries. Yet he had turned his back on all that, renounced it.

' . . . Of the unemployed,' he finished lamely.

'Because the octopus of business management strangles the unskilled worker,' she cried. Her face had taken on a glow that almost made it pretty. 'Join with us. Industrial capitalism must be eliminated completely before we can be free. We must unite.'

'I think I'd better go,' he said.

'No, wait, don't go – '

'I thank you for your help.'

She let him walk a few yards from her before she asked, in a much softer voice, 'Are you afraid of me?'

He paused, looking back with a surprised expression. 'Why should I be afraid of you?' he asked.

She strolled over to him, swinging her hips wide with each step. 'You're a gimp, aren't you?' she asked, glancing down at his twisted foot.

His face turned crimson. 'Go to hell,' he said, starting off once again. His efforts to control his limp only made it more obvious.

'Wait,' she said again, running after him and grabbing his

sleeve. 'What I meant was – wait, damn it, I'm trying to talk to you.'

He stopped again and stood facing her, his expression angry and defiant. 'Well?' he said impatiently.

She gave him a tentative smile. 'The first man I was ever with – I was twelve at the time – ' she added the last with a note of what might have been pride, 'he only had two fingers on his left hand. Said he lost the others in an accident where he worked.'

'What's that supposed to mean?'

'Well, I mean, I never have been with a man who was perfect anyway. I wasn't making fun of your foot, I was just commenting. Like people do with my glasses, you know? I think sometimes men go for me just because of them – like, it's easier with someone who's not so perfect, they aren't so put off, you know what I mean?'

He looked around the warehouse room, and up at the ceiling, managing finally a sideways glance at her. Behind the lenses of the glasses, her eyes were actually pretty, though her thin, colorless lips gave her a spinsterish look. It was her breasts, however, that fascinated him: they were immense, ponderous mountains of flesh that swayed and bobbed beneath her sweater with each movement that she made.

He swallowed. 'Uh, are you trying to say that you would like, uh, you and me . . . ' He nodded toward one of the piles of bedding.

'I wouldn't mind,' she said brightly. Her eyes suddenly narrowed, raking him up and down. 'Say, there isn't anything else wrong with you, is there? I mean, anywhere else?'

'Not a thing,' he said, grinning.

'Well then . . . ?' She shivered, setting her breasts to jiggling and jouncing frantically. 'It's cold in here, don't you think?'

'It'll be warmer in the covers,' he said.

She was undressed before him, choosing the bedding nearest the stove's warmth. He watched her as he undressed, balancing ungracefully on his good foot while he tugged the other free of his trousers. He had never been with a woman before, and the prospect of being with her both attracted and repelled him. She was not pretty, but her thick, well-upholstered body looked soft and warm, her parted thighs forming an invitation.

'You'll stay, won't you?' she asked in an almost plaintive

tone. She had, he noticed, removed everything but her glasses. 'You'll join us?'

'I suppose so,' he said, at the moment occupied with thoughts far removed from the Wobblies or the needs of unskilled laborers.

He stood for a moment looking down at her; then, with the urgency of inexperience, he fell upon her.

49

Ten years earlier, in Chicago, a group of radicals and academics had met to form a new labor organization, the Industrial Workers of the World. Their goal was boldly announced in their constitution: 'The army of production must be organized, not only for the everyday struggle with capitalists, but also to carry on production when capitalism shall have been overthrown. By organizing industrially, we are forming the structure of the new society within the shell of the old.'

In the decade since its founding, the IWW had invaded California in force, concentrating on the unskilled, the foreign born, the poorest and weakest of the workers – the lumberjacks, miners, seamen and bindle stiffs, as the migratory farm workers were known – in short, all those workers neglected by the other labor organizations of the day.

Though their numbers in California never reached more than a few thousand, the Wobblies had managed for a few years to challenge the industrial foundations of the economic system. They were feared by many industrialists and capitalists as wholeheartedly as if they were millions; not only were they passionately devoted to their cause, but their leaders had rediscovered the anarchal truth – that the structure of law and order upon which civilization was based was largely illusory, dependent on the voluntary compliance of the many to the dictates of the few. The technique of 'passive resistance' was born with the Wobblies.

In 1910 the authorities in Fresno had attempted to block IWW recruiting by outlawing meetings and street corner oratory. The Wobblies sent out their call:

Come on the cushions, ride up on top;
Stick to the brakebeams, let nothing stop.
Come in great numbers, this we beseech;
Help Fresno to win Free Speech!

The jails filled rapidly with Wobblies who at once set about indoctrinating other prisoners and singing songs of revolutionary defiance.

Fire-hoses were brought in to cool their passions; the Wobblies took refuge behind their mattresses, and sang louder. Outside, new reinforcements arrived in a steady stream to take the place of those now overburdening the jail system.

Finally the city gave in. The bans were lifted, the Wobblies, quietly released to go on their way, were made bolder by their victory.

In San Diego a year later the confrontation was ugly and violent. Wobblies were forced by vigilante groups to run pick-handle gauntlets which many did not survive; those who did were hauled to jail or escorted to the county line, where they were forced to kneel and kiss the flag and left to fend for themselves on foot. An investigator sent by the governor likened the city's activities to the atrocities of Czarist Russia, but authorities did little more than cluck their tongues, while the Wobblies nursed their bruises.

Los Angeles, with a wage scale thirty to forty per cent lower than that of San Francisco and other cities to the north, was violently anti-labor. The chief opponent of unionized labor was Harrison Gray Otis of the *Los Angeles Times*, he who had given the Wobblies their nickname, and with all the power of the press he had rallied the city's conservative and big business element to his side. In the frequently violent struggle that had ensued, the labor movement had not fared well.

In 1916 in Los Angeles being a Wobbly was not the safest of occupations. Few were willing publicly to admit to being members; most meetings were held secretly, under threat of reprisal from vigilante groups as well as city authorities.

This, then, was the nest into which Roger was welcomed in that damp and chilly spring. At first it was Stella, with her seemingly tireless appetite for sex, that held him, and he remained aloof from the rhetoric of the others who shared the warehouse domicile. These – their numbers and faces varied daily – treated him with reserve but little resentment. He was not the first, after all, to enter the house of labor through the gateway of Stella's thighs.

There was no set time for meetings; people came and went, and when they were there, there was talk, much of it harangues delivered by Stella in a voice flaming with passionate commitment. She disdained the soft approach of the older, more conservative labor unions, with their emphasis on boycotts and appeals to the employers' good natures.

'One must not supplicate, but demand,' was her creed; 'one gets not justice, but what one can command.'

Sitting off by himself on a crate, or leaning against a shadowy wall, Roger waited for her 'sermons', as he called them, to end, knowing that afterward, warmed by the fire of her cause, she would demand sex from him as earnestly as she demanded concessions from her hated capitalists.

It was inevitable, though, that in hearing so many harangues against management and big business, he would begin to listen. He too was one of the disenchanted. If it was true that he had never until now been poor, or that he had become so of his own choice, it was equally true that he was no stranger to alienation or neglect. He had known the abuse of being ignored – his dreams, his needs, his private fears. He had never in his life, since the death of his mother when he was a mere child, felt that he belonged to anyone or anything – certainly not to a French Hills that was being turned into a forest of oil wells where once grapes had grown; nor to his father and his father's Chinese mistress – his father, who could never manage to look at him without that badly concealed and inexplicable revulsion.

Yet here, increasingly, he began to feel a part of something. It was not only Stella and her burning flesh; though he made no close friendship with the Carmens and Alfreds, the Toms and Marios who came and went from the warehouse, he felt accepted by them, in a way he had never felt accepted before. He found the approval that his youth required, in their acceptance, and in turn he began gradually to think of them as his friends, and himself as one of them.

It was only reluctantly, however, that he accepted their radical philosophies. He had no quarrel with the things they had to say about the plight of the working masses. He could see about him in Los Angeles the misery of the disenfranchised, the poor and those who spoke other languages; indeed, though the employees at French Hills had been treated in an enlightened manner, he could not help but see that unionization would have made their lot considerably better.

He disagreed, however, with the radical means by which the Wobblies espoused their cause. They invariably caused violence, which bred more violence. He thought the Wobblies erred in antagonizing authorities and business management instead of conciliating and consulting with them to achieve their goals.

Only once did he attempt to discuss his opinions with Stella. For two nights she slept – and burned – elsewhere, and when she finally returned sulkily to his bed, he apologized and afterward kept his opinions to himself.

He might never have actually joined the IWW as a member, had not he thoughtlessly revealed his full name. In nearly three weeks of living with the Wobblies, everyone remained on a first name basis; it was safer, everyone thought, in the event of a police raid. After a day or two, Roger had grown accustomed to the practice among the men, but it had continued to seem peculiar to him that the woman he slept with night after night was known to him only as Stella. Finally, he asked.

'What difference does it make?' she asked.

'Suppose I want to introduce you to my family some day,' he said, grinning.

'Fat chance.' She gave him a measured look. 'What's your family's name, anyway, maybe I won't want to be introduced?'

'Brussac,' he replied.

Her eyes narrowed thoughtfully. 'Brussac, that sounds familiar – hey, you don't mean the wine people, do you?'

He realized his mistake too late; he ought to have known that name would appear on Stella's mental list of hated capitalists.

'Not exactly,' he said, avoiding her searching look.

'What does that mean, not exactly? Wait a minute – you told me you grew up out in the country, east of here.' She planted herself in front of him, hands on hips, her eyes blazing. 'You're one of the goddamn French Hills Brussacs, aren't you? One of the blood suckers.'

'I'm not,' he said, his voice rising to meet hers. 'Not any more.'

'Since when?'

'Since I left a couple of months ago. What in the hell do you think I'd be doing living here if I was still one of them? Why do you think I was trying to steal some food? I cut out after a fight with my old man.'

'You'll be going back some day – and you'll carry along all sorts of tales about us.'

'No, I won't. I'm not ever going back there. This is where I want to be. This is where I belong.'

'Only you don't belong here,' she said, more calmly. She studied him coldly for a moment. Then she went to the broken crate that served her as a writing-table and brought him the tablet on which she obtained the signatures of new members as they joined the IWW. She thrust it at him.

'Better sign this,' she said.

'What for?'

'I've got to tell the others who you are, it's only fair. For all we know, you might be a spy. I don't know how much they'll like it, they're liable to want to toss you out of here. Of course, if you were a member it'd be different, they wouldn't toss out a fellow member, unless he really was a spy.'

'You know I'm not,' he said hotly.

She thrust the tablet at him again. 'You'd better sign, if you want to hang around here anymore.'

After a moment he took the tablet and reluctantly signed his name, handing it back to her. She took it with a smug expression, staring down at the name, written in a neat, small script.

'This is a red letter day,' she said, carrying the tablet back to her 'desk'. 'This is the first time I've ever signed up a capitalist as a Wobbly.'

50

So long as the Wobblies limited themselves to talk, it was easy for Roger to rationalize his joining of the IWW. It was true that he experienced an occasional sense of guilt. In a way he had betrayed his own origins; French Hills, after all, was one of the local business operations often proposed as a target for Wobbly action, and despite his longtime alienation from his father, fond memories of French Hills – of the grapes, rich and ripe on the vines, of the hills themselves, soft curves like a woman's breasts, washed clean in the spring rains – lingered in his mind.

Still, he reasoned, he had done nothing but sign his name on a sheet of tablet paper. So far as he knew, Stella had not even mentioned his name to the others; if she had, no one spoke of it to him. Nothing seemed changed. Stella was still as passionate with him as ever – indeed, to his surprise, it sometimes seemed to him that she was too passionate. He had begun to sense something almost unnatural in the apparently insatiable lust with which she burned. Of course, he was a young man, with strong drives of his own, and at first her constant urging had been gratifying as well as flattering. Lately, however, he had begun to feel that it was not him personally that she wanted; it was only a ritual in which he was a convenient, but utterly replacable, performer.

He was not entirely unhappy then when she disappeared for a few days in May, explaining that there was 'important work coming up for all of us'.

She returned in the company of two men, strangers whom she introduced as Miller and Druss, union leaders. Miller was a dapper little man with the peculiar habit of looking past whoever he was talking to, as if expecting someone to come through the door at any minute. Druss, a powerfully built German immigrant, had a thick nose and the austere lips of the fanatic. There was an air of sullen obstinacy and cold determination in the tension with which he held himself restlessly in check.

To Roger's surprise, though the newcomers acknowledged their introductions to the others offhandedly, they made a point soon afterward of seeking him out.

'Stella tells us you're a Brussac,' Miller said, glancing over Roger's shoulder with such an air of expectancy that Roger himself nearly looked around.

'What of it?' Roger answered, a bit defensively; he had not forgotten Stella's reaction to learning his identity.

'We think you might be useful to us,' Miller said.

'I'm not interested in doing anything against my family,' Roger said. The remark surprised him; until now, he had believed himself convinced that he owed no loyalty to his family.

'We're looking for someone familiar with vineyard work,' Druss said.

'Why?'

It was Miller who took up the conversation, though Roger had the impression that it was Druss who directed its course.

'There's a large vineyard near San Luis Obispo, belongs to a man named Bergano – are you familiar with it?'

'I've heard of him. I don't know anything about his vineyard. What has this got to do with me?'

'Bergano's advertising all over the state for workers, says he has plenty of work for anyone interested, and at pretty good wages too.'

'That ought to make everyone happy,' Roger said. 'Except the IWW, right? Plenty of work, good money – not much for the Wobblies to work on, is there?'

Druss asked, 'What kind of work do they do in a vineyard this time of year?'

'Plenty. Canes need tying. Suckers have to be removed. Lots of thinning. Plants need spraying with sulfur to protect against mildew. Only . . . ' he hesitated.

'Only what?' Miller wanted to know.

'Nothing. Only, if he's advertising that far and wide, he must have a devil of a lot of acreage. We used to work our vineyards with a dozen men, working hard.'

'That's exactly the sort of thing we want to know,' Miller said enthusiastically. 'That's why we want you to come with us.'

'Come with you where?' Roger asked.

Druss shot Miller a frosty look, as if he had spoken out of turn. 'We want to go up there, to recruit new members,' Druss said.

'I don't know anything about recruiting members,' Roger said. 'Stella's the one you want for that.'

'I'll be going too,' Stella said.

'We want someone who can give us honest information about the situation there,' Druss went on, speaking as if he were explaining to a recalcitrant child. 'Someone who can assess the work situation, someone familiar with the prevailing work conditions. Yours would be a valuable contribution.'

Roger stared at him directly. 'I'm not interested in getting my head cracked open by a pick handle,' he said.

Druss' thin lips formed a faint smile. 'Nor am I,' he said. 'San Diego was a fiasco. We intend to avoid making the same mistakes again.'

'Everything will be peaceful?'

'It will be on our part.'

'Will you come?' Stella asked. Her eyes flashed with the same sort of fire that he saw in them whenever she prepared to make love.

He thought for a moment. Then he shrugged. 'I guess I've

got nothing else to do. Anyway, it'll be good to be outside, and away from this place.'

Though scores of Wobblies, including those Roger had known by their first names, were traveling to San Luis Obispo on foot or in boxcars, he and Stella traveled with Druss and Miller inside the train's second-class compartment. He did not tell them it was a first for him; on those few occasions when he had traveled before, he had never known anything but first class. In that compartment, stylish ladies and elegant gentlemen sat aloof from one another. He found this noisy hodgepodge of humanity strangely refreshing. There were loud conversations in a half dozen languages; children ran up and down the aisles, and somewhere to the rear a baby cried ceaselessly. A rather shabby-looking widow had brought a dog aboard in a basket, from which he had promptly escaped, initiating a chase over, under and about seats in which a goodly number of the car's passengers participated with boisterous good humor.

Not everything was bonhomie, however. He was aware of others whom he might not have seen in the past or, seeing them, not have known for what they were. These were the desperate and the despairing. They were the poorest of the poor, who, having forsworn hope, pursued it like the elusive will-o'-the-wisp. The lucky ones, having cadged or perhaps stolen the price of a ticket, rode with him in the second-class compartment, but they did not engage in cheerful conversations or chase run-away spaniels; they sat with worried eyes watching the windows, anxious to arrive at their destination, clasping work-scarred hands in their laps, in an attitude of prayer, though the supplications had long since dried up in their mouths.

He had known, in some uncaring corner of his mind, that such people existed; indeed, for a time he had lived among them. He heard the lectures of Stella and the others and had comprehended intellectually their plight.

It was only now, however, that he began to see these 'misfortunates', as Stella labeled them, not as abstract ideas, but as people, flesh and blood beings who lived the same life he lived, only cloaked in misery.

They were not only on the train, they walked alongside it in the roadbeds, men, women, children – whole families wending their way northward, because one man had promised work, had offered a living wage for the labor of their hands.

Yet he knew, as they could not, that something was false with the promises. He rode, and saw the increasing crowds of people drifting northward toward San Luis Obispo, and he was certain that there could not be enough work for so many. A large vineyard, of course; a vast vineyard even; work enough perhaps for a hundred, for several hundred – but even to his unpracticed eye, there were too many.

He told Druss this. To his surprise Druss seemed already aware of the discrepancy.

'They've done this before,' Druss said. 'Not only Bergano, though it's something of a specialty of his, but others too. It will turn out there's too many workers there for the work to be done.'

'But what's the point in that?' Roger asked.

Druss gave him a look that said he was a fool. It was Miller, staring past Roger out the window, who answered. 'It lets them manipulate the wages any way they want,' he said.

'But they promised . . . ' Roger paused, realizing suddenly that he did indeed sound foolish.

'It's supply and demand,' Stella said. 'A few workers, a lot of work, high wages have to be paid to get it done. But a lot of workers, more than you need – why then, you can pick the ones willing to work for the least.'

'The most desperate,' Roger said.

'And the hungriest. And those with the most children to feed. Or the sickest wife. Or who've gone the longest without a job or pay.'

'It's manipulating these people – their misery, their basic human needs . . . ' Roger made a futile gesture and grew silent, watching as the train sped by yet another ragged-looking family on the road.

When they arrived at San Luis Obispo they were met by one of those nameless followers who seemed so loyal to the Wobbly leaders; Jim was the only name he had, and he had brought a battered farm cart to transport them to the Bergano vineyards.

Roger helped Stella into the cart, but when he would have climbed on after her, Druss put a restraining hand on his arm.

'I don't know if you should go with us,' Druss said. 'Perhaps after all you ought to go back to Los Angeles. Perhaps even back to your family.'

'Back to . . . but why? I thought you wanted me here?' Roger was genuinely astonished.

'I did – for your own sake as well as for ours. But now . . . '

He shrugged. 'You grew up in luxury, you're soft. Oh, I know, you ran away from home – like a schoolboy on a lark. You've played at being a rebel and a radical – sitting in the shelter of a warehouse, sharing Stella's bed, listening to our talk – it's easy to nod your head, to say, "Yes, this is dreadful, I deplore it" – it takes no courage. But now, here – ' He made a far-flung gesture with his hand. 'This is the real world. I don't know if you've got the stomach for it.'

Roger was embarrassed. The others, waiting in the cart, were listening and watching him. 'You – you think I'm too young,' he stammered.

'No, no – youth is its own strength, its own courage – but you, my son, are young and ignorant – don't be offended. I often wish to God I could trade my knowledge for an ignorance such as yours. Ignorance is a choice, it can be forsworn at will, but what I know, what I have seen and heard, is a curse that I must carry with me forever.'

For a moment Roger regarded the other; then, with a decisive gesture, he shrugged off the restraining hand leaped up into the cart.

'I left home because I wanted to learn about the real world,' he said. 'This is as good a place as any to lose my ignorance of it.'

51

The reality that awaited them at the Bergano ranch was far worse than Roger had imagined. An unseasonal hot spell had driven the temperatures above the hundred mark and turned the camp established for the workers into an odorous jungle. The only shelter provided was in the ragged tents the Berganos rented for two dollars and seventy-five cents a week. There was a sea of these, stretching over the low hills of the ranch, but they could not begin to accommodate all those who had come in response to Bergano's call for workers.

Mostly hatless, dressed in ragged clothes, an army of men, women and children sat or stood about in the pitiless sun. Some lay shoulder to shoulder, trying to sleep in the scant shade provided by their standing comrades. Flies swarmed about them; there was an almost unbearable stench of sweat and excrement.

Roger, who had seen crowds of workmen on French Hills, was unprepared for this bedlam. He stared in dismay, fighting the taste of bile in his mouth. This was inhuman.

'It's horrible,' he said aloud.

Druss, beside him, gave him a grim smile. 'Come, let us go among them,' he said, urging Roger along with a hand on his shoulder.

They made their way down a slope, into the throng. Stella drifted off, striking up conversations here and there, returning to report in a loud whisper, 'They're paying seventy cents a day. Started at a dollar, but the rate went down as more people began to arrive. The betting is it'll drop to fifty cents tomorrow.'

'But they can't do that,' Roger protested. 'Bergano offered two-fifty a day. That's what these people came for.'

'Look around you,' Druss said. 'There must be two thousand, maybe three thousand people here. Bergano can pay what he chooses. There are enough people here who are so desperate they'll take it.'

'Help me, please, for God's sake,' someone cried nearby. Druss looked around and, finding the source of the cry, pushed his way through the crowd in that direction, the others following in his wake.

They found a frightened-looking man kneeling on the ground, with four children, ranging in age from five up to about twelve, standing in a semicircle about him. He was kneeling over a fifth child, a girl of about seven or eight, who writhed on the ground in the throes of some delirium.

'Help me, I beg you,' he cried as Druss strode up to them. 'My daughter, she's in agony – the fever ...'

'Are there no doctors?' Druss asked.

'None – please, sir, if she could only have some water – she's burning up.' He held a rusty tin cup out to them.

'I'll find some,' Roger said, snatching the cup from the man's hand.

He set out through the crowd, pushing and shoving and demanding as he went to know where the water could be found. Most of those he asked only stared at him as if he were mad, though one or two actually burst into laughter.

'Damn it, what's funny?' he demanded of one of these. 'I've got to find some water.'

'There isn't any, sport,' someone told him. 'Not a drop anywhere.'

'But, my God, there's got to be – all these people – the heat – what do you do for thirst?'

This elicited a chorus of laughter and yowls from those about him. 'There's always the lemonade,' someone else shouted, producing another chorus, this time punctuated with jeers and oaths.

'What does that mean?' Roger demanded, but no one wanted to take the time to answer him. One man gave him a shove and, pointing, said, 'Over that way. You'll see.'

He made his way in that direction, gradually become aware that the crowd was thickening as he went. Something was going on up ahead, but it was impossible to tell what from where he was. He forced his way forward, stretching on tiptoe occasionally to try to see over the crowd.

At last he saw three men atop a farm cart, dispensing something from a stack of kegs. 'Is that water?' he asked of some of those pushing forward.

'It's the Bergano's lemonade,' someone explained, and another voice snorted disdainfully and said, 'Lemonade? There's no more lemon in that than my father's whiskers.'

Lemon or not, it was wet at least; he was close enough now to see the liquid streaming from the kegs into the cups and glasses being lifted aloft.

Somehow he managed to make his way to the front. The pouring keg moved toward him and he held up the tin cup. 'I'll have some of that,' he shouted over the din.

'Where's your dime?' the man on the cart asked, managing to miss the cup with the lemonade.

'My dime?'

'We ain't giving this away,' was the explanation. 'It's a dime a cup. Toss it on the cart.'

Roger glanced around and saw others tossing coins into the cart. With almost uncanny accuracy the three men on the cart, each pouring from a keg, kept track of who had paid and who had not.

'Where's the water?' Roger demanded of the man on the cart. 'To hell with your lemonade.'

'Ain't any water. Just the lemonade, and it's a dime a cup. Look, if you don't want to buy any, why don't you move out of the way so some of the others can get up here, there's a lot of thirsty people.'

'You're damn right there are,' Roger cried, his anger reaching the boiling point, 'and they've got a right to something to drink.'

His move was so sudden that the man on the cart was caught completely off guard, merely blinking with surprise as the keg was snatched out of his hands.

A cheer went up from those closest in the crowd as Roger began to pour the lemonade around, filling cups and glasses to overflowing.

The three on the cart were not long in overcoming their surprise, however; a moment later two of them had jumped from the cart and attacked Roger. He had expected that some of the waiting crowd would come to his aid, but to his dismay they backed away. The third man, still on the cart, began shouting, 'Next twenty drinks on the house,' and the crowd swarmed past the fight, pushing toward the free lemonade.

Roger was beaten to the ground. After a few hard kicks, his assailants returned to the task of hawking their lemonade, leaving him half unconscious. Some of those crowding toward the cart actually stepped on him.

Finally a woman knelt beside him. 'Here,' she said, lifting his head and putting a cup to his lips, 'you'd better drink this.'

Ironically, it was the same watery lemonade he had been fighting over earlier. He made a wry grimace as he swallowed. 'They might as well be selling water,' he said.

'They probably will be before this is over,' the woman said. 'Can you get up now? This isn't the best place to stretch out.'

'I'm all right,' he said, getting to his feet. He glanced at the cup from which he had been drinking, and saw that it was still half full. 'Can I take this?' he asked. 'There's a little girl back there, burning up with a fever. I was looking for some water.'

'Go ahead, take it if it'll do some good. My husband and I have decided we'd head back to Los Angeles.'

'That's what everyone should do,' Roger said, looking around at the mob.

She glanced around too, her expression sad. 'Yes,' she said. 'But some of them are worse off than we are.'

He thanked her again and started back in search of Druss and the others. Not until he had lost the woman in the crowd did he realize he hadn't even asked her name. She was one of a nameless horde – the hungry, the poor, the needy. The people whom the IWW sought to unite. He might decry the Wobblies' methods, but at least now he could better understand their purpose.

He had some difficulty finding the spot where he had left the others, and when he did Miller came out to meet him.

'This was the best I could do,' Roger said, indicating the half full cup.

'Give me that,' Miller said. He took it from Roger's hand and, to Roger's dismay, proceeded to drink the cup's contents. He glanced over the rim and, seeing Roger's horrified expression, said, 'She won't need it now.'

Roger turned to look in that direction, but his view was blocked by a ring of men and women that had formed about the spot where the girl had been lying. As he stared, Druss separated himself from the group and came toward him.

'Come with me,' Druss greeted him tersely, his face set in a grim expression. Wordlessly, Roger did as bidden, following the other man through the crowd. The thousands of treading feet had worn the earth bare, so that the dust rose in clouds, filling their nostrils, choking them.

Druss led the way to a slope where a row of flimsy structures had been erected. 'Look at them,' Druss said, gesturing angrily at the buildings. 'These are the "sanitation" facilities.' His voice rose. 'Eight privies, for close on three thousand people. Look.'

Long lines of people stood waiting for access to the outhouses, which looked in danger of falling in upon themselves at any minute. But it was not even necessary to look to know how inadequate the facilities were – Roger's nose could have informed him of that. By this time the inadequate trenches beneath the structures had been filled to overflowing, and the ground round about turned into a morass through which the people must trudge to reach the privies. The air was fetid with the stench of excrement.

The heat, the stink, the brutal mistreatment of hapless humans, all combined were too much for Roger. He turned and began to retch violently.

Druss waited silently beside him, hardly seeming to notice Roger's vomiting. When it was done, however, he wordlessly handed him a clean handkerchief.

'You were right,' Roger said, wiping his mouth, 'I was ignorant. In the name of God, does this go on all the time?'

'Even once is intolerable,' Druss said.

'Is there nothing to be done?'

'There is what we've been trying to do. We can attempt to

turn this ragtag mob into an army, an army of workers that will march across the nation, putting an end to this sort of gross injustice. Look at them – hundreds, thousands – each one alone, impotent, helpless – but joined together, with one vision, one voice, they need never suffer this again.'

'And you're asking me to help?'

Druss looked offended at the statement. 'Human dignity asks you to help,' he said.

'They say your leadership is thick with socialists, even communists.'

'We have not had the luxury of picking and choosing leaders. Few have been willing.'

'People are afraid of you.'

'People were afraid of Jesus.'

Roger smiled; the comparison was not as far fetched as it might have seemed, for there was something messianic about the labor leader. And perhaps, he thought briefly, the same inevitability of martyrdom.

'Where do we start?' Roger asked aloud.

'*We* already have,' was the answer.

52

However much Roger might have disagreed with the Wobblies in theory, he found the actual work of organizing the laborers exhilarating. Here both the problems and the attempts at solutions were real and concrete. It was one thing to discuss on an abstract level the plight of the unskilled laborer at the hand of capitalists; it was quite another to see desperate men and women, and children even, laboring at back-breaking work for wages that would be for the most part eaten up in charges for tents, supplies, food and the ever-available 'lemonade'.

The climate of opinion was fertile for their efforts. The latest count indicated that there were somewhere in excess of twenty-eight hundred people at the ranch, vying for the available work. Most of these on any given day were doomed to disappointment, and to waiting for the following day, when they might have to work for even lower wages. Nor were matters much better for the 'lucky' ones who got work each day, for evening found them little better off, if at all, than when the day had begun.

There was, even among the bindle stiffs, a certain wariness toward Wobbly activity – after all, everyone knew what had happened in San Diego, and those who were here had come for work, not to have their heads cracked open.

Still, it was not difficult to stir up feelings against the Berganos, nor to generate interest in organized action. It was easy for the workers to see that they had been duped and, as Druss and the others pointed out, so long as workers were willing, on an individual basis, to accept Bergano's conditions, the mockery of 'plenty of work for all, at high wages' would continue. It couldn't have been clearer, even to the most reluctant union sympathizer among them, that what was needed here was concerted effort.

And the Wobblies, working virtually day and night, were organizing it. Roger had arrived with the others on Wednesday. By Saturday there was scarcely a worker in the wide valley who did not know of the mass meeting called for the following morning. Druss and Miller would speak, along with a number of local people who had been recruited to provide examples to the others.

Druss had stuck to his promise to keep things peaceful. All threats of violent action had been banned. The meeting was intended only to bargain for better wages and working conditions. Representatives had been sent to Bergano himself, asking him to discuss their requests. He had refused, setting the stage for the mass meeting, at which Druss and the others would urge a general strike. It would be, Roger was convinced, the most peaceful demonstration of IWW policy since the union's birth a decade earlier.

Sunday dawned hot and clear. By ten o'clock, when the meeting was to begin, the temperature was already in the nineties and climbing steadily. This added to the tension that had been building over the last four days. No matter how peaceful the Wobblies intended to keep things, no matter how justified the complaints on which they were voting, everyone present knew that this was the first real Wobbly meeting since the debacle in San Diego. Everyone knew too that Bergano was a tough customer, known to be anti-labor union. He kept on the payroll a number of thugs whose only apparent function was to keep workers in line.

Long before ten the crowds had begun to form. The Wobblies had constructed a crude stage, set atop a knoll that gave them a commanding view of the wide valley where the migrant workers were camped. By the time the leaders mounted the steps to the stage a little after ten, a sea of nervous, expectant faces ranged across the valley before them.

Bergano's people were strangely absent. Sometime during the night the lemonade carts had vanished. The foremen who normally appeared at dawn to begin recruiting the day's workers did not show. From Bergano himself, there was a worrisome silence.

Miller addressed the crowd first. Roger was surprised to discover that the dapper little man spoke well. It was a low key speech, listing the workers' many grievances, which they already knew, but which, as with any troubles, took on an added importance with being chronicled.

Stella followed him. In the days since they had arrived at the ranch, Roger had been so busy that he had had little time to spend with her. Though he missed the regular sexual outlet, he could not help but realize, as he watched her haranguing the crowd in much the same way as she had harangued the Wobblies in the warehouse in Los Angeles, that there was a certain amount of relief in her absence too. There was a tension within her, part of it sexual, part of it her reformer's zeal, that never abated and that made it impossible simply to relax in her company. He noticed now that where Miller had managed to put some of the audience at ease, Stella's appearance was anxiety-producing.

After Stella a trio of workers got up one at a time to address their fellows. One of them was the man whose little girl had died the day they had arrived. He had declined both Roger's and Stella's invitations to speak, agreeing only after Druss had spoken privately with him.

His words were simple and affecting. He made no pleas to join with the Wobblies, nor even discussed their common hardships; instead, he told in a straightforward, almost emotionless manner, his own experiences. His wife had died the year before, of pneumonia. He did not say, though it was understood by those present, that there had been complicating factors – inadequate housing, poor food, not enough warm clothing – the litany of the poor, common to all those gathered to listen.

He had heard, in Indio, of Bergano's offer of 'work for everybody, at high wages', and had traveled northward on foot with his five children, one of whom became ill on the way. They had no money and only enough food for the trip. Unable to pay for a doctor, they had pushed onward, thinking that with their first day's pay they could afford medical attention for her.

They had arrived too late to begin work their first day. The man had begged one of the foremen to let him work, not for wages, but only for some water and food, or a tent in which the girl could rest out of the burning sun. He had been informed that work parties were made up at dawn each day, and if he wished to work he must be among the volunteers the following morning.

'By then,' he said simply, 'my daughter had been buried.'

The audience sat in silence, waiting for him to go on; but after a moment he shook his head and turned from them to leave the stage.

The two workers following him spoke without finesse but with gusto and ardor, urging their fellows to join with the Wobblies in a general strike to better their conditions. Neither of these two added anything that had not been said before, but their listeners could readily identify with their own kind, and their contribution was effective.

Druss, the principal speaker, was to follow these three, but it was while the last of them was speaking that Roger, who was seated on the ground before the stage, became aware that some intelligence was being passed along the lines of those on the stage. He saw Stella look over her shoulder and, with a worried look, nudge Miller, who in turn looked in the same direction. His expression was anxious as he leaned over to whisper in Druss' ear.

Druss did not look at whatever it was the others had noticed, nor did his expression change. He stood, hands folded in front of him, awaiting his turn to speak. Roger had stood, straining to see what it was that had disturbed the others. At first he could see nothing; then, unexpectedly, a new crowd came into view, mounting the knoll upon which the stage stood. Many – but not all – of the newcomers were in uniform, their badges gleaming brightly in the midmorning sun.

There was an uneasy stirring in the crowd of migrant workers. Though the Sheriff and his deputies numbered no more than thirty or forty, there must have been nearly a thousand men following in their wake. The sunlight gleamed on gunmetal as well; most of those approaching were openly armed.

Alongside the Sheriff were two men in business suits,

strangers to Roger but apparently known to Druss. He greeted one of them with an unsmiling nod.

'Mister Bergano – glad you could make it to our little gathering.'

Mister Bergano removed his hat to wipe his brow with a monogramed handkerchief. 'Up to your old tricks are you, Wilfred?'

The Sheriff led the way onto the stage, with Bergano and the other suited gentleman following, and after them a dozen deputies, hands resting on the handles of their revolvers.

'Okay,' the Sheriff said, taking up a bullhorn that had been used by some of the speakers, and addressing the crowd with it, 'the party's over, time to break it up.'

'Just a minute,' Druss interrupted him. 'We are committing no crime in gathering here . . . '

The gentleman with Mister Bergano stepped forward, tugging a sheaf of official-looking papers from inside his coat. 'I'm the District Attorney for this county, and this here is private property . . . '

' . . . The U.S. Constitution guarantees the right of free speech and of peaceable assembly . . . '

'This is no peaceable assembly,' the Sheriff in turn interrupted him, still speaking through the bullhorn. 'We know the kinds of stunts you bastards pull, and we ain't having no San Diego here, nor no Fresno. Anything gets started, people are going to get hurt.'

'We've done no wrong,' Druss insisted, trying to wrest the bullhorn from the Sheriff's hands. 'The only weapons here are yours.'

This last was not entirely true, Roger reflected – many of the migrants carried with them their rifles and squirrel guns, and probably the majority had hunting knives or pocket knives. Around him, he saw a half dozen knives slipped unobtrusively from pockets. The crowd had begun to buzz with low-voiced but angry conversation. On the stage, three of the deputies had drawn their guns without any orders, and the others were watching their leader anxiously. The posse that had accompanied the Sheriff and his deputies had begun to spread out forming a ring around the crowd; here too weapons were coming into view.

Druss, the Sheriff, and the District Attorney were all trying to talk at once. The Sheriff had snatched the bullhorn back from

Druss, but now it was Bergano himself who came forward and took the horn.

He turned to face the restless crowd. He was unknown to most of them, only the few in front having been close enough to hear Druss greet him by name. Now, perhaps misjudging the weight of his authority or the depth of the crowd's anger, he made the mistake of introducing himself.

'I'm Ed Bergano,' he shouted through the bullhorn, 'and this here is my ranch.'

There was an immediate chorus of shouting and jeering. Bergano, apparently encouraged by the show of strength behind him, for by now all of the deputies on the stage had drawn their guns, tried to shout the crowd down.

'I'm here to order . . . ' was all Roger heard; the rest was drowned out. For several seconds pandemonium reigned. In the audience, hundreds upon hundreds of hot, hungry, thirsty men and women, angered not only by the frustrations of the past few days but by years of indifference and mistreatment, rose to their feet, giving vent to their rage and resentment. On the stage one of the workers who had spoken earlier came forward to attempt to wrest the bullhorn from Bergano's hand, and was immediately seized and thrown to the floor by three burly deputies.

Afterward, Roger was never entirely sure what had happened; he knew that Bergano was struck in the forehead by something – a rock, he suspected – thrown from the audience; but as to how the gunshots started, or who fired first, he could never honestly say. The Wobblies, those who talked publicly afterward, blamed the Sheriff's men, and the posse that surged forward as soon as the bedlam erupted; the Sheriff and his men blamed the crowd.

The meeting, only a few minutes before a peaceful one, had become a melee. Shots rang out. The posse and the deputies charged into the largely unarmed crowd of farmworkers, firing guns and swinging clubs.

When the fighting began Roger leaped forward, meaning to help those on the stage, but before he could reach there, one of the deputies fell or was pushed from the platform, landing on Roger and knocking him, dazed, to the ground.

He struggled to his feet, only to find himself set upon by two club-swinging men from the posse. One of the two went down suddenly, felled by a blow from behind. Roger ducked the club of the other man and again fought his way toward the stage.

Stella materialized unexpectedly before him, pushing her way through a knot of fighting men. 'We've got to get out of here,' she cried, throwing herself into his arms.

'I can't run,' he said. 'Got to stay and fight with the others . . . '

'No.' She caught his shirt in her hands and held him when he would have shoved past her. 'Druss' orders. Someone's got to stay out of jail, else there'll be nobody to tell the story. Come with me.'

For a second or two he hesitated, looking behind the stage. Druss had vanished in the confusion; he saw Miller, his arms held by two men while a third punched him with unvarying rhythm.

'You can't help them, except by staying out and keeping up the work,' Stella said, tugging at his sleeve. 'Come on, there's no one over here.'

He let her pull him along. Beyond the stage, the knoll was all but empty, the fighting having surged to the front. Once in the open, they began to run, in the direction of some distant trees. Behind them someone shouted, and once a bullet made the dirt jump in front of their feet, but their flight was otherwise unhindered.

They sat in the shade of an oak, washing themselves in the water of a muddy creek. He was surprised to discover how much blood was on him, very little of it his own. He had a bad cut on one cheek, and a bruise the size of a baseball on a forearm, but otherwise he had fared surprisingly well.

Stella's glasses were gone, lost in the melee, and her lip was cut and badly swollen from a deputy's fist.

She had been swearing steadily for several minutes, surprising him with the diversity of her vocabulary, much of which was entirely new to him.

He was trying to bring some order to his scattered thoughts. The meeting, had been intended as a peaceful one – or had it? Had Druss intended all along that violence should be provoked? It was not unlike the violence that had scarred the Wobblies' efforts throughout the state; but were they to blame, or only the victims?

'What about the others?' he asked aloud.

'Miller'll be arrested, if there's anything left of him to arrest when those goons finish punching him.'

'Druss . . . ?'

She gave him a cold, angry look. 'Druss is dead,' she said.

He shuddered involuntarily – Druss – the man had been unfathomable to him, and yet – messianic, yes, that was the word he'd thought of before.

'Are you sure?'

To his surprise she laughed, loudly and coarsely. 'Oh my God, have you ever seen anyone shot at close range with a forty-five, it took half his head off. That's his brains I've been trying to wash out of my blouse – the great treasure of the Wobblies, nothing but a stain on my clothes.'

He felt nauseous, he would have liked to retch, but could not. 'Jesus,' was all he could say, shaking his head to and fro, 'Jesus.'

After a while she sat forward and put a hand on his shoulder, shaking him as if to wake him from a trance. 'They'll blame all this on us. Miller'll be hanged, if he's lucky – we would have gotten the same if they'd caught us there.'

'We'll get lawyers,' he said. 'We'll testify. The truth . . . '

'Don't be an ass,' she snapped, jerking her hand back. 'They don't want the truth, they want comfort, and revenge – the comfort of knowing they've driven the evil Wobblies from their land, revenge for our disrupting their scheme of things.'

She got up, brushing the dirt from her skirt. 'We're going to get as far away from here as possible. There's a farmhouse just over that hill. As soon as it gets dark, we're going to steal some fresh clothes and some food, and head out of here.'

'Head where?'

For a long moment she stared down at him, as if weighing him in the balance. 'There's a place,' she said, speaking slowly, 'another vineyard, one of the biggest. Druss wanted to go there – it's what he wanted to groom you for, if you passed the test here.'

'Where is it?'

'Brussac-America, in Sonoma.'

She held her breath. His eyes dropped from hers, went to the front of her blouse, to a wide stain that the creek waters had not entirely removed. He thought of what Druss had said to him, about his ignorance; he understood it better now. Like Druss, he would have happily traded his present knowledge for his former blindness. But it was too late. Knowledge once gained could not be forsworn. Druss was gone. So too was his innocence, gone with the boyhood he had left at French Hills; but what he had seen and experienced today would remain with him for all his life.

'We'll have to travel cross country,' he said. 'The roads won't be safe.'

'I know people in Santa Barbara. We'll be all right once we get there,' she said.

He felt flushed and feverish. He got up, removing his shirt, and went to the creek to splash water on his face and chest.

'Roger,' she said.

He turned and saw that she had removed her blouse, with its offensive mark. Her eyes, unfocused without her glasses, were gleaming, her breasts rising and falling with hurried breath.

He watched her undress, waited until she was lying upon the ground in the shade of the oak. Then he rose and came to her, tugging his trousers down about his hips and mounting her with all the pent up ferocity seething within him.

It was a release, and a welcome one; and yet, even as his body slapped against hers, it seemed to him that she stank, for somehow in his mind she had merged with all the blood and the violence and the ugliness that were the children of the day.

53

'Alexandra, didn't you hear me calling? I've been looking all over for you – have you forgotten Mrs Collins is coming to dinner?'

Alexandra made a face as her mother walked up. 'Mrs Collins is an old crow,' she said. 'I suppose she's looking us over, to see if I'm the proper sort she wants at her school – isn't that kind of impertinent of her?'

'Very,' Jolene said with a laugh. 'But on the other hand, our family history isn't exactly the sort exclusive schools are built on. I'm afraid there's enough skeletons in the closet to furnish a good graveyard.' She paused to look around the vineyards. 'What are you doing out here anyway?'

'Watching the workers.'

'Well, they'll be quitting soon. Come along, won't you, Mrs Collins might think I've got you working as a field hand.'

They started toward the house together. Mother and daughter were a handsome pair. With Alexandra the golden hair had darkened to a warm brown, glinting copper in the sunlight. She was taller than her mother by several inches, a strong, healthy-looking girl whose love for the out of doors was evident. Perhaps not as pretty as her mother, Alexandra had a vivacity and a ready smile that made her immensely appealing.

At the moment, though, she was not smiling. She kept glancing around, looking for someone, as she had been earlier when her mother had interrupted her. It was like a game she was playing, a sort of hide-and-seek among the vines.

There he was, finally, the handsome young stranger, working the vines along with their regular workers. The faint limp made it easy to pick him out, even at a distance, and gave him too a certain world-weary air.

At the moment he was engaged in earnest conversation with two others – or rather, he was conversing, making emphatic gestures with his hands, while they listened intently. From the corner of her eye she saw Dan, the foreman, notice the three and begin to walk toward them.

Would he . . . yes, just as before; the young stranger had seen Dan too, apparently, though he gave no sign of it. Instead, the conversation seemed to end of its own accord and all three went back to work, the other two where they were, the one with the limp drifting nonchalantly, unobtrusively, farther away. The foreman, seeing that work had been resumed, lost interest.

'But I haven't,' Alexandra thought, smiling.

Fair weather and foul, she lived in these fields; she knew every plant – and every man or woman who worked them. Not a one of their shacks she wasn't welcome into, not a child's birthday she forgot.

Of course, that was the regular workers. There were those who worked temporarily, now and at harvest time – the bindle stiffs, though Brussac-America kept a rather large force on at all times, and thus needed fewer migrant workers than other vineyards of comparable size.

The answer to her mystery, Mother would tell her, was obvious – he was one of the migrants. It had been her own initial conclusion when she had first caught sight of him, shirt off, his broad chest gleaming with perspiration in the afternoon sunshine.

Only, why hadn't he come to the dinner-table with the others? She had watched for him, wanting a second look at this godlike creature who had suddenly appeared in their midst. He had not appeared that night, nor the next day, for she had watched at each meal. Nor had he come to a meal in the three days since he had first materialized. One might skip a meal – she sometimes did so herself – but three days of meals, while working the vineyards?

The second day, she had noticed something else about him – he was avoiding the foremen; avoiding everyone, in fact, but the field workers themselves. Watching from the edge of the field, from the porch of the big house, even from the window of her bedroom, she had observed that every time one of the foremen, or her father, came in his direction, the stranger managed to slip away long before they arrived at the spot where he had been.

Last night she had gone down to the workers' shacks – this was not so unusual as to cause comment, and she had the excuse of bringing a jar of cough remedy to Mrs Estrada, who had been under the weather.

Tentatively she had broached the subject of migrant workers, of new faces among this year's lot, but Mrs Estrada had seemed to think these were all the same people who had been there the year before. It was true, though, that Mrs Estrada had been abed for three days with a cold and might not know of a new-comer, and – Alexandra hadn't wanted to seem too interested – better, she thought, not to arouse too much curiosity on anyone else's part, until . . . but truth to tell, she didn't know what it was she was waiting for. What, after all, was there for anyone to be curious about? A new worker, one that Mrs Estrada hadn't met yet, who didn't like the foremen, who declined to take his meals with the others – perhaps he didn't even know that his meals were included.

Nor was he, she had noticed, among those who greeted her from the front stoops of their shacks. He seemed to vanish with the day, like the sun springing full blown upon the morning.

Watching him as now, well away from the foreman, he once again resumed the work of trimming the branches to let more sun onto the forming fruit, she saw him accidentally knock his hand with his shears. He put his hand to his mouth, sucking the wound clean, before taking a dirty kerchief from his pocket and wrapping it about the cut.

Not a god, then, nor a phantom, but a man, who bleeds like any other, she thought. A man who must eat like any other, who must sleep somewhere. She wondered where – and why.

She realized with a start that her mother had spoken to her, was awaiting a reply. 'I'm sorry,' she apologized.

'Good Heavens, you might as well be walking in your sleep,' Jolene scolded her. 'Is anything the matter?'

'No, nothing,' Alexandra said. 'What did you ask just now?'

'I asked what you were wearing for dinner – I think that white dress might be best, the muslin with the daisies.'

The bell at the great house rang, signaling the end of the day's work and summoning the men to their evening meal. The workers began to collect their tools, removing their hats and wiping their brows. It was the moment when they began to relax, to laugh and shout to one another, sometimes plans for the evening, sometimes just ribald jokes, a release from work-day tension. Singly, in twos and threes, they began to drift toward the shacks, or toward the pump and the trough where many of them would wash up, or toward the row of trestle tables, set out of doors in good weather, where there were bowls heaped with rice and ham and beans, and children shooing the flies away with paper fans.

He too was making his way in from the vineyard, except that while the others were heading in a more or less straight line toward the buildings clustered around the big house, he was traveling at a diagonal that carried him inconspicuously farther and farther from them, though in the same general direction. As she watched, he disappeared among the outlying buildings, the full yard apart from his fellow workers. Those particular buildings housed the presses, unused just now. Had he gone in there? But at this time of year, the buildings stood empty, except for the few days involved in cleaning the equipment preparatory to the fall harvest.

A babble of sound greeted them as they came through the yard; the workers and their families were eating at the long tables. Many of them called out greetings. Jolene returned them by name, taking pride in knowing each of their employees.

Again Alexandra looked about carefully, thinking the man she had been watching might simply have taken a roundabout way and joined the others for dinner after all; but there was no sign of him at the tables.

'Are you looking for someone?' her mother asked.

'No, no one in particular,' Alexandra replied quickly. 'I was just wondering about the new help this year.'

'There isn't much, I'm afraid, just one family, and Mister Dolgedo again. Your father wants to keep the number of migrants down, he thinks we do better paying our regulars for the extra work, except at harvest.'

'The new family – how many are they?'

'Father, mother, a boy ten, a girl about eight.' Jolene glanced at her sideways. 'Alexandra, what is all this about the help?'

'It's nothing, Mother, really,' Alexandra said, not even sure as she did so why she was hiding her curiosity from her mother. Was there really something mysterious about the young man in the fields, or was she only romanticizing, as her mother so often accused her.

Still, thoughts of him stayed with her as she dressed for dinner. She found herself going to the window, from which she could see the sheds housing the presses. Was he there, at this moment, perhaps even gazing up at the house, at her very window?

Mrs Collins arrived, the modern woman in her own shiny new Ford. Alexandra barely noticed the arrival. She had made up her mind – she must know.

She waited until they were in the parlor; she could hear their voices, her father's deep, confident, her mother's with its distinctive timbre – and Mrs Collins', sharp, almost nasal.

She went down the back stairs. Cook, busy preparing dinner, gave her no more than a quick glance as she darted out the back door and down the steps.

The workers had finished their meal, and most had retired to the yard where their shacks stood. They sat about in groups, men with men, women with women, the children playing in the dirt. Someone had brought out a guitar and was strumming disconnected chords that floated ghost-like on the evening breeze.

The sheds were dark. She tugged one wooden door open and hesitated, peering into the black cavern of the interior. Not a sound, not a sign of life.

She was mistaken, then, he must have been going somewhere else, perhaps after all to the shacks. She was about to leave, when she heard a noise from within, a faint rustling in the distance.

Rats? She dreaded the thought of encountering one in the darkened shed; on the other hand, if she left without knowing, it would torture her all night long.

She stepped inside, pausing in the shaft of light, waiting for her eyes to adjust to the gloom. The air was stale and sour in here, never entirely free of the odor of crushed grapes. The presses themselves, shiny clean, loomed in the darkness like so many giant beasts, rows of them waiting in polished stillness for her passing.

She went between the rows, her heels making faint clicking noises on the cement floor. She was wishing she had brought a lamp; there were electric lights here, as in all the buildings, but they would undoubtedly attract the attentions of others, one of the foremen, or her father even, and if anyone were here . . .

He came upon her so suddenly that she scarcely knew what was happening. An arm about her throat, a knife-blade gleaming in the pale light from the door – she was pulled, dragged almost, about one of the giant vats, through a door into one of the store rooms, where a single candle was burning. She saw a crumpled pile of bedclothes, the heel of a loaf of bread, an opened bottle of Brussac-America wine.

He let her go, so abruptly that she fell against the table, making the candlelight dance and bob on the wall.

'What the hell are you doing here?' he asked in a low voice.

She turned to face him, rubbing her throat where his arm had hurt her. 'I might ask you the same thing,' she said, too surprised and angry at being roughed up to be afraid.

He ignored her remark and countered with another question of his own. 'Why have you been spying on me?'

'Who says I have?' She studied him with frank interest. This was the first she had seen him close up, and the glimpses across the field had not prepared her for this.

He was almost unbearably handsome, with the dark hair falling in reckless curls about his sculptured bronze face, and the eyes, now gray, now green, that regarded her with anger and suspicion. He wore no shirt and his bare chest glistened with sweat.

'I've seen you,' he said, 'following me around the fields – what are you doing here now, if you aren't spying on me?'

'Do you know who I am?' she asked, managing a sweet smile for him.

The smile left him apparently untouched. 'Princess of the realm, aren't you?' he replied dryly. 'Lady Alexandra, I believe.'

Her smile faded in the wake of his sarcasm. 'At least I am a lady,' she said. 'It is obvious you are no gentleman.'

He made a mock bow from the waist. 'You're right,' he said, turning to the table and spearing the heel of bread with his knife. He lifted it to his mouth and tore off a bite of the crust. 'I've got no manners at all,' he said, speaking with his mouth full. 'That's a luxury the poor can't afford.'

'You don't look poor,' she said.

'That's a dumb thing to say. Here I am in rags, working in a vineyard and eating stale bread, and you think I'm a railroad baron, I suppose.'

'Poor people look different – they act different,' she insisted. He tore off another bite of the bread. 'Is that all you've had to eat?' she asked.

'First I'm not poor enough for you, now I'm too poor.' He washed the bread down with a long swallow of wine.

'Why didn't you eat with the others?'

He gave her a scornful look. 'The generous fare of the patrons? What was it, let me think – rice, and beans I suppose, and oh, yes, plenty of tortillas. Thank you, my stale bread will do.'

'That's not fair, it's perfectly good food, we . . . .'

'Why weren't you eating it then?' he asked, pointing the knife accusingly at her. 'You and your family.'

'We own this place, there's no reason why we should have to . . . ' She stopped, her mouth forming a perfect O.

' . . . have to eat peasant food,' he finished for her. 'But it is good enough for them. For those who aren't good enough for you.'

She was silent for a moment, regarding him in the flickering light. 'What is your name?' she asked finally.

'What does that matter?' he said, continuing to eat.

'I can find out, you know. I can ask the foremen, they must have found out your name when they hired you.'

His eyes darted nervously around to her, giving him away. 'That's it, isn't it?' she said, smiling triumphantly. 'You've never been hired. You aren't even supposed to be here.'

He looked displeased. 'That's stupid,' he said, a trifle too emphatically, 'why would I be breaking my back working in your fields, if I hadn't been hired?'

'I think I'll find out,' she said, turning as if to go.

In an instant he was before her, blocking the way. 'I just wanted to talk to people,' he said, his eyes holding hers, his voice low. 'I wanted to find out what conditions were like here.'

'You're spying on us,' she accused him, dropping her own voice instinctively. 'For some other vintner.'

To her surprise, he laughed. 'I'm no friend of any vintner's,' he said. 'Not any more.'

'Who, then?'

'Maybe for them – for all those people eating your rice and beans and sleeping in your drafty, dirty shacks – '

'I've been in those shacks, there's nothing wrong with them,' she argued.

'They stink. The wind blows through them all winter long and when it rains everything gets dampened, including their spirits – why don't you spend a night in one sometime, preferably a cold, wet one?'

'I – ' She hesitated, confused by his anger and his accusations, for which she hadn't any ready answers; confused, too, by the closeness of his half-naked body, by the intensity of his gaze when he looked at her, by the unfamiliar longings stirring within her. 'I don't know what to say to you,' she admitted, forcing her eyes from his. 'You've got me all mixed up.'

He laughed again, though less bitterly. 'The poor, sheltered rich girl,' he said, putting out a hand to tilt her chin gently upward, till their eyes met again. 'Afraid to deal with life on its own terms.'

'I'm not afraid,' she said, though she had begun to tremble at his touch.

'Christ, you ought to be, you ought to be afraid of all kinds of things, of what's going on in the world, and of the way those workers of yours really feel, and – and you ought to be afraid of being alone in a barn with a half-dressed stranger.'

This last slipped out without any intention on his part; he saw her eyes widen slightly, but she made no attempt to move away, not even when his hands moved to her shoulders, kneading the tender flesh gently at first, and then with increasing force.

'I'm not afraid,' she said again.

He hadn't intended to kiss her – had meant, in fact, to hate her; but somehow his hate failed him in the reality of her presence, her vulnerability. He wanted to crush her in a passionate embrace, and at the same moment to cradle her gently and protect her from the cruel truths of the world. He felt for a moment as if he were drowning in the wide eyes regarding him with a mixture of fear and longing and innocent wonder.

He pulled her close, the lace of her bodice scratching against his bare chest. Her lips parted involuntarily as he lowered his to them.

In the distance a woman's voice could be heard, calling 'Alexandra. Alexandra.'

She freed herself from his embrace. He let her go, surprised by his own actions; surprised, because a moment before he'd had every intention of taking her, and he still wanted her. With an odd feeling that combined both reluctance and relief, he watched her move to the door.

'I'm not afraid,' were the last words she said before she vanished. He stood, staring into the darkness, straining at the suddenly unwelcome silence until he heard the outer door open and close after her.

54

'You're sure no one has noticed your coming here?'

'No, I'm too clever,' Alexandra said, running one finger along the length of his bare arm.

Roger pushed her hand impatiently away. 'Don't be facetious,' he said. 'I don't suppose you've got any idea what they'd do to me if they caught me here? They'd probably hang me.'

'Now you're being facetious,' she said. 'You haven't even seduced me yet.'

'Jesus,' he swore, 'don't you know anything? Haven't you ever been off this stupid ranch?'

She looked hurt, but she did not move or turn away. 'Not very often,' she said.

He tugged a cigarette from a crumpled pack in his shirt pocket and lit it. Something stirred in the immense darkness surrounding them. He sat tense, listening, but the silence returned; a rat, he decided, on some nocturnal expedition.

'What makes you so sure I'm going to?' he asked. 'Seduce you, I mean?'

'Aren't you?'

He left the question unanswered. 'Do you know what a Wobbly is?' he asked, reclining with one hand behind his back.

'A Wobbly? Aren't they – they're anarchists, aren't they, or anti-American, something of that sort.'

'They are labor reformers,' he said. 'They – no, *we* are trying to unite the working class against the capitalistic class.'

'You mean, you are one of them?'

He inhaled deeply on the cigarette, blew the smoke in long twin streams from his nostrils. He had learned to smoke only a few weeks before.

'Yes,' he said finally.

She thought for a moment. 'And that's why you've come here, why you've been talking to our workers? You want them to unite, to rise up against us – against my parents – and me too, I suppose.'

'Christ, I didn't even know you until two nights ago.'

'Does that make a difference?'

'Don't be a fool, of course it does,' he said angrily, stubbing out the cigarette on the cement floor.

'You're against all capitalists, except those you know – is that it?' she asked.

'Anyway, it isn't you I want to see brought down, it's the ones who use and exploit other people, it's the ones who won't talk or listen, who shut people out, it's men like . . . ' he caught himself, about to say, ' . . . like my father.'

Was that it, he wondered? Was his anger really righteous anger on behalf of the suffering, or did he only want someone to rise in his stead against the man who ruled French Hills? How involved would he be in the Wobbly cause if his father had not shut him out all those years? Was he seeking justice? Or revenge?

'Surely you've seen that my parents aren't like that?' she said.

'I've seen – ' Again he paused; why was he even here? Why, of all the vineyards in California, had Stella picked this one? Surely she must have known that it was better than most, far better than many? What was he expected to prove? Was the challenge to enlist workers even on a model farm? Had she only wanted to test the family connection, to see if he was loyal? Or had he simply failed to get beneath the surface, to discover abuses just as unfair, but more subtle? He had been tormented by an endless stream of such questions, all without answers.

'I've seen too little to make a judgment,' he finished lamely.

She stared at him for a moment; then, with a faint smile on her lips, she lowered her face and kissed him.

'I don't think you should come out here anymore,' he said, breaking the kiss.

'Why not?'

'Someone will see you, it will make trouble – for yourself as well as for me.'

'Liar,' she said. 'That's not the reason.' His shirt lay open. She kissed his throat, ran her lips over the bare expanse of his chest.

'What are you doing?' he asked, his voice husky.

'I've decided, if you won't seduce me,' she said, 'then I shall have to seduce you.'

'Now they *will* hang me,' he said later.

She lay with her head on the flat of his belly, running her fingers lightly through the thick bush of hair at its base. He was the first man she had known, the first she had even seen there, and she was fascinated by what she had discovered.

'They'd run you off,' she said. 'And I'd go with you.'

He was still damp from the sweat of their lovemaking and the scent of his sex was strong in her nostrils. She kissed him there, circling the V formed by his thighs, the wet warmth of her tongue descending his legs.

He jerked involuntarily as she kissed the twisted ankle of his bad foot. 'Don't do that,' he said.

'It's a part of you,' she said, kissing it again. 'Is there some border beyond which I am not to venture? At the thighs, say, or the knees?' She kissed each of these in reverse order. 'What about your arms? Are the elbows forbidden – or your hands, may I not kiss your hands?'

'Stop it.' He caught her head in his hands and lifted it till her eyes met his. 'Damn it, can't I make you understand? You're the enemy.'

She laughed softly in her throat and brought her face down to his, her hair cascading like a curtain of privacy about them.

'How can I be the enemy,' she asked, 'when I love you?'

He had never known anyone like her, nor anything like the experience of making love with her; it was so natural, it was hard to equate it with that frantic, almost destructively passionate act he had experienced with Stella, though it was no less intense or less torrid.

He did not try again to tell her she should not come to the shed to see him. No matter the danger, he would have to see her.

He went with her to the door, not speaking, but holding her in a long embrace before she finally slipped from his arms and disappeared across the yard. He watched her go until there was nothing to be seen but the moonlight filtering through the trees.

There was a noise behind him. He turned to find Stella there, watching him with a coldly angry expression.

'Touching scene,' she said.

'I'm glad you enjoyed it,' he said. He swung the door shut, plunging the interior of the shed into darkness. He had committed the building's interior to memory, so that he could find his way easily in the darkness to the little room in the rear where his single candle burned.

To his surprise Stella found him with the ease of a cat, suddenly materializing in his path. He noticed, not for the first time, the strong scent of womanly sex that clung to her; noticed too that what had been a perfume with Alexandra was with her an odor.

She clasped his wrist, her nails biting his flesh. 'Who was that girl?' she asked, her voice a sibilant hiss in the blackness.

'Some sort of cousin, a long way removed,' he said.

'Kissing kin, it would seem.' There was venom in her tone, so real that he seemed to feel it between them.

'It's no concern of yours,' he said, snatching his wrist free of her grip.

'Damn you.'

Her nails raked his cheek, leaving the wet warmth of fresh blood. He struck out blindly with his open hand, the blow catching her squarely and echoing in the cavernous room.

She was not the sort to cry; her only discernible reaction was a loud sucking in of her breath.

'We can't stand here slapping one another in the dark,' he said, making his voice more gentle. 'I've got a private suite back this way – give me your hand.'

'I know where your room is,' she said.

He expected her to lose her way or run into some of the building's equipment, but like some nocturnal wraith she floated before him to his room. He waited until they were there to speak to her again.

'Has there been any word?' he asked.

'Miller's been charged with murder,' she said. 'They caught up with him in Arizona.'

'They'll have to extradite him. We'll fight that, raise money – '

'They don't bother with such niceties where Wobblies are concerned. He's already back, they've got him at Santa Barbara.'

He was silent for a moment, remembering the dapper little man who had seemed at first meeting so inconsequential. His crime had been to attempt to help a friendless and exploited group of migrant workers; his reward was a murder charge.

'How many others?' he asked.

'A dozen, last I heard. Seff in Los Angeles and Morton in 'Frisco – neither of them were even at Bergano's. The National Guard's combing the state – they want us all. They're calling us all murderers.'

Five men – including the Sheriff and the District Attorney, as well as Druss and two migrant workers – had died in the rioting at Bergano's ranch. Since then it seemed as if the entire state, indeed the entire country, had mobilized against the Wobblies, who were universally blamed for the trouble.

'Have you been all right?' he asked aloud.

'They won't find me, if that's what you mean,' she said.

'Where have you been?'

'In 'Frisco. That's a labor town, though they haven't been very sympathetic to the IWW.'

'I'm afraid I haven't accomplished much here. Most of the workers seem pretty contented, although I haven't gotten around to talking to many of them yet. Have to keep out of sight, I don't want to attract any undue attention with things the way they are just now.'

'It looked to me like you'd accomplished plenty,' she said dryly.

'I told you, that doesn't concern you.'

'It's unimportant anyway,' she said, dismissing the matter with a wave of her hand. 'San Francisco is where it's going to happen. They're staging a big parade in support of the European war.'

'What are you going to do?'

'Show them that the Wobblies are still a force to be reckoned with, despite their efforts to eradicate us,' she said.

He recognized the fiery tone of her voice; it gave him an unexpected chill. 'Look,' he said, 'I want no part of any violence.'

'You were a part of it at Bergano's.'

'We didn't start that, regardless of what they say. And if I could do it all over, I'd do anything in my power to prevent what happened.'

'You're a fool. Force is the only thing the capitalists and the warmongers understand.' She stopped abruptly, the passionate expression of her face softening somewhat. 'I want you to come to 'Frisco with me,' she said.

'I haven't finished here,' he said.

'You said yourself, you haven't accomplished anything.'

'That's all the more reason to stick with it.'

Her eyes took on a hard, set look. 'I say you're coming with me,' she said.

'Look,' he said, 'I agreed to work for the cause, not for your sake, or my own, but because I want to see right done. But I never agreed to work for you, or take orders from you. I came here at your suggestion, to investigate conditions here, and until I've learned for myself the whole story, I'll stay here.'

She came closer, her face contorted with anger. 'You're lying,' she said, 'it's the girl. That's what you want to stick around here for . . .'

'Stop it.' He spoke sharply; for all the intimacy that he had shared with Stella, he found her presence now grating. There was something about her that was not sound; it was impossible to know what to expect of her next.

As if to confirm this assessment, she began of a sudden to cry, not softly and disarmingly, but with loud snuffling noises, great tears washing down her cheeks.

'You've got to come with me,' she cried, raising her voice to an alarming level.

'You're getting hysterical,' he said. He took hold of her shoulders, meaning to shake her, but she threw her arms around him so violently that he staggered a step backward.

'You've got to,' she insisted, trying as she talked to kiss his mouth, his cheeks, his throat, 'I don't know what I'll do if you don't, I'll do something horrible, I mean it, I'll make everyone suffer with me, I'll kill someone, I'll kill myself . . .'

He managed to get her at arm's length, and slapped her again. She stared at him with wide-eyed surprise that became, as he watched in the flickering candlelight, a burning anger.

'Damn you,' she swore in a whisper. 'God-damn you to hell.'

She turned and was gone, disappearing into the main room of the shed.

Frightened by the intensity of her rage, he went after her. 'Stella,' he called her name, his voice echoing in the open room.

'Go to hell,' she called back.

He went in the direction of her voice, but to his surprise it was he who lost his way, banging into a crate and stumbling to his knees.

'Stella,' he called again, but this time there was no answer, and though he searched for several minutes it was in vain – she had gone.

55

'I want to go to that parade – that getting-ready-for-war parade in San Francisco.'

Jolene, in the act of writing a letter to her husband, paused thoughtfully to consider her mother's remarks. 'Do you think we should?' she asked. 'There's talk there may be some trouble with the labor people. After that riot down south – and they still haven't found all those people. There's a girl, they say, and a young man.'

'The Wobblies?' Her mother snorted with disdain. 'I'd like to see them start that sort of trouble here. I'd have José . . .' She stopped abruptly.

'Now, Mother,' Jolene said, 'you know father's not here anymore.'

'You don't have to mince words,' Mary snapped, turning her face away, 'I know he's dead, he's been dead for six months, and I'm not so addled I can't keep things straight. One does simply forget from time to time, you know.'

'Especially when you're tired and overdue for a nap,' Jolene said, beginning to collect her things. 'I'm sorry, I should have gotten out of here long ago.'

'I wasn't sleepy,' Mary said petulantly, still turned toward the wall. 'I'm still not.'

Jolene had gotten used to her mother's pettishness, which had increased steadily since José's death. She came to the bed and gave Mary's cheek a gentle pat.

'You'll see, as soon as I'm gone, you'll drift right off. Shall I tell Sloan you said hello?'

'Tell him anything you like,' Mary said. Then, as if remembering something, she turned to look at her daughter. 'What I would like,' she said, 'is the sales figures.'

'They're about the same as last month's.'

Mary's eyes glinted. 'What about French Hills?'

'I haven't heard how they're doing lately,' Jolene said, avoiding her mother's penetrating gaze.

'Liar.'

Jolene sighed. 'They're still down, I've heard.'

'What about their damn fool oil, are they making any money on that yet?'

'Not much, not so far,' Jolene said.

Mary gave a triumphant bark of a laugh. 'Good,' she said, smiling blissfully and closing her eyes. 'Now I *can* sleep.'

To Jolene's surprise, she proceeded to do so almost at once. For a moment Jolene gazed at her with a mixture of impatience and affection. Mary had never gotten over her bitterness toward French Hills and those she thought had robbed her. Adam, David, Jean were all in their graves now and still Mary spoke of them with an anger as fresh as if they had just quarreled the day before.

And Philip, Jolene thought, remains; she glanced at the half-finished letter in her hand, the letter to Sloan. Congress was considering anew the question of tariffs on imported wines, and Sloan had accompanied a California delegation to lobby for their interests. She thought of her husband, and the years they had spent together. Happy years, for the most part, good productive years. If she had chosen the other path, if she had gone with Philip, what would those years have been? It was impossible even to imagine; some dark cloud of destiny had hovered over them from their first meeting. The Brussacs – rich, powerful, blessed in many ways, envied by many; yet in their blood and through their lives ran that Stygian thread of tragedy and heartbreak that could not be broken, forever linking them in a hellish alliance.

A soft tap at the door interrupted her gloomy thoughts. She found their head foreman in the hall, looking embarrassed as he usually did at being in the house.

'Beg pardon, Ma'am,' he greeted her, shuffling his feet and leaving drippings of mud on the carpet, 'sorry to interrupt, but something's come up.'

'It's all right, my mother's gone to sleep, and I was just leaving. Let me close the window and get my things, and I'll be right out.'

He waited, ill at ease, while she closed the window all but a crack, and took a final peek at her sleeping mother. Finally she came into the hall, closing the door softly after herself.

'Now then, what seems to be the matter?' she asked, starting along the corridor with the foreman at her side.

'We caught someone, a labor agitator – a Wobbly, I think,' he said.

'A Wobbly – here?' She remembered at once the riot that had occurred a few weeks before at the Bergano ranch to the south; a dreadful incident, and like every other grower, she was glad that the perpetrators had been brought to a speedy justice. But here, at Brussac-America . . . ?

'What makes you certain that's what he is?' she asked aloud.

'He's been skulking around here, talking to the men out in the fields, slipping away whenever the wrong person got too close. Then this morning two of the fellows, Raoul and Pablo, come to me, told me this fella's been trying to interest them in a strike.'

'Indeed?' Jolene said, becoming angry as she considered the damage being done by stealth under their very noses. Wasn't that just like that cowardly sort, nothing done openly, just a campaign of whispers and lies?

'We went out to talk to him,' the foreman went on, 'but he saw us coming and tried to slip away again. This time we kept an eye out and saw where he went. He's been living out in number two press shed, got himself a regular little apartment out there in the storage room.'

'Where is this – this person now?' she asked, wrinkling her nose with disgust.

'We brought him in to the Mister's office, figured we ought to turn him over to the Sheriff, but I thought you might want to have a talk with him first.'

'I'm glad you did,' she said, 'I do indeed want to see for myself what sort of person spends his time promoting violence and death.'

They had come down the front stairs as they spoke. The door to Sloan's office stood open on the left. She paused in the doorway; two of the workmen were standing just inside, holding a third man between them. He stood in a slumped position, letting them support his weight, and his head was down, his dark curly hair hanging down to conceal his face.

'Is he conscious?' Jolene asked.

'Damn right he is,' the foreman said. 'You, this here's the mistress of the place, you look at her when she talks to you.'

'I hadn't heard her say anything to me,' the stranger said in a slow, langorous voice. He lifted his head slowly, tossing the curls back from his face, and looking directly at her.

Jolene gasped and took a step backward, as if she had been struck a blow; one hand went to her breast.

'Philip!' The name rang in her head like a shout, though it was spoken in the faintest of whispers. The room seemed to recede around them until there was only her and that face, those burning eyes she remembered, the two of them at opposite ends of a long, dark tunnel . . .

'You all right, Miss Jolene?' The foreman, alarmed by her suddenly ashen pallor, took a step toward her.

Jolene recovered enough to say, 'Yes, yes I'm fine, thank you.' She gestured them from the room. 'I'll handle this – no, don't look worried, I'll be all right.'

Roger, staring at this incredibly beautiful woman, sucked in his own breath in surprise. Her name – and his father's – forgotten snatches of his mother's drunken ravings, of another woman 'up north' – and a name, an unusual name he'd never heard before or since – 'Jolene'.

He stared, and knew with some unrecognized instinct that this was the woman his father had loved, still did love; the woman whose name had haunted his mother's marriage, and in a sense brought about her death.

'Jolene.'

The others had gone, he had hardly been aware of their departure. She had closed the door, leaning against it as if suddenly wearied. Now, hearing her name from his lips, she turned slowly, her eyes wide and luminous in her pale face.

'Who are you?' she asked, her voice nearly inaudible.

'I'm his son.'

She came across the room to him. 'What in the name of Heaven are you doing here – like this?' she asked.

His eyes went downward, from her wet, parted lips, to the agitated rise and fall of her breasts. 'It's not in Heaven's name that I'm here, Madame,' he replied.

'I don't understand – '

'I'm here for the sake of the poor devils who work for you, and for all the other growers, the working man, the poor and the helpless, the exploited . . . '

'But we exploit no one. Our people are well paid, well fed, well treated . . . '

'Animals, that's what they are to you, to the people like you and Bergano and the rest, animals to be beaten if necessary, or even shot . . . '

'Bergano!' Her eyes went still wider. 'You – a Wobbly – the

young man they've been looking for – surely you don't mean . . . ?'

'That I was there? That I'm the young man? And what if I am? Will you have me shot? Your men, I think, are not far beyond that door, you have only to shout, to summon the authorities – shall I open the door for you?'

He moved as if to do so, but she misinterpreted the move, thinking he meant to take hold of her; she shrank back from him.

His eyebrows lifted. 'Are you frightened of me, Madame?' he asked in a faintly mocking tone. She did not answer, staring in silence at his face.

'Do I look so much like him?' he asked after a pause.

'Exactly as I remember him,' she said, closing her eyes suddenly as if the memory pained her.

'And you loved him?' She nodded. 'And still love him?'

The eyes opened again, this time flickering with annoyance. 'That doesn't concern you, I'm afraid.'

'But it does, I'm afraid. Do you know, Madame, that yours was the first name I recall learning, even before my family name? Jolene. An easy name to recall, it rolls so prettily from the tongue.'

She put a tentative hand on his arm. 'Did he – did he speak of me often?' she asked.

'My father?' he laughed. 'He spoke rarely to me of anything, and never of you. But my mother – did you know my mother?'

'No. She was not . . . ' She hesitated.

'Not of your social class, is that it?'

He stared at her for a moment, seeing not only a beautiful woman but a symbol of his whole unhappy youth: the woman his mother hated, and his father loved. It was easy to blame her for the failure of that miserable marriage; his father had never loved them, neither his mother nor him, because he had loved only this woman.

He was angry, angry at the men who had caught him, angry at himself for not being more clever; angry too at knowing that hereafter he would be unable to hold Alexandra in his arms and feel her lips warm and moist against his.

All of the accumulated angers rose up in him like a gorge, and it was this woman that he was angry with, in the name of all of them.

'I meant she was simply not – of my acquaintance,' Jolene said.

'My mother was a drunkard, and a tramp – I have it on my father's authority. And she loved him, Madame, knowing as she did so that it was you he loved, you he wanted, you he dreamed of – you who made a mockery of their marriage, who made him despise her –'

'No, I . . .'

'She called you a temptress from hell.' He paused, his eyes drinking in the dark cleft above the bodice of her dress, the fullness of her breasts, the still-narrow waist. Even in his anger he was aware of her incomparable beauty, which only fueled his temper.

'And she was right,' he added in a husky voice.

Their eyes met, his with a new light in them, hers wary now and still pained. 'What is your name?' she asked.

'Call me Philip if you like, Madame – if it will make things easier.'

'Make things easier? I don't understand . . .'

He seized her suddenly, taking her in his arms. She was surprised, too startled to resist at first. She felt his lips on her cheek, on her throat.

'God in Heaven, no,' she cried, struggling against him, but he was like a man possessed, crushing her to him, his hands tearing at her clothes.

There was a horsehair divan behind her, against the wall; he half led, half dragged her to it, flinging her down with such violence that the wind was knocked out of her. In an instant he was upon her.

'Please, don't, I beg you,' she said, her eyes filling with tears.

He seemed not to hear her. She looked through her tears up into his face – so like Philip's face – Philip's chin and mouth, Philip's eyes, angry now, filled with hate, and with desire – she could close her eyes and believe that it was Philip whose weight was upon her, Philip whose mouth fastened so savagely upon hers – Philip – Philip – Philip . . .

'Mother, are you all right, I've been knocking, I . . .'

Alexandra stopped just inside the door, at first unable to take in the scene before her. For a long moment the two on the divan were frozen as if in a tableau; at length, Roger rose, crimson-faced.

'They told me they'd brought Roger here,' Alexandra stammered, turning her face away. 'I was afraid – I thought you might have him harmed, I wanted . . .'

'Alexandra – ' Jolene said, trying to think of something to say.

Alexandra did not wait to hear, however. She clapped her hands to her face, muffling her cry, and turned to dash from the room.

56

Jolene turned on the young man, now standing shamefacedly in the center of the room. 'I should have you hanged,' she said.

To her surprise, he agreed. 'You're entirely right,' he said, without looking at her. 'It's what I deserve.'

She saw, with a sense of shock, that there were tears trickling down his cheeks. He wiped them away with a furtive movement of his hand.

That single gesture of shame and repentance did more to soften her anger than anything he might have said. She saw, almost for the first time, that he was only a youth – his resemblance to his father had blinded her before.

'Close that door,' she said, indicating the door left open by Alexandra's hasty exit.

He looked surprised. 'Do you want me to call your men?' he asked.

'In due time. Just close it for now, please.' She went to Sloan's desk, removing the pistol that he kept in the drawer and setting it loudly on the desk between them. 'That's in case you get carried away with yourself again,' she explained.

He glanced from the gun to her, and back to the gun. Without a word, he went to the door and closed it. When he turned back to the room, she was pouring two drinks from a decanter atop the desk.

'I think we both need this,' she said, taking one of the glasses and indicating the other for him. 'Drink it, I won't poison you.'

He drank, steadily watching her over the rim of the glass. The liquor left a fiery trail down to his stomach. He grimaced, lifting the glass to the light to examine the remaining contents.

'It's poteen,' she said. 'Irish whiskey.' He watched with respect as she half-emptied her glass.

'Now then,' she said, setting the glass down beside the gun, 'You'd better explain to me how you know my daughter.'

'She's a better detective than your foreman,' he said. 'She found me out a few days ago. Followed me around the fields.'

'And followed you to where you've been living – ?'

'Yes.'

'And?'

'And, nothing much.' He got the impression she knew what had gone on with him and the girl, but she did not pursue that aspect further. 'We talked. I told her who I was, and how I got here.'

'Perhaps you'd better tell me how you got here,' she said.

He sighed. 'It's a long story.'

She finished her whiskey and refilled both their glasses. 'I've got time,' she said.

It was, in many ways, a story familiar to her: disenchanted youth; rebellion; striking out, and finding the road less roseate than it had appeared from afar. It was easy to see herself, about his same age, leaving home for what seemed at the time unimpeachable reasons; that was the way of youth, making mistakes.

She heard him out, making little comment except to encourage him with an occasional question. When his glass was empty, she quietly refilled it. He spoke slowly at first, weighing his words, but as he warmed to his story the words came faster.

He finished with a description of the events that had transpired at Bergano's ranch, an entirely different story from what she had heard heretofore; oddly she did not for a moment doubt the truth of this young man's narrative.

'After that, we made our way north,' he explained. 'The girl went on to San Francisco. I came here.'

'Why?'

'Because – ' He hesitated.

'Because you thought you'd find conditions here as they were at Bergano's?'

'Something like that, I suppose.' He avoided her gaze.

'I trust you have learned differently.'

'I – ' Again he hesitated. 'Forgive me, I have already offended you sufficiently.'

'You need have no fear of speaking your mind here,' she said.

'Conditions are better here, infinitely better, and yet – damn it!' He got up abruptly, pacing the floor before her desk. 'They're rotten. The food is lousy, the pay is worse, the living quarters – would you want to live in them, Mrs – Jesus, I don't even know your name, except – '

'Jolene will do very well.' She too stood, her manner decidedly cooler. 'And I have lived in worse. We have always treated our people well . . . '

'There, that's it,' he said, almost shouting. ' "Our people", like they were slaves, like you owned them – our house, our vineyards, our workers. It isn't right, they're entitled to be their own people. They've a right to decide too what's fair for them, not merely to exist on your generous patronage. They've got a right to live decently, not just well for migrant workers. They've got a right to a real wage, the sort of wages people make in cities, the sort of wages union workers make for far less work. They've got a right to buy the kind of food they want, not what the company chooses to give them. Damn it, don't you see . . . '

He was interrupted by a tap at the door. The housekeeper appeared, casting apprehensive glances in Roger's direction. 'Begging your pardon, Ma'am,' she said, 'but Cook's been holding lunch, she wants to know if you'll be much longer.'

'No, we'll be right there,' Jolene said. 'And, Mrs Wright, would you have another place set? This is our cousin, Roger, from Los Angeles. He'll be visiting with us a few days. You'll see that the green room is made ready for him, won't you.'

'Yes, Ma'am, at once,' Mrs Wright said, bobbing her head.

'And ask Dan to come in, please,' Jolene added.

The foreman appeared a moment later, glancing uneasily in Roger's direction. 'Housekeeper said you wanted to see me?' he said.

'Yes. You've already met our cousin, Roger . . . '

'Your cousin?'

' . . . This is our foreman, Dan Sanchez. Roger is going to be staying with us for a while. I've given him complete freedom to look over our operations. I want you to give him your full cooperation.'

'But – but this man is . . . '

'Is going to organize our workers into their own labor union,' Jolene stated firmly.

Both men stared aghast at her. 'You're turning this place over to the Wobblies,' Dan said at last.

'I'm not turning this place over to anyone,' she replied. 'I'm simply giving the people who work here and produce the wine for us what they're rightfully entitled to – a voice in the management of Brussac-America, particularly in regard to wages and working conditions. This will be an independent union, with no ties to the Wobblies.'

'You're crazy,' Dan said hotly. 'The Mister'll . . .'

'That will do,' Jolene said. 'Mister Morrow will be back in a couple of weeks. If you've got any complaints, you may discuss them with him. In the meantime, please see that our cousin gets full cooperation from everyone; I shall hold you personally responsible.'

For a moment the foreman looked as if he would like to say more; then, with an angry shake of his head, he turned on his heel and strode from the room.

When he was gone, an astonished Roger said, 'You'd do this, after what I did?'

'My husband and I have talked many times about the plight of the farm worker in California,' she said. 'This whole issue is like a giant powder keg; what happened at Bergano's is a warning to all of us that, unless something is done, someday the workers – not just the grape pickers, but those in the other fields and the orchards, that unnumbered army of workers that keeps our farms producing – will rise up against us and take for themselves what we've refused to give them. We've always tried to be generous here, and until you spoke to me today, I honestly believed we had done our share, but now I see that I was naïve, cruelly so. It's only that, until now, we had few choices. The major labor unions haven't wanted the farm workers, and as for the Wobblies, I meant what I told Dan, I want no Wobbly insurrections here. I warn you, should that happen, I'll be the first to start shooting – and you'll be my first target.'

To her surprise, he suddenly dropped to one knee, clasping her hand in his and bringing it to his lips.

'You're a great lady,' he murmured.

'Get up and don't be a fool,' she snapped, snatching her hand back from him. 'I'm only trying to save my neck, mine and my grandchildren's. And anyway, unless we move quickly, you're going to be faced with your first case of discontent among my employees.'

'What do you mean?' He got quickly to his feet.

'Cook is furious when her meals are spoiled, and lunch has already been delayed considerably. Perhaps you'd like to wash up, there's a washroom just under the stairs there, in the hall – I'll tell her we're on our way.'

Alexandra had flung herself across the bed in her room. Jolene came to sit on the edge of the bed, patting her daughter's hair gently.

'You mustn't be too angry,' she said. 'It wasn't entirely what it seemed.'

'I don't see what else it could have been,' Alexandra said into her pillow.

'It had very little to do with me, actually. It was his father he was really attacking.'

'His father?' Alexandra lifted her head and regarded her mother with damp eyes.

'He's very bitter toward his father because he feels betrayed. His father and I were once close. Attacking me was a way of hurting his father indirectly – I think he feels worse about it than either of us.'

Alexandra took a moment to digest this information. 'Who was he?' she asked finally. 'His father, I mean.'

'His name was Philip. He was my uncle's illegitimate son.'

'Were you very close?'

Jolene hesitated briefly. 'Very,' she said. 'At one time, we were to be married.'

'Did you love him?'

Again, she hesitated; even now, so many years later, the pain had not altogether left her.

'Yes,' she said. The two were silent for a few moments, each following her own thoughts. 'Your father and I have sheltered you,' Jolene said finally. 'We meant to protect you from the sort of troubles we both had when we were younger – I suppose it was inevitable trouble would seek us out here. This young man – he is not, you understand, the tranquil sort? I do not think loving him will ever be an easy proposition. If you're unsure, or if you're frightened, it might be better for me to send him away now.'

'And I can go back to being sheltered and protected?' Alexandra asked dryly.

Jolene smiled despite herself. 'I suspect it's rather late for that. But I've no doubt that we could find some, shall we say, safer candidates for your affection, if you like.'

Alexandra got up from the bed, pushing her hair back from

her face and smoothing her rumpled skirt. 'I'll tell you what I told him,' she said. 'I'm not afraid. Where is he?'

Jolene got up from the bed also. 'Waiting for us to come down.' She sighed, and added, 'for what I fear will be a very cold lunch.'

57

'Señor, our children get no education because there are no schools for them. If they could be taught while they are here . . .'

'There is no health care for our people. When they take sick, they must suffer, or travel all the way into the city, for doctors they cannot afford . . .'

'Here, there is plenty to eat, but we worry, is it the best food . . .'

The questions and the complaints rang in Roger's head, till he could hear them in his sleep. In the first flush of success, it had seemed that the job Jolene had given him was a simple one. He had only to bring the workers together, explain to them that they were to have their own union, and then set about running one.

It had not immediately occurred to him how little he – and they – knew about organizing labor unions. He, after all, had been drawn into the movement only lately, and reluctantly at that. He had become, through circumstances unforeseen by himself, an activist, even an agitator; but while this cast him on the side of the workers, it hardly prepared him for the management of such an enterprise.

As for the workers at Brussac-America, he might as well have told them that they now had management's permission to travel to the moon, an enterprise for which they were nearly as well prepared as for forming a labor union. Indeed, the very suggestion of the latter was enough to frighten them. They knew, some of them first hand, what happened when workers began to talk of unionizing. The incident at Bergano's, though the latest and the bloodiest, was not the only such tragedy. To the farm worker in California's fields in 1916, unionization meant Wobblies; no other labor organization had any interest in the bindle stiffs; and wherever the Wobblies went, it meant trouble. At the very least, those who flirted with Wobbly sentiments could expect to be fired. The less fortunate ended up with bandaged heads, or stretched out in a pine box, with their widows weeping over them.

His first meeting drew a crowd of three, despite the fact that Jolene had acquiesced in his request that the workers be given the time away from the work to attend.

'They don't trust me,' he said glumly.

'Trust must be earned,' Jolene informed him.

Since his interview with her, he had remained as a guest in the *casa grande* – the big house; he had taken his meals with the family and in general dressed, and acted, like a Brussac.

Now he went into the fields. He took a blanket and a change of clothes and appeared at the door of one of the workers' shacks, announcing that he would be living there with that family.

They made him room in a corner for his bed, and fed him, greeting his attempts at conversation with polite silence. In the morning he woke to find that he was the shack's sole tenant; the family had moved in with another.

He worked among the men, as he had when he first arrived, but then they had assumed him to be one of them; now, he was an enigma. They knew him to be part of the Brussacs – they continued to refer to him as El Señor, and occasionally even El Patron, despite his protests to the contrary. He talked to them of banding together to form a union. They smiled, and nodded their heads – and shied away from him.

His second meeting brought an audience of two.

It was after this second meeting that Rodriquez approached him.

'Señor?'

Dispirited, Roger had been on his way back to the shack in which he lived alone. He stopped and turned to find one of the Mexican workers following him across the yard. This was a rather unprepossessing fellow, nearly as wide as he was tall and with a great drooping mustache which could not help but give him a comic appearance.

'What is it?' Roger asked wearily; at the moment, he was

silently cursing all the workers for their reluctance and their stubborn refusal to do as he exhorted.

'I am Rodriquez. I wish to talk.'

Roger shrugged and started off again. 'Talk away,' he said.

Rodriquez fell into step beside him; though Roger was not walking particularly fast, the difference between his long-legged stride and that of the much shorter man was so great that Rodriquez had almost to run to keep up with him. Though this added to the comic effect, it seemed not to deter him at all.

'Señor, your talk of organizing the workers, this is not a joke?'

'Am I laughing?' Roger asked.

Rodriquez grinned to show that he got the humor of the question. 'The people, they fear it is a trick of some sort. They fear it will lead to trouble.'

Roger stopped dead in his tracks, so abruptly that Rodriquez went on a few paces beyond him and had to turn back.

'Jesus,' Roger swore, 'what do I have to do to convince these people?'

'Make me *el presidente*,' Rodriquez said, with a broad grin.

'What?'

'*El presidente*. Of the union. You will need a leader, no?' Rodriquez spread his hands expansively.

'I thought that's what I was going to be,' Roger said.

Rodriquez shook his head, the mustache flopping. 'You speak, Señor, of our union. Of our needs and our wants. But you, forgive me, Señor, are not of us. Is it to be our union, or yours?'

Roger was silent for a long moment. Finally, he asked, 'What in the hell qualifications have you got for the job?'

'I am Chicano.'

'That's not enough. There's some sense to what you say, but – no offense to you, but whoever heads the union will have to be a real leader, someone dynamic, someone who can get things done . . .'

Rodriquez' grin broadened. 'I can get things done,' he said. 'Anyway, Señor, there is no other choice. No one else will take the job. They are afraid that if the winds change, if the people in the big house turn against our union, it is the leaders who will be beaten or hanged. So, they say no. And they will not follow you. So . . .' He shrugged.

'And what exactly am I supposed to do?' Roger demanded, 'just bow out?'

'Not entirely. You are not of us, you are of them,' he gestured toward the main house, its windows glowing now as dusk deepened around them. 'You will be our – how do you say it? Our bridge – '

'Liaison?'

'Yes, that is it, our lay – layson with the owners. The people will trust you to look out for our interests.'

'I thought you just got finished saying they wouldn't trust me, now you say they will?'

'In the right place, *si*. But even dressed as a hen, a fox is not welcome in the coop.'

Roger was silent for another moment. It occurred to him that in the few minutes they had been standing talking, Rodriquez had lost much of his comic posture and had grown quite serious. The wide, bright eyes that had seemed to be laughing at everything looked deadly shrewd.

'All right,' Roger said, reversing his direction and starting back toward the house, 'take the job, it's yours.'

Rodriquez called after him, 'Thank you, Señor.'

'Don't thank me,' Roger answered without looking back. 'Like the people said, if the winds change, it's your neck.'

'Our necks,' came the answer.

Three nights later, eighty-seven men, women and children crowded into one of the pressing sheds, and a union – The United Workers of Brussac-America – was formed.

'Your union's doing very well,' Alexandra said.

'Not my union, their union – or, to put it more accurately, Rodriquez's union,' Roger said.

They had come to stand at the edge of the vineyard and watch the workers. Even a casual observer could have seen the difference in the way the men worked. Roger, who was more than casually interested, knew that work output had increased dramatically, though as yet nothing had been negotiated between the fledgling union and Brussac-America.

'Do you trust him?' Alexandra asked.

'Rodriquez? I've got no reason not to. Why?'

The great bell that stood in the yard by the house began to toll, marking the end of the work day. There was an unmistakable haste, a sense of purpose, with which the workers began to hurry toward the yard where their shacks stood. Roger began to stroll along the quickly emptying field.

'There's talk among the household help,' Alexandra said,

walking at his side. 'They say he's planning a big demonstration, a confrontation with the family. They say it could get ugly.'

' "They say." A lot of busybodies, imagining things. Let's go in here.' They had come to the low iron fence surrounding the family cemetery. Without waiting for her assent, he pushed open the newly oiled gate and went in. For a moment or so they wandered among the neatly trimmed graves.

'Who's this?' he asked, pausing beside one marker. 'Albert McInnis? Doesn't sound like family.'

'That's Weasel. He was our one-man household staff when I was young – nursemaid for me, cook – oh, a wonderful cook. He was with father forever, from the time they were both young.'

'Nice name,' Roger said. He went on, stopping at another. 'Your grandfather?' he asked.

'Yes. He was from French Hills, you know.'

'So your mother told me.' In the past few days, he had learned a great deal of Brussac history from Alexandra's mother, and from Alexandra herself. They seemed never to tire of the subject, and it astonished him that they could tell tales of things that happened generations before, all the way back in France, with such enthusiasm and such vividness of detail that it was difficult to credit that they had not been there at the time.

'Will you go back?'

The question surprised him. 'To French Hills, you mean?' She nodded. 'I don't know.'

'Mother says you will.'

'Your mother says a great many things.' He smiled. 'Does she say why I'll go back?'

'That's easy. Because you're a Brussac. She says Brussacs are tied to the earth, to their own special dirt.'

'Brussacs,' he said disdainfully. 'I'm no more a real Brussac than I am a real cousin to you – the son of your mother's uncle's illegitimate son – the Brussac rules don't apply to me.'

'That doesn't matter,' she said. 'It's the blood that counts. Grandmother Perreira says it isn't blood at all, she says it's wine in our veins. She says that's our curse.'

'You're forgetting, I've never made wine. I ran away from winemaking.'

'And ran right to it, too. And anyway, from what you've said, it's French Hills that's run away from winemaking. Would you have left if it hadn't been for the oil?'

'I didn't run away from French Hills, I ran away from my father.'

'But you can't run away from your father, that's like hiding from your reflection in a mirror, or denying your shadow.'

'More of Grandmother Perreira's wisdom?'

She laughed and said, 'No, that's pure Cousin Alexandra. But it's true, I know it is. There's something about fathers and sons, same as with mothers and daughters. It's like, when you come into a room and catch an unexpected glimpse of yourself in a mirror – or you're walking down a street, and suddenly see yourself in a store window, and you don't even recognize yourself, and yet you know it's you you're seeing. I look at my mother sometimes and I think, "Who is that woman?" And yet, she could be me, we're so much the same, or I her.'

'I could never be my father,' he said, a note of bitterness creeping into his voice.

'You *are* your father. Though I've never met him, I know his eyes look out from your face, his voice speaks from your mouth – '

'You're practically saying I don't exist.'

She shook her head. 'You don't, not apart from the rest – from your earth and your blood and your birth – it's all a part of what you are, all a part of what I love in you . . . '

He grinned suddenly and seized her in his arms. 'Now that,' he said, 'is the sort of argument I like to hear.' He kissed her, loving not only taste and the scent and the feel that were her, but also the smell of new-mown grass and the distant caw of a blackbird winging his way homeward. For the first time, he was in love with life, as if his love for her had changed the tint and hue of all about him, letting him see now a different world, through different eyes.

'I love you,' he murmured, and thought as he mouthed them how inadequate words were. If only he could take her inside his breast, to share the beating of his heart, or into his mind, where she could see the rapturous heights to which her kisses carried him. He wondered why, with all the ways that man had devised to express and state and communicate, he had not managed to find a more impassive way of expressing these the most important of all the things in his life.

The tender moment was interrupted by a shout from afar. They looked and saw one of the house servants waving from the porch.

'That's Selena,' Alexandra said. 'She looks as excited as all get out.'

'We'd better go see what's happening,' Roger said.

Holding hands, they started back in the direction of the big house. At first they did not hurry, but as they came closer across the fields, both of them became gradually aware of something out of the ordinary. It was Alexandra who first put into words the question that was beginning to puzzle both of them.

'Where is everybody?' she asked aloud.

Still holding her hand, Roger began to hurry her along at an increasing pace. 'I've been wondering the same thing myself,' he said.

It was the time of evening when ordinarily children could be seen playing in the yards, and women stood about gossiping, while their men exchanged yarns at their stoops. Tonight, however, there was no one to be seen in the area of the workers' shacks. An ominous silence had fallen since the end of the work day.

'Look,' Alexandra said, pointing. They had come in view of the wide clearing about which the shacks were clustered. The clearing itself was crowded with people, the workers and their families forming a moving, colorful mass about a central figure who stood slightly taller than they.

'Rodriquez,' Roger said aloud, pausing to watch. 'Looks like he's trying to get them riled up.'

'Let's go listen,' Alexandra said.

'No.' He spoke more sharply than he had intended; he knew from first-hand experience what could happen when a mob became aroused. At the moment, those below looked peaceable, but there was no doubt that Rodriquez was haranguing them, and some in the crowd had begun to raise their fists in the air. Shouts, indecipherable at this distance, could be heard occasionally.

He saw that he had frightened her, and managing a grin, he said, 'I'll come back down myself and see what it's all about, just as soon as I get you up to the house.'

She looked about to argue, but he started off for the house again, fairly pulling her along.

They found the house in an uproar. Jolene ran down the steps to meet them, Dan Sanchez close behind. 'Thank Heaven, there you are,' Jolene cried, embracing her daughter. 'I got frightened when no one knew where you were.'

'What's wrong?' Roger demanded. 'What's going on?'

'It's them damn pickers,' Dan Sanchez answered. 'I knew there'd be trouble over letting them have a union.'

'Cook was down to the shacks to visit her sister,' Jolene said. 'Rodriquez has called everybody together for a big meeting.'

'We saw them,' Alexandra said, 'but we couldn't hear what it was all about.'

'Rodriquez is exhorting them to march on the house,' Jolene said.

'I told my men to get the guns out of your husband's cupboard,' Sanchez said. 'If they want trouble . . . '

'No.' Jolene said firmly.

'Now, Missus, you let me . . . '

'I'll handle this myself,' Jolene said, 'and there will be no gunfire. Leave my husband's guns where they were.'

'Look,' Roger said, 'why don't I go down there myself and find out just what Rodriquez has got planned.'

'It's too late for that,' Sanchez said, pointing behind them. 'Look.'

They did and saw a long column of men and women marching up from the shacks. Four and five abreast, they came slowly but steadily, and in an almost eerie silence.

Roger glanced around. There were, counting himself and Sanchez's men, a dozen of them at the house. The advancing throng numbered at least ten times that.

'I think we'd better get up on the porch,' he said, his expression grim.

58

Jolene was remembering a story about her great-grandmother in France during the revolution – Aunt Marie had told it to her when she had been in France, a story of a mob advancing on the chateau, and great-grandmother Anne had been alone –

'Dan,' she said aloud, remembering the rest of the tale, 'tell your men to bring wine, two – no, make it three casks.'

The foreman looked as if he meant to object, but she forestalled him with a firm look, and added, 'Tell them to be quick about it.'

He gave the orders and his men left the porch looking relieved to be doing something. Jolene started out to meet the advancing throng.

'I'll come with you,' Roger said.

'No. I am the mistress here, and I assume that it is I they've come to see.'

She did not wait for argument but went across the lawn. The workers, seeing her, came to a halt, looking momentarily uncertain. Rodriquez, at their head, came forward without a pause.

'Señora,' he greeted her, removing his hat and bowing.

'Mister Rodriquez.' She smiled and glanced past him at the nervous-looking throng. 'And this, I take it, is your new labor union?'

'*Si.*' He flashed his teeth in a wide grin, then quickly grew sober again. 'We have come, Señora, to discuss a contract.'

Jolene breathed a mental sigh of relief; so that was it. And Rodriquez had wanted to make a show of strength, of unity before discussing terms, in case she did not take their new union seriously. What might have happened, she wondered, if she hadn't prevented Sanchez's men from arming themselves? Or if she had simply refused to meet with these people?

A sudden shout went up from the crowd. She started, thinking that there might be trouble after all, but then she realized that these were shouts of pleasure. She looked around and saw that Sanchez's men had arrived with the wine, and were in the process now of tapping the casks.

'Very well,' she said, turning back to Rodriquez. 'Would you like to come in?'

He shook his head. 'I think it better if I discuss in front of my people. And,' he added, 'I think there is not room enough inside for so many.'

'Yes,' she said, nodding soberly. 'Will you all have some wine?'

'Business first, wine later,' Rodriquez said.

'Fair enough.' To his surprise, she seated herself on the cool lawn. 'I'm afraid I haven't got chairs enough – there are so many of you – but I don't mind sitting on the grass, if you don't.'

There was a great deal of laughter, some of it embarrassed,

and some expressions of admiration for the 'beautiful señora'. Rodriquez, looking a trifle flustered for the first time in the meeting, seated himself rather stiffly before her. The others dropped to the ground in more relaxed postures, a few even climbing the trees to sit overhead on the branches.

'Mister Rodriquez,' Jolene said, becoming quite businesslike, 'I think it only fair to give you a warning.'

Rodriquez's smile vanished; around them, the waiting crowd grew silent once more.

'And what is that, Señora?' Rodriquez asked cooly.

'I drive a very hard bargain,' Jolene said, with just the faintest trace of a smile.

'It's father. Father's home!'

Roger, hearing Alexandra's shout, went to the window of his room in time to see a tall, handsome gentleman step down from his motor car. He felt a pang of jealousy as he saw Alexandra run from the house and fling herself enthusiastically into her father's arms. A moment later Jolene came out to greet her husband with scarcely more decorum.

Watching the family reunion, Roger's jealousy faded to a general sense of unease. The weeks since he had been welcomed into this house by its mistress had been happy ones for him, perhaps the happiest of his life. He was hopelessly in love with Alexandra, and only slightly less so with her mother. Jolene's fair and generous dealings with her workers had alleviated much of the bitterness of what he had seen before coming here.

He was fully aware, however, that this happy idyll might end with the arrival of the gentleman at that moment mounting the steps to the house. He had begun his visit here by seducing the man's daughter, and had gone on to assault his wife. Sloan Morrow would be entirely justified in having him whipped, or worse.

'Well, might as well face the music,' Roger said aloud. He was about to leave the room when he caught sight of himself in the mirror over the dresser. He was wearing, as he had been since moving into the house, clothes that Jolene had provided him – a few things her husband seldom wore, as she had put it.

It was too much, to face the offended husband in the man's own clothes. He went to the closet, where his own clothes had been stored on a shelf. He had nothing but the one outfit in which he had escaped northward from Bergano's. It had been washed and mended but nothing could redeem its threadbare condition.

Dressed in his own clothes, Roger paused once more to examine himself in the mirror. It was incredible, he thought with grim amusement, what a change a suit of clothes made in a man. A few minutes before he had looked like a proper scion of the Brussacs, a gentleman, a businessman. Now he looked as he had looked when first he had arrived here; he looked like a migrant, a bindle stiff.

'That's the trouble,' he thought. For all his traveling about, for all that he had experienced since he'd left French Hills, he still didn't know where his rightful place was – where did he belong anyway? In the world of business suits and elegant parlors? Or in a vineyard? He knew there was aristocratic blood in his veins; the blood of the Brussacs – wine, Alexandra's grandmother had called it, but noble wine, surely. Yet in him, as in all the Brussacs, there was peasant blood as well. His mother had been a tramp. Even his father, whose family link to the Brussacs was undeniable, had been illegitimate, product of a loveless mating between aristocrat and servant.

What did that make him? Who was he, and where did he belong? These questions had begun to haunt him. There was the real reason he had left French Hills; the quarrel with his father had only been an excuse. He had wanted to find himself, to find his rightful place.

What he had found was a place where he had been very happy, a place where he had discovered love, a place where he had begun to contemplate his own worth and to think of himself as something more than a waste of life and flesh.

But it was not, alas, *his* place. He was still what he had always been, an outsider looking in upon others, admiring their world, savoring and even envying it, but never truly a part of it, just as the elegant clothes he had worn were not his at all, but only borrowed from another.

Stripped of pretensions, of foolish fantasy, he had what he had always had – nothing.

Thus chastened, he went down to meet Jolene's husband, and Alexandra's father.

They were in the parlor. He stood for a moment in the doorway watching them, wishing that he could be truly a part of that happy group, as he knew he was not.

It was Morrow himself who first saw him. For a second or

so the older man regarded him somberly, with an expression Roger was unable to read.

Alexandra saw him then and with one of those musical laughs of hers, said, 'It's Roger,' and came to greet him taking his hand and leading him into the room. 'This is Roger, father, I've told him so much about you.'

'It must have made for boring conversation,' Sloan said, shaking his guest's hand.

'Your daughter's very devoted to you,' Roger said.

'Yes, she's very gullible.'

There was one of those awkward pauses, where the animation of the conversation that went beforehand only makes the silence more intense.

'My wife and daughter tell me you've been rather actively engaged in our business,' Sloan said finally.

'I've tried to make myself useful where I could.'

'I was about to take a walk about, have a look at things. Maybe you'd do me the honor of accompanying me?'

'Glad to,' Roger said. He nodded at the two women, pretending not to notice Jolene's strained expression.

'You've done a good job with this union business.'

It was almost the first comment Sloan had made since they had come out.

'Thank you, sir, but the real work was done by one of your men, Rodriquez,' Roger said.

'Yes, I remember him. Funny, I never thought he had that sort of stuff in him.'

'Sometimes it just wants the opportunity to come out.' After a moment, Roger added, 'It was your wife who handled the contract negotiations. I think everyone was satisfied.'

The demands that the new union had made had been modest and fair; the contract under which they were now working had made some reasonable changes in wages and working conditions, yet its chief difference could be seen in the attitudes of the men working in the vineyards, men who held their heads up with new pride, who laughed often and sang while they worked.

'I'm afraid, though, that unionizing your workers and giving them a contract have made you and your wife something of outcasts among the other growers.'

Sloan gave a disdainful snort. 'My wife and I are used to being outcasts. Let them complain. The day will come when they'll have to do what we've done, and the delay will cost them. I understand you're wanted by the law.'

The abrupt change of subject caught Roger off guard. 'I'm afraid so,' he stammered, coming to a halt. 'You could have me arrested, you know.'

'Yes, I know.'

'Sir, I – ' Roger hesitated, then forced himself to go on, studying the other man's shoes as he spoke. 'I'm afraid I have to tell you this. I – I assaulted your wife when I first came here. It's only out of the goodness of her heart that I wasn't strung up by your workmen.'

'My wife is a very generous woman and one well acquainted with the less pleasant aspects of life.'

'I'm deeply ashamed of what I did.'

'So she told me. She also said you've worked hard to try to make amends.'

'I'll always be in her debt – and yours as well.'

'What of my daughter?' Sloan asked sternly. 'I won't have her innocence sullied simply to satisfy your – what did my wife call it? – your rage against life.'

'Sir, I love your daughter,' Roger said, forgetting his shyness.

'And?'

'And, I would beg your permission to marry her, if only . . .'

'If only what?'

Roger turned away, kicking a clod of dirt with the toe of his shoe. 'If only I were worthy of her. Look at me, I'm nobody, I haven't got a thing but these rags I'm wearing. I don't even have a home.'

'You're young yet,' Sloan said. 'You've got plenty of time, and I expect you'll try a number of paths before you find the one meant for you. But you're wrong on a couple of counts. You are somebody, even though you may not yet know who. Neither my wife nor my daughter would have taken you into our home if they hadn't seen something of worth in you. And, anyway, you do have a home.'

'You mean French Hills? I'll never go back there.'

'That would be a pity, because part of yourself is still there, and without it you'll never be whole. And now, I think I shall go back in, I've been several months without the company of my wife, and beautiful though these fields look to me, I've got better fruits to harvest.'

He started for the house, but when he had gone a few paces, he paused to look back.

'You're welcome to stay here as long as you need to,' he said, 'but I think you know, this isn't the end of the search for you; that destination lies elsewhere.'

If only I knew where, Roger thought, watching him make his way back across the field. In that vast world that lay beyond the gates of Brussac-America, that world from which he had taken refuge here, lay not one but scores, hundreds, thousands of paths from which to choose. How did he – how did any man – know which one to choose, which one was the right one for him? He was like a blind man, feeling his way through an unfamiliar room, bumping here, banging there, stumbling forward without knowing whether he was making progress, or heading toward disaster. Was this the way it was with everyone, or was it this that set him apart from others?

Was it only he who didn't know where he was going?

59

'Mister Brussac?'

'Yes?'

'Message for you.'

Surprised, Roger took the slip of paper from the bellboy and unfolded it. The address written inside had been smudged, as if too hastily folded; there was no name and no message, but the handwriting was familiar to him.

'From a secret admirer?' Alexandra asked, with only the slightest edge to her bantering tone.

'No, just an old acquaintance,' Roger said, folding the paper and thrusting it into his pocket. 'Look, something's come up, I'm afraid I'll have to leave you for a short while.'

'Oh dear,' Alexandra said, and Mary said, querulously, 'The parade'll be starting anytime now.'

'Never mind that, we can manage,' Jolene told her mother; to Roger she said, 'I hope it's nothing too drastic.'

'Just some loose strings that I should have attended to before this,' he said. 'Are you sure you'll be all right? I promised your husband I'd drive you in the parade.'

'Dear Roger, I've been driving motorcars almost as long as

they've been making them, and do, please, be gallant and not ask how long that is. I'm only sorry you're going to miss all the fun.'

'Not all of it, I hope,' he said, 'I'll make it as quick as I can. With luck, maybe I'll still join you in time to drive.'

He gave Alexandra a disappointed look. 'I hope you'll forgive me, too,' he said.

'I'll try,' she said, managing a wan smile. Her face brightened momentarily. 'But wait, I'll come with you,' she said.

'And waste that pretty patriotic shawl,' he chided her. He took it from her arm and draped it gracefully about her shoulders; she had crocheted it herself in bright bands of red, white, and blue when she had learned that they were to drive in San Francisco's much heralded 'preparedness day' parade. 'Not on your life.'

The Palace Hotel's lobby was jammed, as all the city's hotels were. He took her arm and guided her to the protective shelter of a huge potted palm, where he gave her cheek a quick peck.

'You go along with your mother and grandmother. I promise I'll join you before the parade's over.'

'It isn't fair,' Alexandra pouted. 'First father has to tend to business, and now you've got to go dashing off on some mysterious errand.'

'Nothing mysterious about it,' he assured her, guiding her back to her mother and grandmother. 'Just an old bill that has to be settled.'

'So, you came,' Stella greeted him.

'Wasn't that what you wanted?' He glanced around as he came in; the house was decrepit, both outside and in; there was a sour smell, like cabbage cooked too long.

'It's late to talk about what I want,' she said, curling her lip in a sneer.

She had led him down a narrow, dimly lit hallway and into what had once been the drawing-room of the decaying mansion. Two men were at work at a little table. Roger saw an array of electrical wires, but little else that he recognized. The two glanced at him uneasily as he came in.

'It's all right,' Stella told them, 'an old friend of mine.' To Roger she said, 'Sorry I can't offer you a drink. Not all of us have been living off Brussac wealth.'

'Look, Stella,' he said, 'I didn't come here to trade barbs with you. What is it that you want?'

'The same thing I've always wanted – justice,' she said.

'Justice.' He sighed. 'I'm not even sure what that is anymore.'

She came closer, her eyes glinting in the way he remembered. 'But you did know, not so long ago. In your heart, you still do. We accomplished good before, we can again. Work with me.'

'I – I committed myself. I've got responsibilities to the people at Brussac-America. Obligations. I can't just walk out on them.'

'No one's asking you to do that,' she said, smiling. She paused to light a cigarette, blowing the smoke through her nostrils. 'That was a neat piece of work you did, incidentally. I hear your new union's already negotiated a contract.'

'It isn't my union.'

'You were instrumental in its birth. You still wield influence, with the workers and management alike.'

'You're awfully well informed,' he said.

Again the smile, with not a trace of humor in it. 'I stay in touch,' she said. 'There are people even at Brussac-America who are sympathetic to our cause. Aren't you?'

'I suppose so, in principle anyway.'

'Then?'

'Look, Stella, this conversation is going no place – what exactly is it you want from me?'

'The union,' she said simply.

He stared, taking a moment to consider her answer. 'What you mean is, you want me to turn the union over to the Wobblies.'

'Bring them into the IWW. For their own sakes.'

'In a word, no.'

'Why not?' she demanded angrily.

'Because I gave my word not to,' was his answer. 'No, save your breath, there's no point in arguing about this. If that's all you wanted, I've got another engagement . . . '

He started to turn toward the hallway. 'Wait,' she said, putting a hand on his arm. He gave her a suspicious look, but her expression was one of innocent friendliness.

'All right, I'm not surprised,' she said, 'I suspected that would be your answer, but I had to ask, right? No hard feelings?'

She looked so genuine that some of his antagonism melted. 'No hard feelings,' he said, smiling in return. 'And now, I really do have people waiting.'

She did not remove the hand from his arm. 'Aren't you even

interested in what I've been doing?' she asked.

'I supposed pretty much the same as before. I've never considered you the sort to change course once it was set.'

'True enough,' she said, with a laugh. 'But there have been some interesting differences lately. For one thing, this parade.'

'I figured your people would jump on that,' he said.

In the last few months the United States had been edging closer and closer to the war in Europe, and preparedness parades, designed to display patriotism as well as eagerness to support the upcoming war effort, had become fashionable. Like many other cities, San Francisco had decided to stage its own parade, but with an extra ingredient: the parade would demonstrate not only patriotic enthusiasm, but also the desire of the city's employers to bring back the open shop of the good old days. Employees working in non-union shops had been ordered to march in the parade under threat of dismissal.

In a city where labor was as strongly entrenched as it was in San Francisco, such activity was certain to arouse passions. Newspapers and city officials had received a flood of threatening letters, which had been ignored. The plans for the parade had gone forward. For a time many of the city's citizens had viewed the situation with apprehension, but as the actual day for the parade had drawn near the militant voices had grown still, and everyone had begun to breathe easier; the crisis, it was generally assumed, had passed without incident.

'It was something we couldn't ignore,' Stella said. 'Come look what Josef has made for us.'

She led him to the table where the two silent men had resumed their work. Spread out before them was an array of wires, timing mechanisms and electrical gadgets, which they were installing in an ordinary-looking suitcase.

'What is all this?' Roger asked; something about Stella's manner made him uneasy. She was too friendly, too confident – he knew her well enough to know that she did not give in so easily.

'They're making a bomb,' she said.

He felt the hair rise on the back of his neck. 'A bomb? What in God's name for?'

She did not answer directly, but instead tugged him over to a door, opening it to reveal stairs going down to a basement.

'Look, you'll really like this,' she said, urging him to the head of the stairs.

'I can't see anything,' he said, shrinking back from the musty darkness below.

'Wait just here,' Stella said, 'I'll get a light for you.'

She disappeared behind him. He stood staring unhappily into the gloom, thinking perhaps after all that Stella was mad. He would have somehow to dissuade her from her current course of action, convince her . . .

He was suddenly struck hard in the middle of the back. He fell forward, losing his balance, to topple down the stairs. Even as he fell, he heard the door slam shut above him and a bolt slide into place.

He struck his head falling, and for several minutes lay stunned at the foot of the stairs. From the house above him he heard muted voices, and finally the slam of a door; then all was quiet.

'Hey,' he shouted, stumbling to his feet. He felt his way up the stairs and tried the door, pounding on it when it would not open and shouting for Stella and Josef. There was no answer, and after a moment he concluded that they had all gone, and he was only wasting breath he might need for getting out of where he was.

He felt along the walls for a light switch, finding only cobwebs. At last he remembered the matches in his pocket and struck one, to survey his surroundings. There was a light fixture overhead, but the bulb had been removed; apparently Stella had had this fate in mind for him all along, he concluded grimly.

The match burned his fingers. He shook it out and lit another, lighting his way down the stairs with it. There was not much to his prison – a furnace, its pipes raised as if in supplication. There was a coal chute, and light could be seen through its opening, but it was obviously too small to allow him escape; the same was true of the two tiny windows high up in the walls.

He went back to the door, putting his shoulder against it to test its strength; it yielded but held. He dropped another match, and when it did not go out went to step on it; as he did so, he saw sawdust on the floor.

He lit a fresh match and knelt, examining the floor, the door, the woodwork.

Termites, he thought, his spirits rising. This old house must be riddled with them. He lit yet another match and examined the door frame more closely. With his fingernail he was able to break away splinters of rotted wood.

Smiling to himself, he took out the pocket-knife he had carried with him since French Hills, and with its sharp blade began to dig away the wood around the door's hinges.

It took less time than he would have guessed, no more than a quarter hour, before he was able to yank the hinges loose from the wood and shove the door aside. He stepped into the room beyond, and nearly fell over a bundle left lying near the door – wires, a clock, explosives. Stella and her companions had intended to destroy the house and any evidence they might have left behind – himself included.

Gingerly he pulled the wires loose from the explosives and carried the entire assemblage to the kitchen. He found a sink there, with an old-fashioned pump and after submerging the bomb in water, he went back to the drawing-room.

The suitcase, with the bomb that Josef had been building into it, was gone. They must have planned to disrupt the parade with it. Jolene was driving their new motor car in the parade, with Alexandra and old Mary, at the head of a contingent of workers from Brussac-America representing their new union. The idea had been the workers' own, intended in a small way to offset the anti-labor tone of the parade. Sloan had been against it, afraid that the appearance of the union group in a blatantly anti-union parade might lead to trouble, but Jolene had insisted; Alexandra and Mary too had wanted to participate, and when the furor had seemed to die down Sloan had given in reluctantly.

By now, Roger thought, leaving the house and beginning to run along the street, the parade must already have started; and somewhere along its route, Stella would place an innocent looking suitcase . . .

60

Damn them, Stella thought, damn them all. She watched the motor cars with banners on their sides sporting anti-union sentiments and calling for open shops, and felt a gorge of hate rise up in her throat.

An open cart, this one pulled by horses, went by, made up as a float, A matronly looking woman in a Miss Liberty costume balanced precariously on a platform, holding a cardboard sword, slightly bent, in one hand and brass scales in the other. Bands played a cacophony of conflicting tunes, all of a patriotic nature.

Damn Roger Brussac most of all. Stella picked up the suitcase and began to walk again, glancing at her watch as she did so. Five minutes yet to go. Josef had been precise regarding the time. She could not afford to be neglectful. She needed to find exactly the right spot where the bomb would do the most damage; and she must stay with it until the last possible minute, lest some passerby pick it up and take it home, thinking it contained valuables. A bomb along the parade route would produce national headlines; a bomb in some tenement apartment was worthless to the cause.

She walked along Market Street, actually moving faster than the parade. The sidewalks were crowded, thousands of people cheering as the floats and the bands passed by.

The parade turned at Polk Street. She watched a float make the difficult turn, filling nearly the entire intersection. Yes, this was the place. She found a spot to stand near a street light, setting the suitcase at her feet. Again she glanced at her watch. A little more than two minutes.

Now that the actual moment was at hand, she was calmer than she had been earlier. She even smiled at the antics of a clown going by.

The smile became a trifle sad as she thought of Roger; poor Roger. By now he was dead, the house and everything in it blown sky high. She had really hated doing that to him. At one time she had been very attached to him, too attached. Perhaps she might have loved him, under other circumstances.

Roger had been a fool, though. In his heart, he had never really been dedicated to the cause, not truly, deeply dedicated. Else he would not have abandoned it so abruptly. And in so doing, he had made himself a menace to her. So long as he had remained one of them, he had been safe; but a reformed Roger, who knew too much, too many people – who knew her and her involvement in the IWW, and even where she might be found – no, she had known since her last visit to Brussac-America, since she'd seen him with that girl, she had known then that Roger would have to be disposed of.

She had hated the knowledge. She had even given him a final chance; if he had agreed to bring that union into the IWW, she could have convinced the others to let him live. But he had been stubborn; he had offered no hope of reconciliation. What had followed had been necessity.

Someone jostled her. It brought her back to the present. She checked the time and saw that there was now just a little over a minute. Silently she counted the seconds until it was a minute, then less. Then she turned away from the parade and began to walk back down Market Street.

'Lady.'

She had gone only a few yards when she heard someone behind her. She tried to hasten her steps, but the crowd was thick here and it was impossible to move very quickly.

'Lady – hey, lady.' Someone grabbed her arm, and she turned to see a short, balding man, out of breath from trying to catch up with her. 'You forgot your suitcase, lady,' he said, holding up the bag. 'Thought I'd never catch up with you – what's wrong?'

'Get away from me,' she shouted, backing away from him. 'Leave me alone.' People had begun to turn and look at them.

'Hey, I ain't doing nothing,' the man protested, embarrassed by the peculiar looks he was getting. 'I just brought you your suitcase, you left it back there by that lamp post.'

'It's not mine,' she cried. 'I've never seen it before in my life.'

'Are you crazy, I saw you walk along with it, you were walking in front of me for three blocks dragging this thing, then you set it down, and you left it there. What is this . . . ?'

Without even looking at her watch, she knew it was within seconds of the time. People were watching them now, wondering what was going on. She turned from the stranger and pushed her way through the crowd lining the street, meaning to dart across the parade route to the other side.

'Let me through,' she cried, elbowing those in front of her. 'Please, I've got to get through.'

A path parted. She dashed forward, looking neither right nor left. 'Look out,' someone shouted, but it was too late, she had dashed right into the path of a car. Something struck her, not violently, but hard enough to throw her to the ground.

'Good lord,' Mary said from the back seat; Alexandra gave a little squeal of fright.

Jolene, seeing the figure dart out from the curb, had tried to stop the car, but there simply had not been time, even at the slow speed they were traveling. There was a sickening thud as the car's fender struck the girl, knocking her to the ground.

She pulled the big parking brake and jumped from the car; Mary and Alexandra had already jumped down from the rear and were bending over the fallen girl.

'Is she all right?' Jolene asked, joining them.

'Just stunned, I think,' Mary said. 'She needs some salts.'

'I put a kit in the car,' Jolene said, 'in case of any emergency. I'll get it.'

'I'll try to find a doctor,' Alexandra said.

Mary, bending over the girl on the ground, said, 'Give me your shawl, she's shivering.'

At first, Roger thought it was another of California's frequent earthquakes. The ground seemed to shake, and the windows in the store he was passing rattled violently. It took him a minute to recognize the explosion for what it was; when he did, he began to run, shoving people out of his way.

The parade had come to a halt now, people anxiously asking one another what had happened. Ahead, he saw a crowd of people. It was harder now to make his way through. He pushed and elbowed, ignoring the curses and occasional blows of those he shoved aside.

Suddenly he was through the crowd, and before him was a horrible scene of destruction and carnage. An area half a block long had been razed by the fire. The windows had been blown out of the shops along the street; a lamp post had fallen across the street, crushing a float beneath it. Smoke curled upward from a half dozen fires started by the explosion.

The street itself was a nightmare. Pieces of floats and motor cars were strewn everywhere, and amid that even worse debris. Roger stumbled over something, and glanced down to see that it was a human leg, severed from its body.

Hysteria reigned. People screamed and sobbed, and from the wounded came a chorus of cries and moans. Roger staggered forward, hoping against hope that Jolene and her family might already have passed by this spot, might be safe somewhere along the remainder of the parade route.

Then he saw the car, or rather, the wreckage of the car.

'Alexandra.' He tried to shout, but the sound came out nothing more than a whisper. He pushed on, unable to take his eyes from the shiny deck of the car. Perhaps they had not been in the car, perhaps the car had broken down and had to be abandoned . . .

He reached the car, steadying himself with a hand on one fender and not noticing that the metal was scorching hot.

There, on the ground virtually at his feet, lay a body, or rather what was left of one. Only the shawl – the red, white, and blue shawl she had finished crocheting a few days before – made it possible to identify her. Nothing else was recognizable.

He clutched his stomach and retched violently, feeling as if it were his very life he was spewing out. Alexandra – dead! And the blame was his. If he'd been with her – if he'd agreed to Stella's demands – if he'd never gone to Brussac-America in the first place – this might not have happened, they might all be still alive.

He wished he'd never left French Hills; or better yet, that he need never have been born. He turned from the carnage and stumbled and staggered through the debris, through the thickening crowds. Sirens had begun to sound; the city was beginning to respond to the emergency. There would be police, ambulances, doctors – too late!

He staggered along in a daze, not knowing where he was going or how far he had come from the site of the explosion. He ran into people, into buildings even, and still he went on, unaware even that he was sobbing openly, tears streaming down his cheeks.

At last his breath and his legs gave out. He stumbled and fell; he dragged himself to his feet, and turned into an open doorway, colliding with someone standing there.

'Hey, there, you all right, fellow?'

'I – yes, I'm all right.'

'You sure look determined – say, you didn't come here to sign up, did you?'

Roger lifted his head and willed his eyes to focus. He found himself literally hanging on to a burly man in a uniform. The face, though chiseled, was kindly, and the blue eyes watching him filled with concern.

'Sign up?' His mind refused to grasp the situation; he felt numbed, drugged.

'To join the Army – go overseas, fight the Hun,' was the answer. 'This is a recruiting office – didn't you know?'

'Recruiting . . . ?' Somewhere in the distance, a band had begun to play 'America the Beautiful'; through the offkey playing he could still hear the wail of sirens.

'I could sure use a recruit,' the uniformed man was saying. 'I thought this parade would bring 'em in in droves, but so far no luck. Whatdaya say, son, you want to see the world? Like they say, Uncle Sam needs you.'

The world – a place, somewhere where he belonged, there had to be a place for him. 'Yes,' he said aloud. 'Yes, I want to see the world.'

61

'Alexandra?'

There was no answer. Jolene opened the door to her daughter's room and stepped in. Alexandra was seated by her dressing-table. She blinked as if waking from a dream and turned toward the door.

'Yes, mother?'

'Alexandra, you simply cannot sit in here every day, pining away,' Jolene said, coming across the room. 'I know, I know what you're going to say, you can't bear to face people, but you must some time. You're very young, you've got your whole life before you, and someday you'll be grateful that you didn't waste it.'

'You'd never understand,' Alexandra said.

'But I do, my darling, I have a pretty fair understanding of the human heart, particularly its considerable capacity for pain. But Alexandra, Roger is gone, for all we know he may be dead . . .'

'I'll never believe that,' Alexandra snapped. More thoughtfully, she added, 'It would be easier, I think if it were true, at least then there'd be nothing to wait for, nothing to wonder about. But I'd know it in my heart if it were true, and it isn't, I'm certain of it.'

Jolene sighed; as well talk to a wall, she thought, as a young girl in love. 'Very well then,' she said, 'he's gone away, it's one and the same, isn't it? It's three years now. Wouldn't he have gotten in touch with you by now, if he could?'

'I don't know,' Alexandra cried, jumping up from her chair. 'I've asked myself that a thousand times. That day of the parade

– Grandmother Mary – the explosion – where could he have gone? And why?'

Jolene winced at the mention of an incident she herself would sooner have forgotten. She too was haunted by that day in San Francisco. Hitting that girl with her car would have been bad enough of itself; but just afterwards had come that horrible explosion that had killed not only her mother and the strange girl, but eight others as well. It was only by the grace of God that she and Alexandra had escaped serious injury. She herself had been at the rear of the car, getting the first aid kit; Alexandra had started across the street, looking for a doctor. The car had shielded them from the worst of the blast.

Tom Mooney, a labor radical, had been convicted of the bombing on what to Jolene's mind had been nothing more than a fabrication of evidence.

'You know, Alexandra,' Jolene said, 'there are many people who feel that Mister Mooney was not responsible for the bombing that day.'

'What are you suggesting?' Alexandra asked hotly.

'People think the Wobblies were involved – and Roger was once a member of that organization.'

'He was no longer a part of that, you know that as well as I do,' Alexandra said.

'I thought not, at the time. But he had been sympathetic to their cause. And he did disappear immediately after the bombing.'

'I won't listen to this,' Alexandra cried, clapping her hands over her ears. 'You're horrible to think such a thing.'

'Zan . . .'

'No, leave me alone. I don't want to see you. I don't want to see anyone except Roger.' Alexandra threw herself across the bed and began to sob noisily.

Jolene stared at her for a moment, wanting to go to her and comfort her, and certain at the same time that her sympathy would be rejected, as it had been thus far. She went out, closing the door softly after herself.

She knew from experience what it could mean to pine for a love that could never be, and she dreaded seeing her daughter repeat her own youthful mistakes. If only she knew, really knew, what had happened to Roger. She had been so certain that he truly loved Alexandra, so certain too that he had outgrown the excesses of rebellious youth. Yet he had vanished, suddenly, inexplicably.

She wondered, as she had wondered over and over through the passing years, where he had gone – and why.

'Ou est le Château Brussac?'

The boy, a surly faced urchin, shrugged. 'Never heard of it,' he said, casting a covetous eye on Roger's cigarettes.

'Merci,' Roger said. He tossed him the pack; the boy caught it neatly and took off at a run along the street.

'Monsieur.' It was the woman at the news kiosk. 'You want the Château Brussac?'

'Yes – do you know where it is?'

'Straight along that road, about five kilometers.' She hesitated, sizing him up. 'There's no one there, you know. It's been empty for years.'

'I know. *Merci.*'

She watched him start in the direction she had indicated, noting that he walked with a slight limp. His uniform was dirty and torn. Probably, she thought, a deserter; this was hardly the sort of place a soldier would come to on leave.

Ah, well, she thought, mentally shrugging, it was no concern of hers, so long as he wasn't a Boche. Now, if she'd been a few years younger, and the handsome American had approached her . . .

The road was hot and dusty. Roger had lost his pack days ago; and though he still carried his canteen it was empty. When he came to the river he went down and knelt at its banks, and drank from the green water. It had an aftertaste of rot and filth, but it was cool and wet, and he dabbed it on his sunburned face and neck.

He almost passed the Château without finding it, hidden as it was from the road. Only the crumbling gate posts warned him that something lay beyond.

He followed what had once been a lane, but was now so overgrown as to have vanished altogether in stretches. Just when he was about to abandon the search, he came over a knoll and there before him lay the ghostly shell of a house.

There had been fighting here; the scars were everywhere. Here a number of men had camped; the latrine had not been filled in and it plagued the air with stench and great clouds of flies. There some trees had been hastily felled for firewood.

As he came closer, he saw that the windows were gone from the house, the door hanging open on one rusted hinge. Streaks of black ran upward from several of the openings, indicating that a horrible fire had burned inside; even from a distance, one could smell the burnt wood.

He went in, his footsteps echoing on stones trod by centuries of slippered feet. Here and there the warped and stained paneling had been prized from the walls, perhaps as fuel for the immense fireplace along one side. A stone passageway led toward the rear, no doubt to a kitchen; he chose the wide stairs leading upward.

Everywhere was desolation. The few furnishings not carried from the house had been slashed and broken; silken draperies hung in tatters at the glassless windows. Human waste dotted parquet floors that might have graced museums.

From room to room he strolled, sickened and yet fascinated. He kept hoping in the face of all reality that something might have been spared, some room, even a single piece of the furnishings.

When he finally found something, it was not at all what he had expected. In an attic room, draped across a splintered trunk, lay a piece of yellowed lace. It might once have been a dress, perhaps even a wedding dress; but when he went to pick it up, to feel it in his fingers, it crumbled at his touch. It had been spared the ravages of man, but time was not to be denied.

The outer buildings had been razed to the ground, the vineyards trampled under the feet of marching troops. Everywhere it was a nightmare of waste and ruin, and yet – and yet, there was *something*, how could he explain it? A sense of familiarity, as if he had trod these fields before, had walked in those once elegant rooms in grander days. He felt as if someone he had known and loved, a beautiful girl, had been sullied by those passing armies. He knew this place, with something more than memory, something more than sight and touch and smell.

There was Brussac here, pure and untainted, not only blood but aura, soul, spirit – the very roots of the vines from which he had sprung.

He could not explain, did not know himself, why he had come here, though it was not as a deserter. It had taken days of plodding over battlefields grown cold with dried blood; he had slept in ditches, eaten what he could find, spoken to no human but to ask directions; all for this – and now that he was here, he counted it worth everything, and more even. As a farmer knows not the crops without knowing the soil, so he suddenly knew himself in a way he had not known before.

In the cellar, amid the debris of tumbled racks and broken bottles, he found one bottle still unbroken. He carried it to the kitchen and prized the cork out with his penknife. The wine was vinegar, yet its acrid tang seemed to clear his buzzing head.

He carried it into one of the front rooms. Had this been the parlor? The music room? How comfortably, how elegantly those earlier generations of Brussacs had lived, without the agonies and the turmoil that beset those in California. Perhaps the transplantation had damaged the vines, tainted the fruit.

The vines. The fruit. He laughed silently to himself. Old Mary had been right, it wasn't blood in the Brussac veins, it was wine. Try though they might, they could not change it. He had fled, but always he had come to the vineyards, to Brussac vineyards, as if his whole world, his life, were encircled by vines.

He sat on the floor, leaning against the shreds of what had once been a tapestry, and drank, tilting the bottle up, leaning his head back, like a peasant.

That voice – was it in his head, or had he actually heard it? Something rattled nearby. He started, sitting abruptly upright, in time to see a rat scurry from one pile of rubbish to another.

Ghosts. The place was crawling with them, they'd been hovering about him since he'd arrived, whispering, mocking. He closed his eyes, suddenly tired; tired not only physically, but tired of the spirit – tired of thinking, of wondering, of puzzling. Who was he? Where did he belong? Surely not here; but if not here, then where?'

The voices again – was he drunk? Who was that, Druss? '. . . You ought to go back . . . back to your family . . .'

'But my family is here.'

Alexandra – the voice he dreaded the most – '. . . How can I be the enemy, when I love you . . .'

He started again; he'd fallen asleep. He shook his head, found the bottle where it had fallen on the floor, and drained the last few drops from it.

The voices, the voices, always, when he slept, when he was alone, they came to haunt him. What was it, something that he'd just heard, something he'd heard and heard again, but could not quite remember. He frowned, trying to dredge the words from receding memory. Whose voice . . . ?

As suddenly as the sun can spring from behind a cloud on a

clearing day, he seemed to see Sloan Morrow before him, to hear him speaking clearly:

'You are somebody . . . You do have a home.'

French Hills!

'I'll never go back there.'

'That would be a pity, because part of yourself is still there, and without it, you'll never be whole.'

French Hills. So subtly, so patiently had it been woven into the fabric of his life, he had not known that it mattered to him; and yet when he had thought to tear it from his heart, it had raveled. He must go back, he must pick up those broken threads, if he was ever to be whole. At last he knew – and knowing, he could go home.

He paused at the top of the knoll to look back upon the house. He was the last Brussac who would tread those ancient halls; but the land would remain. The land was forever. The war was nearly over. Someone would come to claim this place. Sons and daughters would marry and raise their sons and daughters to run in the open fields, to swim in the cold green water of the river.

And always, forever, in the air they breathed, in the soil upon which they trod, in the food and the water they took from the earth, would live the blood – the wine – of the Brussacs; for this was their place and would be forever.

He lifted his hand to his cap in a salute, to all those who had come here before him, to those yet to come. Then he turned away and began to walk toward the town, never once looking back.

62

'I've come home.'

For a moment Philip did not even recognize the young man in the doorway as the boy who had left two, or was it three, years before.

'Roger?'

'The same – may I come in?'

'This is your home. It always has been,' Philip said. He had been remembering another homecoming in this same room, except that time he had been the young man, and his father had not exactly welcomed him. Now it was he who was confined to a chair, while a handsome stranger advanced into the room.

Roger paused. 'Are you ill?' he asked.

'A broken rib. I fell from a rigging a few days ago. What of you? Have you been well?'

'I was in the army,' Roger said, as if that answered the question. 'In France, among others. I went to Château Brussac.'

'I'm afraid to ask what it was like – no, don't tell me. I think that's all that enables a man to survive the horrors of existence, being able to forget. I'd forgotten that place. Let it stay forgotten.'

For a moment he stared off into space, seeming to be miles away. Roger, who had come prepared to do battle with the giant he remembered, was shocked by the sight of this aging man confined to his chair. Had all that he remembered – the hate, the fear, the bitter conflict – been only in his perception?

A log snapped in the fireplace, bringing them back to the moment. Philip blinked and brought his gaze back to the man standing before him. Not only his son, but his nephew as well, a child he had wronged before the seed had grown fertile in his mother's womb. It was far easier to forgive the wrongs another has done to you than to forgive the wrongs you have done to him.

'I came back thinking you'd have some work for me,' Roger said.

'It's all oil now. I sold off the last of the growing land last year.' He grunted with disdain. 'Oil – it's dirty stuff, black and smelly. You can't get it out of your nostrils any more than you can your clothes. How those ghosts at the Château must have howled. But we've begun to make some money, not much but a little. That's something I wasn't able to do off wine. Maybe I just didn't have the Brussac touch. Or maybe the world's just too much changed. Old Master Claude frowns at me every time I pass by his portrait, but it was easier in his time. You know, they're talking about making it illegal for a man to have a drink?'

'They'll never pass a law like that,' Roger said, grinning. 'The people'd rise up in arms against it.'

'People are stupid. Look at this war they just finished, what did it prove? Ten million men dead, another twenty million wounded, and for what?'

'Germany's learned her lesson. We all have. There'll be no more wars, the world's too small for them now.'

There was a long silence between them. Philip forced himself to look at his son carefully; yes, he could see Elena in the boy, it made him want to turn away, but he resisted the impulse.

'You weren't wounded?' he asked.

Roger shook his head. 'Not in the war,' he said.

Philip took a moment to digest that.

'I could use some help around here,' he said finally. 'We've been short-handed since they started drafting men for the army. Haven't been able to get anybody since but kids and winos.'

'I'd be honored to help where I can,' Roger said; he hesitated slightly, then added, 'Dad.'

Philip's reply fell somewhere between a question and a statement: 'Son,' was all he said.

It was not so much a reconciliation as it was a truce. In his heart, Roger doubted that they would ever be close; there was too much bad blood between them, nor could he fail to see that whatever had caused their estrangement still existed. Once or twice he would turn and surprise his father watching him, and in those few seconds before the mask dropped into place he could still detect traces of the old revulsion. Something in himself, in the very sight of him, sickened his father.

In the past, this might have been enough to drive him away again; but he had learned in the years of his sojourn, and he could see too that this was something his father could not help, something he was powerless to overcome, try though he might – and he did try, that too was obvious. There was no real closeness, no show of affection, but he could see the earnestness with which his father strived to make him feel welcome, and he settled for that.

Philip had married his mistress. Roger, who had been in love himself since then, observed them and was puzzled. They were polite to one another, always considerate, always kind; but he saw nothing of passion in their marriage, neither fire nor wind. He supposed they were intimate when alone; in the company of others, they might have been nothing more than good friends.

For Philip too, the experience of working closely with a son he scarcely knew was a difficult and sometimes unsettling one. He watched with increasing respect Roger's quick mastery of the jobs given him, and quickly came to defer to his son's judgments.

The irony of his situation was that, had he had the luxury of choosing a son, he would no doubt have chosen someone very like the one he now had. He wished that there were some way to undo the past; yet, even as he wished it, he would glance at Roger, he would see something of the boy's mother in the way he held his head, in the line of his nose, and the old shame would come over him.

Gradually, as the years since Elena's death had lengthened, a mist had crept over his memory of the past, softening its harshness. It was like standing at a distance in the evening and observing a city you knew well; as the evening deepens, the mist softens the city's lines, and at last obscures them altogether in a gray, impenetrable night.

He had tried on many occasions to talk to Anna of these matters, knowing that she of all the people in his life would have been the most likely to understand. But the right opportunity had never presented itself, and as he had grown older he had become more silent. In his youth, he had been ready to pour himself out of the world. He had felt an intense kinship with others.

That power had gradually faded; he had come to see others as strangers. Then he had centered all his love on one person, making the effort to join her soul to his. With all his might he had drawn her to him, wanting to know her and be known by her, to the bottom of his heart.

Little by little, however, he had come to see that it was impossible. However ardently he had loved her, however intimate they had been, they had remained strangers. He saw that not even the most devoted man and wife really knew one another.

At last he had retired into himself, and in silence built a world of his own, kept from the eyes of every living soul, even from Anna, because in his heart he knew that she would not truly understand it.

He would like to have welcomed his son into this private world, but the time had grown too late, and the path to the inner garden too labyrinthine to follow. So he worked with his son and treated him, as he did his wife, with cordiality and respect, and rarely recognized his own longing for love.

'You were right, it's sure dirty work,' Roger said. They were washing up at the old trough once used for watering horses. The horses were gone now, replaced by a somewhat decrepit Model T that stood in the barn when not in use, in the spot where the horses' stalls had once stood.

Roger had learned a great deal in the month since his return about the workings of an oil field and especially about its filth. The stench of oil permeated everything. He seemed to smell it even in his sleep, and he could not help but compare it to the changing perfume of grapes, growing from new-formed buds to harvest ripeness. Experienced growers claimed to be able to judge the state of the crop by its scent alone.

He had been careful not to say much of this to his father, though, lest he seem to be criticizing. He was surprised, therefore, when Philip brought it up.

'It ought to be grapes out there,' he said, gesturing toward the sprawling field of derricks. 'The Brussacs are grape people, always have been.'

'They'll never grow there now,' Roger said. Between the derricks, the earth was shiny with pools of oil, and even the grass grew sparsely. The earth had yielded up one treasure, but at the cost of another. It would be centuries before this land would grow again.

Philip, arduously scrubbing his hands, which now bore a permanent patina of black, said, 'There's another piece of land, been lying fallow for years. Up near San José. Someday we'll make wine again, we'll grow our grapes there. It's good land for it, all it wants is someone with the time and the will.'

He paused and looked up at Roger. 'I'll leave it to you,' he said, as if the idea had just occurred to him. 'On that condition, that you plant it in grapes.'

'Done,' Roger said. Then, grinning, he added, 'It's funny, when I ran away from here, I thought the last thing I ever wanted to be involved with was a vineyard – and when I got to Château Brussac, I realized that was the one thing above all that I did want.'

'A man always comes back to what he is,' Philip said. He glanced over his shoulder. 'Looks like we've got company.'

Few visitors arrived anymore on horseback. Most of them drove motor cars up the long lane, or got down from cars on the road, as this one did, and walked up.

'Anna will be sore,' Philip said, 'she hates having supper wait till it gets cold.'

'You go on in,' Roger said, drying his hands on his trousers, 'I'll see what this fellow wants.'

'Don't be too long,' Philip said, heading for the house. At the porch, he paused to look at the distant figure starting up the lane; for a moment, there was something familiar about the walk, slow, indolent.

'I must be getting old,' he thought, going on in. 'It's getting to where everybody reminds me of somebody else.'

Roger waited until the stranger had reached the edge of the yard before going out to meet him. Seemingly unaware of his approach, the man had paused to study the oil derricks stretching across the hills that had once been planted in grapes.

'Howdy,' Roger greeted him, walking up. 'What can I do for you?'

The man turned and gave him a cold look. 'Who the hell are you?' he demanded.

'I was about to ask the same of you,' Roger said. 'More politely, of course. My name's Brussac. What's yours?'

'Brussac?' The stranger grunted, ignoring the question. 'You must be the bastard's kid.'

'I don't take kindly to that sort of talk,' Roger said, bristling. 'Maybe you'd better explain what you want here.'

'This is my home,' the man said, pushing past him and strolling toward the house. 'My name's Harvey, Harvey Brussac.'

63

'Hold it right there.' Philip came out the front door onto the porch, a rifle balanced on one hip.

'Well, I'll be damned, if it ain't the frog,' Harvey said, laughing unconcernedly.

'What do you want here?' Philip demanded.

'Why, I've come home,' Harvey said. He made a wide gesture with one hand. 'I heard you had taken over the whole place, turned it into an oil field. Found that interesting. I been doing a lot of roughnecking – working the oil rigs, in case you didn't know – Oklahoma, Texas – wherever they were drilling.'

'Why didn't you stay there?' Philip asked.

'Well now, you see, the boss's wife, she kind of got a light in her eyes, wasn't anything very serious, but he came to the conclusion I ought to do my drilling someplace else – so, to make a story short, I came back to see what was happening in California. Then I heard what was going on out here – so I thought I'd better come and see for myself.'

'Well, you've seen it,' Philip said, brandishing the rifle. 'Now git.'

Harvey continued to smile, but his eyes were cold and menacing. 'Now you ain't even trying to be hospitable, froggie,' he said. 'To tell you the truth, I was kind of figuring on staying around a while.'

'We don't want you here. Roger, throw him off the property.'

Harvey half pivoted, so that Roger was in his range of view also. Roger, however, was still trying to sort things out.

'Who is he, really?' he asked aloud.

'His dad was my dad's brother, Jean,' Philip said. 'We're cousins, but in my estimation he's no more than a snake, to be shot if it threatens you.'

'By rights,' Harvey said, seemingly unperturbed by the threats or the lack of hospitality, 'this place's half mine.'

'I'll give you six feet of it,' Philip said, lifting the rifle.

'No,' Roger said, mounting the steps and pushing the gun barrel aside.

'Are you crazy?' Philip asked. 'I'm telling you, we got to get him off this land or put him under it, one or the other.'

'It's his home,' Roger said. He did not like the looks of his new-found cousin; Harvey was big and husky, and as mean looking as any man he had ever seen. But he had learned a lot in the last few years about a man's roots, his need to identify with the place from which he had sprung. 'Maybe he needed to come back to it.'

'All he wants,' Philip said, 'is a chance to plant a knife in my back – yours too, if you don't look out.'

'I expect the Sheriff would see things my way,' Harvey said, picking his teeth with one dirty fingernail.

'He's got a right to be here,' Roger said, 'as much right maybe as you and me.'

'More, maybe,' Harvey said, grinning. 'Least my Pa was married to my Ma.'

Philip swore and again tried to lift the rifle, and again Roger shoved it aside. 'You saying we should let him stay here?' Philip asked angrily.

'I don't think we got any choice,' Roger said. 'Not legally – nor morally. Besides, we could use a good roughneck.'

'You're a fool,' Philip said, lowering the gun. 'Mark my words, he'll be nothing but trouble.' With that, he went into the house. Anna, who had been waiting just inside the door, tried to put her arms about him, but Philip pushed her aside and disappeared along the hall.

'Well, cousin,' Harvey said, 'glad to see you got some sense at least.'

'How long you planning on staying?' Roger asked.

'As long as it suits me.' Harvey gazed once more in the direction of the oil derricks.

'You'll have to help with the work,' Roger said, 'we're short-handed.'

'I don't mind, gives me a chance to learn about the oil business.' He started up the steps. 'Tell your Pa I've taken my old bedroom back. No need for him to move out of the master bedroom – not yet, anyway.'

Summer came early. The pools of black oil became mirrors, catching the sunlight and sending it back in hues and tints of green and gold and red. Roger worked from dawn till after dark, but he had come to mind the oil fields less; though he was there physically, his thoughts had turned in another direction.

Since the day his father had promised him the land at San José, he had begun to think of the day when it would be his – his own piece of the earth, Brussac land to be sure, with the ties that stretched back through the generations, and yet in a sense fresh land too, land that had lain fallow, land he could mark with his own imprint in a way that he never could mark French Hills and its oil wells.

French Hills, though, had helped to heal the wounds of his soul. He had written at last to Jolene, telling her where he was, and of the reconciliation with his father, which he felt sure would please her. He had wanted to write before, had not meant to cut from his life that lovely woman who had been so gracious and so generous to him. He had tried a hundred times and thrown each letter away. Since that moment when he had seen Alexandra lying dead on a San Francisco street, he had been unable to bear anything that reminded him of her, of the warm, happy days of the all-too-brief summer they had shared. He had taken all his memories of her – the sweet, clean fragrance of her hair; the touch of her lips, like the brush of butterfly's wings; her love, like a child bringing pebbles in her hand, and saying, 'Look what I've brought, and these are all for you' – memory upon memory, and he had shut them away in a dark chamber of his mind, where he could not see or feel or touch them, and he had pretended that the pain was gone.

Now, at last, he could open the door upon that chamber of treasured griefs, he could remember again, and ache with the memory, but he could live with it too. So he had written.

His relations with Harvey remained touchy. Philip flatly refused to work with his cousin, but he no longer argued with Roger's insistence that Harvey had a right to be there.

As for Harvey himself, his scorn for his relatives was mostly silent – a look, a snicker, even a coarse bark of a laugh to show his opinion of some proposal forwarded by Roger or his father.

'But give the devil his due,' Roger said more than once, 'he works, and works hard.'

Indeed, it soon became clear that Harvey's knowledge of oil drilling was as good as anyone's on the place, maybe better, and his determination to produce profitable wells matched by no one's.

'I worked for a couple of years in Oklahoma,' Harvey explained. 'Them boys are first rate when it comes to tracking down the real oil.'

It was Harvey who first suggested, then insisted, that they start wildcatting. A wildcat well was one where no oil was known to be, guided more often than not by some specific instinct.

'What we need is one good gusher,' Harvey argued, 'and there's got to be one here. All we got to do is find it.'

Philip opposed any further drilling, but Roger, swayed by Harvey's apparent knowledge of his subject, supported the proposal.

'It's your funeral,' Philip grumbled, and proceeded thereafter to ignore that aspect of their operations.

Harvey and Roger together turned their attention to the as yet untapped land surrounding the wells. 'It's here,' Harvey said, indicating the downward slope of one hill. 'I can feel it in my bones. This is where we drill.'

Even with additional help, the work was hard and dangerous. Constant encounters with oil-slick riggings, falling pipes, snarled chains and straining steel provided a constant threat of lost limbs or worse. Ever present too was the danger of explosion or fire, from the combination of volatile fuels and the dynamite Harvey introduced for use in their search.

'They been working with this back east,' he explained. 'You dig a bunch of holes, fill them with dynamite, pack 'em good and tight so the blast goes down and not up – then you measure what happens on this here instrument – they call it a seismograph. That shows where there's rock formations underground that are likely to be holding oil.'

To Roger it sounded simple enough, until the first series of explosions sent a plume of dust a hundred feet into the air and showered them with rocks and dirt.

'Must not have got it packed right,' Harvey said, apparently unconcerned, while Roger rubbed a shoulder bruised by a flying rock.

For two weeks the hills shook with the thump, thump of dynamite blasts. Philip, who pronounced the method 'suicidal', came each morning to watch the holes being packed with their explosives, and left grumbling before the blasts were detonated.

For all the success they were having, though, they might have been chasing an errant gopher. Each blast brought new pronouncements from Harvey as to where the oil surely would be found – and each new wildcat well proved fruitless. By now the hill they had been exploring looked like a battlefield, pockmarked with the evidence of their blasting. The main house sported a half dozen cracked windows, and Anna, silent and grim-faced, had carefully packed away all her father's old treasures in the attic.

'Maybe we'd better give this up,' Roger said finally. He knew, as Harvey did not care to know, that they were already behind on loan payments. French Hills was mortgaged to the hilt to provide the money that had been needed for early drilling and exploration. The sluggish wells already in operation had provided enough to make the payments, and a little over. But the heavy expense of blasting and drilling unsuccessful wildcats had left them in a bad way.

'It's here, I tell you,' Harvey said, thumping the ground with a booted foot. 'This time I got it down to a pinpoint.'

'Give it up,' Philip snapped. 'We're already broke from chasing your will o' the wisps.'

'Willow my foot, you ignorant greaser bastard,' Harvey returned.

'Damn you,' Philip swore, starting for him.

Roger had to move between them to prevent a fight. 'He's right,' he said to Harvey, 'we can't afford to keep this up. We'll wind up losing everything.'

'It's right here,' Harvey insisted. 'I'd stake my life on it, there's oil straight down from where we're standing, a big pool of it, just waiting to come out.'

There was the ring of sincerity to his words. Of one thing Roger was certain; this time, Harvey really believed what he was saying.

'This is the last one we try,' he said wearily, heading off to get the dynamite.

They began drilling three days later. It never failed to give Roger a queasy feeling as he saw the giant bit begin to chew its way into the once-proud earth. He had never gotten used to what he saw as the rape of this splendid land that had been so treasured by generations of his family. Was this – this valley peopled with ugly scarecrows that were the riggings – to be the heritage of the generations to follow? Once again he thought of the land to the north, land he had never seen, but which now loomed in his imagination like the promised land to some weary pilgrim.

For weeks they tore a path downward into the earth. As the drill sank, so did Roger's spirits. Another failure could ruin them.

'Damn it, I know it's here,' Harvey insisted, delivering a hard kick to a steel beam.

'We're two hundred feet down now,' Roger pointed out. 'None of our other wells are more than a hundred and fifty feet.'

'None of the other wells are producing more than three, four barrels a day,' Harvey replied. 'That's why you're going broke.'

'That, and the fifty thousand we've sunk in these wildcats.'

'It's here,' Harvey said stubbornly. 'Damn, what's that Chink want now?'

Roger glanced toward the house and saw a figure, recognizable at the distance only as a woman, picking her way across the pockmarked slope.

'Probably a message from Pa, telling us it's time to give up on this well,' Roger said gloomily. 'Damn, that bit's stuck. Come on, let's give it one more try.'

Somewhere in the ground beneath them the earth had

flinched, spilling rock into the hole gnawed by the drill's conical teeth and binding the probe. The derrick shuddered as steel fought rock.

They began pumping mud down the pipe, forgetting the approaching figure altogether. At last the pipe broke free. Swearing and slipping on a derrick floor slickened with mud and oil residue, they worked to screw on another length of drill pipe, to reach still deeper into the earth.

Finally the drill was operating again. Roger wiped the sweat and mud from his brow, and turned toward the house.

It was like a blow to the stomach. He staggered backward, closing his eyes hard. The heat, fatigue . . . He was seeing things: for a moment, it wasn't Anna crossing the field, beginning to run toward him; it was Alexandra.

'Roger!'

He opened his eyes, blinking. It was her! Good God, was he dreaming, or losing his mind . . . ?

And suddenly, it didn't matter if it was a dream, or real; nothing mattered but that lithe, lovely form racing toward him. He gave a shout and leaped down from the derrick, beginning to run to meet her. A moment later he had seized her in his arms, swung her up and around in a dizzying spin. The two of them tried to laugh, cry, talk and kiss, all in the same miraculous instant.

Harvey remained oblivious to their ecstatic reunion, however – for at the moment of Alexandra's shout, his ears had been attuned to another siren's call, one for which he had listened over the many weeks of their search.

'We've got it,' he said in a hoarse cry, unaware that Roger had not heard him, was no longer by his side. 'Jesus God Almighty, we've got it.'

At first, an untrained ear might have noticed nothing different. Then, abruptly, the entire derrick seemed to tremble, as if in the throes of some cataclysmic orgasm – and finally, it erupted, a great geyser leaping skyward, mud and oil and then, increasingly, just oil, a spewing, spitting gusher of it.

Harvey gave a great whoop of joy and turned to say something to Roger – only to find him gone. He looked, and saw him with a girl, the two of them locked in a passionate embrace, oblivious to the deluge of oil that poured down upon them, like some primeval rainstorm, until both of them had been dyed the green-black of the oil itself.

64

'All this time, I thought you were dead.'

'It was some other girl, a stranger,' Alexandra said. 'Grandmother Mary borrowed my shawl to put over her. I had just gone around the car when the bomb went off – the car shielded us, but Grandmother . . . it was horrible.'

Roger got up from the bed and went to the dresser, lighting himself a cigarette. Some other girl – he wondered if it had been Stella. He supposed it was just that she should die in the tragedy she had spawned, but he could not help feeling a sadness. They had, after all, shared a part of their lives. Like himself, she had been searching. Her search perhaps was ended. His was for something he had not yet found.

Alexandra came to stand behind him, putting her arms about his naked body and leaning her head against his back. 'You've changed,' she said.

'I'm older. I've been places, seen things.'

'And I've done nothing but wait.'

He turned around, taking her in his arms. 'That's the hardest of all, isn't it?' he asked. 'Anyway, I don't want you to change, I want you just as you are.'

There was a chorus of shouts from outside, the men coming in from the field. Harvey's gusher had been capped; judging from its healthy appearance, it would provide the sort of output they needed to put French Hills on a sound financial footing again.

'Dinner'll be ready soon,' Roger said. 'Time for you to meet the family.'

Alexandra giggled. 'I think just this once I had better change. You may like me just as I am, but I suspect your family might prefer me with something on.'

'Well, my father always had an eye for beautiful women,' Roger said. It suddenly occurred to him that this was the daughter of the woman his father had loved for many years. Alexandra had already explained that she had stopped at the house only to ask after him, and when they had come in from the gusher they had not paused for introductions, so for the moment his father knew nothing. But how would he react when he learned that she was a guest in his house?

Philip and Harvey were already at the table when they came down. Anna was just coming in from the kitchen, carrying a steaming tureen; though there were still a few servants to help with the house, she had always insisted that she preferred serving her husband herself, and in recent years that had proven a welcome economy.

Though Harvey remained seated, Philip got up as they entered the room. 'I want you to meet my father,' Roger said, 'This is Alexandra. She's Jolene's daughter.'

There was a loud crash and everyone turned to find Anna standing empty-handed, the tureen broken at her feet.

'I'm sorry,' she stammered, 'it was so hot – excuse me, I'll get someone to clean that up.' She disappeared into the kitchen.

Philip went after her. He found her rummaging in the cupboard for a fresh tureen, her eyes glinting with moisture.

'It's all right,' he said, taking her into his arms.

'That name,' she said. 'I know what it means to you. And her daughter is so lovely . . .'

'Never mind,' Philip said, patting her reassuringly. 'I'm married to you.'

She tilted her head to look up at him. 'Do you regret that?'

His answer came without any hesitation. 'No,' he said, firmly and evenly. 'That's one of the few things I don't regret.'

'And – and her?'

'Anna . . .'

'Do you still love her?'

'Anna, don't.' He let her go and turned away from her, not wanting to hurt her, unable to lie to her. There was a long moment of silence; then, the rattle of crockery as she resumed her search for another tureen.

'Let me help with those,' Alexandra said.

Anna was in the act of clearing the table. 'If you like,' she said, nodding.

Philip was about to suggest that they leave that chore for one of the servants, when he glanced at his wife and saw she was actually pleased by the offer.

'I'm going to have a drink before I turn in,' he said instead, pushing his chair back from the table.

'Think I'll check the wells, make sure everything's running smoothly,' Roger said.

Harvey remained sitting when they had all gone out. For a long moment he stared toward the kitchen from which he could hear the faint murmur of women's voices.

The girl was a beauty, there was no denying it; and he too recognized the significance of her mother's name. Years before, Elena had told him of a woman up north, Jolene, whom her husband loved, a woman Elena blamed for the failure of her marriage. Anna, it seemed, had the same sort of problem with her husband.

He found the information interesting. Working closely with Roger, he had developed a grudging respect for the young man; but Philip he still hated with a passion that had not wavered over the years. Philip had alienated him from his father, murdered his brother, all but stolen his birthright from him. It was hatred as much as greed that had brought him back to French Hills. He wanted to make French Hills his own, not only for the fortune that represented in his mind, but even more importantly, to take it away from Philip.

His memory had gone back, far back, to their childhood. He remembered his father's sister coming for a visit – that was at the death of his grandfather; she had brought a girl, her daughter, with her. The girl had been Jolene; it was an easy name to remember; and even then, there had been something between her and Philip – Felipe, he'd been then.

Imagine, Harvey mused, sipping coffee already grown cold in the cup, imagine that lasting all these years – and now, here was Jolene's daughter, all dreamy-eyed over Felipe's son.

Interesting, he thought, pushing his own chair back from the table and getting up, damned interesting.

Like Philip, he decided, he would have a drink, but he did not head for the drawing-room, where he knew Philip would be. He had taken to keeping his own whiskey in the barn, where he could drink in solitude. Tonight he would be celebrating. He was already, in fact, a little drunk, not on liquor but on the success of his search for a well. He'd shown them, both the bastard greaser and his son, found the oil they hadn't been able to find. In the end, he'd come out on top, because he was smarter and stronger than both of them. He had made up his mind just today, watching his gusher spouting toward the sky – he wasn't going to take any orders in the future. Hereafter, he was running things. And those that didn't like it would have to lump it.

Starting tomorrow, things were going to be different.

'Your mother must be very beautiful,' Anna was saying. They were just finishing up the dishes.

'She is,' Alexandra said.

'And your father – what sort of man is he?'

'Oh, he's just as beautiful as mother – in a fatherly way, of course.'

'Of course,' Anna said.

'I wish you could see them together, they're such a happy couple. I hope when Roger and I are married so many years, our marriage will still be as happy and untroubled as theirs. I don't believe they've ever had a day's difficulty.'

Anna, looking truly pleased for the first time since their introduction, nodded and said, 'Yes, every marriage should be like that.'

'There, that's the last of them – shall I help put things away?'

'No, please,' Anna said, 'you go and be with Roger; he should be back by now.'

Roger apparently was not back, though. She saw his father sitting alone in the drawing-room, but she did not feel quite comfortable alone with him. Instead, she went out onto the porch.

The sky had clouded over. The full moon vanished and reappeared among the clouds, like a fat lady playing at hide-and-seek. She had a glimpse of the oil field in the distance. Roger had said he was going there; perhaps she would stroll out to meet him.

She had gone only a few feet from the porch when someone stepped from the darkness of the barn. Thinking it was Roger, she turned in that direction. A moment later the moonlight returned, revealing Roger's cousin, Harvey.

'Evening,' he greeted her, coming forward; she thought that his walk seemed a little unsteady and wondered if he had been drinking.

'I was just looking for Roger,' she said, stopping. 'Have you seen him?'

He was oddly thoughtful, as if considering the question. Finally he said, 'Sure. Want me to take you to him?'

'Oh, I would appreciate that,' she said. 'I was a little uncertain of wandering about here in the dark – no telling what I might run into.'

'That's right,' Harvey said. 'He went over this way. Come on.'

Up close, she could smell the whiskey on his breath, which made her a bit nervous. He did seem, though, to be in control of himself, and she dismissed her fears as childish. A cousin of Roger's was unlikely to be a nuisance, after all. She fell into step beside him, picking her way gingerly over the unfamiliar ground.

Anna, who had just taken some scraps out to the dogs, heard a distant murmur of voices. Curious, she went to the corner of the house and looked around to the front.

She saw Alexandra and Harvey crossing the wide yard together, in the direction of the oil field. She frowned thoughtfully, wondering where Roger was. She didn't like that other one, he had an aura of violence about him, seemingly ready to burst into action at any moment. She was not happy having him about the place; she was even less happy seeing him escorting that nice young lady into the fields at night.

Just then the moon vanished again behind a bank of clouds. Still frowning, Anna started back to the kitchen.

'Goodness, shouldn't we have found Roger by now?' Alexandra was breathless from the long walk. 'You're sure he's out here?'

'He came this way. What'd his old man say when you asked him?'

'I didn't, I just came on out. What if we tried shouting for him?'

'These hills can play tricks with shouts, make it hard to know where a sound came from,' Harvey said. 'We might have missed him.'

'I can see that would be easy to do out here,' Alexandra said. They were among the wells now, the derricks like ghostly scarecrows towering over them. 'Maybe we ought to go back.'

To her surprise, Harvey took her arm. 'Let's just look over here,' he said, steering her even deeper into the fields of derricks. After a moment, he asked, 'You fixing to marry that one?'

'Yes, I am. Why?' She was becoming nervous again; something about Harvey's manner – and the hand on her arm was so firm, almost hurting her.

'You're marrying the wrong man,' he said, dropping his voice almost to a whisper.

'I don't know what you mean.'

'I'm the one who found that gusher you saw,' he said, liquor slurring his words. 'And I'm the one who's going to be running this place in the future.'

'I don't really care what Roger does, or where he is, so long as I am with him,' Alexandra said coldly. 'I think we'd better start back now, if you don't mind.'

She came to a halt. Harvey halted with her, but he did not turn back nor release her arm.

'You ought to be marrying me,' he said. 'I'm a Brussac, the real thing too.'

'Roger's a Brussac – I think you're drunk.'

He gave a disdainful laugh. 'Him a Brussac, don't make me sick. You want to know about him, I'll tell you – his old lady was a tramp, wasn't a man for twenty miles around here didn't lay on top of her. I had her myself more times than I can count. And his old man's nothing but a bastard . . . '

'I don't want to listen to this,' Alexandra said, 'let go of me.'

His expression turned hard and ugly. He held tight to her arm, pulling her close and leaning over her. 'What's the matter, I ain't fancy enough for you or something? You know, I think you and me are some sort of cousins too – maybe you just ought to give me a little kiss, for family's sake.'

He leaned down as if to kiss her. With her free hand she slapped his face, the sound like a shot in the night.

For a moment he only stared, his eyes expressing first surprise, then mounting anger. 'Bitch,' he swore. He seized both her shoulders and shook her violently, making her head snap to and fro. Suddenly he flung her to the ground.

For a moment she was so stunned and dazed that she could only lie there staring up at him with terrified eyes. Harvey glowered back at her. Liquor, long-festered hatred, animal lust, all inflamed his senses. For a confused moment he thought it was not she but Jolene lying before him – Jolene, whose name had been so intertwined in the lives of those at French Hills; Jolene, whom Philip had loved with a desperate, hopeless love throughout his life; Jolene, of whom Elena had spoken with such bitter resentment.

Here at last was the way to hurt Philip, to repay the wounds that Philip had inflicted upon him. Here at last the means to avenge himself upon all those who had looked down their noses at him, finding him coarse and vulgar and not good enough for their company. Faces and names flashed in a blur through his mind.

Like an animal he fell upon her. She tried to cry out, but his mouth covered hers, muffling her screams, his tongue invading her. She felt his hands tearing at her clothes, clawing at her bare flesh. She fought against him, the rough ground scraping her arms and legs.

Suddenly he had ceased struggling with her. His mouth left hers and she could breathe again. She saw that he had turned his head to the right, and when she looked in that direction, she saw Roger's father standing there, a rifle in his hands.

'Get up,' Philip ordered.

Harvey moved off her, kneeling in the dirt. She started to scramble to her feet; as she did so, she made the mistake of getting between the two men. In an instant, Harvey had seized her again and given her a violent shove, knocking her into Philip and throwing him off balance.

By the time Philip had gotten her on her feet again, Harvey had gone, vanishing into the darkness.

Philip made a move as if to go after him. 'Please,' Alexandra cried, 'let him go.'

The look that Philip gave her was every bit as hard and ugly as that she had seen on Harvey's face earlier. 'No,' he said, shoving her aside. 'This is something that's needed to be settled for a long time, and I think tonight's as good as any night to settle it.'

He ran after Harvey. The clouds had again obscured the moon, and in a moment both of them had vanished to sight. Alexandra stared after them for a second or two – then she turned and began to run toward the house, stumbling on the uneven surface of the ground. She must find Roger, before something horrible happened; even without knowing all that had gone before, she could see that those two were acting out some long-standing feud. If they found one another in the darkness of the field . . .

A weapon – he needed a weapon, Harvey thought. He should have brought his gun with him, should have known better than to be without it with that one around.

He paused in the shadow of the supply shed, snatching up a shovel; not much against a rifle, he thought. His eyes scoured the area, looking for something better – and fell on the pile of dynamite they had been using for their explorations.

He smiled to himself. Just the thing, to blow the greaser bastard to kingdom come, be rid of him forever; and nobody could say afterward it hadn't been an accident; accidents happened all the time with dynamite.

He snatched up two of the sticks and began to run again. As he did so, a shot rang out, and he felt the wind as a bullet just missed his head.

'Harvey!' It was the greaser. 'Harvey, I'm coming after you. This time it's you or me.'

'Go to hell,' Harvey called back. Another shot rang out, this one missing him by a mile.

Harvey ducked into a shadow, crouching down. Too hard, he thought, to try to throw something amid all these derricks. He needed a vantage point, someplace where he had a good view, and room to throw.

He leaned back and felt the touch of cold steel, one of the girders to the derrick beside which he was crouching. He stared at the girder for a few seconds, his eyes moving upward.

Upward – that was the answer. He stuffed the dynamite into his pockets and jumped up onto the girder, beginning to climb.

He had climbed maybe forty feet when Philip shouted again, and another shot rang out. Pausing to look down, Harvey saw Philip darting across an open space between two derricks.

Harvey yanked one of the dynamite sticks from his pocket, fumbled for and found matches. One arm crooked over a beam for balance, he managed to get the fuse going. He counted mentally as the fire burned along the fuse.

From below, Philip could see movement but little else. Thinking Harvey had drawn a gun, he crouched for cover and sighted along the rifle's barrel.

High above, Harvey waited until the dynamite's fuse was almost burned down. He lifted his arm to throw – and a shot rang out.

The initial pain was little more than a sting; for a second or two he didn't even realize he had been hit, until he felt the wet warmth seeping through his shirt and looked down to see the dark, widening stain.

He remembered to throw the dynamite, but his aim was wide of the mark. It fell far from Philip, but only inches from the supply shed and the stack of dynamite there.

Philip saw the figure above sway, leaning crazily out from the steel beams. Then, with a cry that sounded more surprised than frightened, Harvey fell, rolling head over heels as he hurtled to the ground.

'They're somewhere over here – oh, Roger, please hurry, I'm so afraid of what might happen,' Alexandra said.

'So am I – maybe you ought to go back,' Roger said. He had gone earlier from the main field to check the gusher, and back to the house by a circuitous route, to hear from Anna an alarming story of Philip's following Harvey and Alexandra into the fields; and no sooner had he started in search of them than an hysterical Alexandra had come running into his arms, to tell him that Philip and Harvey were trying to kill one another.

From somewhere ahead of them he heard another shot and what sounded like a cry. He hesitated, thinking he should really send Alexandra back.

Suddenly they were both thrown to the ground by the force of a massive explosion; it sounded as if all the dynamite on the place had gone off at once. Rocks and dust showered down upon them mercilessly.

On the heels of that explosion came another awesome one, making the earth tremble and sending a geyser of smoke and flame leaping skyward.

'The wells,' Roger shouted, flinging himself across Alexandra to protect her. 'The explosion must have ruptured the pipes, they're going off like a string of firecrackers!'

It was like Armageddon, the end of the world. The angry earth itself seemed to erupt in a swift chain of explosions, making the hills tremble, turning the night into a horrible sun-scape of leaping flames and great balls of black smoke. Like the gasps of some great god emerging from the bowels of the earth, the wells for which they had toiled and suffered dissolved one by one into the holocaust.

Huddled on the ground with Alexandra, Roger watched the desolation, feeling the hairs singeing on his arms and brows, and knew that it was more than oil that was being destroyed – it was French Hills, and the reign of the once mighty Brussacs. This was their Götterdämmerung. What had been wrought through years of petty quarrels and foolish arrogance was being finished now in the conflagration.

The explosions ended; the earth ceased its shudders. Alex-andra sat up, holding one arm that had been badly burned.

'Your father . . . ?'

Before them, a hundred different fires blazed, punctuated with black spaces where there had been nothing to burn, or where the fires had already burned themselves out.

Roger got up, brushing dirt and soot from his clothes. The

hat he had worn had protected him somewhat, but where his head and face had been exposed the hair had been burned away.

'I'm going to look for him,' he said.

'Do you think he's still alive?'

Roger shook his head. 'I'm afraid,' he said, 'that's between him and a God that never understood him.'

65

'Mother.'

'I came as soon as I heard,' Jolene said. 'How is he? Is he all right?'

Alexandra shook her head, her eyes glistening with tears. 'The doctor's with him now. He was burned so badly – I just don't know.'

Jolene took off her gloves and hat as she came in. Her still-glorious hair had been bobbed in the latest fashion, and she wore one of the new hobbled skirts, revealing an exquisite pair of ankles. On a woman of her age the effect might have been ludicrous, but in fact she looked scarcely older than her daughter, and lovely despite the strain of worry etched on her face. She had driven all night by herself, leaving within minutes of the call she had received from a woman she didn't know, who had said only that she was Philip's wife and that he had been critically burned. The sun had been mounting the horizon as she had driven up the lane.

'He's in the master bedroom,' Alexandra said, 'down here.'

'I know the way,' Jolene said, starting along the hall. She came to the parlor, her senses suddenly assaulted with memories. It was here she had first set eyes on Philip. He'd been only a small boy, known then as Felipe, and she only a girl. Together they had stolen along this very corridor, to the same bedroom, where another man had lain dying.

She put a hand on the woodwork to steady herself, her vision all at once blurred by tears. Philip – all of her life, from girlhood to the present, he had been there, deep in her heart, a presence as vital to her existence as breath itself, thrumming with every heartbeat. A score, a hundred, a thousand memories came rushing in upon her – Philip . . . Philip . . . Philip.

'Mother, are you all right?' Alexandra put a solicitous hand on her shoulder.

'Yes – thank you.' She steeled herself, taking the deep breaths of a drowning person, and forced her footsteps along the hall, dreading her destination, yet drawn to it by a need stronger to her than life itself.

She saw Roger in the corridor. He took her hand wordlessly, and she kissed his cheek, but it was the woman with him to whom she went.

'You are Anna?' Jolene asked.

'Yes.' The dark eyes searched her face, as if memorizing every line, each feature.

'It was so kind of you to call me.'

The long lashes dropped over the dark eyes, then lifted again, as though with immense effort. Anna's gaze met hers frankly, firmly.

'From the time they brought him in,' she said, 'he begged to see you.'

'I'm sorry.'

'Why should you be? He promised me no more than he could give. I have asked no more than he promised.'

The bedroom door opened and a man, clearly the doctor, came out. He went directly to Anna, shaking his head gravely.

'His mind's clear for the moment,' he said. 'He's asking for you.'

'Did he speak my name?' Anna asked.

The doctor seemed surprised by the question. 'Why, over and over,' he replied. 'It's Julie, isn't it, something like that?'

The two women exchanged a glance. 'You go in,' Anna said.

Jolene hesitated only for a moment. Then, with a quick nod, she went past them and into the bedroom. Philip lay with his eyes closed. There was, oddly, only one small burn on his cheek; the other, critical, burns had been on his body, covered now by the bedclothes. He looked, at a glance, untroubled and unharmed.

Standing beside the bed, staring down at him, she remembered again that first meeting. What children they had been, innocent, their lives as yet untainted.

'Jolene – ' He spoke her name even before he opened his eyes, as if he had sensed her presence at his side.

'I'm here,' she said, kneeling on the floor beside the bed.

He looked at her then, peering hard as if uncertain it was

truly her. He put out a hand; she leaned toward it and he gently ran a finger down the curve of one cheek.

'I – I had to tell you – to explain, about Elena,' he said in a faltering voice.

'It isn't necessary,' she said, trying to hide her tears from him. He felt them on her cheek, smeared them with his fingertip.

'I should have told you long ago, but I was afraid, and ashamed.' He began to talk, pausing every few words for breath; it was evident that the task was difficult for him, but he went on.

Jolene, not daring to interrupt, experienced a full range of reactions to his story – shock, initially, at what he had done, even a momentary sense of revulsion; then, gradually, understanding of the motives and the tricks of fate that had obliged him to act as he had; and, finally, pity for what he had suffered from his guilty secret.

There was a lengthy silence when he was done. 'Can – can you forgive me?' he asked at last.

'My darling,' she murmured, seizing his hand and pressing it to her lips, 'it is I who should beg for forgiveness. What you must have gone through.'

'I did love you, you know.'

It was strange, she thought, kneeling on the hardwood floor at the side of his deathbed, but for the first time with Philip she felt free – not of his love, but of the bitter hold that it had held on her for so much of her life.

Resentment, jealousy, frustration, had combined to weld a chain of their love that had bound her day and night to dreams of the past, and blinded her too often to the realities of the present; but as the fresh air will blow the stale from a room when it is opened, so had the revelation of his secret stripped away the foolish fantasies and petty resentments that had so enslaved her before.

She could love Philip – *would* love him, for all her life – but she could forgive the past, and in doing so see their love and themselves for what they were, and for what they had been.

They had been children, not only when they met but for most of their lives. It was a girl whom he had loved, and who had loved him, as a boy. Perhaps it was true that she would never love Sloan as she had loved Philip; but it was equally true that Philip could never have filled Sloan's place in her life, even had they not gone their separate paths.

For her, she knew that the path had been the right one. She

had been through so much since, and so much of that she had been through with Sloan. She had come to understand that marriage was a partnership in which love was only one of the investments, and perhaps not even the most important.

She had, in a phrase, grown up at last. It had been the ghost of a girl who had longed all those years for the ghost of a boy she had known; but it was a woman now who knelt beside a dying man, and in her heart, along with her undying love for him, was the knowledge that it was the wrong man.

She saw that he was looking at her, waiting for an answer. 'I told you once,' she said, 'that I would never love anyone as I loved you, Philip – and I have not. But I have learned since then that there are many kinds of love, and ours may not have been the finest – the fiercest, perhaps, the most all-consuming, but not the finest.'

'Jolene, before I – will you kiss me, one last time?'

Fresh tears had begun to flow. Wordlessly she bent above him, lowering her lips to his. For a second or two, all else had vanished. Things were as they had been. Twenty years of heart-break and misunderstanding had fallen away, and she was young again, and kissing her beloved.

Then it was over. She was a middle-aged woman, however beautiful, and this face so near to hers was not the face of her memory, but the lined and careworn face of a stranger.

'I would like to see my wife now,' he said with evident effort. 'And my son. There are things I need to tell him.'

She stood. At the door she paused, meaning to say goodbye, but the word would not come. She saw him one last time through a veil of tears; his eyes had closed, and once again he looked as if he were asleep. He showed no awareness of her leaving.

66

'Roger's gone,' Alexandra said.

'Gone? I don't understand.'

'He left this morning. He said something about a gift his father had given him, in San José.'

Jolene smiled. 'I think I understand,' she said. 'Look, it's not out of the way – why don't you come with me, and I'll take you to him.'

Alexandra was hesitant. 'Don't you think, if he'd wanted me with him, he'd have asked me to go along?' she asked.

Jolene laughed and took her daughter's hand. 'My dear,' she said, 'I have loved and been loved by two wonderful men in my life and never, in any time of crisis, did either of them know what it was they truly wanted. Come along. When he sees you, he'll realize he wanted you there.'

She found the place with surprising ease, considering how long it was since she had been there. The building that had once been a winery was nothing but a pile of rubble; the fields ran rampant with weeds, but on the hillsides some vines still grew, long untended and grown wild.

Roger was there. The pickup truck from French Hills was parked in the overgrown drive, and when they had climbed the hill behind the ruins of the winery, they saw him on the far slope, kneeling and digging in the earth.

'You go to him,' Jolene said. 'I'll just wait here for a moment.'

Alexandra ran toward him, but as she drew nearer, she shyly slowed her pace and strolled up to greet him. She was nearly there when he saw her and smiled in greeting; he did indeed, as her mother had promised, look as if he wanted her there. Her shyness vanished, and when he stood, she ran happily into his arms.

He had been digging at the roots of a vine, and his embrace showered her with loose dirt, ruining her dress, but she didn't mind.

'Look,' he said, stepping back and showing her one of the roots he had dug up, 'they're still here, still growing – the vines planted years ago by my grandfather.'

'Is this Brussac land?' she asked, gazing at the hills surrounding them.

'It's my land, now,' he said. He stared at the piece of root in his hand. 'Someday,' his father had said of this land, 'we'll make wine again, we'll grow our grapes there.' It was good land, this earth that was his, peopled with living vines, waiting only the touch of a master's hand.

'Years ago,' he said aloud, 'when my ancestors came to this

country, they had nothing but some land and some vines – and a will to survive. I was just wondering how you'd feel about a husband with nothing more than that.'

'It's all that I've ever wanted,' she answered, 'so long as the husband is you.'

Jolene, seeing them embrace again, knew that she was no longer needed there, and turned back toward her waiting car. At any rate, she was growing impatient to be home again, with Sloan and everything that was familiar to her.

Last night, sleeping in Philip's house, she had dreamed her dream of old. It was the same dream, yet different too. There was the road and there the walled city toward which she hastened; but all at once she had realized that this time the jostling throngs were absent and she traveled the road alone.

And when she had looked, she saw that the city gates stood open, and that someone stood there in the shadows, waiting; as she watched, he had stepped into the sunlight, opening his arms; and, calling his name, she had run sobbing into them.

She quickened her step. Sloan; he was there, at home, at their home, waiting for her. The wind whipped her neck-scarf about her face, and suddenly she had begun to run toward the waiting car at the bottom of the hill.

Book
Tokens